SPIRALLING

CAL SPEET

Harper North

HarperNorth
Windmill Green
24 Mount Street
Manchester M2 3NX

A division of
HarperCollins*Publishers*
1 London Bridge Street
London SE1 9GF

www.harpercollins.co.uk

HarperCollins*Publishers*
Macken House, 39/40 Mayor Street Upper
Dublin 1, D01 C9W8, Ireland

First published by HarperCollins*Publishers* Ltd 2025

1

Copyright © Cal Speet 2025

Cal Speet asserts the moral right to
be identified as the author of this work.

A catalogue record for this book is
available from the British Library.

ISBN: 978-0-00-876778-5

This novel is entirely a work of fiction. The names, characters
and incidents portrayed in it are the work of the author's imagination.
Any resemblance to actual persons, living or dead, events or
localities is entirely coincidental.

Typeset by Amnet ContentSource

Printed and bound in the UK using 100% Renewable Electricity
by CPI Group (UK) Ltd

All rights reserved. No part of this publication may be
reproduced, stored in a retrieval system, or transmitted,
in any form or by any means, electronic, mechanical,
photocopying, recording or otherwise, without the
prior permission of the publishers.

Without limiting the author's and publisher's exclusive rights,
any unauthorised use of this publication to train generative artificial
intelligence (AI) technologies is expressly prohibited. HarperCollins
also exercise their rights under Article 4(3) of the Digital Single Market
Directive 2019/790 and expressly reserve this publication from
the text and data mining exception.

This book contains FSC™ certified paper and other controlled
sources to ensure responsible forest management.

For more information visit: www.harpercollins.co.uk/green

For Anita Lounsbach,
let's face it - we got there in the end.

PART ONE

1

Let Go

Leaving the sanctuary of your duvet is a horrible necessity at the best of times. At the worst of times – January – and when you're in the nucleus of a devastating, explosive and scandalous breakup, it's nigh on impossible . . .

I wriggled my shivering body out from the IKEA bed set and headed to the bathroom to brush my teeth. Ah, and there he was. Bold as brass but nowhere near as shiny. In unforgiving HD. My reflection. I quite liked him, once, but things had become difficult. He'd put on two stone of heartbreak weight and had avoided any unnecessary social interaction for weeks, and the result was a mop of dark brown curls that would've looked more at home in The Shire than central Manchester. My freckles, which I usually found endearing, were interrupted at intervals by patches of adult acne. At least I still had the threat of a bone structure. Aquafresh. Face wash. Moisturiser. Hair serum. My beauty routine might've been somewhat chode-ish when measured against the relentless skincare marathons of my girlfriends, but compared to the personal hygiene of all the straight men I knew (four!), I was Patrick Bateman.

[07:39] **Evie:** Morning, girlies!
[07:50] **Gabriel:** Hello
[07:50] **Evie:** How are you doing, beautiful boy?
[07:50] **Gabriel:** Had a weird nightmare
[07:51] **Evie:** About Seamus?
[07:51] **Gabriel:** Actually, no, Evie, you'll be surprised to know that I'm still capable of maintaining thought space that doesn't revolve around my ex

I wasn't.

    [07:52] **Evie:** That's a relief!
    [07:52] **Tasha:** And a massive fucking lie

Damn.

    [07:52] **Gabriel:** Morning, Tash
    [07:52] **Tasha:** Morning!

Preparing for the first day back after an *extended* break, I continued the clockwork ritual of getting ready for work. Water bottle, filled. No coffee (caffeine leads to spiralling). Cig on the Juliette. Banana. Slate-grey, contrast-stitch trousers. Low-top Dr. Martens, scuffed. Maroon crew neck. New fleece that Dad got me for Christmas after 'noticing I'd been going on a lot more walks'. It was a thoughtful gesture by his standards but also rude because I'd only been on two. Keys. Laptop bag. Phone. Out the door and to the lift. I lived in a second-floor apartment, but the stairs seemed a little bit too much like exercise, and everyone knows that the only people who exercise in the morning are Andrew Tate fans, boomers who are training for a half-marathon, and power lesbians. I wondered if there was a person who existed in the centre of that Venn diagram. Ellen Degeneres?

'Gabe – hold the door!' The voice of my two-doors-down, five-foot-six, four-drinks-and-dinner-together-once-and-now-overfamiliar neighbour Mitchell ricocheted across the corridor as he bounded into view and fell gasping into the lift, quiff first.

    [08:15] **Gabriel:** Mitchell alert, in the lift.
    It's the first time I've seen him since before
    what happened at Christmas
    [08:15] **Evie:** Aw! Say hi from me
    [08:16] **Tasha:** It's so weird to imagine him
    existing in daylight. I thought he only left his
    apartment after dark

'Thanks, babe.' He was panting, and leaned forward to press the ground-floor button. 'I'm a sweaty mess before 9 a.m. and NOT for the right reasons.' He laughed, turning to face the mirrored wall. 'Oh god, am I bright red?'

'More of a radioactive terracotta,' I said. Mitchell would never be seen without several layers of St. Tropez mousse that gave him, to be kind, a tan that would be described as 'unseasonal' and, to be honest, one that would result in his international cancelling if published on the platform formally known as Twitter.

'You cunt!' He cackled, playfully slapping my arm. I laughed, too. 'I've not seen you in months!'

'Wasn't it just before Christmas?'

'Oh, yeah. Weeks, then, but that was only to drop a parcel off. It hardly counts. Anyway, how are you, babe?' he asked, doing his best impression of earnestness.

Although most of my interactions with Mitchell had been limited to our pre-work run-ins in the lift and a single instance of drinks at my place, those experiences were enough to glean that he was comically self-absorbed. This was the first time he'd ever asked how I was. There had to be an ulterior motive. He was, after all, what many eminent Oxford psychologists would refer to as 'a messy bitch that lived for drama'.

'I'm alright, Mitch, yeah,' I said, with the ghost of a smile.

'Sure . . . but you've not been at work?' continued the Tannish Inquisition.

'I have; you mustn't have seen me,' I lied. 'I've been taking the stairs. New Year's resolution, more exercise and all that! Health kick.'

'Gross.' He winced, withdrawing his phone to glance at the time. The lift stopped at Floor One, signalling a chance at salvation from a potential interrogation. Even Mitchell, in all his directness, wouldn't push for details about my personal life in front of a stranger. I hoped. I watched as the doors opened, desperate for the most effective interruption against his prying. I crossed my fingers behind my back. Come on, Broadgate Towers. Please give me a family with an impressionable young child. Give me a man with an agitated and invasive dog. Better yet, kill two birds with one stone: give me a senior member of the NAACP to arrest this man and throw him into a maximum-security exfoliation facility.

The doors opened.

A moment passed.

The audible sound of Mitchell chewing gum.

Another moment passed.

No one entered.

The doors closed.

Shit.

'Anyway, how are you *really*, Gabe? I saw the removal van at the start of the month . . .' Mitchell tilted his head to the side, his peroxide tsunami of a hairstyle remaining stoic, and jutted out his bottom lip in a faux-sulky expression. His motive became clear. He wanted to extract any possible detail about my breakup. Mitchell seemed to absorb energy from gossip like palm trees do from the sun – and this strange photosynthesis was complete once he'd relayed the gossip to anyone with a pair of ears and a spare minute.

'And you've been getting a LOT of Deliveroos. Like, a lot. Plus – I thought you said you were on a health kick?'

We reached the ground floor, and the doors opened once more, revealing the bustle of the lobby. Stepping out of the lift, I tried to focus my energy on imagining the anaemic leftover Christmas tree that stood in the corner bursting into flames, rather than swatting at the annoying little Mitch that was hot on my heels.

'They're salads.'

'Sure. But Gabe, if you—'

'Got to run, Mitch – late already! See you soon, though. Text me next time you're out!' I added the platitude, knowing that a barrage of double-ticked and ignored messages would greet him when he opened our text conversation. I strolled out of the lift at a speed that would be considered fast,[1] even for the most seasoned CityGay™. I'd almost reached the automatic double doors of the exit when:

'Oh, by the way, Gabe. I know what happened with Seamus! *Everybody* at Kiss does.'

I stopped walking, rooted in place. Mitchell dropped the statement with nonchalance, but it hit me like a tonne of bricks. It was innocuous enough – Mitchell was drawn to drama like some kind of tropical orange moth to a flame and probably just wanted to insert himself – but his words made me instantly spiral. How did he know about what happened with my ex? I felt my jaw tense. Why did everybody at the third most popular bar in The Village also know? Did Seamus tell them? My heart rate switched from a pulse to a vibration, and my limbs stiffened. Were they all talking about it? Were they laughing at me? Did they, for some reason, hate me? When would I see them next? Was I about to have a heart attack? In front of Mitchell? That really would give them all something to laugh about. How embarrassing. Paul, the Broadgate concierge, to whom I'd grown close, would have to hold my hand while the ambulance came. Mum wouldn't make it here in time; she'd have to get a train because of her motorway anxiety. Dad's not my emergency contact; he'd only find out after it was too late. Manchester man dead. Beloved son and brother. Cherished friend. Aspiring writer. Pathetic ex. No kids. I didn't even have a will. What would I have left in a will? Minus £500 in an overdraft and a Nintendo Switch?

'Gabe – are you okay?' Mitchell's voice was muffled and distant, like the sound waves were moving through jelly. My mouth was arid.

---

[1] It is widely accepted that homosexual, city-dwelling men have the fastest gait amongst all human sub-types. The reasoning hasn't been verified but it's probably down to either a fear of being hate-crimed or a lack of driving licence

Not a heart attack, I hoped, but perhaps the early stages of a panic attack. This wasn't my first, and I'd learnt a tip from TikTok on how to deal with it. I needed to ground myself in my body by finding something that aligned with each of my senses.

I could **hear** traffic moving up and down Oldham Road, rhythmic, comforting.
I could **smell** citrus floor cleaner.
I could **feel** the tension from the straps of my rucksack against my shoulders.
I could **taste** toothpaste and Amber Leaf.
I could **see** Mitchell's denim jorts moving ever closer.

I shut my eyes. Deep inhale. Hold. Deeper exhale. I could feel Mitchell's hand on my shoulder, and my heartbeat started to return to normal. Deep inhale. Hold. Deeper exhale.

'Babe, do you need me to get you some help?' he asked. Opening my eyes, I noticed a gleam in his at the prospect of a crisis.

'No, thanks. I have to go, Mitch. I'm running late for work, and it's my first day back.'

'Are you sure? That was so weird. You didn't move for like, ages, and your eyes went wide. It was giving *That's So Raven*, but scary.'

'I'm fine.'

'Wait! Gabe, you said you'd been at work! What are you on about, "first day back"?!'

'See you later,' I shouted over my shoulder, not caring that I'd probably confirmed all of his suspicions as I walked through the automatic doors and into the city.

★ ★ ★

The journey from the flat at Broadgate to my place of work took a quarter of an hour, but this could alter by about two minutes on either side depending on whether I was listening to Beyonce's *Renaissance* or

Lana Del Rey's *Norman Fucking Rockwell!*. That morning, however, it would have to be the natural chorus of Piccadilly Gardens – the anaemic beep of a tram cutting through the pitter-patter of winter drizzle, a squabble of sodden teenagers dragging their feet across cigarette end-strewn paving, homeless men asking for change from apologetic yuppies – that would be the soundtrack to my commute. I needed to focus on collecting my thoughts after my near panic attack in the best way I knew how.

```
[08:28] Evie: It's not that I don't want
one. it's just that they ruin your life. it's
like having a child. Lauren got a Ragdoll, and
they're meant to suit being flat cats
[08:29] Tasha: Yeah, I've seen it all over her
socials
[08:29] Evie: She's had to put it on Pet-
s4Homes because it's chewed through the wires
of her Dyson Airwrap and only drinks from the
toilet
[08:34] Gabriel: She's kink-shaming her own
kitten? I never liked her vibe
```

I stopped at a corner shop and quickly nipped in to buy a depression breakfast of Reese's Peanut Butter Cups.

```
[08:36] Evie: Maybe she just wanted a
companion!
[08:36] Tasha: I think she just wanted an Ins-
tagram post
[08:37] Evie: How was Mitchell, Gabe?
[08:37] Gabriel: Well, he didn't talk much
about himself, actually
[08:37] Evie: That's not like him
[08:38] Tasha: It's a post-Christmas miracle!
```

[08:38] **Evie:** So, was he just quiet?
[08:39] **Gabriel:** God no, come on, Evie let's not be insane. he was just asking me a lot about Seamus
[08:39] **Evie:** How did he know that Seamus wasn't at Broadgate?
[08:39] **Gabriel:** He saw the removal van and he said he'd noticed I'd been getting a 'lot of Deliveroos'
[08:39] **Tasha:** Prick
[08:40] **Gabriel:** Right? They're mostly salads anyway
[08:40] **Evie:** Of course!
[08:40] **Tasha:** We know, Gabe

I swallowed the last peanut butter cup whole and stuffed the wrappers deep into my trouser pockets before licking my fingers clean.

[08:41] **Gabriel:** I nearly had a panny before
[08:41] **Evie:** Oh no. are you ok? It's been so long since you've had one
[08:42] **Gabriel:** No, it's fine, I'm fine, I think
[08:42] **Evie:** Are you sure you're feeling well enough to go back to work?
[08:43] **Tasha:** He's had two weeks off, Evie. It's not a choice at this point unless he wants to be on 'can't pay, we'll take it away'
[08:43] **Gabriel:** Thanks for the reminder, Dad. yeah, I need to, I miss the routine
[08:43] **Evie:** What triggered it?

The car park parallel to the offices loomed into view. I wandered through my colleagues' parked vehicles and waved at the cleaner as I stopped outside the rusted back entrance for a sneaky roll-up.

[08:46] **Gabriel:** The whole situation this morning. It's the first time I've come close to having to discuss the breakup with anyone except you guys and my family. even most of them don't know the full story. I hadn't planned what to say if anyone asked me about it

[08:47] **Evie:** You don't owe anyone an explanation, Gabe

[08:48] **Tasha:** Tea[2]. if anyone except us asks, feed them some media-trained bullshit that a Love Islander would fart out on a podcast. 'we're no longer together, but I wish him all the best.'

[08:48] **Gabriel:** But I don't

[08:49] **Tasha:** Obviously, but I think 'we're no longer together, and I hope he dies after being attacked by a swarm of Japanese murder hornets' would probs invite follow-up questions

[08:49] **Evie:** Omg, have they reached the UK? Japanese murder hornets?

[08:49] **Tasha:** What?

[08:49] **Gabriel:** What, no, Evie

Boddlies was the fast-fashion company I had reluctantly worked at since graduating university. Originally, I'd been part-time, with contracted hours slotted around my studies. My glamorous role during that era was completing menial duties around the offices and store rooms for minimum wage. After graduating, however, they offered me the prestigious title of 'Studio Assistant', where it was my sole responsibility to Photoshop away minuscule flaws from the faces of local models. Not *exactly* what I'd envisioned when analysing Robert Louis Stevenson's

---

[2] Tea. Truth, or gossip, depending on the context. Kind of diametrically opposed, but no one ever claimed that slang made sense

depiction of the duality of man during my three-year English Literature course. Jumping into a degree-relevant career immediately after graduating was normally a privilege reserved only for those who had upper-middle-class parents *with connections*, those who had upper-middle-class parents *who pay their rent for them while they get an internship*, or those who got their BSc in Computer Science, so I accepted the offer and became a slightly less tiny cog in the FastFashionClimateDeathMachine. Aside from being repulsed by the industry's terrible ethics, it wasn't ideal for several other reasons. The hours were long. The workload was intense due to how quickly new styles were introduced to meet the latest influencer-trickle-down trends. There was no window in the studio, meaning no daylight, and it also meant being trapped in an airtight room with Steve, the resident photographer, who – although charming, kind, and occasionally interesting – did have a tendency to develop a venomous strain of BO during Spring/Summer. That aside, it paid the bills at a time when the job market was stagnant, and the repetitive nature of the role was therapeutic. I needed that today. I'd hoped that having a job which occupied very little of my thought space after 5 p.m. might give me the opportunity to start forging a career around my chosen vocation, but pursuing freelance writing opportunities fell down my priority list once my relationship began to crumble. Steve wasn't in the studio when I arrived that morning, and the model wasn't due in for another hour, so I sat at my desk and began the herculean task of responding to the endless barrage of crucial correspondence I'd no doubt received during my absence:

Inbox (3 Unread):
becci.wains@boddlies.co.uk - **First floor men's toilet out of use**
chloesmith@ultramodels.co.uk - **RE Jenson Availability**
simon@boddlies.co.uk - **A 'Happy Holidays' surprise from Boddlies**

Three whole emails. How did they survive without me? The third was from December – and still unopened – after I'd naively taken a few days' annual leave in the run-up to Christmas to spend some extra quality time with my ex. What a festive fucking fool. Still, a 'happy holidays' *surprise*? From the CEO of Boddlies, no less. We were due a bonus, and I was overdue some good fortune.

> Hi All,
> Happy holidays to all at Boddlies, from me and mine to you and yours. I want to thank everybody for their hard work and commitment this year.
> As many of you know, our sales team missed their target – if only by a whisker! They've not had an easy job of it; markets everywhere are still suffering from ripple effects of the current climate and Boddlies margins are, unfortunately, another casualty.
> As the sharp amongst you (looking at you, Courtney!) may have deduced from this, there will be no official Christmas bonus this year.
> However, against the advice of the finance team, I've decided to, dare I say it, go a bit rogue – and reward everybody with a little unofficial bonus in the spirit of the holidays. If I get fired – you know why!
> I am attaching a £50 Amazon voucher to spend on whatever you please, and – totally unrelated – do remember your 20% staff discount on Boddlies sale items while finishing your Xmas shopping ;)
>
> *All my festive best,*
> *Simon*
> *Christmas Elf Officer*

I lifted my jaw up from the floor, took a picture of the computer screen and sent it to the group chat.

    [09:02] **Gabriel:** Guys - what do you think is
    the worst part of this email?
    [09:04] **Tasha:** This is like Sophie's Choice

[09:06] **Evie:** It has to be Christmas Elf Officer, that made me gag
[09:06] **Gabriel:** Ho Ho Ho!
[09:06] **Tasha:** No. NO. NO!!!
[09:08] **Evie:** What will you spend your voucher on, Gabe?
[09:08] **Gabriel:** Fifty quid? Our bonus is meant to be over five hundred. It's an insult. I feel like I can't accept it out of principle
[09:08] **Tasha:** You will, though
[09:09] **Evie:** You did say you wanted an air fryer
[09:09] **Gabriel:** Yeah, but not one that's handed to me by Simon Claus while I lie across his lap, giggling with my arms outstretched
[09:10] **Tasha:** Visceral. have you had this fantasy before?

There was a knock at the studio door.

'Come in!'

The ominous Silhouette of Janet, head of HR, appeared in the doorway.

'Good morning, Gabriel,' she drawled. Her voice sounded like Siri, if Siri was from Bury. Janet, as heads of HR often do, inspired a specific type of discomfort from any P45-fearing employee with a modicum of common sense. She had been a fixture at Boddlies since it opened its doors forty years ago. In those four decades, she'd dismissed seventeen junior merchandisers, eleven sales representatives, nine design interns, five heads of menswear, two samples management executives, and a partridge in a pear tree. I hadn't had many interactions with her, owing to my phobia of authority figures but, once, I panicked and offered her a Skittle as we passed each other in the corridor.

'Absolutely not,' she'd chuckled without stopping. It was the only time I'd ever heard her laugh.

'Hi Janet, it's nice to see you. How was your Christmas?' I asked, pocketing my phone, minimising the email from Simon, and opening Photoshop in one fell swoop.

'Yes, fine. Thank you,' she said with the enthusiasm of someone who'd just agreed to have their dog put down. 'How was yours?'

I would've sobbed if anybody else had asked that question and told them the truth: that it was the worst Christmas of my life, that my heart was broken and that I was terrified that I wouldn't ever be able to love another person again.

'Lovely, cheers. The only thing that would've made it better would've been some snow. Shame I got ill towards the end but I'm feeling much better now, thank you.' I forced a smile.

'I'm glad. Well, look, Gabriel. I need to have a word with you.'

'Sure, I'll grab you a chair, just—'

'No, no. I'll stand.'

'Okay. Heads-up, though, Steve will be here soon, and we've got a model coming in shortly as well, so if you'd like to go some—'

'It's fine. Steve won't be coming into the studio today, and we've rescheduled the model for next week in your absence.'

I looked up at Janet but avoided eye contact. Now, she stood parallel to me, her hands clutching a black leather clipboard against her midriff, and I got a sudden, sickening feeling that this wasn't a standard return-to-work interview.

'Gabriel, there's no easy way to say this, especially with your recent ill health.' Her lifeless eyes met mine momentarily, and I detected the hint of a challenge. It was as though Janet, a woman who had spent her adult life on the receiving end of sick calls, both genuine and fake, might've managed to figure out that my 'undercooked Christmas turkey leading to two weeks of intense food poisoning' story wasn't entirely true. 'But Simon has made the difficult decision to render the role of Studio Assistant redundant as of today. Steve will be taking over the editing. Budget has to be taken into account, especially with the markets in free-fall. He feels he has to prioritise frugality. There are just so many factors to consider.'

'What about my career here, is that not a factor?' I blurted. It was surprising that I didn't get struck by lightning on the spot as I'd spent most of my time at Boddlies daydreaming about being elsewhere.

'Gabriel . . .' Janet's lips thinned, and her mouth tightened until it looked almost exactly like a cat's arsehole. 'I think we both know your commitment to a "career" at Boddlies has been . . . fragile . . . at best. You currently hold the record for most sick days amongst any employee in the history of the company.'

I felt a twinge of pride.

'We're letting you go, Gabriel, effective immediately.'

The twinge disappeared. I thought of Steve and some of the models I'd become close to, and remembered sitting on my sofa many years ago watching Davina McCall send shockwaves through the *Big Brother* house by announcing a surprise eviction. 'You have ten seconds to say your goodbyes – I'm coming to get you!' But she wasn't. And there wasn't any opportunity for goodbyes, no potential fanfare, no comforting hug from a charismatic mother figure. It was just me, Janet, and her irritatingly stylish asymmetrical bob.

'You'll get two months' severance pay, which I think you'll agree is very generous.'

I stood up, steadied my shaking knees, picked up my backpack, looked Janet directly in the eyes and said, 'I'd expect nothing less from the "Chief Elf Officer". Goodbye, Janet.'

I walked past her and out into the corridor. My head was swimming, and my body could barely maintain balance. Yes, I was nauseous at the thought of an uncertain future and paralysed by the trauma of my recent past. But I'd maintained my dignity and composure at a time when most would've lost them. Not only that, I'd stood up to Janet and finished with a cutting remark that, frankly, I was ecstatic had come to me at the opportune moment. I was leaving triumphant, with my head held high. I hoped Mina in reception had heard my zinger; they'd all be talking about this for months.

'Gabriel?' Janet's voice reverberated through the hall. I turned to face her one last time.

'What, Janet?'

'You're, erm . . . you're flying low,' she said, nodding towards my crotch. I felt my ears burn. 'And you've got something on your chin. I think it's chocolate, but I'm not sure.' She looked disgusted.

For fuck's sake.

2

Goodness and Grief

Monday/Tuesday (Denial)
I couldn't believe this was happening. Who manages to stop getting laid, then gets laid off in the space of a month? It's often posited that processing a breakup can feel similar to processing a death. If that were the case, how was processing a breakup, losing your job, and inadvertently showing the head of HR a glimpse of your ancient Calvin Kleins supposed to feel? This multiple grief was impossible to navigate. I felt like I was the one remaining baby hamster whose mother had panic-eaten my siblings and left me bewildered, naked and alone in an entirely new world. And so, like a hamster, I scuttled to my wheel and entered a cycle of comfort and distraction. Sofa. Relentless scrolling through social media. Chain-smoking. Rudy's Deliveroos. Scroll while eating. Re-runs of *Game of Thrones* while scrolling. Bed. Porn wank. Sleep. Vivid nightmare about being locked in a submarine at the bottom of the ocean with Bradley Walsh, wherein I had to answer general knowledge questions to make the submarine rise to the surface. Woke up just as I got a question about the capital of Pakistan wrong. Imagination wank, that, in parts, included a fantasy version of Naval Officer Bradley Walsh with giant hairy pecs and ridiculous abs. Sofa. Felt weird about the Bradley Walsh reverie. Watched *Countryfile* to regain some wholesomeness. Scroll. Lied to Evie and Tasha (who were insistent upon coming around to check if I was okay) and told them I was staying at my Mum's 'for a reset'. More *Game of Thrones*. Bada Bing sandwich ordered on Deliveroo. Bed. Scroll. 'Ancient Library Ambient Sounds' playing in the background. Sleep.

Wednesday (Anger)
Signing a flat contract with your then-boyfriend, only to have the relationship explode part way through, is an experience I would only

recommend to my enemies[3]. Less 'Live, Laugh, Love' wall art and more 'Die, Cry, Resent'. The emotional fallout from the blast had rendered me incapable of thinking about – let alone addressing – any pressing logistics. It wasn't ideal then that, three weeks after the breakup, and after my sudden foray into unemployment, I was woken up by a hard rap at my apartment door. I slithered from bed, threw on a crumpled hoody from my floordrobe and meandered into the living area. Unplanned social visits are a rarity for people like me (Zillennials with a myriad of undiagnosed mental health problems), so it could only be one of three things. As I looked through the peephole, I morning-breathed a sigh of relief as I realised it was the best possible option: Paul, one of the building managers who usually manned the front desk. I spent a lot of time in reception because of the whole 'always losing keys' and 'addicted to consumerism so regularly collecting packages' situations, so we'd grown close quickly.

'Gabe! 'appy New Year, mate,' beamed Paul as I opened the door. He leaned forward over the threshold, ignored the green stink lines wafting from my shoulders and the cloud of cartoon flies buzzing around my head and locked me in a bear hug.

'Happy New Year, Paul,' I mumbled into his enormous neck.

''ow are ya, kid? You look a lickle bit *on edge*,' he said, overly enunciating the last two words in his thick Mancunian accent. Paul was an absolute diamond – funny, thoughtful and refused to suffer fools – but he only had two volume settings: loud and louder.

'I'm alright, you know.' It was becoming increasingly difficult to say this with conviction. 'I was worried you were the TV licence people. Or Mitchell.' I forced a smile.

Paul guffawed. 'Have they bin sendin' you letters again? The Beeb? Bastards. I've not paid mine ever since the whole Corbyn *Newsnight* fiasco. Impartial, my hairy white arse.'

'Yeah, I'd love to pretend mine was a political protest, but to be honest, Paul, I've never paid it. Anyway, how was your Christmas?'

---

[3] Amateur DJs

'Ah, yeah, it was alright, mate. Same old for the most part. Kristen – my daughter, you know – came back from Oz, so it was nice to see 'er. She's got a new fella 'n' all, brought him along without letting anybody know beforehand. The wife wasn't best pleased. We'll blame the state of Christmas dinner on that.' He laughed.

'What was he like? Kristen's boyfriend?'

'He's sound, good lad. Well-paid job. Not tight or anything like that. He seems to worship her, as 'e should. No complaints. Except . . .' There was always an 'except'. 'Except after we'd finished dinner, after a few bevvies . . . he did this thing where 'e kept on slapping the back of me head! Out of nowhere!' He was shouting, his prominent brow furrowed. Paul was very tall, very round, and was one of those unfortunate men who started growing hair at three years old, started losing it at nineteen and, by their mid-twenties, looked like someone had ironed Ross Kemp. At fifty-three, though, he'd grown into it, and it was almost impossible to imagine him any other way.

'That's a bit weird?'

'Well . . . yeah! That's what I thought. He did it a couple of times, usually after someone cracked a joke and we were all having a laugh . . . you know, almost like how we might slap each other on the back and that? So I thought it might just be an Aussie thing, at first.' He started rubbing the back of his bald head while he spoke, as if soothing a war wound.

'But 'e just kept doing it. Harder and harder, as well, so I flipped. I said, "Excuse me, my mate, have you lost something? Because you're not gonna find it on the back of my bonce!"' Paul's tone had lightened slightly, and I was laughing now. 'Shat himself, bless him. Never heard an Aussie with a stammer before. He said, "Nah, mate, sorry. I wasn't trying to be funny but . . . you've got tinsel sticking out of your jumper. I was tryna pick it out for you without anyone noticing!"' he finished, trying to imitate an Australian accent but instead sounding like Robert Irwin after a gap year in Mumbai.

Once we'd both stopped laughing, I invited him in and put the kettle on.

★ ★ ★

'Stinks in here, Gabe. Crack a window or something, mate,' said Paul, awkwardly perched on the only sofa space that wasn't covered in miscellaneous items of clothing or empty snack packets.

'Oh yeah, sorry. I've not been feeling well. Here.' I handed him his brew before doing as he said, then moved an empty multipack of Wotsits to sit next to him.

'Cheers. You don't seem yourself. Where's your fella?' he asked. Paul never used Seamus's name. Even when we were together, it was always 'your fella' or 'your hubby'. Behind closed doors, Seamus insisted that Paul didn't like him, but I'd reassure him that he was paranoid and that Paul liked everyone.

'He's not here. He's . . .' I thought about lying to Paul or giving him the 'we're no longer together, but I wish him the best in all his future endeavours' line that Tasha had suggested earlier in the week. He was looking at me with such kindness that I didn't. I caved and told him everything, from the details of the breakup with Seamus to being laid off.

'That little shitstain!' boomed Paul once I'd finished the entire sordid tale. 'I never liked him. Never. Wouldn't give anyone the time of day and always thought he was a cut above. The utter bastard. Turns out 'e's below. WAY below. He better not show his face in these parts again, or it'll be you and me both out of a job.' He slapped his meaty hand onto my shoulder. 'You're gonna be alright, 'r kid. I promise. You're such a light, Gabe. You were too bright for him, mate. And the job, you're better than that 'n' all. You know I'm only downstairs for a chat. We can go for a pint when you're feeling like yourself again. Whatever you need, mate, whenever.'

I wanted to respond but was momentarily overwhelmed. I wished I could cry, to create little tributaries for the reservoir of pain that had burst its banks inside my mind, but I couldn't. All I felt was anger. Waves of unfathomable frustration at the injustice of it all. The betrayal. The time wasted. All the memories that used to pop with colour, as if the saturation had been dialed up to max, had turned blurry, poisoned and purple. I saw Janet from HR's smug face as she delivered the news and thought about Simon, laughing to himself as he typed the 'Chief Elf Officer' pun with one hand and signed off on my redundancy with the other. Then, my thoughts drifted to that place I'd done my utmost over the last few days to stop them from reaching – to that moment in the kitchen on Christmas Day. To the notification on Seamus's phone.

I stood up from the sofa and screamed 'FOR FUCK'S SAKE!' not caring for the neighbours' opinions, the chances of me developing a vocal polyp like Adele in 2011 or for poor Paul – who was dumbfounded at first but then stood up next to me and joined in at twice the volume.

'WHAT A PAIR OF TWATS!' he roared. His face, whose resting shade was puce anyway, turned beetroot. This went on for a while until we both fell back, exhausted.

'Do you know what, Gabe?' Paul said, struggling to regain control of his breath.

'What, Paul?'

'It might make you feel better if you get yourself down to the gym. Great way to get all the aggression out, you know. Endorphins and that too. Plus . . .' he nodded towards my belly, visible through the now ill-fitting hoody I'd thrown on earlier. 'You'll end up like me if you're not careful, and you don't want that. The sight of me own todger's a distant dream at this point.'

Thursday (Bargaining)

I woke up to my 10:00 alarm without hitting snooze. This small victory made me feel more human and less worm, so I decided to shower (the first in a medically dangerous amount of time) and began to emerge from my disgusting chrysalis. After washing, I cleaned the entire flat from top to bottom. This took two and a half hours and was soundtracked by Radio 1 DJ Nat O'Leary's 'noughties and nothing else', with a rare burst of serotonin courtesy of Natasha Bedingfield during the floor-sweeping portion.

[13:04] **Gabriel:** Hi guys
[13:04] **Tasha:** Hello stranger!
[13:05] **Evie:** Gaaaaaabe!
[13:06] **Gabriel:** I've woken up and had a shower and I've just finished cleaning the flat. she looks gorgeous
[13:06] **Tasha:** Brilliant! I was beginning to smell you from Didsbury
[13:06] **Evie:** Proud of you!!! i thought you were at your mum's?

I was shit at lying.

[13:10] **Gabriel:** That was a lie, sorry. i needed to stew for a bit.
[13:11] **Evie:** I get it. you should go to your mum's, though, she always cheers you up. and just say in the future, Gabe! Lying doesn't suit you, and you're shit at it

She was right, I really was shit at it.

[13:11] **Gabriel:** SEEING Mum cheers me up, staying at her house does not. too many ghosts.

Returning home with my tail between my legs would also feel like an admission of defeat. Like life had beaten me.

[13:12] **Evie:** It might be healing for you, though, Gabe, to go home for a bit. regress to progress, you know
[13:12] **Tasha:** Evie, that sounds like something you've stolen from a fridge magnet in the staffroom. Anyway, Gabe, does this mean we can come over?

[13:14] **Gabriel**: I'm going to the gym today. i want to start running again. i've also got my nicotine patches on. i'm quitting. then, I'm going to go to the shops. i'm starting to get cabin fever. then I'm going to ring my mum. Just to speak to her. Not go to home and stay. Just a call. Then, after that, maybe

[13:14] **Evie**: Is this a 'new year, new you' kind of thing?

[13:15] **Tasha**: Evie, that's for 48-year-old women who're stuck in pyramid schemes to put as their Facebook status

[13:16] **Gabriel**: It's more of a 'maybe if I wasn't a lazy recluse who smokes his body weight in cigs and can't stop eating his feelings I wouldn't have been shat on by the only man I've ever loved and then fired' kind of thing

[13:17] **Evie**: Come on, Gabe, neither of those things were your fault

[13:17] **Tasha**: He's got a point though

[13:17] **Gabe**: Why don't you eat my ass, Tasha

[13:17] **Tasha**: I will if you shut up and let us come round

[13:18] **Gabe**: I'll text you later on!

With that, I threw my packet of Amber Leaf into the bin and headed to the gym, taking the first steps on the road to glory.

Friday (Depression)

The road to glory ended up being a short alleyway to disappointment. I only managed a twelve-minute run before getting out of breath and going on TikTok. I caved and bought a new packet of tobacco at the shop, tore my nicotine patch off by dinnertime and forgot about calling Mum. However, the instant access to cigs turned out to be a lifeline the next afternoon. I was cooking a nutritious superfood dinner (bacon barm) when I received an unexpected message in my Instagram inbox:

Cathrynnn: Hi Gabe! Long time. I've not got Shay on socials, but I've seen that you guys are living together . . . please could you tell him how much I adored the poem he uploaded onto his blog last night? I broke up with my boyfriend recently (some might call it an anxious attachment style, I'd call it fucking exhausting!) and it resonated. It's great that he's sticking with his writing. Hope you are too!

Suddenly, the living room felt cramped and claustrophobic. My ex and I had met and fell in love as course-mates studying English Literature at university. Seamus had always kept up with his writing – his outlet was poetry – and regularly updated his blog to an audience of over a hundred subscribers, one hundred people who could now have access to intimate parts of our relationship. I'd been checking it almost every day[4]. Was it going to be some kind of diss poem about me? Was I now, non-consensually, part of the gay white British equivalent of a *rap beef*? My palms were sweating, knees weak, bacon barm was heavy as I hurriedly typed the URL to Seamus's poetry blog.

http://theotherseamus.poetblog.com
18 January
the claw

> look at you
> shaking
> sweaty hands out
> pleading

---

[4] Every night, actually. Right before I fall asleep. As anyone with a broken heart knows - this is the most appropriate time for self-flagellation

little lips
trembling
begging for one of those I love yous

                                  look at me
                                 knackered
                        eyes tired of rolling
                      primed to start dolling
               the familiar hollow platitude
                        an earthquake
                        zero magnitude
                where the utterance falls
                       and dissipates
                                  flaccid
                                prostrate

look at you
expectant
infantile
insecure
green
like one of those desperate little aliens
from toy story
silently screaming
pick me!
pick me!

                                  look at me
                        falsely reassuring
                                      cold
                                  metallic
                                dangling
             like i'm the pizza planet claw
                    and i pick you up
              and you shut the fuck up
there's no deus ex machina for us.

Every line felt like Paul's Australian son-in-law running behind me and slapping the back of my head at full pelt.

    [18:09] **Gabriel:** Guys, I need to see you. i
    need to get out of the flat. something's hap-
    pened. meet me at Flawd in an hour.

★ ★ ★

Flawd was a trendy wine bar in an idyllic spot on Ancoats Marina, not far from my flat, with a calming view of the water and the barges bobbing along it. It was always packed and popping, so we could chat at a tipsy volume without being overheard.

'You're going to have to translate this for us, I think, Gabe,' Tasha said, looking across the tiny, circular table at me expectantly. 'Poetry isn't my forte; even if it was, I'm not fluent in prick.' By day, Tasha worked as a data analyst at one of the 'big four' firms. She would make little to no effort with regards to her in-office appearance, often opting for a severe bun and a lot of black but it was an entirely different story when she was in town. Her ice-blonde hair was parted at the middle and fell in loose curls past her shoulders, which were draped in a chestnut faux-fur jacket. She wore minimal makeup on her already flawless alabaster skin, but a hint of bronzer beneath her high cheekbones, dark red lipstick, and a thin feline cat eye to accentuate her hazel eyes. She was strikingly beautiful – and knew it – but never wanted to acknowledge or discuss it. Not because she was particularly insecure – and certainly not through modesty, which she viewed as dishonest – but because it was uninteresting to her, and that was one thing she couldn't stand.

'Is he saying that you look like an alien?' Evie asked, frowning with concentration. Evie was the polar opposite in both appearance and personality to Natasha. Tall and willowy, Evie was a teaching assistant at a local primary school who dressed more like a wood nymph that had escaped from a glade in the Peak District than a faculty member. Her auburn hair was long and flowing, with twists and braids peppered throughout, a style that both framed her warm face and recalled old illustrations of princesses in Celtic folklore. If you were to compliment Evie on any aspect of herself, she would blush, disagree, mumble a reluctant 'thanks', and then treasure it forever.

'He's *saying* I was a needy, tragic, reassurance-seeking child that he had to force himself to love. On the internet, to all our old classmates.' I groaned, sipping the Lithuanian wine that Tasha had chosen from the bar. It was crisp, dry and very, very bitter.

'And do you know what the worst part is?' I asked.

'The "pick me, pick me" bit?' Evie offered.

'The line about you having sweaty hands?' suggested Tasha.

'No. Well, yeah, those are mortifying. I'm not sure the sweaty hands line was supposed to be literal. I think it's meant to convey how desperate I was for him to love me. My hands only sweat when I'm anxious. Maybe it is literal, but anyway, this only further illustrates my point. The worst part is that it's *layered*. The worst part is that it's a good poem, and it's about me — on the internet.'

'I think if it was *really* good, Gabe, it would be published in an anthology, or whatever, rather than sat on his lonely little blog,' Tasha said. 'The whole thing comes across like an arrogant post-grad who thinks that every insignificant feeling they have should be screamed to an audience, transcribed onto a stone slate and put in a museum for normies to gape at in wonder, but like I said, I don't get poetry.' She took a large sip from her glass for dramatic effect.

'What does he mean by "there's no *deus ex machina* for us"?' Evie was squinting at the poem on her phone screen.

'Do you know what *deus ex machina* means, Evie? Do you understand the term but not the context? Cause I don't want to mansplain, but then you are incredibly thick.' I smirked. Both Evie and Tasha burst out laughing. Evie's intelligence level was a running gag within the group, which she revelled in. She was intuitive, astoundingly creative, and emotionally intelligent, but she often misunderstood things or tuned out if the conversation surrounded a topic she wasn't invested in. She would insist this had nothing to do with her functional cannabis addiction.

'I know it's Latin, but I've not got the foggiest. Go on, Gabe, just go! Mansplain, you're chimping at the bit!' She was right. She may have got the idiom wrong, but she was right.

'*Deus ex machina* is a concept used in film or literature whereby the characters are stuck in a situation that appears to be hopeless, and then some kind of godly figure or previously unknown power materialises out of nowhere to save the day. It's considered cheap. They use it a lot in *Doctor Who*. The Doctor will suddenly work out the solution to a problem that's been present and unsolvable throughout the episode, using nothing but a sudden boost in intelligence that allows him to piece together clues that didn't exist to any of the other characters or the viewers at home.'

'But you *don't* want to mansplain?' laughed Tasha.

'So in this context,' I continued through pursed lips, ignoring the interruption, 'Seamus is saying "there's no *deus ex machina* for us" as in, nothing could save us by that point. Which is true. And an effective closing line to an effective poem.' I could feel my cheeks turning red and my toes curling under the table.

'Look, Gabe. It's bad. No one wants to be insulted online. No one wants their dirty laundry aired, even if it is cryptic,' Evie began.

'I don't care that it's cryptic. It feels like there are magazine articles with the headline GABRIEL AND SEAMUS SPLIT, AND IT'S GABRIEL'S FAULT! stuck to every lamp-post in Manchester.' I was shouting now, panic seeping into my words. I thought about all of our mutual friends at university reading the poem. Would they be able to decipher it? Taylor Swift fans manage to decode all of her lyrics – surely people who are studied in poetry would be able to put two and two together. What if it was published? Would my first foray into the literary world be as a flaccid, fumbling, feeble muse? I began to picture memes emerging – photos of my face superimposed onto the tiny aliens from *Toy Story*.

'This is my worst fear,' I groaned, tapping my foot under the table with anxiety.

'I thought your worst fear was getting stuck in a long conversation with David Beckham?' Tasha said.

Evie swallowed a smirk at Tasha's comment.

'That's still up there.'

'Gabe, I get that you feel embarrassed. He shouldn't have done this so soon, or at all really. But you have to remember . . .' Here, Evie paused and leaned across the table to grab my (perfectly dry) hand. 'The people who matter know that the only one who deserves to feel embarrassed is him. Not you. You did nothing wrong, Gabe. He should be so ashamed of himself.'

Evie rarely lost her temper, but she was gripping my hand fiercely now. Her eyes had turned to a steely glaze, her voice had lost its musical mellowness, replaced by a rough half-growl that verged on frightening. Sometimes I'd wondered how, in all her airy mellowness, Evie managed to retain control over a class of boisterous Mancunian children, but when she slipped into this mood it became clear.

'You should feel lucky to have got away. He's the loser, Gabe. He's a despicable person. He doesn't have the self-awareness to learn from this, so he'll stay a despicable person. I could strangle him for what he did to you. I hope he never darkens *any* of our doorsteps again. He pulled the wool over our eyes – we loved him too, Gabe. But none of that matters anymore. He's nothing but a low-life piece of shite who's probably rotting in some overpriced, rat-infested London flatshare! He had to run away! And good riddance.' Evie's grip loosened from 'hydraulic press' back to 'gentle support'.

'*He* lost *you*! What could be worse than that?' she asked, eyes filling with tears. For the first time since everything began to unravel, so were mine.

'I just can't stop thinking . . . I can't stop feeling like . . .' I paused to try to catch my voice and stop it from breaking, but failed. 'I'm trying to distract myself constantly because, if I sit with my brain for too long, I come to the same conclusion every time.' Tears flowed freely, and I felt grateful that we'd chosen a table tucked away in the corner. 'That I'm a shit person. I must be. I must be shit at my job. I must be shit to live with. I must be a shit shag. I must be a shit boyfriend. Just be honest with me, guys.' I looked up at the faces of two of the people I loved most in the world. Evie's, blotchy and devastated, and Tasha's, uncomfortable yet concerned. 'Am I just shit?' I burst into uncontrollable sobs.

Of course, my best friends sprang into action. Evie bounded to the bar to grab two bottles of wine. Would we have preferred a budget-friendly Sainsbury's Taste the Difference? Yes. But time was of the essence: I hadn't managed to regulate my emotions and people were starting to stare. Tasha escorted me away from our table at Flawd, throwing terrifying glances at any of the well-dressed punters who looked our way, and out onto the frostbitten marina. Even though it was within walking distance, we grabbed an Uber, and I cried for the entire four-minute journey back home. A new personal best.

★ ★ ★

It was a testament to my fragile emotional state that Tasha didn't comment on my living conditions as we huddled together under the duvet, glasses of wine in hand. She had been quiet since my minor breakdown, with Evie doing almost all of the emotional lifting, but now it was her time to shine.

'OK, Gabe, you're overwhelmed. What you need are some *solutions*. Here.' She reached into her black leather handbag and pulled out a tatty notebook before tearing out a page and handing it to me along with an old biro. Tasha was ready for everything. 'Write down the five reasons why you're feeling depressed, and we'll come up with some ways to get through it. Go.'

'Am I limited to five?' I asked, withering under Tasha's glare before starting to scrawl. When I was finished, I handed the paper to her, and she disappeared into the living room. She was gone for about fifteen minutes, which gave Evie and me just enough time to watch Shakira and Jennifer Lopez's half-time show on the iPad (again). Tasha returned as Shakira triumphantly shouted 'Muchas gracias!' to the cheering crowd, and thrust the piece of paper into my hand with just as much gusto and pride.

DEPRESSION LIST
1. **I am unemployed.**
   Don't worry about this for now. I've just spoken with Scott, and he's going to see if he can get you a job at his place. First, go back to your mum's and rest.
2. **I am unhappy with the way that I look and feel because I can't stop eating and won't start exercising.**
   Don't worry about this for now. You have a gym in your apartment building. When the time is right, you can start prioritising your physical health again. First, go back to your mum's and rest.
3. **Paul came round earlier today. It was nice to see him, and we jumped around screaming for a bit, but then he told me that Seamus had taken himself off the council tax. I need to find a replacement flatmate or I'll fall into financial ruin.**
   I'm struggling to imagine Paul airborne. Don't worry about this for now. I rang your mum. She says your brother is looking to move back up North so he could take the spot. She wants you to go back to hers first, though, and rest.
4. **I am single and alone.**
   You are not alone. God knows why, but you are surrounded by people that love you.
5. **On Tuesday, I accidentally had a wank over Bradley Walsh.**
   Oh my god, Gabe. Please go back to your mum's and rest.

So I did.

★★★

Spiralling 33

Exposition Weekly!

www.exposition.co

17 January

ONLY AVAILABLE AT 2 A.M., INSIDE THE MIND OF GABRIEL LANES!

GABRIEL AND SEAMUS SPLIT!

A N G E L DOWN . . . *Exposition Weekly!* can exclusively reveal that in the early hours of Boxing Day, Gabriel Lanes broke up with his then-boyfriend, Seamus Monks, in explosive and scandalous circumstances. In an unprecedented scoop, we sat down with the recently fired flop to get all the juicy details of the breakup on *everyone's* lips.

Q: Why did you agree to this interview so soon after the events of Christmas Day?

A: Well, it was two in the morning, and I couldn't sleep, so I had no choice. You wouldn't leave me alone. I'd replayed the scenes from Christmas in my head so many times that I assumed my brain was coming up with new ways for me to explore them. Maybe it was torture. Maybe it was catharsis.

Q: Maybe it was Maybelline! (Turn to page 3 for 10% off the new WONDEREYES Mascara.) So, Gabriel, set the scene. How did everything begin that fateful festive Friday?

A: Okay. The lounge at my father's house was buzzing with merriment and anticipation; the festive scent of roast turkey, bubbling cauliflower cheese and several Jo Malone candles wafted around the open-plan kitchen. Wine, Baileys and Guinness had flowed freely for hours, and it was almost time to eat.

Q: Who was there?

A: My whole family. Well, my parents got a divorce, so obviously, no one from my mum's side. It was my brother, Dan. My older sister, Anna, who's pregnant—

Q: WOW. That's an exclusive! Will Exposition Weekly! have rights to the first photos of the little cherub?

A: Erm . . . sure, is it normal for an interviewer to interrupt like this?

Q: Yes, it is when it's *your* brain! Answer the question.

A: Right. My brother, my sister and her boyfriend. Then, my father, Jeremy, my stepmother, Ivy, and her son, Luca.

Q: Many people struggle to connect with a new stepfamily; what's your relationship like with yours?

A: I haven't known them for too long; my Dad and Ivy only married a few years ago. Ivy, my stepmother, has been lovely. She always makes us feel welcome. She spent a lot of money transforming the house for the festive period. She always spends a lot of money. Mum doesn't like her, obviously. It was usually tastefully decorated, but during the last week of November, it became this kind of garish winter wonderland.

Q: And what about your stepbrother, Luca? Do you get on with him?

A: Sure, I mean, I... He's a few years younger than me. But he's gay, too, the only other one in the family, so that always helped. It meant that my father could increase his 'number of homosexuals interacted with' tally from one to two. It also meant that I had somebody to roll my eyes with if anyone ever used the term 'woke' pejoratively. He's very different to me, though. Obsessed with the gym. He's also fucking enormous. Bright red hair.

Q: Sounds like you need our 10 WAYS TO GET SHREDDED FOR SPRING! guide, Gabriel! (Turn to page 9). How had things been, up until that point, with your boyfriend, Seamus?

A: We'd had a... tumultuous year. Our honeymoon phase, if we'd ever had one, had ended. We moved into a city-centre apartment together, Broadgate Towers. It was stressful. I worked, but he just wanted to pursue writing. Finances became an issue. The last dregs of romance were swilled away with the dirty dishwater while we argued over washing up; long conversations about our shared creative goals were replaced by unsuccessfully trying to hide farts with coughs. But, I thought it was salvageable. By Christmas, I'd thought we were over the hump, so to speak.

Q: And speaking of, how was your sex life?

A: Inconsistent. But it was getting better.

Q: That's great! Many are calling the reasons for your breakup 'outrageous', 'sordid' and 'something that seemed more like an extract from a badly written porn film than reality'. Can you tell us exactly what happened that led to the split? Start at the beginning.

A: Will you let me speak this time? I like to retread every single detail to relive the pain over and over again in an agonising cycle that causes endless harm and anxiety and makes it impossible for me to move on.

Q: Go ahead!

A: Thank you. So, it was late afternoon, and dinner was almost ready. Dad was in the kitchen, finishing up the cooking. Dan had gone for a sneaky spliff behind the shed and then been cajoled into a prosecco by my stepmother, so had fallen asleep in the armchair. The rest of us played charades. It was hilarious. Ivy tried to act out the word 'mockingbird' in To Kill a Mockingbird, *but no one could guess it. Her arm movements looked more like a Boeing 747 crashing than a bird. Luca and I figured it out eventually. I was surprised because he's not very well read, prefers weightlifting, you know?*

Q: You can't have it all! (Turn to page 14 for an extract from Girlboss: HOW TO HAVE IT ALL!). Go on?

A: I noticed Seamus was being quiet. So, when my whole family went to sit for dinner, I pulled him aside to have a word. He'd been glued to his phone for a lot of the day. It was rude. I didn't like how he did that when it was just us two, never mind in front of my family.

Q: And on Christmas!

A: Exactly! And he'd been doing it so much recently, since the move. Hunched over the screen, couldn't hold a conversation. So I pulled him up on it. He agreed and put his phone on the kitchen counter out of reach to charge. We said we loved each other, then went into the dining room for dinner.

Q: AH! So this must be the scene of the crime? *The Dining Room* **– the last supper, so to speak!**

A: You're very irritating. No, we were eating dinner, which was a picture-perfect family scene. Hearty food was interrupted only by drunken belly laughs and playful banter. Once we'd finished, Ivy brought in three bottles of champagne and did this toast. It barely made sense, but her heart was in the right place. My sister, Anna, read through a list of potential baby names and got pissed off if she didn't get a loud enough 'aw!' after every single one. Luca and Seamus swapped tips for increasing your protein intake; Shay started the gym a few months back, so he was hungry for information. Dad brought in more champagne. Everyone did a performance of 'Fairytale of New York'.

Q: Did they sing the F slur?
A: Of course.

Q: Brilliant!
A: Then, I excused myself to wash the dishes. I wanted to help out, and my social battery was close to zero. Some time alone felt like a good idea.

Q: Then what happened?
A: Well, there were piles of gravy-stained plates, half-abandoned glasses, and fat-encrusted baking trays. It took me ages. My hands were raw from scrubbing.

Q: It's a hard life.
A: It is. But I could hear everyone in the next room having a great time, which was nice. That feeling. Of family.

Q: Aw.
A: Then I heard someone running up the stairs (they back onto the kitchen so you can hear each step and identify who's on them). That's another thing with family, isn't it? You know how everyone goes up the stairs. Just by the sound.

Q: Who was it?
A: My stepbrother, Luca. Like I said, he's massive, so he does these big, galumphing strides that make the house feel like it's going to cave in. It used to make me laugh.

Q: Was the nail-bitingly scandalous reason you and Seamus broke up because he didn't help you with the dishes?
A: I wish. No, I leaned forward to flick the kettle on. I remember this part perfectly. The steam from the kettle unfurled into translucent plumes. They were swirly, like 'Starry Night' by Van Gogh. Then, a bright light shone through them from the kitchen side.

Q: What was it? The light?
A: Seamus's phone, which he'd left charging. He was getting a couple of WhatsApp notifications.

Q: Did you look at them?
A: No.

Q: Did you want to?
A: Yes.

Q: Then what?
A: Then I carried on washing up, unaware that my life was about to be torn into a million pieces. After another few minutes, his phone buzzed again. And again. WhatsApp. It was past midnight at this point, during Christmas. I thought I trusted him, but apparently, I did not.

Q: So you looked?
A: Yes.

Q: And what did the messages say?
A: I need a moment.

At this stage, our interview paused. We were unsure whether Gabriel had fallen asleep, but after a few minutes, he returned.

Q: Hello again.
A: Hi.

Q: So, back to the messages on Seamus's phone. Did you know his passcode?
A: I did, but I'd only ever used it to put a song on the speaker. Or set a timer, or whatever. I'd never invade somebody's privacy like that.

Q: But you did.
A: But I did then, yes.

Q: And what did they say? What were the messages?
A: I saw two. The first said: 'Quick, we've not got long. He's in the kitchen doing the washing up. I'm in the study like last time.'
Q: And the second?
A: The second said: 'Come up, I want you.'

Q: And who were the messages from, to your then-boyfriend, Seamus?
A: They were from my stepbrother, Luca.

3

Mum's the Word

I had always envied the people in their twenties who, when life forced them to stay for longer than a week at a parent's house, remained unfazed or even . . . happy. Like ninety per cent of gayboys, I adored my mother, and we had always had a tight-knit relationship, even if it had probably evolved from parent/child to friend/confidant far too soon. Stepping back into the home of my teenage years – a place where the walls had drunk in a hundred arguments, the ceilings had shrunk back as I lay in bed paralysed with angsty depression staring at them for hours, and the sofa had slowly adapted to the grooves of my body after months foetal on the PlayStation – was triggering, to say the least. I didn't visit my mother's house for longer than a weekend unless there was a special occasion or an emergency, so it had become a kind of crisis centre in my psyche. It wasn't the home of my early childhood that I'd lived in with my siblings when my parents were together; it was the refuge Mum had built post-divorce. I'd never been happy there as a teenager. It existed to me now as a stark, bricks-and-mortar reminder of a broken half-child who hated himself and whose self-hatred spilt outwards, infecting anyone who came within close proximity. It was the house whose mortgage payments had crippled my mother, who had struggled to care for two teenagers and one young adult while holding down a minimum-wage job as a care assistant. It was the place where I had tried to come to terms with my sexuality, but was only after I had left these confines, only once I had wriggled and fought until I flopped out of the goldfish bowl that was Romiley, only after I had fled to a city and connected with likeminded people, that I experienced enough empathy to burn the shame of growing up queer in a small town to a crisp like a mosquito under a magnifying glass. In Romiley, being queer meant being infamous. There were only about four openly gay boys in my generation who showed up at the house parties or local bar crawls of our late teens – and all of us, for the most part, had a time of it. If we weren't being goggled at by gammons[5], we were being interrogated by lads our own age who we barely knew, cornering us to prise us open and coax out intimate details about our sex lives for their own cruel amusement. None of us leaned on one other, me and the other gay boys. This was before *Rupaul's Drag Race* was popular and we discovered that it was okay, even amazing, to be mates. The pervasive mentality was more *Little Britain*'s 'Only Gay in the Village'. We were taught to hate ourselves, so we hated each other. I started university after Evie and Tasha so, in my loneliness in Romiley, I found myself creating personas just to survive – Gabriel the Self-Deprecating Jester who laughed at himself before anyone else could, Gabriel the Attention-Starved who would seek every eye and ear in the room rather than have them directed at him due to something he couldn't control, Gabriel the Edgy with a seemingly manageable but actually pretty destructive drug and alcohol problem. We were perceived and judged, and it was negative, and it was constant and it was, at the time, addictive. This feeling – this strange, shitty microcosm of celebrity – made me hypervigilant, hyperaware, and hyperanxious. The feeling of comparative invisibility in Manchester made me feel free. It was a reset. A new beginning. Eventually, once I met my course-mates, once I got to spend my time with Evie and Tasha again, once I started going out with Seamus, I found who I was again. No personas needed. In Manchester, I had been seen in all my truth, and accepted – even loved – for it. Crawling back to my mum's house in Romiley may at first have seemed antithetical to what my friends wanted for me (and what I wanted for myself), but it wasn't. I knew how to be depressed

---

[5] A 'gammon' refers to a particular subset of males: over fifty, with a face that resembles a ham hock due to overconsumption of alcohol and the *Daily Mail*

in my mum's house. I'd done it before and survived. The regression felt comfortable, something familiar and stable amongst so much instability. A dark, derelict, debilitating port in a storm – but a port nonetheless. A port whose harbourmaster would stand proudly – steadfast through any weather – wearing a £3 anorak from Oxfam, with outstretched arms ready to hoist me up and pull me in from the rain. My wondrous, incomparable, salty sea dog of a mother. It was her love. Her unconditional, all-engulfing, magnetic love that was powerful enough to pull me back from the safe haven I had built for myself in Manchester and into a freezing box room with an abandoned exercise bike in the corner, a floor covered by plastic storage boxes brimming with hoarded miscellanea and an abandoned application of some hideous wallpaper. That unfathomable love picked up the pieces of my broken soul over the next month and started to put them back together. For the first fortnight, I was catatonic. The full force of the events of the last few weeks had finally caught up to me, knocked me off my feet and under a tatty old duvet with a faded picture of the New York skyline across it. My fight-or-flight that had stood firm enough to keep me going since Christmas finally gave in, and I crumbled.

Mum knew I couldn't talk about what had happened with Seamus or my job, so she would come in occasionally and sit by the bed in silence, and she'd stroke my hair as I slipped in and out of sleep, just to let me know that she was there. I was in full-throttle depression by this point. Curtains drawn. No phone. No thoughts. No energy. No feeling. A sedate, decomposing zombie who slept eighteen hours a day. A mindless husk that had to be force-fed oven pizza and only remembered to have a gulp of water when his tongue had started to glue itself to the roof of his mouth from dehydration. After a few days of silence, Mum opened the plastic storage boxes on the floor and shared some contents. It was a bit like when someone gets into a car accident and falls into a coma. Scientists say that some of the brain can still respond to positive stimuli during a comatose state, so families will do things like organise a favourite football player to visit the hospital wing to jolt their loved ones back to consciousness. Except I wasn't in a coma, I didn't have a favourite football player because I was a homosexual, and Mum couldn't afford to fly Lady Gaga to Stockport, so instead she just shared with me little glimpses from my childhood.

'Bloody hell, do you remember this, Gabe? This takes me back,' she said, pulling out a battered copy of *The Rainbow Fish* by Marcus Pfister. I nodded into the pillow.

'Your nana bought it for you on your first birthday – fat lot of use that was. You were still filling up nappies every hour and screaming the house down crying if I didn't rock you back and forward over my shoulder, never mind reading. Oh wow! Look at this, Gabe!' She opened the book and revealed a biro inscription on the inside cover:

> *To my precious grandson on his first birthday.*
> *All my love,*
> *Nana (Daisy)*

'Of course, she had to go and put her name in there. She couldn't have had you growing up thinking it was off your dad's side,' laughed Mum. 'You loved it when you got a bit older, though. Do you remember why?' she asked. I raised my head off the pillow to get a closer look. Mum opened it and pointed at the multicoloured fish inside, a full watercolour illustration except for the holographic silver scales that leapt from the page.

'Because you were obsessed with anything sparkly. The glitter phase was the worst – when you were in Year 1. I was still finding it in the carpet for years later. No, that wasn't the worst, now that I think about it. There was a time I got a frantic call from your reception teacher because she'd caught you stealing sequins from the arts and crafts box and stuffing them into your pockets. We should've known, really,' said Mum, with a half-wistful, half-wry smile.

'Known what?' I croaked, my voice hoarse from underuse.

'That you were . . . you know . . .' She let her wrist go limp, and her hand flapped forward. 'A rainbow fish.' I laughed at that, albeit weakly, before falling into a dreamless sleep.

★ ★ ★

Seeing the positive reaction, Mum continued the trip down Memory Lane. Every day, after her long shift, she would come in, open a box, and sift through the contents within. We pored over baby records and school reports, laughing at the consistent note from every one of my teachers – 'Gabriel is intelligent but talks too much and is a disruption to the rest of the class.' We picked through photo albums, pausing to cringe at shots of Dan and me with our tiny genitalia wobbling about on the North Wales shore. We read through my final university submissions – which Mum could not finish without shedding tears of pride. As this process continued, I had no choice but to reconnect with myself. My breakup with Seamus had sparked the belief that I was a worthless nothing who deserved to have my relationship and career implode, but this time spent with Mum and our memories managed to stamp out those embers before they caught alight. Bit by bit, I stopped living like I was in a full-body cast and started to come back to life. Mum suggested a Saturday trip to Lyme Park.

'Come on, enough's enough,' she'd snapped through her signature thin 'Mum lips'[6]. 'A bit of nature will do you good, and I need to air this room out. It reeks.'

We walked over the sprawling hills, the winter winds clearing our sinuses. We reminisced about the time that we'd come here years ago

---

[6] Many Northern Mums' lips become thinner as they get angrier. When they're at peak frustration, their mouths are nothing but wrinkled slits

when Dan had stood in dog poo and only realised after we were trapped in the tiny Ford KA together on the drive home.

'Shit Sticks. Do you remember when we used to call him that?' Mum asked.

'You still do, Mum,' I said.

'That's because he still is. It's not intentional; it just finds him anywhere and everywhere he bloody goes. Mess. He's back home next week, you know.'

My heart, which had felt like an ACME anvil only weeks ago but was shedding weight daily, rose further in my chest. Dan had been studying at university in London, and I'd missed him dearly. We had barely kept in touch during his studies. He wasn't a texter, didn't have social media, and made little to no effort to uphold any interpersonal relationships that weren't in his immediate vicinity – in other words, he was a straight man in his twenties. Nevertheless, I knew that, as soon as I saw him, we'd drift back into our old ways, and to have him around would be the final defibrillation that I needed.

After he arrived, Dan and I stayed up until the early hours, chatting shit about the current political climate, bitching about his privately educated course-mates and playing *Crash Bandicoot* on the dusty old PlayStation 2. He told me excitedly about the new job he'd secured in Manchester city centre, which would begin in Spring.

'So, have you found anyone to live with yet?' I'd asked him over a drink in the local. Twelve months ago, if someone had told me that I'd be spending the next Valentine's Day single, jobless, and sat with my brother in the Duke of York having a warm pint over a plate of soggy onion rings, I'd have jumped off City Tower.

'Haven't thought about it much. Mum did mention the other day that you've got a spare room at yours?' Dan's voice was hesitant. I wasn't sure whether his trepidation stemmed from nervousness about broaching the subject of us moving in together, because he'd inadvertently referenced the Seamus situation for the first time, or . . .

'Wait, have you and Mum been bitching about me?'

'What? Bit— Gabe, no. Obviously not. You're being paranoid,' insisted Dan through a mouthful of greasy batter.

'How's that obvious?'

'Why would we bitch about you? You've not done anything wrong, not too much bro. He did, like. Your ex. I could kill that little weirdo. We just feel bad for you.'

'I don't need you to feel sorry for me,' I said, eyes narrowing. Dan burst out laughing. 'What's funny?'

'Well . . . it's a bit hard not to, Gabe.' He gestured around at the scene before us. The pub was all but empty except for Mr Ron, an elderly mechanic who used to pay Dan and me for stealing dust caps from parked cars around our estate when we were children. He was half-asleep at the bar, head resting on one hand, rolling a drinks mat between his fingers with the other. 'Endless Love' by Luther Vandross and Mariah Carey played through a tinny speaker. Everything stank of vinegar. I laughed too.

'This is how you're spending your Valentine's Day, too, you know.' I laughed. We had a couple more pints, Mr Ron entered the REM phase, and the speaker ran out of battery, so I re-broached the subject.

'Tasha found a couple of Master's students to sub-let my apartment while I've been at Mum's. They move out end of March, so if you wanted . . .' I let the sentence hang for a moment.

'I could . . .' He did the same thing.

'You could move in with me?' I finished.

'Go on, then.' He grinned.

'Do you think we'll end up killing each other?' I asked.

'Probably. I'll bring my PS5, that should help.'

'You've got a PS5?!'

'Of course! *Crash Bandicoot* all night, my dude!' He laughed.

'Not *all* night. I will have to start dating again at some point.' It was the first time this thought had even occurred to me – and I was surprised that, although daunting, it came with a murmur of exhilaration.

'Ey, Gabe! That's great news.' Dan raised his pint glass. 'If anywhere will make you believe in love again, it's this place.'

Mr Ron lifted his leg to audibly fart before returning to his slumber.

'So you're not worried about living with me . . . and the potential for . . .' I let the sentence hang in the air again.

'For you to be bringing home Dom tops on the reg?' he finished.

I was shook[7]. 'Well . . . yeah. How do you know what a Dom top is?' I asked, dumbfounded.

'Darling! I'm a *Londoner!*'

Sunday (Acceptance)

The last week at Mum's was filled with enough administrative tasks to keep my brain occupied before the big move back to the city. Mum took Dan to Home Bargains on no less than three separate occasions to ensure he had enough toiletries, cleaning supplies, and bedding to survive his first venture into adulthood. I set up the council tax, arranged the vacate date with the Master's students, and even – in a move that hovered somewhere between ambitious and deluded – started buying some new clothes for warmer weather in preparation for the upcoming spring. On the eve of the move, I took Mum and Dan out for a meal to say thank you at the inauthentic but undeniably tasty local tapas restaurant, La Canza. Mum spent most of the evening running through a checklist to make sure Dan hadn't forgotten anything, even after I'd reassured her that, in the horrifying event that my brother did leave a toothbrush behind, there were, surprisingly, shops in Manchester.

As I rolled under the aged duvet for the last time, there was one final task I knew I had to complete before I left. I opened WhatsApp and scrolled down to my conversation with Seamus. I hadn't dared to enter this territory since everything had happened. It felt like picking a half-healed scab, but I knew that, like with any wound, I needed to let it air out if it was to start healing. I ripped off the metaphorical plaster and opened 'the last texts':

---

[7] Adjective: to be shaken to your core

26 December:

[01:01] **Seamus:** I cannot believe you have just kicked me out onto the streets on Christmas Day. this taxi is going to cost a fortune and you know I'm skint

[01:01] **Gabriel:** YOU CANNOT BELIEVE THAT? do you think that THAT is more unbelievable than me letting you stay and have a festive fucking sleepover with my stepbrother? go fuck yourself

[01:03] **Seamus:** I'm not going to talk to you while you're being hysterical

[01:04] **Gabriel:** Then don't. i hate you. i hope your taxi crashes and you die

[01:11] **Seamus:** Are you going to tell your family

[03:32] **Seamus:** Gabriel, please don't tell your family

26 December (cont.):

[10:41] **Gabriel:** Hello. i hope you're having the worst Christmas imaginable cause god knows I am. no, I'm not going to tell my family. i'm not going to tear my family apart on your behalf. you're not worth it. they know you've cheated, they don't know the full story

[11:20] **Seamus:** Can we talk about this?

[11:39] **Gabriel:** What is there to possibly say? I can't talk about it, I feel sick even thinking about it

[13:40] **Seamus:** Can I call you?

[13:43] **Gabriel:** No

27 December:

[17:28] **Seamus**: Gabriel, this is ridiculous. we have a home together

[22:10] **Seamus**: Gabe, please. it was a stupid mistake

28 December:
(2 missed calls)

29 December:
(6 missed calls)

31 December:

[23:04] **Seamus**: Hi, gabril. Happy new Year. I'm so sorry - I love you

[23:11] **Gabriel**: It has taken you nearly a week to apologise. You do realise that. It has taken you almost a full fucking week to offer me a misspelt, pissed-up, shitty little apology. Do you have any idea what you have done to me?

[23:14] **Seamus**: I tried to call you Gabe. Please can I come to the flat just so we van talk

[23:21] **Gabriel**: You are not stepping foot in that flat ever again, I never want to look at you again, Shay. You are dead to me. I mean it. Stay the fuck away from me. You've broken my heart. You are a meaningless nothing. You're a disgusting pervert and your poetry is shit. Your blog is an embarrassment and your poetry is so bad

[23:24] **Seamus**: At least i. Can actually write

[23:26] **Gabriel**: What's that supposed to mean?

[23:30] **Seamus**: You can't read either, apparently lol. I said AT LEAST I CAN ACTALLY WRITE. You can't even do that, you just finish work at your silly bottomy fashion job and sit in front of a tv rotting. You think I wanted to live like that ??

[23:40] **Seamus:** I didn't mean that please can I come back home

[23:48] **Gabriel:** I HAD TO SIT AND ROT TO DROWN OUT THE THOUGHT THAT WE WERE FALLING APART AT THE SEAMS AND YOU DIDN'T GIVE A FLYING SHIT, SEAMUS

I looked away from the phone for a moment and fell back through time to those evenings in the six months prior to Christmas – Seamus with his head in a MacBook slaving over his poetry, me back from a shift at Boddlies, worn out, uninspired, unable to support. Together, but distant. Resentment creeping in, bubbling, twisting my idea of who he was, who I was.

[23:51] **Seamus:** And you domnt think that hurt me too? Sorry that I put it into my art

[23:55] **Gabriel:** You put it into my STEPBROTH-ER you self-obsessed cunt

[23:57] **Seamus:** Where was I meant to put it? My hand for the rest of my life? You didn't want it

[23:59] **Gabriel:** Because I was sick of being your mother. I would've worked on us. I was trying to make us work, you were railing a member of my family

[23:59] **Seamus:** Whatever Gabriel. Fine. What're you gonna do. I love you.

[23:59] **Seamus:** And you love me

[23:59] **Seamus:** I'm sorry

1 January:
   (9 missed calls)

2 January:
   [16:03] **Seamus:** Please talk to me, Gabriel. You at least owe me that

5 January:
   (1 missed call)

I took a deep breath, deleted the conversation, and blocked his number.

★★★

We'd hired a moving van to accommodate Dan's stuff, as the only other option was to try and force a forty-inch television and two-metre-wide desk into the back of Mum's Ford KA, which we all agreed was impossible. Once the van was loaded, Mum had stopped offering the driver brews at two-minute intervals, and we'd all made sure to have a final forced piss, we started to say our goodbyes. Dan went first, wrapped Mum in a gangly hug, planted a kiss on her cheek and scurried to the van so he could make sure to get the front seat. Dickhead.

'Come here, love,' Mum said, pulling me into a warm embrace. 'Look after your brother. You know what he's like. Make sure he stays off that wacky baccy; it's no good for him. Don't let him near our Evie. Those two would put enough ganja smoke into the atmosphere to blow another hole in the ozone layer. I mean it.' She looked at me sternly.

'He's a grown man, Mum. He can look after himself. He knows what a Dom top is and everything,' I said, still unable to mask how impressed I was.

'Well, I've got no clue what you're going on about, but I suppose that means I'm not a grown man. Thank god.'

I looked at my mother as she laughed, her crow's feet deeper than the last time I'd seen her, with new lines and creases on her forehead and neck. Strands of grey hair peppered her choppy, home-dyed bob. I swallowed a lump in my throat as I was reminded of the fact that I would never be able to face — she was getting older and there was nothing I could do to stop it.

'Mum, I . . .'

I wanted to express how much her support meant to me. I tried to find the words to express how grateful I was to her for the last six weeks. I wanted to let her know that nobody *my* age was wearing ripped skinny jeans anymore, let alone a woman in her fifties. But I couldn't. Instinctively, she placed her hand on my cheek.

'Thank you, Mum. For everything,' I managed.

'I'm so proud of you, Gabe,' she said as her eyes dampened.

'For what? For crawling back here like a man-child at the first sign of trouble and putting you through all that worry?'

'Don't you dare. Don't you *dare*,' she said fiercely. 'Man-child? I know full-grown men three times your size who wouldn't have survived half of what you've been through. I'm proud of you for doing what you've always managed to do. For taking the hand you've been dealt and turning it around. You have no idea how I feel when I bump into your teachers at Morrisons or see your old mates' mums at the park and tell them about what you've been up to in the city. And they always ask; they always remember you. Do you know why?'

'Why?'

'Because you're a good man. Because you light up every room you're in, son. You always have. It's your gift; it's your curse, too, probably. Because you shine too brightly, and then your batteries run out.'

'That's funny,' I said tearfully, remembering what Paul had said to me on the sofa. 'One of the guys at Broadgate said something similar to me recently.'

'Is he single?'

'Sadly not.'

'Ah, well. Come here, son.' She pulled me into one final hug. 'I'm gonna miss you. Call me whenever you get the chance. Don't spend any time worrying about what that piss-fart of an ex did, or thinking about what he's up to now. He's not worth it. Don't go anywhere near that stepbrother of yours, either. Trust your dad to bring someone like that into your life. Look after Dan, though. I mean it.'

'I love you, Mum.'

'I love every hair on your head, Gabriel, and don't you forget it.'

We cried into each other's shoulders as we rocked back and forth for a moment, just as we had done when I was a child all those years ago.

Observations from the plastic nostalgia boxes

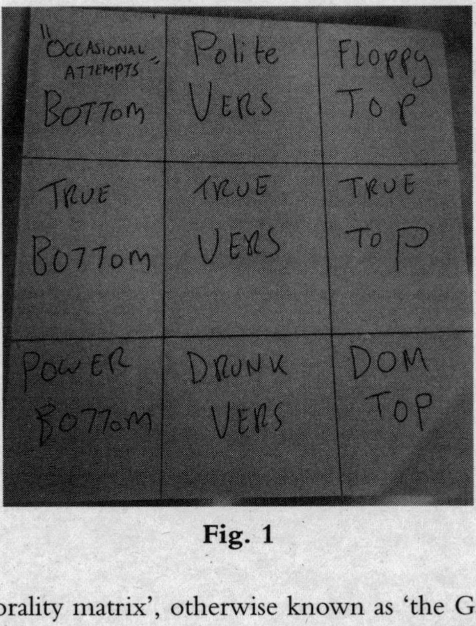

"OCCASIONAL ATTEMPTS = BOTTOM	Polite VERS	Floppy TOP
TRUE BOTTOM	TRUE VERS	TRUE TOP
POWER BOTTOM	DRUNK VERS	DOM TOP

Fig. 1

The 'gay morality matrix', otherwise known as 'the Gayscale', that Gabriel, Evie and Tasha devised four years ago, had somehow found its way in amongst the heirlooms. Gay people are labelled 'top' if they prefer to be the active partner or 'giver' during penetrative anal sex. They are labelled 'Bottom' if they prefer to be the passive partner or 'taker' during penetrative anal sex. They are labelled 'Versatile' or 'vers' if they don't have a major preference and enjoy both positions. In the gay world, the position you label yourself with is crucial and will dictate the type of men you date and the type of sex you have. Below are the definitions for the sub-categories of positions illustrated in Fig 1.

'Occasional Attempts Bottom'

A homosexual man who will not, by default, take it up the arse. Every so often, though, when the mood calls, he will take a sojourn to the magical world of bottoming out of sheer curiosity, although rarely successfully.

'Power Bottom'

A homosexual man who may still be the receptive partner but is certainly not the passive participant. These excitable fellows will often dominate sexual proceedings with a hearty vigour, electing to go in 'the driver's seat', so to speak. They do not baulk at the sight of a large penis and, instead, anticipate with glee the creative ways with which they will bring it to completion.

'Polite Vers'

Where a True Vers enjoys both top and bottom positions, a Polite Vers has a definite preference but will align with their partner to help them reach ecstasy. For example, Kyle is a top who will not bottom. Andrew is a polite vers who prefers to top but will bottom because of Kyle's preferences. Thus, all have an acceptable time.

'Drunk Vers'

A drunk vers is a homosexual man who usually stays within the parameters of top or bottom, but when inebriated, will explore the opposite position to the one that they are usually comfortable with.

'Floppy Top'

A floppy top is a homosexual man who much prefers, and is used to, bottoming, but will attempt to top from time to time. This can often start off strong but, in their heart of hearts, the floppy top is a bottom; therefore, before long, it's a flop.

'Dom Top'

A Dom top is often considered a rare and coveted specimen amongst homosexual men. They refuse to bottom (or be submissive in any sense during sexual interactions) and instead prefer to send your prostate to the high heavens. Goodness gracious me!

Fig. 2

Here, we can observe a family portrait that Gabriel completed over the course of a week when he was just four years old. Since completing this masterpiece, Gabriel has shed many of his excess fingers, and the club foot present in this artwork has miraculously healed. Daniel, Gabriel's brother, who appears here as a cigarette-end, eventually evolved into a human being. As Gabriel matured, he realised, to his disappointment, that – much like men – women have feet, not wheels.

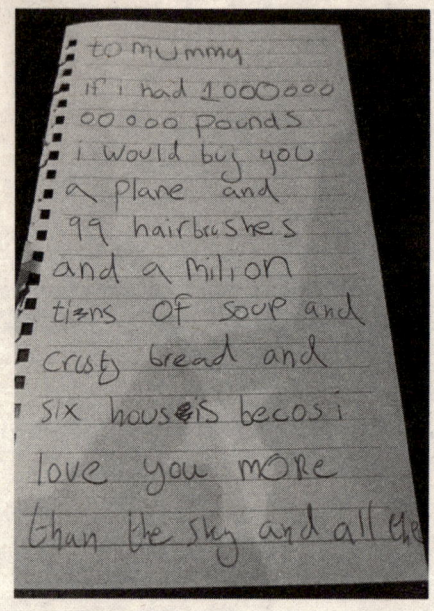

Fig. 3

Gabriel wrote this heartfelt letter to his mother, aged six, before beginning an unsuccessful campaign for his parents to buy him a Dalmatian.

4

You've Got Male

'We need to do something to celebrate, Gabe,' Dan had said two weeks after we'd moved back to Broadgate Towers. The move had gone swimmingly enough; Dan had transformed what had been a sparsely decorated spare room into his bedroom by putting up a triptych of pop-art *Sopranos* prints, dotting a few fake plants from IKEA on the bedside tables and hanging up his closet of (mostly Carhartt) clothes. I'd done a complete bedroom clear-out, scouring the drawers for remnants of my previous relationship and throwing them in the bin. I bought a new bed set, threw away Seamus's remaining toiletries and donated his old books to the RSPCA on Oak Street. Before long, the ghost of my relationship was exorcised from Flat 264, and it had started to feel like a cosy home. Although the living area could have been tidier, we maintained a good level of cleanliness, and that worked for us. I'd given up my diet of Doritos and despair and had restarted the regular cooking of balanced meals for two – something I enjoyed and was quite good at. After only a fortnight, we'd reached a level of homemaking symbiosis that Seamus and I never managed – so Dan was right: we did have reason to celebrate.

'We should! Seamus and I already did a housewarming when we moved here last year, though,' I said, noting with pleasant satisfaction how mentioning his name no longer made my nervous system behave like the Fukushima power plant.

'Why don't we go on a night out? I'm dying to get pissed.' Dan was in dire need of letting off some steam after almost finishing the first week at his new job. I was in dire need of letting off some steam after finishing my sixth week of being unemployed and intermittently spiralling about my slowly increasing credit card debt and fast-approaching job interview at Tasha's boyfriend Scott's workplace. Me and Dan, like most brothers, harboured a healthy undercurrent of competitiveness. I was glad to see him thrive at his new job, but I would've been gladder if I had one myself. Everybody who knew us both said that he resembled me. He had the same freckles and bone structure, but his hair – a much lighter brown and straight where mine was curly – was cut into a skin fade, with a horizontal, textured fringe at the front, like Friar Tuck had discovered salt spray.

'You're stoned every day. Isn't that mind-numbing enough? But, yeah, let's. I'm busy this Saturday with life admin, but shall we do the one after?' I replied.

'Sound. Who's coming? The boys will be in Malaga then, so the guest list is on you.' 'The boys' in question were Dan's two best mates from home who had studied up North and now lived in Manchester.

'Probably just Tasha and Evie. Tasha might want to bring Scott, her boyfriend,' I said.

'Ah shit, yeah, they've been together for quite a while now, no? What's he saying?' Dan fiddled with the zipper on one of our new forest-green sofa cushions.

'Stop playing with that zip, or you'll break it. Yeah, a couple of years. He's alright. He's a bit . . .' I searched for the right word. 'He works in sales and is *fantastic* at it.'

'I see.'

'I've not spent that much time with him, but he's been weird whenever I have; I don't know. There's something fake about him. Don't say anything.'

I added the proviso after remembering Dan drunkenly telling our Aunty Diane what I'd said about her amethyst earring set during her vow renewal three years ago.

'I won't.'

'Well, you know those people who seem like they're pretending to be a good person? Like, as soon as the door closes and they're by themselves, they ditch the pleasantries and unzip their skin and they're actually just a reptile in a human costume?'

'Erm . . . no?'

'Tasha loves him, though. Evidently,' I continued. 'They're "the perfect couple". Renting a house together and everything in Didsbury.' I walked over to pluck the cushion from Dan's hands. 'He just irks me. I don't know. But then, he has sorted that interview for me next week, so he can't be all bad. He's just arrogant and controlling,' I finished before placing the cushion neatly on the armchair just out of Dan's reach.

'Right,' laughed Dan. 'Are you sure you're not just being possessive?'

'That doesn't sound like me.'

'It's not as if Tasha takes any prisoners,' said Dan, picking up his house keys from the side and playing with them absent-mindedly so he had something to keep his hands busy.

'She's different around him,' I replied, pausing to think. 'No, you're right. Besides, good vibes only, right?'

'Cringe. Is Evie still single?' Dan was suddenly more interested in the keys he was jingling.

'Yeah. She dated someone for a while last year, but it didn't work out. She was cut up about it. Why do you ask?' I said, narrowing my eyes.

'No reason!'

'I know you've always had a thing for her.'

'Woah, woah, woah! She's always had a thing for *me*.' Dan smirked.

'So, you don't think she's hot?'

'I wouldn't say . . . hot. She's pretty. Like a fairy. Or a bunny. I don't know. That rack[8] is undeniable, though.' He laughed.

'Dan, do you know what kind of men compare women favourably to prey animals?' I questioned, then continued without giving him pause for answer. 'Predators. Stop being such a perv.'

---

[8] One of far too many terms used by heterosexual males to refer to a pair of boobs. Gentler options include breasts, love globes or Yorkshire puddings

'Relax! You know I love Evie. I was just curious. It's fine, there's plenty more fish in the sea. Wait, do fish count as prey animals?'

I laughed reluctantly.

'Anyway, if you're interested in the relationship status of *any* girl, you need to do something about that facial hair,' I said. Dan's wide chin was peppered at inconsistent intervals with mousy strands of stubble of various lengths.

'I'm trying something. Let me live. You just worry about yourself, yeah?'

'What? Have I missed a spot?' I asked, rubbing my face, which I always kept smooth because the ability to grow consistent facial hair was absent from the gene pool.

'No, not the shaving department, you idiot. The dating one.'

'Oh. Where shall we go, then? Next weekend?' I asked, keen to change the subject from my current relationship status (dumped).

'Why are you asking me? I've only just got here. It's your city!'

Dan meant nothing by these words – but they had a gravitational pull, a grounding quality – they made me feel safe. He was right. Seamus was in London, the trauma of Christmas felt like a lifetime ago, and Manchester felt like it did the first time I'd stepped foot on its streets, buzzing with potential for adventure.

★ ★ ★

Before I headed out on Saturday morning to complete my errands, I stopped at reception to chat with Paul. He'd been instrumental with the move, organising a lot of the behind-the-scenes admin and helping to quickly transfer our stuff from the van to the flat so we wouldn't be charged extra. I took him a bottle of whiskey to say thank you, but he informed me that whiskey gave him gout. I reassured him that I could exchange it for a bottle of something that didn't cause agonising sodium crystals to form over his ankle.

'By the way, Gabe,' he said in his best attempt at a whisper, and taking the bottle of whiskey from my hands anyway before smuggling it beneath his desk. 'I did some jiggery-pokery on't computer. I've moved it so you can pay January and February rent at the end of the tenancy, just to give you some time to get back on your feet.'

'What? Paul, that's such a relief. Thank you. How did you—'

'Never mind how. Say no more. And don't let your mate Mitchell or any of the others know.' He tapped his nose.

I huffed. 'He's not my mate, Paul, he's my neighbour.'

'And you two have never... you know...' Paul said, raising his eyebrows.

'What the HELL! Eugh, Paul, I'm going.' I left him guffawing at his desk.

I quickly overcame Paul's horrifying assumption as spring had sprung and I was blessed with that most elusive of miracles – a sunny Manchester Saturday.

```
[08:18] Gabriel: Guys, are you up for a night
out next weekend?
[08:21] Evie: YES! It's been ages
[08:22] Tasha: Morning girls. Yes, Gabe,
absolutely
[08:22] Gabriel: Will Scott be coming, Tasha?
[08:23] Evie: Is Dan coming, Gabe?
[08:23] Gabriel: Yes! he can't wait, I think
he's already picked out a plain black crew neck
and plain grey trousers, especially
[08:24] Tasha: No, Scott's busy. he's got this
work thing
[08:25] Gabriel: Can he not fuse the two?
could be good to meet a couple of his colleagues
before I do that interview
```

It was a long shot, but I was also hypervigilant, – I didn't want Tasha to clock my reservations about Scott's suitability as a partner. Though I feared I'd come across *too* enthusiastically.

[08:26] **Tasha:** I'm not sure there's much crossover between the sales team of an insurance company and the gay village
[08:27] **Evie:** That's very presumptuous, Natasha
[08:27] **Tasha:** No, I've met them. they're all straight, only one is under forty, and he'd spend the whole night asking Gabe questions like 'does it hurt getting bummed'
[08:27] **Gabriel:** Ah, one of them
[08:28] **Tasha:** Does it, Gabe?
[08:28] **Gabriel:** Try something other than ar-rhythmic, clunky missionary and you might find out, Tash!
[08:29] **Evie:** Gabe! You're feeling better <3

I grabbed a chai from Nomad and walked past a group of students in fancy dress waiting at the tram stop. They were all dressed as different Harry Potter characters but with a now ironic LGBT twist. A boy with a ginger mullet and long, dangling earrings made an eye-catching non-binary Dobby. I instinctively knew they'd be catching a tram to do the Didsbury Dozen[9].

[08:40] **Gabriel:** Remember when we did the Didsbury Dozen last year
[08:42] **Evie:** Barely :(
[08:43] **Tasha:** That's because you were cross-faded[10] by the sixth pub and ended up going home with my best friend from work

---

[9] Manchester's most famous pub crawl
[10] Cross-faded is the state you reach when mixing weed and alcohol — a combination so horrible that I wouldn't even recommend it to amateur DJs, but one that Evie often found herself in the throes of

[08:44] **Evie:** Stop it. again, I'm so sorry for that
   [08:44] **Tasha:** It's not me you need to apologise to, is it, Evie?
   [08:45] **Evie:** I apologised to him millions of times
   [08:45] **Gabriel:** Guys what the hell happened? I don't remember you telling me about this

Shafts of sunlight illuminated the ancient sandstone of the Portico Library, giving glowing golden borders to the broad, cobbled street as I strolled towards the post office. This area of the city was handsome in any weather, but under this kind of light, it came alive, providing a dramatic backdrop for smartly dressed financiers on their morning commute. A teenage boy was busking on the pavement, singing a gravelly rendition of 'Live Forever' by Oasis as passersby dropped coins into his open guitar case.

   [08:51] **Evie:** I was too mortified to bring it up at the time
   [08:51] **Gabriel:** I'm sure it's fine. What did you do?

There was a pleasant spring breeze, but the temperature was mild, and a little girl with blonde pigtails was pulling at the hem of her mum's skirt, asking for an ice cream.

  'It's still a bit too cold for that, love. Oh, go on then, seeing as you asked so nicely,' I overheard her reply as they sprang off towards a corner shop. I took a deep breath and smiled, basking in the timely reminder that Manchester could produce timeless art, striking architecture and, most importantly, beautiful people.

   [08:53] **Evie:** I threw up on his dick

Right.

    [08:54] **Gabriel**: What?! Oh nooooo, Evie
    [08:54] **Tasha**: Hahahaha
    [08:55] **Evie**: Yeah. I don't even like giving blow jobs, but I was drunk and he was pretty
    [08:55] **Gabriel**: Did you . . . carry on after that?
    [08:56] **Tasha**: Yeah, Gabe. she jumped on top and rode him while projectile vomiting
    [08:57] **Gabriel**: Ah, number 27 in the Kama Sutra - The Linda Blair. still need to try that one
    [08:57] **Tasha**: I'll add it to the list
    [08:57] **Evie**: Of course I didn't, he went for a shower and Tasha rescued me
    [08:57] **Tasha**: He hasn't brought it up to me since
    [08:58] **Gabriel**: Not the best Monday morning water-cooler conversation is it
    [08:58] **Evie**: True
    [08:58] **Tasha**: Tea

★ ★ ★

Seamus had left his driver's licence, DSLR camera and inhaler at the flat. Although I'd discarded or donated most of his worldly goods, my vengeful callousness didn't extend far enough to deprive him of legal documents or life-saving devices. I'd never been to Seamus's family home in Hertfordshire nor met his parents, though not for lack of trying. He'd always kept us at arm's length, ready with an arsenal of excuses prepared for whenever the opportunity to merge his relationship and his family presented itself. In hindsight, another enormous red flag, willfully ignored by yours truly. Luckily, his older sister had visited him while we were at university together, and I still had her on Facebook. I messaged her, managed to acquire their home address, then deleted her. Thus, Spring Gardens Post Office became the venue where I would sever any lasting ties to my brotherfucker ex-boyfriend. The post office was spacious, with over a dozen individually numbered service tills, yet you always somehow ended up queueing for at least twenty minutes. Coming on a Saturday morning was probably not my most innovative idea. Throngs of stressed Mancunians milled around with brown paper packages clutched under their armpits. The air inside smelled like old carpet and glue.

A hard-looking man from Salford loudly argued about postage prices with an Eastern European mailwoman. A sausage dog, which I'd noticed tied up outside on the way in, had somehow escaped from his bollard prison and had bounded into the post office to a chorus of 'awwws' and a couple of raised feet. In amongst the chaos, I remembered I had to box Seamus's items before posting them. Flat-packed cardboard boxes of varying sizes covered the shelves. Luckily, this section was empty except for a tall man standing nearby, busy duct-taping at the packing table, so I got the pick of the bunch. I selected the smallest, cheapest, ugliest option and went to the packing table. As I took Seamus's possessions from my backpack, the tall man's aftershave cut through the post office's natural scent. It was heavenly. I glanced at him as he was now facing me and only a few feet away. He was *so* sexy that I considered puffing on Seamus's inhaler. A tan leather smoking jacket hung off his broad shoulders. He had clear skin and long eyelashes, which made his chiselled face look almost angelic as he glanced down to continue duct-taping his parcel. I would've placed him in his late twenties or early thirties. His fingernails were immaculate, even though his hands appeared broad and strong. He pulled the brown tape and slapped it onto the top of the box before him.

[09:11] **Gabriel:** Guys, there's a ten[11] in the post office
[09:11] **Evie:** Spring Gardens? I always see hot people in there
[09:12] **Gabriel:** That's because you think everyone's hot
[09:12] **Evie:** Is he gay?
[09:12] **Gabriel:** His fingers look manicured
[09:13] **Tasha:** Ask him out
[09:13] **Gabriel:** Don't be unhinged

I placed the flatpack box on the counter, ready to say 'fuck off' to the last remnants of Seamus. There was a weird assemblage process that involved folding things along serrated edges that suddenly my flustered brain couldn't figure out. I looked over to the tall man's package to see if I could spot any cardboard construction hints. His gorgeous hands weaved the tape and cardboard together with the precision of a surgeon, creating a geometrically flawless cuboid. He was like an outrageously fuckable version of Postman Pat. Our eyes met accidentally, and he grinned at me. Returning the smile, I felt my ears turn red. Underneath the box there were no instructions. This was humiliating. The first time I'd registered an attractive man in months, and I was behaving like an arthritic Neanderthal.

'Do you need any help with that? They can be really annoying,' the man said as he stepped towards where I was standing.

'Please, yeah. I usually just use a Jiffy bag, but all this wouldn't fit.' I felt my ears turn red again as I realised that 'I usually just use a Jiffy bag' could be a candidate for the least sexy sentence of all time.

---

[11] Generally, I detest the trend of assigning a numerical rating to people based on their attractiveness, which is of course completely subjective and always multi-faceted. It's a quick way to convey a message, though, so shut up and stop being so sanctimonious

'Yeah, you just have to . . .' He leaned across me and started working on my box. 'Pull the corners like this and . . . Voila!' he exclaimed, holding it up high. He wasn't French, so he must be gay.

'Thanks so much. I would've been stood here for hours,' I said with relief.

'No problem.' It was a natural end point to the interaction, but neither of us walked away.

'I'm Marcus,' he said, holding out a hand for me to shake.

'I'm Gabriel,' I said, shaking his hand, which was a lot rougher than it looked.

'Three extraordinarily random items that you're posting there,' Marcus observed.

'Yeah. I've killed someone. This is the evidence,' I replied.

'I see, so I'm an accomplice now?' He smirked. I had enough butterflies[12] to give Asia O'Hara a chance at redemption.

'Unfortunately. Sorry for dragging you in,' I said. Realising he'd taken most of the initiative so far, I had to be brave. 'So, when you're not aiding and abetting a murderer, what do you do?'

'Ah, I'm a chef. I'm off to work now once I've posted this,' said Marcus.

The surgical precision from earlier made sense. Creating beautiful meals is an art form, it's all connected.

'I LOVE food,' I all but barked. He laughed.

'Funnily enough, so do I. Kind of comes with the job . . . Anyway, it's been nice chatting, but I've got to dash,' he said, holding up his package and nodding towards the service tills. I'd ruined it with the

---

[12] Asia O'Hara was a frontrunner during *RuPaul's Drag Race* season 11. Her chances of winning were dashed during the finale, when, during a lip-sync performance, she opened a hidden cage in her bodice to set free hundreds of butterflies in the hope that they would fly free and astound the audience, but they all died. She wasn't cancelled, because no one cares about insects, but she didn't win, and the moment lives on in infamy

bark; I knew it. 'I love food'? Jesus Christ. He started to walk towards the tills but paused before passing me.

'If we're accomplices now, it's probably best if we stay in touch, you know, so we can keep our stories straight. Could I take your number?'

I read it out while he inputted it into his phone. I posted Seamus's things and left the post office with a tracking receipt and a semi.

★ ★ ★

I completed the rest of my errands with such a spring in my step that I all but skipped around town. Even a spice[13] head shouting 'faggot!' at me as I bounded through Piccadilly Gardens couldn't quell my elation. I had done it. I had successfully flirted and secured the number of a hot man. I was no longer 'dumped', I was 'dating'. Of course, Marcus hadn't texted me yet, but I was quietly confident that he would. I was about to declare this the best day I'd had in months until I rounded the corner before Broadgate and was faced with an unsettling pairing: my brother Dan, standing outside the entrance holding a bin bag, in conversation with somebody petite and blonde who, when the afternoon sun touched his skin, glowed with the light of a thousand bottles of St. Tropez mousse.

'Gabe!' My neighbour Mitchell waved his arms erratically and beckoned me over. It was fourteen degrees, and he was wearing a vest. If the spice head had called me a faggot for wearing a salmon Fred Perry polo, god knows what he'd have done to this poor soul.

'Hi, Mitch. How're you?' I said. The quality of my mood made it much easier to mask my disinterest.

'Amazing, babe. You never told me you had a gorgeous brother, Gabriel!' exclaimed Mitchell with a high-pitched giggle. 'We've

---

[13] 'Spice' is a slang term for synthetic cannabinoids, a research chemical that took the homeless community of Manchester by storm and rendered anyone who smoked it an aggressive wraith

been having a right old laugh, right, Dan?' My brother's nonplussed expression suggested that he'd bumped into Mitchell while taking out the rubbish.

'We have. He's a riot, Gabe,' said Dan, flashing me a befuddled glance when Mitchell wasn't looking.

'Shut up!' crooned Mitchell, slapping Dan on the shoulder before returning to face me. 'Anyway, Gabriel, Dan mentioned you're all going out next weekend?' He widened his eyes, which were a bright shade of blue that contrasted unsettlingly with his skin tone. Before I could think of an excuse, I felt my phone vibrate in my hand.

```
[14:09] Marcus: Hello. If you've not got any
more bodies to bury, fancy coming to mine next
week for dinner? How's Tuesday? I'll cook.
```

I felt a sudden surge of affection for the world around me and everyone in it.

'Yes! You should come, Mitch. We'd love to see you!' I grinned.

Both Mitchell and Dan looked slightly taken aback.

'Well . . . slay! See you then, boys!' Mitchell said before sauntering into the city. Dan disposed of the rubbish in the bin nearby, and I walked with him back to the flat, brimming with anticipation and excitement.

5

Spaghetti

When Tuesday arrived, I completed my pre-date ritual with an enthused reverie that could only be caused by a man I'd already decided was 'boyfriend material'. I rummaged through my wardrobe, trying on four shirts with two pairs of shoes, pausing for the mandatory check-in with the girls. These check-ins were a strange yet necessary vacuum in which Tasha turned into some sort of cut-throat Manchester's Next Top Model judge, and Evie expressed her disapproval politely.

[16:54] **Evie:** It's striking. I think that outfit would be better for maybe a third or fourth date

[16:58] **Tasha:** You look like a Blue Peter presenter with a questionable sexual past

[17:01] **Evie:** Try the pleated trousers with the Basquiat print shirt

[17:15] **Gabriel:** He seems intelligent, though, Evie. what if he asks me something about Basquiat, and I have no idea? I know nothing about his art or life I just thought the print was cool

[17:17] **Evie:** Do a quick Wikipedia search on him before you go!

[17:18] **Tasha:** I think this might be cultural appropriation in real-time

I uncorked a bottle of red that had been sitting on the side for a day too long, emptied the third that remained into a wine glass and began considering the slight amendments I would make to my personality for the evening. I was a staunch proponent of 'be yourself' in daily life, but that rule went whistling out of the window on a first date. Especially when 'being yourself' means getting cheated on and betrayed by members of your own extended family. No, tonight, Matthew, I would be the New Me. A shinier, less squawky, effortlessly flirtatious version of myself that wasn't aggressively opinionated and sometimes lecturey. The football was on, so Dan was out having a few mid-week pints with his colleagues, meaning I had complete control over the speaker. I played three songs to get me in the mood for the date with Marcus: Neiked – 'Sexual', Dusty Springfield – 'Son of a Preacher Man' and Miguel – 'Adorn'. I didn't *intend* to shag him, but it had been ninety-eight days since I last had sex and over eighteen months since I was properly satisfied; plus, the initial chemistry would've burnt the brows off Robert Oppenheimer, so if it did happen, I wasn't going to shed any tears. I needed to be prepared if there was even a ten per cent chance of going all the way. It is a fact of life that the only orifice available for gay men to have penetrative sex is the anus and that the only orifice in the human body that involves the presence of poo is – in the cruellest twist of fate – also the anus. Thus, unless you have a specific fetish, it is best to do your utmost to divorce the two. And it is with that primary aim that I began the obligatory pre-sex ritual that was a rite of passage for many gay men.

* * *

The Obligatory Pre-sex Ritual that is a Rite of Passage for Gay Men
By Gabriel Lanes

Optional step: Masturbate. If you're somebody that gets too excited too quickly, pre-empt this by having a wank! Don't watch porn. You'll desensitise yourself to the potential ecstasy that is to follow. You also run the risk of subconsciously entering the 'faux porn star' mindset, which will result in performative, unfulfilling sex that involves a lot of disproportionate moaning, an uncomfortable amount of time spent in the doggy position and, in the most severe cases, breathless exclamations of 'Daddy!' Affected American accents may vary in intensity.

STEP ONE – Anus Maintenance, with Specific Reference to Anus Hair. If possible, do this the night before in the shower. This step can vary based on your own preferences, but you mostly have three choices:

The Bald Eagle: Shave it all off. Maximum aerodynamics, minimum friction. Squat in the shower and work in gentle, outward motions away from the hole. For the love of god, don't forget the gooch.

The Groomed Gentleman: For those amongst you who are particularly furry, give it a trim with appropriately sized scissors. Please be careful. If you have to go to A&E with any anus-related problems, the receptionists will assume that you were trying to insert something weird into it. Every A&E front desk worker has a story about a man coming in who 'accidentally' fell on a LEGO Darth Vader.

Can't Be Tamed: Some like to lean into a primal essence of manliness and leave their anus hair at its natural length. This is so far removed from my personal experience that I can't give any reliable advice – but perhaps a deep-treatment conditioner to replenish amino acids and leave it full-bodied and glossy? You're worth it.

STEP TWO – Douching, Some Basic Instructions for the Uninitiated. Do this half an hour before you leave for your date.

Disassemble your douche. Fill the bulb with tepid water. TEPID. If it's too cold, the walls of your anal cavity will permanently contract and harden to stone, meaning your ass will transform from a place of pleasure to a penis pencil sharpener. If it's too hot, you'll steam-cook your internal organs and die until the police come searching for you and find a six-foot gyoza on the bathroom floor.

Reassemble. Coat the tube of your douche with a water-based lube. Insert tube into anus. Squeeze water into sphincter by pressing chamber. Remove douche, but hold water inside anus by tensing sphincter, like you're holding in a fart during a funeral. Wait on the toilet for at least a minute. Eject water into toilet bowl by relaxing sphincter and pushing slightly.

Repeat until water is clear. Obviously, it's never going to be VOSS. Just make sure it's closer to Highland Spring than Peroni.

STEP THREE – Shower. I assume and hope that this step doesn't require further instruction.

★★★

Seven o'clock loomed. I'd decided on pleated black trousers, but with a red revere-collar short-sleeved shirt from one of my favourite slow-fashion designers, Lorenz. The colour made my skin glow, and the front had a graphic of a port bottle being poured, which was a cute homage to Marcus's profession.

```
[18:40] Gabriel: Went with the Lorenz shirt.
The one with the port bottle. could be a cute
homage to his profession
[18:42] Tasha: Could also look like you're in
a fancy dress costume for 'date with chef'
[18:44] Evie: Hahaha. that shirt really suits
you, Gabe, a fine selection!
[18:45] Tasha: It does suit you. Is it
temperature-appropriate, though?
[18:48] Gabe: We'll be in his apartment, which
I assume he'll have been cooking in all day. I'm
sure I'll be fine. besides . . .
[18:49] Evie: Hoes don't get cold!
```

[18:50] **Gabe:** Exactly
[18:51] **Evie:** Speaking of hoes, do you think you'll shag?

I sprayed a tasteful amount of Thierry Mugler on my wrists and hair, grabbed my coat, and booked the Uber. The driver who picked me up complimented my shirt but didn't start a conversation, which was ideal because I was too nervous for small talk with strangers. The inevitable 'What time are you on till?', for the first time in my long and storied career as an Uber passenger, remained unspoken.

[19:04] **Gabe:** I'm not sure, you know. He's gorgeous, and I'm slowly but surely reaching 'meet up with a married man on Grindr' levels of horny, but idk
[19:04] **Evie:** Did you douche?
[19:05] **Gabe:** Yeah, just in case
[19:05] **Tasha:** Then you'll shag
[19:05] **Gabe:** I'm nervous, though. It's been a century since I shagged anyone that wasn't Seamus
[19:07] **Evie:** You'll be fine! Sex is like riding a bike
[19:07] **Tasha:** Except more tiring
[19:08] **Gabe:** And it doesn't make every motorist in the country hate you
[19:08] **Tasha:** And it's less likely to make you orgasm
[19:09] **Evie:** Hahaha. Gabe, if it happens, it happens
[19:10] **Gabe:** I also think there could be potential there, so I don't want to give it all up on the first date
[19:10] **Tasha:** Okay, Heteronormative Harry
[19:10] **Gabe:** We'll see. To be fair, I did have a semi when he asked me out

Spiralling

```
[19:12] Tasha: You must be the first person in
history to get a boner in a post office
[19:14] Evie: I got fanny flutters in Greggs once
```

Before we could attempt to unpack what Evie had just revealed, the driver spoke.

'Think it's here, mate. If you just walk around that corner, you'll get to the entrance.'

I quickly tipped him and gave him five stars in the app. This was the first time I'd been to this particular apartment building; it was just off Spinningfields, an area where I spent little time. Deansgate and Spinningfields contained the highest concentration of both Blazer/Brunch/Bulldogs[14] girlies and Ralph/Races/Racist[15] lads, so they were best avoided if you didn't want to get stuck in a conversation about Pretty Little Thing or cryptocurrency.

I took a deep breath.

```
[19:18] Gabriel: Hi, I think I'm here
```

'The Henley Building', read the plaque outside the double-door entrance to the apartment building, next to a numerical keypad and

---

[14] Blazer/Brunch/Bulldogs are a specific yet widespread conglomerate of girlies, usually in their early to mid-twenties, who leave the comfort of their Cheshire new-builds to come to the city for the day and have Instagrammable brunches, in brightly coloured blazers, to chat about their French Bulldogs and Molly-Mae. They are harmless if consumed in moderation.

[15] Ralph/Races/Racist are a specific yet widespread conglomerate of lads, usually in their early to mid-twenties, who leave the comfort of their Cheshire new-builds to come to the city after either a group hike or day out betting their parents' money at the races, before inevitably descending into attacks on 'woke culture' and, eventually, the marginalised. They are best avoided generally, but should definitely be swerved after 5 p.m., which is when the first bag of cocaine is usually collected

a modern intercom system. I could see through the glass that the lobby was decorated tastefully, with dark wood flooring and colourful furniture. There was no 'Spinningfields Beige' in sight.

```
[19:21] Marcus: The Henley Building?
[19:22] Gabriel: Yeah
[19:22] Marcus: I'll buzz you up, I would come
to the door but I've got things frying
[19:23] Gabriel: I'm intrigued!
[19:23] Marcus: Ha, wait and see
```

The electronic locking mechanism in the doors clicked, and I walked into the heated lobby. The concierge behind the desk flashed me a warm smile and gestured towards the lift.

```
[19:26] Marcus: 11th floor, Apartment 3
[19:26] Gabriel: See you in a sec
```

As I got closer to apartment 1103, I experienced the heady cocktail of emotions that are exclusively served before a first date: a shot of intense nerves, three drops of adrenaline, and a wedge of self-confidence that came after putting an unusual amount of time into perfecting your appearance, all mixed in with the excitement of potential. I ruffled my newly cut hair slightly, licked my lips, and knocked twice. The soft, indiscernible hum of music. The clang of a spatula against the side of a pan. Muffled footsteps coming closer, and then, as the door swung open:

'Gabriel!' All six-foot-something of Marcus appeared in the doorway. 'Good to see you.' He leaned forward and embraced me, patting me on the back and then holding me at arm's length.

'Come in! Food won't be long.'

'Hope so; it's the only reason I'm here. I'm leaving immediately after dinner.'

'I doubt it.' He smirked, patting my back as I walked into the flat. 'What would you like to drink? Wine? Beer? Something else that I don't have but will happily go to the shop for?'

'All the way to Spar? For me?! A glass of red would be amazing. Cheers.'

He laughed. 'I should've known, really.'

It took me a moment as he glanced down at my shirt.

'Yeah, this was a hint.'

'It's a cool shirt.'

I hung my jacket, took off my shoes, and sat on the sofa. The flat was immaculate, with a wide south-facing window, exposed brick walls with creative neon-light art installations, and the smell of something mouth-watering wafting from the oven.

'Is this to your taste?' asked Marcus, who had appeared holding two wine glasses in one hand and a bottle of Chateauneuf du Pape in the other. His voice was warm, and his eyes smiled even when his mouth didn't.

'It's one of my favourites, actually,' I replied. It was one of the only wines I knew by name, having won a bottle in a charity raffle at Boddlies' summer party a couple of years ago.

'Ah, same. In some circles, I'm known as the 'Chateauneuf du Papi'.' He looked at me, wincing as if he regretted the joke as soon as he'd verbalised it. I winced back, then burst out laughing.

'Sorry – cheesy, I know. It's a joke my dad says to my mum every Christmas. She hates it too,' said Marcus.

Ah. Potentially Tory family. I would have to investigate further.

'I don't hate it. I'm just curious to know what circles you're known as that in?' I asked, raising an eyebrow.

'Post offices all across the country.'

'I wouldn't be surprised if that were true after your little display the other day. Very smooth.' I smiled at the memory of our previous encounter.

He grinned back at me. The butterflies returned. Marcus was beautiful the other day, but now he was drop-dead gorgeous. He wore wide-legged brown trousers with an unbuttoned, cadet-blue linen shirt, and his sculpted chest was just visible through the undone buttons, peppered with curls of dark hair. The chestnut hair on his head fell in a lazy middle parting, just two strands at the front gently swinging in time with his gesticulations. As he poured the wine, my eyes wandered to his lips – full, with a perfect cupid's bow. He'd shaved, but there was a shadow from the facial hair that had been there this morning. His skin had a sheen from the heat of the kitchen. He was the most classically attractive man I'd ever had any kind of romantic interaction with.

'Cheers!' He beamed.

'Cheers.'

'To a first-class evening,' he said.

'Gross. You can't blame that one on your dad,' I said, rolling my eyes.

We laughed and clinked glasses. He sat next to me on the sofa, just close enough so that our knees were touching.

'Can I ask you a personal question?' I enquired with a faux-sombre expression.

Marcus shifted slightly and seemed somewhat anxious for the first time. 'Hit me.'

'What on earth' – I leaned forward and picked up the black iPod Classic that had been lying dormant on the coffee table – 'is this?'

Marcus chuckled. 'It's my music!'

'I've not seen one of these in years. Didn't want to front the subscription fee for Spotify?' I asked incredulously, though I doubted it was the case considering our surroundings.

'Not quite.' He took the iPod from my hands, his skin brushing against mine as he pulled his hand back slowly and intentionally.

'Nostalgia?' I offered.

'Sort of. To me, this is the best way to own music. No one does it like Apple did back then. It has the convenience of streaming but some of the tangibility of a CD collection. It doesn't take up much space or cost a bomb, like vinyl. It has no other features besides my music library, meaning I can listen for as long as I want without getting stuck doom-scrolling. But it still feels personal because I'm downloading and curating a permanent collection. You own the music. It isn't transient like streaming, but it's still accessible.'

I wasn't sure whether this was endearing or pretentious. Maybe somewhere in between.

'I've never thought of it like that,' I said.

'Did you have one?' he asked while doing the 'uninterrupted eye contact' thing that objectively attractive people seemed to do subconsciously, but that takes a degree of effort from mere mortals (that harbour even the shadow of insecurity). His eyes were royal blue, and he had a spattering of dark freckles on one side of his face that made them pop even more.

'Of course! Well, an iPod Nano. It was purple, Christmas 2011. My name was engraved on the back.'

'Wow.' He laughed kindly. 'Not tacky whatsoever.'

'It was a present. Are you calling my Mum tacky?'

'Well, it's not that; it's just the—'

'I'm only messing. She is tacky. She's amazing but also tacky. When I was growing up, she had a NO FEAR bumper sticker on her car. I used to cringe when I imagined people reading it on the motorway.' Was this oversharing? Whatever. If he can do a short speech about wanting to *Saltburn* Steve Jobs' grave, I can tell a mumecdote.

'What was the car?' he asked.

'A bright red Ford KA.'

He dropped the iPod and started belly-laughing. So did I. Time and my first-date jitters all but disappeared as we exchanged alternative bumper stickers for my mum's Ford KA, intermittently bursting into fits of laughter. It had started to feel effortless. SHIT.

★ ★ ★

After finishing our first glasses of wine, Marcus poured us another and then headed to the kitchen to finish dinner. He apologised for his inability to chat during the final stages of cooking. 'You're too witty. I won't be able to keep up with the conversation, but I promise it will be worth it in the end.'

I wanted to say, 'I didn't realise you were making a bullshit sandwich', but he'd just called me witty, and the sudden weight of expectation gave me stage fright.

'I guess I'll go through your collection, then!' I said, as I picked up the iPod from the Indian jute rug.

'Feel free. Put whatever you want on the speaker.'

This was the perfect opportunity to do two things:

1. Text the group chat to feedback
2. Explore his music library for further hints of where Marcus fell on the Gayscale[16]

[20:38] **Gabriel:** Guys, are you there? quick, he's cooking, and I've got his iPod

[20:38] **Evie:** HERE! his what?!

[20:39] **Gabriel:** No time to explain, we need to see where he falls on the Gayscale

[20:39] **Evie:** Ok . . . how's it going generally?

[20:40] **Gabriel:** Very well. he looks fucking phenomenal. the food smells outrageous. he's laughing at all my jokes. we've been taking the piss out of my mum

[20:42] **Tasha:** What's a first date if you don't do that, I guess

[20:43] **Gabriel:** Right?? Okay, I've got access to his whole music library and a visual of his

---

[16] See page 67

living space. I'll tell you factoids, and you
say where you think he falls on the Gayscale
  [20:44] **Evie:** Oh!!! So, he still listens to
his music on an iPod? That's cute
  [20:44] **Tasha:** Bit pretentious. why don't you
just shag him to find out his position?
  [20:45] **Evie:** Because if they're both bottoms,
then they're fucked!
  [20:46] **Gabriel:** Quite the opposite. But yes,
that's it. two plug sockets do not make a working iron.
  [20:47] **Tasha:** Sexy analogy

'What's funny?' Marcus's muffled voice asked from across the kitchen. I looked over to see him balancing pans in both hands and holding a clear cellophane package containing an indecipherable ingredient in his mouth. 'Hope it's not my music collection!'

'No, just remembered something from earlier. I'll put some music on now. Eyes on the prize!' I said, pointing towards the stove.

'Yes, chef!' he shouted back.

Weirdly hot.

  [21:00] **Gabriel:** Ok, scrolling now. On his recently played artists. Oh god, Charli XCX
  [21:00] **Evie:** Power Bottom
  [21:02] **Tasha:** How OLD is this guy?
  [21:03] **Gabriel:** He's 31. You're right; Charli is too young for him. He's a Top who was recently dating a younger Power Bottom Zoomer and listened to their music recommendations.
  [21:04] **Tasha:** Okay so good in the sense that you might be compatible, but bad in the sense that he might be a sex offender

[21:06] **Gabriel:** I'm on his most played, you won't believe it guys
[21:06] **Evie:** Is it Gaga?
[21:07] **Tasha:** Is it R Kelly?
[21:07] **Gabriel:** It's Pink Floyd. Where does that fall?
[21:09] **Evie:** Oh wow. Maybe he is a Top. My uncle listens to them, and he's a mechanic
[21:10] **Tasha:** Gabe, are you on a date with Evie's uncle again
[21:10] **Evie:** Again?!
[21:11] **Gabriel:** That does feel Top or potentially True Vers
[21:12] **Evie:** You're so annoying, Tash. Gabe, what about his flat? Are there any clues there?
[21:14] **Tasha:** Has he got a coffee table book?

I downed the remaining wine in two gulps and inspected the living room, surveying it properly. Gone was the doe-eyed, anxious naivety of 7 p.m., only to be replaced with the forensic gaze of a three-drinks-in ruthless investigator.

[21:18] **Gabriel:** The apartment is beautiful. a lot of it is because of the building - so beyond his control. exposed brick. big awning window. modern light fixtures. warm hues.
[21:19] **Evie:** He still chose the apartment. Great taste in interior design!
[21:19] **Tasha:** What in god's name is an 'awning window'
[21:20] **Gabriel:** There are three potted plants
[21:20] **Evie:** Bottom! he has to be. I like the sound of this guy, though
[21:21] **Tasha:** What kind of plants?

Spiralling

   [21:22] **Gabriel:** Do I look like Alan Titchmarsh?
   [21:22] **Evie:** Don't answer that, Tasha
   [21:24] **Gabriel:** There's a candle on the table
   [21:24] **Evie:** What flavour?

I checked to see if Marcus was still busy with dinner. It looked like he was plating up. Time was running out. I picked up the candle and checked the label.

   [21:25] **Gabriel:** Tobacco, cedarwood and leather
   [21:25] **Evie:** That's so Dom top! This is confusing
   [21:26] **Gabriel:** I'm sure he's about to serve the food, have we not decided?
   [21:26] **Tasha:** THE COFFEE TABLE BOOK, GABE. CHECK THE COFFEE TABLE.

Sure enough, on the table just in front of where I was sat lay a large hardback coffee table book – face down. I leaned forward and flipped it over. I gasped quietly before putting it back in the same position.

   [21:29] **Gabriel:** Guys, the coffee table book
   [21:29] **Tasha:** WHAT IS IT???
   [21:29] **Evie:** ???
   [21:29] **Gabriel:** Omg, you won't BELIEVE IT guys. it's S —

'Right! Dinner is served. Take a seat. I'll top up your wine,' said Marcus. I pocketed my phone and headed to the table.

★★★

Even if I didn't plan on having sex that evening, the first forkful of the food Marcus had prepared was close enough to ecstasy for it not to matter.

'This is one of the best things I've ever eaten. I can't stop. Did you put crack in it?'

'No. But lots of casein, so close enough,' said Marcus, dabbing at the side of his mouth with a folded napkin.

I paused. It was the first time my fork had hesitated before reaching my mouth since the meal had been in front of me. 'What's casein?' I asked, wracking my brain to remember if I'd heard of any new party drugs doing the rounds. Surely he wouldn't have spiked my *pasta*? He didn't seem like the type, plus he could've put something in my drink earlier with ease if he'd wanted to. Maybe the whole murderer/accomplice banter was closer to the truth than I'd initially assumed.

'It's a protein that's found in most cheeses. It's what makes it so moreish,' he said matter-of-factly. False alarm on the old spike-o-gram. 'Casein activates the opioid system; that's why some people can become addicted to cheese. There have been studies that say it's as addictive as some hard drugs.' At any other time, I'd have revelled in the opportunity to talk to FRANK, but the pasta was too incredible for me to listen. I didn't give a shit. He could've told me that he'd just received a BBC News notification announcing that Parmesan was highly carcinogenic, and I would've nodded absent-mindedly and finished the bowl.

'Well, I'd choose this dish over a gram of coke any day. Except maybe Friday.' I laughed, washing my latest forkful down with a swig of red.

'You like drugs?' he asked. The words hung heavy in the air for a moment. This was a difficult question to answer, especially in your twenties, especially in Manchester, especially on a first date and especially in Gay World. It could go either way. For all I knew, Marcus could be a devoted fan of PNP[17]. He could have pasta for his main and poppers for dessert. He might be the Chateauneuf Du Papi on

---

[17] 'Party 'N' Play', a term some gay men use to denote their desire to get high together and have sex

Wednesday and Pinot Ganjio on Saturday. Or, he might have never so much as sniffed a spliff in his sheltered chef life. He may have coughed on his first drag of a cigarette, forced upon him by an older student at Le Cordon Bleu, and recoiled at the thought of any mind-altering substance outside of the wine-pairing at a Michelin bistro. Hopefully, it was somewhere in between.

'Not really. I don't mind getting involved if they're there and the situation calls for it. But it's not something I, like, actively pursue.' This was – for the most part – an honest answer. 'How about you?'

'No, not for me. Don't get me wrong, I dabbled a bit in my twenties' – that meant he took MDMA once, was sick during the come up and went home to google his symptoms – 'but it doesn't sit well with me now.'

He was pensive for a moment, eyes glazing over. This gave me the perfect opportunity to wolf down the final tubes of penne.

'One of my best friends got cannabis-induced psychosis a couple of years ago. He had to be sectioned for a while.'

I rushed to swallow my food so I could respond and accidentally let out an audible gulp that verged on slapstick. 'I'm so sorry.' It was a double apology.

'That's okay.'

'What happened? If you don't mind me asking.' If he did mind, he shouldn't have brought up complex trauma over dinner.

'Of course not. It was a combination of things. I suppose he wasn't in a good place for a long time. Started self-medicating, smoking a lot of weed. Seemed innocuous at first, nothing too intense.'

I was trying to remain attentive, to be empathetic, but there was something about him being vulnerable – yet sage and articulate – that was making him even more attractive as the seconds went by. His hands were so big and veiny.

'Do you mind if I smoke?' he asked.

'Not at all.'

'I'm partial to the occasional one after a heavy meal. Would you like one too?'

'I've quit . . . so yes. Please.'

He passed me a Marlboro Gold (what a treat!) and topped up our wine glasses. This was the fourth glass of the evening. The food would've helped to sober me up, but I still made a mental note – in faint pencil – to not drink much more.

'At first, it was just the usual stoner conspiracy theories,' Marcus continued. 'You know: 9/11 was an inside job, the FBI killed John F Kennedy, there's a hidden group of financial elites controlling banks and governments across the world. That sort of thing.'

Thanks to Evie, I was always unsure about JFK, and the last one is just late-stage capitalism, but this wasn't the time for that discussion.

'Then it got strange. He, well, Kalem is his name. He started to have delusions of grandeur. Started believing that he was the centre of the universe and that companies on social media were communicating directly with him through secret codes. At one point, he bought a plasma ball from Amazon and was convinced that Nicki Minaj was sending him messages through it, warning him of an impending apocalypse. He stopped sleeping and started looking directly into the sun for energy every morning.'

'Sounds like a normal Tuesday for a Barb[18]. Jesus, he thought he could photosynthesise! Are his eyes okay now?'

'Luckily, yes. He's got an astigmatism and needs reading glasses, but they suit him. Anyway, it culminated in him running through the centre of his home town in his underwear and posting his passport through the church door as a message to God to come and collect him,' Marcus finished.

I couldn't help it; my mouth was agape. Marcus burst out laughing.

'It's fine. We laugh at it now.'

---

[18] A 'Barb' is a nickname for a devoted fan of the US rapper and celebrated biologist credited with the invention of the Brazilian Butt Lift, Dr. Nicki Minaj

I smiled with relief. His sense of humour was, thankfully, almost as good as his food. We chatted a bit longer at the table and then returned to the sofa, tipsy and stuffed.

* * *

'That was one of the best things I've ever eaten,' I told him again once our food had settled. We were close now, leaning into each other on the suede sofa. 'How do you decide what to cook for pleasure? I can imagine that's quite hard, as a chef.' I had reached the level of drunk-horny that even the utterances of the words 'hard' and 'pleasure' made me want to throw my glass of red wine onto the rug and kiss him aggressively.

'When I'm cooking for myself, it's based on convenience. But when I'm cooking for somebody I'm trying to impress . . .' He was stroking my thigh now with those big, rough, perfect hands. 'Then it's different,' he continued, holding eye contact with me. 'For you, I wanted to cook something wholesome, hearty, complex in flavour, but simple in execution. That's the best kind of food, I think. Food that feels like you're home.'

'Mmm hmm,' was all I could muster as he increased the pressure on my thigh. 'How did you make it so layered? It was very . . . complex,' I said with a gulp.

'The sauce, I use four different cheeses. Each is from a different European country, but they balance one another perfectly. I grate in nutmeg, smoked salt, and two different types of mustard. It has to be perfectly thick.' He had started running his other hand through my hair. I was rock hard, and his thigh-rubbing was edging perilously close to my groin.

'The leeks, I sweat off in butter until they fall apart. The pancetta is from the butcher's in the Northern Quarter; I fry that off, low and slow in its own juices.' I didn't know whether it was the alcohol, hearing a beautiful man speak with such passion, authority, and tenderness, or my current sex drought – but this was one of the most sexually charged moments I'd ever experienced. To someone else, he might've sounded like the voiceover from the early 2000s Marks and

Spencer's adverts, but to me, he was irresistible. I wanted to bite him and feel those hands all over my bare skin.

'And the crust. The crust is panko breadcrumbs, grated Parmigiano Reggiano and a dash of cayenne pepper. I grill that until it's hot and crisp and bubbling.' His face was an inch from mine now, and I could feel his breath against my lips. I couldn't resist any longer. I pulled him in hard, and we kissed. His tongue was wet and soft, ebbing and flowing against mine as he pulled my body on top of his. I mounted him, and he slid his hands up the back of my shirt, lightly scratching my back while we kissed with feverish passion. He pulled away, grabbed my hand, and led me to the bedroom for what I was sure was about to be the most earth-shattering sex of my life.

Disappointment Non Cuit

Servings: 2
Preparation time: 3 hours
Cooking time: 17 minutes

Ingredients:
- *10 glasses of wine*
- *A condom*
- *One bottle of Durex lubricant*
- *2 bottoms*

STEP ONE – *Head into the bedroom, hand in hand. Sigh with anticipation as the hot chef you're on a date with pushes you back onto linen sheets and tears his top off, revealing a sculpted chest and washboard abs, before pouncing on you to remove your shirt and unveil a pigeon chest and one-pack.*

STEP TWO – *Feel suddenly insecure as you realise that the man you are about to have sex* with is only eight percent body fat, and you are thirty-eight per cent pasta. Feel the insecurity fizzle away as you see the hunger in the hot chef's eyes. He fancies you. You fancy him. You now fancy you. Lie back as he pulls down your trousers, grabs your underwear, his fingers grasping firmly on your rock-hard dick and begins to suck your nipple.

STEP THREE – Continue foreplay until you are both close to the point of ecstasy. Smile as he unpeels his glistening form from yours at the last possible moment, standing upright with a perfect six-inch erection that bounces gleefully with every one of his movements. Watch with shuddering anticipation as he reaches into his bedside drawer with his massive, veiny hands, rummages around for a second and pulls out a condom and a bottle of water-based lubricant.

STEP FOUR – Feel so aroused that even the upcoming awkward process of him having to wrap his penis in a latex balloon doesn't quell your horniness. Lie back, turn over, and raise your ass into the air very slightly, like a nervous gazelle in the African savannah presenting to a mate for the first time that summer.

STEP FIVE – Wait to feel the curious sensation of cold lubricant on warm fingers. Be surprised, as it doesn't come. Instead, feel the mattress dip slightly next to you as the hot chef's body lands parallel to yours. Turn to see his beautiful face, cheeks flushed rose against olive, as he smiles at you and bites his lip, reaching over to hand you the condom and lubricant with a raise of one eyebrow.

STEP SIX - Look at his outstretched hands filled with sexual paraphernalia, then back to his beautiful face, then back to his hands. Allow the feeling of confusion to run through your body. Notice as he places the condom and lubricant in front of you, then nods his head back, gesturing for you to look around.

STEP SEVEN - Turn to see the hot chef's perfectly formed ass pointing northwards, his golden back arched like an ostentatious lion stretching out beneath the blazing heat of a Next lamp. Gasp as the realisation of the hot chef's expectations becomes clear. He is also a bottom. Fail to mask your surprise. Push the condom and lubricant back in his direction. Watch as he lies flat, defeated. Raise your ass again, more confidently this time. Try to emulate the arched lion back, unsuccessfully avoiding looking like a frightened alley cat.

STEP EIGHT - Stir in some flashbacks of previous sexual disappointment in a past relationship with a horrible ex. Feel yourself go rapidly flaccid. Watch same thing happen to hot chef. Sit momentarily in the crushing realisation that this is unsalvageable.

STEP NINE - Get dressed, making small talk about his bedroom decorations. Thank hot chef for a wonderful evening. Leave with a steaming portion of Disappointment Non Cuit.
 - Pairs excellently with a warm mug of unhealed trauma.

6

Debriefs and Dickheads

'So, after all that, you didn't even get a shag?' asked Tasha the following evening. She'd invited me to her home in Didsbury under the guise of a takeaway and chill, but I knew her real motive — to extract the sordid details about my date with Marcus. This worked for me, as I'd needed someone other than my brother to vent to, *and* I was hoping to bump into her boyfriend, Scott, before my interview for 'Executive Copywriter' at his workplace, EnsureInsure, on Friday.

'Nope. Left with purple wine lips and blue balls,' I said, biting into a piece of boneless chicken from Wingstop.

'What I don't get, Gabe,' began Tasha, through mouthfuls of fries. She had two small blobs of toothpaste on her face to dry out the stress spots she'd developed over the week. Her white-blonde hair was tied up in a stern bun juxtaposed by a set of baby-pink satin pyjamas. It was 6 p.m., and many would argue that it was far too early to wear nightwear, but those people didn't have a 5 a.m. alarm or a ruthless career in data-handling[19].

'Is, if the date was going so well, and the foreplay was as good as you say it was, then why didn't you end up having sex?'

I considered it for a moment. The only way the initial date with Marcus could've gone better was if he'd revealed that he was a fully trained masseur, pulled a set of aromatherapy oils from under his coffee table and ironed out the two knots I'd had in my lower back since move-in day. We'd connected on all the key levels: humour, emotional intelligence, interests and even sexual until it came to the moment of penetration.

---

[19] I have no idea if data-handling is a ruthless career. Tasha has tried to summarise her job to me countless times, but I still have no idea what it involves and — to be frank? — no desire to

'Well, you see Natasha . . . I'm a bottom, and—'

Before I could finish my thought, Tasha had swallowed her last mouthful of lemon pepper fries and clasped her hands to her mouth.

'NO!' she screamed.

'And I've never actually topped. It's just not for me,' I continued, ignoring her sarcasm. 'Seamus would ask me to, sometimes. But I never felt like it. I think I'm just a passive sexual partner, to my core,' I finished, feeling my cheeks turn red. Tasha leaned over and put her hand on my shoulder earnestly.

'Gabe. There's no need to be embarrassed. You're a gentle, submissive flower swaying softly in a sexual summer breeze, and that's okay!' She smiled.

'You've got lemon pepper in between your teeth,' I lied.

She frowned and started cleaning them with her tongue.

'I would like to try it, eventually, I suppose. With the right guy. But the pressure got to me last night.'

'Why didn't he just top you, then?' Tasha asked.

'He might've done . . . maybe . . . but, as I said, the pressure got to me, and I started thinking about Seamus, and spiralling about how I evidently never satisfied him. Then I lost my boner, and Marcus lost his, and by that point, it wasn't exactly an atmosphere that was conducive to any kind of fucking.'

'Are you going to see him again?'

'I don't think there's any point. I'm not in a position to start experimenting with my sexual identity at the moment. I'm horny and lonely. I want to be railed – hard – and cuddled. I'm not sure which one takes priority.' I sighed. It wasn't until I'd spoken it out loud that I realised how true it was or how pathetic that truth sounded.

'Jesus,' laughed Tasha. 'Okay, so if the only reason Marcus didn't top you was because the ghost of your ex-boyfriend materialised to make you both floppy, who's to say he wouldn't if you met up again?'

I cast my mind back to the night before when I'd been texting Evie and Tasha about Marcus's potential to be a top or bottom. The details were blurry, but an image rose to the forefront of my mind like a photograph floating to the top of a developing bath in a darkroom.

'Do you remember you both asked me to check the coffee table book for a clue about where Marcus fell on the Gayscale?' I asked. Tasha moved to the edge of the sofa.

'Yes . . .' she said.

'Well, it was . . . it was *Selfish*,' I finished, bracing for impact.

Tasha looked dumbfounded. 'It was selfish? What, selfish to have a coffee table book? You've lost me, Gabe.' She frowned.

'No, Tasha. *Selfish*. The coffee table book, *Selfish*,' I said, watching as realisation dawned on Tasha's face and she collapsed with laughter.

'*Selfish* . . . Kim Kardashian, *Selfish*?' she managed to wheeze.

'Yes. *Selfish*, by Kim Kardashian.' I could barely finish the sentence. *Selfish* was a coffee table book released by the omnipresent chieftain of the Kardashian Klan, Kimberly, in the spring of 2015. It contained, in its entirety, different selfies that she had taken over the years, accompanied by pearls of ancient wisdom in the form of captions telling us how much she loved contour, or that she took a selfie at a red light while driving and thought that may be illegal now. I was aware of the captions in detail because Evie and I were owners of the iconic tome at the time of publication. The Kardashians often became a cause of contention in our triad, especially when there was alcohol involved. Evie and I had been fans of their show since we were younger. Tasha saw them as figureheads of an industry that was instilling damaging values in impressionable girls and gays everywhere. During a memorable afters[20] at Evie's uni house in Fallowfield

---

[20] An 'afters' is the post-amble that takes place after the main event. They often end up being the most enjoyable, but most difficult-to-remember part of a night out. They are varied in their location – from a close friend's living room, to a stranger's kitchen, to a lock-in at a pub, but almost always include the surprising presence of a person who you've never met before and never will again

many years ago, we had been having one of our typical debates, this particular one around the validity of Kanye West's statement that Kim Kardashian was 'the new Marilyn Monroe'. Tasha had accompanied her argument, that this assessment by Yeezus was 'delusional bullshit', by drunkenly plucking *Selfish* from Evie's coffee table and doing a dramatic reading of Kim's captions with the same vocal stylings as Marilyn Monroe's 'Happy Birthday Mr President'. Evie, who was mid-way through a course of antibiotics for cystitis and at the end of a bottle of Gordon's pink gin, had burst into tears and run upstairs to bed, slamming doors behind her and screaming about how Tasha 'wouldn't be such a bitch about the Kardashians if she understood what Khloe was going through with Lamar.' The following morning, the politics and history student, Claudia, whom Evie had been dating and who had witnessed the entire performance, sent Evie a text about how she wouldn't be able to see her as much as she 'didn't think their values aligned'.

'So, you think that, because Marcus had Kim Kardashian's book on his coffee table, he's definitely a bottom, and you definitely won't be able to have good sex?' asked Tasha, eyes pink from tears of laughter.

'Don't be ridiculous. I don't think that at all. I *know* that,' I said. Suddenly, I felt a burst of dizzying excitement. This was a new feeling for me. After years of living vicariously through my friends' dating stories, advising them, being furious with them, maligning the duds, and being excited by the good ones, it was my turn. The prospect of being single for the first time since my breakup with Seamus didn't feel scary and overwhelming; it felt loaded with potential. Although the date with Marcus hadn't gone entirely to plan, it had reminded me that I was capable of being fancied and flirted with and that, if it didn't work out with the guy I ran into at the post office, it might work out with the man across the bar or the receptionist at the gym. Even if every man I ever dated turned out to be a flop for whatever reason, the silver lining of recounting the experiences to my friends and converting disappointment into laughter would make it all worthwhile and remind me of a truth that so easily slips away when you're spiralling about singledom – that as long as you have good friends to laugh with, you're never really alone. Without thinking, I leapt forward and wrapped Tasha in a bear hug.

'Gabe, what the FUCK!' she shouted, half laughing, as we both fell over with such surprising force that we knocked a pot of buffalo dipping sauce onto the eight-month-old alabaster carpet. There was a bang from the floor below as the front door opened, then closed, and heavy footsteps thumped upstairs towards the living room. The door swung open, and Tasha's boyfriend, Scott, entered, panting in a four-button trench coat, holding a laptop bag in one hand and a bouquet in the other.

'What's happened?' he demanded, shooting me a concerned glance as I stood to my feet and started wiping sauce from my elbow with a napkin. 'I heard shouting. Are you alright?' He turned to Tasha.

'Hi. Yes, yeah. Obviously.' She swallowed her final laugh. 'We were just messing around. I'll get the stain remover.'

'Don't you dare?' Scott smiled, dropping his laptop bag and handing her the bouquet. 'I'll sort it.' He kissed her on the cheek.

'What have I done to deserve these?' Tasha asked, waving the bouquet above her head and momentarily resembling a deranged serial bridesmaid.

'Do I need a reason to treat you?' His tone was sickly sweet. He had that kind of neutral southern accent that sounded more like money than geography.

'I guess not . . .' said Tasha, quietly. As Scott headed to the kitchen to grab the stain remover, she turned to me, and repressed a grin. I stood up to arrange the flowers in a vase on the table, unable to look directly at Tasha for fear of The Giggles[21]. By the time I'd completed my impromptu flower-arranging performance, Scott had returned and began to scrub at the buffalo sauce with the bristle-brush end of a stain remover.

'This is how you repay me, is it, Gabe, for getting you an interview at EnsureInsure? Dying my new carpet orange?' He looked up from his scrubbing. For a moment, there was a flash of genuine fury across his face. Then he smiled at me, his Invisalign showing across a set of white teeth. Scott was, by all accounts, a good-looking man. He had a strong, prominent chin, dimples, with the build of somebody who grew up playing sports, and the arrogance of someone accustomed to winning them. His yellow-blond hair was tousled, and a five o'clock shadow played across his arrow-shaped face.

'Sorry, Scott. Do you need any help?' I asked.

'No, no, don't worry. You just sit there and try not to spill anything else. How are you, anyway?' he said, scrubbing ferociously as white foam built over the spillage. Something had changed in the atmosphere since his arrival; the air felt tighter, like an invisible force was pinching the corners of the room and pulling them outward.

'Ah, you know. Thriving. Living with my brother. On the verge of having to take out a third credit card. Potentially developing erectile dysfunction. I love that trench coat, by the way,' I said. This was me in ultra-fake Regina George mode. I hated the coat. It made him look like Inspector Gadget had moved to West London and started a hedge fund.

'Yeah, Tasha mentioned Dan had moved in. It's been ages since I've seen you, mate. Wasn't the last time at Ramona in summer?' Scott had finished scrubbing and was leaving the chemicals to work their magic.

---

[21] The Giggles here meaning the specific type of uncontrollable laughter that occurs only when you know it's not allowed

'I think it must have been, yeah,' I said, struggling to resist an eyeroll. I knew what was coming.

'God, you were sloshed. Surprised you remember it. You *do* remember what you were saying to the bouncer?' he asked with a judgmental half-grin.

I had no idea what I'd said to the bouncer – my memories from that night were blurred, and all I had to focus on the morning after was a smudged recollection of the Ramona doormen shoving me down Swan Street and the words 'Captain Tom', 'disrespectful' and 'barred'. Scott had texted me a picture of myself the following morning, stumbling away from the scene with one shoe on, which didn't help with the hangxiety. I hadn't replied, which would've been enough to make most people realise that it wasn't a comfortable subject. Still, Scott seemed to like trying to make me feel uncomfortable.

'I do, sadly. Anyway, do you have any tips for the interview on Friday?' I attempted to change the subject.

'Well, don't drink beforehand. Let's start there!' He laughed. Tasha returned from the kitchen and a wave of relief washed over me. I didn't know how much more of his American Chat Show Host humour I could take. I listened to Scott's tips for the interview, made an excuse about needing to get back to the flat to help Dan with something and left.

★★★

14 May, 2016
```
[09:09] Claudia: Morning, Evie
[09:21] Evie: Good morning Baltimooooooore
[09:22] Claudia: Lol, what?
[09:23] Evie: How are you, babe?
[09:24] Claudia: I'm good. I've been thinking,
```
and I think for the rest of the term I'm going to focus on my studies. I'm just not sure our values align. hope you understand x

[09:25] **Evie:** Is this about last night? About the Kardashians?
[09:26] **Claudia:** What? No, it's not about the Kardashians. It's just about my future.
[09:27] **Evie:** It's about last night, I know it. Do you know what, Claudia
[09:28] **Claudia:** What?
[09:28] **Evie:** If you can't take me at my defending Khloe Kardashian, then you don't deserve me at my knowing more than you expected about the battle of Hastings. It's over
[09:29] **Claudia:** Are you still drunk?
[09:30] **Evie:** Farewell, Claudia

★ ★ ★

Friday reared her head rainy, grey and wet. I'd spent yesterday prepping for the interview with the help of Dan, who had slipped into the role of 'head of marketing' with unnerving ease. We role-played, he quizzed me on my CV so that I'd memorised all the half-truths and exaggerations, and I'd thoroughly researched EnsureInsure. (I knew the year it was founded and generally what they did.) Scott had given me the helpful heads-up that Eric, the actual head of marketing who would be interviewing me that afternoon, hated swearing and loved Christopher Nolan films. By the time the interview had finished, it was almost 6 p.m., and I was ready for a drink. Paul and Dan met me at The Crown & Kettle, one of my favourite pubs in Ancoats, and, by extension, the city. The weather wasn't generous enough to allow us to sit on the benches outside, so we'd found a cosy little nook nestled in a warm corner beneath the timeworn tiled ceiling that looked like it had been excavated from the shipwreck of the Titanic's dining hall.

'The ceiling in here is fire,' said Dan. 'How old is it?'

'Couple 'undred years. Used to be a courthouse. There was a fuck-off fire, though, and a lot of it burnt down. They 'ad to restore it. Took fifteen years. My cousin did some of the brickwork,' said Paul.

'Nice use of an adjective, idiot,' I said to Dan.

'Don't cancel me!!!' he mocked.

'Well, maybe in future, if you use more varied vocabulary instead of just describing everything as 'sick' or 'fire', you'll be better off. Not even varied, just appropriate. Who calls ancient architecture 'fire', honestly? It's like being related to Shaggy from Scooby-Doo.' Dan also had the same flecks of patchy, non-committal facial hair on his chin.

'Christ, Gabe, the interview went well, then, did it? Have a bit of your pint!' Paul said.

'Firstly, I've had a spliff, so leave me alone. Secondly, you're insane, mate.' Dan turned to Paul. 'He's such a hypocrite. Do you know what he said when I told him I'd graduated?'

Paul shook his head.

'"Slay queen!"' Dan said.

'In my defence, that was ironic.'

'Just what you need when trying to celebrate with your family – irony,' Dan said.

'Sorry if I'm being a bitch, it's just been a weird couple of days.' I sighed. 'The interview went alright, I think. I hope. Didn't fumble any of the questions. Scott, Tasha's boyfriend, gave me the head's-up that he's into film, specifically Christopher Nolan, so we bonded over that towards the end.'

'What's 'is favourite Nolan?' asked Paul.

'*Dunkirk*?!' I replied.

Paul tutted.

'Weirdo,' Dan said.

'Sound of that Scott to give you tips. Seems like a top geezer,' said Paul.

'Hmm.'

'What? You're not sure on him?' Paul asked.

'Not really. I went to give Tasha a hug yesterday, and we knocked a bit of buffalo sauce onto the new carpet he'd paid for. He came back and saw it, then looked at me like he wanted to strangle me. I know it's annoying, but it was an accident, and he had murder in his eyes. Then did this fake smile. Tasha went all shy too. She doesn't act like herself around him. If that was me or Evie, she'd have said some cutting remark. He just weirds me out,' I said.

'Has he said anything specifically bad to you, mate? This Scott?' Paul asked.

'He asked me when I chose to be gay once,' I said. Dan laughed and rolled his eyes. Paul looked confused.

'I can't believe that still happens,' Dan said.

'Same.'

'What's so bad about that?' Paul's hammy features contorted into a frown.

'Wow, Paul. Now you're cancelled, too,' I said.

'Unbelievable, Paul. Gabe, shall we contact ResidentLiving? I don't know if this man should be allowed to work in our building.' Dan laughed. Paul looked nonplussed.

'It's not necessarily *so* bad, Paul; it's just annoying. It's something ignorant straight people say, and it plays into old religious beliefs that your sexuality is something you choose rather than something that happens subconsciously or that you're born with. It's like me asking you when you *chose* to be straight?'

'In my second year at Ellesmere High when Claire Johnson wore a skirt three sizes too small,' Paul said, immediately.

'Right,' I said.

'I'm only messing. But understood. Cheers lads, for being patient with me. Never too old to learn!' Paul let out a hollow laugh. His eyes drifted, and he looked momentarily crestfallen. He cleared his throat. 'Anyway, Gabe, there's always gonna be people you don't get on with in life, and there doesn't always have to be a reason. Between us, Benny at work, he does my head in.'

'Why?' asked Dan.

'Yaps too much while I'm eating me lunch.'

'Gotcha,' I replied. 'Right, just going for a cig. It's your round, Dan.'

'I got the last one!' Dan said.

'I've cooked every night this week and mopped up twice because, for someone who smokes enough cannabis to paralyse Damian Marley, you've still not figured out how to roll a spliff without decorating the floor with baccy. I'll be your skivvy, reluctantly, but I won't do it for free. Mine's a pint of Sessions,' I said, standing up to leave.

'Slay queen?' Dan frowned.

'Bloody hell, you two sound like me and my missus,' Paul boomed. 'So, have you got anyone on the go, Daniel?'

'There were these three girls back in London, but now I'm . . .'

The sound of my brother relaying his dating exploits melted into the buzz of the pub as I headed to the smoking area. I didn't want to hear about Dan's latest sexploits. As a feminist, I found the disposable way in which he treated women repulsive. I'd witnessed it enough times to see a pattern – he would feign emotional interest (or convince himself that it was there) just long enough to be having regular sex, then move on when he got bored (or the spectre of any kind of commitment hovered over him). This cycle tended to last between two and nine weeks. As a brother, though, I'd always remember his drunken admission that he 'didn't think love was real'. This had stuck with me, and left me with the worrying belief that our parents' divorce had fucked him up, leaving him with a disconnect from his own feelings, a disregard for other people's, and a functional cannabis problem to numb it all. I lit up a cig, and my phone rang.

'Hi!'

'Hi mate, how are you? How do you think it went?' asked Scott.

Jeez, that was quick. 'I'm not sure, to be honest, Scott. I answered the questions well, and we had a good conversation about films at the end. Thanks for the tip.'

'Well, I've got good news and bad news. Which do you want first?' he asked. I always hated this question. It was for people who go power-mad the moment they have a tidbit of knowledge that you don't. Waiting to receive news was nerve-wracking enough without a delay in the form of a minigame.

'Good, please,' I said.

'The good news is – you got the job! Eric wants you to start the Monday after next. He said you came across well, and he thinks that "if you manage to bring the passion and articulation you showed when discussing the *Interstellar* soundtrack to copy about EnsureInsure, then you'll excel". Reckon you're up for it?'

I dropped my cig into a puddle with elation.

'Of course!' I replied, telling my first corporate lie. I didn't believe for a second that I could get as passionate about insurance policies as I could about Hans Zimmer. 'And thank you so much, Scott. For everything. I really, really appreciate this.' Maybe I had misjudged him slightly.

'Great!' said Scott. 'Okay, so, on to the bad news, and I'd appreciate it if you kept this between us.'

'Yeah, sure. What is it?' I said.

'And by that, I mean, if you could make sure this doesn't get back to Tasha, I'd be grateful, mate.' His voice had lost all life and, in its flatness, sounded menacing. 'Do you promise?'

My breath felt shallow, and my heart rate increased to panic levels for the first time that day. I'd never conspired against my best friend in such a way.

'I promise. What's up?'

'Well, Gabe, Tasha told me what happened last night. That you lunged at her and that that's how the carpet got stained. She was a bit upset about it, mate.'

I was too stunned to speak. Why would Tasha lie? In all our years of friendship, she had never lied to me yet, as far as I'd known. What would she have to gain?

'I don't want to offend you, mate,' he began. 'But sometimes you think you can handle women differently, or whatever. I've seen it before, from your lot. That it's okay for you to push them around, or feel their tits, or slap their ass or whatever, because you're gay. It's not a big deal; you do you, but not with Tasha. She doesn't like it. You understand, right, Gabe?' He sounded cheerful enough, but it was fake. I was thrown for six. The last thing I wanted to do was jeopardise this new job after just finding out I'd got it, so I needed to keep Scott on my side until I at least found out a bit more as to what the fuck was going on.

'Sure, Scott. No worries at all.'

'Great. You're all out on the town tomorrow night, aren't you? Canal Street, is it?' he asked, switching back into normal human mode.

'We are! Can you not make it?' I asked.

'Sadly not, but have a great night, Gabe. And remember what I said! I'll see you when you start. Bye, mate.'

'Bye, Scott.'

7

Out!

'Okay girlies, fuck marry kill – David Attenborough, Alan Sugar, Paul from downstairs. Go!' squawked Mitchell before taking a shot of some Tequila Rose he'd brought for everyone to share. I considered the options, as Evie popped half-frozen ice cubes into glasses on the kitchen side, and Dan howled with laughter. Having Mitchell for prinks[22] had so far been, admittedly, hilarious. I knew how fickle he was, so I wasn't worried that he'd start quizzing me about my breakup, as he'd probably already forgotten and was fixating on someone else's business or a different micro-drama. Since his arrival, Mitchell had spent fifteen minutes trying to convince Dan, whose skin tone was about nine shades lighter than his, to put some of his foundation on; he'd told me my hair 'reminded him of *Downton Abbey*', and asked Evie if her skirt was from a car boot sale. So far, he'd been a tonic, and everyone was enjoying his company, as well as the music he was blasting through a SONOS speaker he'd brought in a Sainsbury's carrier bag.

'Okay, so I'd fuck David Attenborough . . .' I started.

'Babe, he's literally four hundred years old,' said Mitchell with unease.

'I think fucking him might also kill him,' said Tasha, who so far had seemed utterly unaware of what Scott had said to me after my interview at EnsureInsure and was behaving normally. 'Which would probably be considered grand treason. Not a great choice, Gabe.'

---

[22] Afters' little sister, prinks, here means pre-drinks. The time before a night out where you congregate in one place, chat shit, discuss outfits, and have enough alcohol so that the thought of engaging with strangers or dancing to old Britney Spears songs doesn't seem quite as intimidating

'Well, that's alright, isn't it, because it's mine. You can explain your reasoning when you answer the question,' I huffed. A chorus of sarcastic 'wooooos' reverberated across the walls of my apartment.

'As I was *saying*, I'd make gentle and dignified love to David Attenborough at a pace with which he was entirely comfortable. I'd kill Alan Sugar by taking away his ghost-written puns on *The Apprentice* so that his brain would short-circuit when making up one of his own, and I'd marry Paul.'

'Is Paul married, Gabe?' asked Dan.

'He is babe, yeah,' replied Mitchell, who had formed a habit of responding to everything Dan said, even if it wasn't directed at him. 'Has been for years, and he's got two kids, but one of them lives in Australia now, and I dunno about the other one. Gabe?'

'He's got a son, but he doesn't talk about him much. I don't think they're close. But yes, for the hypothetical, I would marry lovely Paul,' I finished, taking a glug from my gin and tonic.

'How old is David Attenborough actually, though? Gabe, google it! And play something fierce on the speaker; I need to poo in the jacuzzi!' cackled Mitchell, throwing me his diamanté-encrusted phone case and strutting to the bathroom. I put on his most recently played song on Spotify (Kim Petras – 'Icy') and headed to google. I began to type 'h', and Mitchell's recent searches popped up underneath:

    BBC weather Manchester
    Does lip filler hurt
    Lip filler prices uk
    Charli xcx tickets
    Is there a brat spring
    Popcorn lung from vape
    Popcorn lung symptoms
    Watch real housewives of pontomac online free
    Is Tom Jones black
    French bulldog puppies manchester

Shawn Mendes topless
Ozempic uk
Ring of fire rules
Salmon en croute recipe
What does en croute mean

'Ok, I've got another one!' said Mitchell, returning from the bathroom triumphant. He plucked his phone from my hands, the David Attenborough quandary forgotten, and began to pour himself another shot of tequila rose.

'Dan. Daniel,' he said, looking over at Dan and pouting. Mitchell had the attitude of a particular type of Gayman in that he openly flirted with straight men, but in such an innocuous and obtuse way that it only ever served for the amusement of the flirt, the flirted, and the captive audience. Dan, who had quickly become accustomed to Mitchell, revelled in the attention.

'Daniel, Daniel, Daniel. Fuck marry kill – me, Natasha, Evie,' Mitchell announced, clasping his hand to his mouth in faux surprise when the room erupted into a chorus of 'Mitch!' And 'No!' And 'Not this'. Evie, who was only on her second drink and required at least four to have any kind of romantic interaction, started intensely fidgeting with a bead on her gipsy skirt. Tasha wrinkled her nose and pulled a face that looked like she'd just smelled manure. Mitchell had moved forward slightly in his chair. Dan was unfazed.

'Ah, that's easy. No offence, guys,' Dan began. 'So I'd kill you, Mitch. Sorry, bro.' Mitchell shook his head to indicate his unbotheredness. 'I'd probably fuck you, Tasha . . .'

'You'd "probably fuck me"? It's a mystery that you're single, Dan. Has Gabe been teaching you how to be poetic?' Tasha's tone was playful, her eyes glinting.

'And I'd marry Evie in a heartbeat,' he finished, flashing Evie a grin while she turned beetroot and took a large gulp of her drink to mask her embarrassment.

'Right, guys, we should probably get going soon,' I said, eager to put a stop to whatever the hell that was.

'It's so early!' exclaimed Mitchell. It was ten past eleven.

```
[23:10] Tasha: Everything OK?
```

The message flashed across the screen from our private chat, mostly used for administrative purposes like arranging meet-ups when Evie was busy, brainstorming birthday presents for Evie, or forwarding funny spelling mistakes Evie had made. The truth was, everything was not okay at all. Since Scott's confrontation after the interview at EnsureInsure, I had wracked my mind trying to replay events and understand what on earth had happened. As far as I was concerned, I had tried to hug Tasha, she hadn't been expecting it, and we both fell over in good spirits into a pot of mildly spicy sauce. According to Scott, though, Tasha had told him that I'd 'lunged at her' and that she was upset. There were three potential options here:

Option 1:

Tasha had lied to Scott, telling him that I'd lunged at her and that she was upset.

Potential reasoning:

1. Tasha did not want to take any part of the blame for the buffalo sauce spillage. This seemed insane; it was an innocent mistake that was relatively easy to remedy, and Scott was not an abusive husband from 1920s New York who flies off the handle at any mild spousal misdemeanour.
2. Tasha was tipsy and sensitive, so she misinterpreted the hug as aggressive. This was wildly unrealistic, as trying to imagine Tasha feeling sensitive was like trying to imagine a wasp being shy. Even if this was the case, she would not have sullied my relationship with Scott by exaggerating, and she would have confronted me about it since.

3. Tasha hated me and was in the early stages of a grand scheme to have me arrested or sectioned.

Likelihood of Option 1: 17%

Option 2:
> **Scott was lying, and Tasha did not make any kind of accusation.**

Potential reasoning:

1. Scott wanted to establish a power dynamic between us that positioned him as the dominant party.
2. Scott sounded pretty homophobic with his 'your lot like to grab women' hot-take[23], so he may have been using me as a lightning rod for his anger towards the gays.
3. Scott was jealous of my closeness with Tasha and wanted to drive a wedge (or should I say . . . buffalo chicken wing[24]) between us.

Likelihood of option 2: 81%

Option 3:
> **I didn't know how to hug properly. I had misjudged my own strength and had a violent aura without realising it.**

---

[23] There is a problem with latent misogyny in the gay community as a whole. Because we grow up having strong bonds with women, some gays feel like they have unchecked access to women's bodies. I don't, however, think for a second that Scott has ever paused to ruminate on intersectional feminist issues because I have heard him cite Jordan Pearson as a reference twice in the past and Tasha says he's 'obsessed' with the Joe Rogan podcast

[24] I'm so sorry

Potential reasoning:

1. I am Lennie from *Of Mice and Men*

Likelihood of option 3: 2%

As I wasn't entirely sure about any of the options, I decided I'd sit with them for a bit longer. I didn't want to bring a shotgun to the party and set a weird vibe for our first night out together in a long time.

```
[23:10] Gabriel: Of course! Are you?
[23:11] Tasha: Ok, just checking. Yeah, I'm
worried we might have to get Mountain Rescue
to collect Mitch from the top floor of G-A-Y if
he doesn't pace himself, but that's on him, I
suppose
```

'Right ladies, one more shot, then we'll hit the town and let them bitches have it!' Mitchell shouted before attempting to do a Death Drop[25] and landing in a tangle of limbs on the floor, his glass smashing beside him.

★ ★ ★

Canal Street in Manchester, 'The Gay Village' as it's known to straight people, or 'The Village' as it's affectionately referred to by regular frequenters, is a kaleidoscopic drop-kick of colour. The bar fronts are

---

[25] A 'Death Drop' is a dance move often performed by drag queens, wherein they will purposefully buckle one of their legs and instantly drop to the floor, usually to the beat of a song. It is not for the faint-hearted, takes years of practice, and has been the cause of many a sprain for uninitiated gays worldwide

adorned with luminous signs, their lettering interrupted by the neon wigs of eight-foot drag queens. The canal side has a ribbon of trees running parallel to it, each adorned with hazy emerald fairy lights. The throngs of eclectic punters, tourists, and bar reps that dance and weave along the cobbled lanes in brightly coloured outfits and effervescent makeup contrast the stark red brick and murky canal: a poignant nod to how the gay community has risen from the oppressive grip of heteronormativity to create its own thriving, eclectic, vibrant sanctuary – or a testament to how every queer person is, at heart, an attention-seeking little bitch. The squad for the evening – me, Evie, Tasha, Dan and Mitchell – were five such bitches, and we strutted around the corner of Princess Street and onto Canal Street with the drama and intensity of a group of Marvel superheroes walking in slow motion after a victory in battle:

Mitchell (Orange Thunder)
Height: 5 ft 6
Look: Ronseal skin. Blond quiff artificially straightened downwards into full fringe. Daisy Dukes, white patent leather heels, crop top, cowboy hat. Glitter covering dark under-eye circles.
Superpowers: Blinding tan. The ability and near-constant willingness to twerk like a frightened rabbit with osteoporosis.

Gabriel (Razor Quill)
Height: 6 ft 1
Look: Hair curly and dark, pushed back into waves. Distressed brown leather jacket, open with a graphic T-shirt underneath. Caramel wide-leg trousers. Low-top Dr. Martens, obviously.
Superpowers: Can temporarily suppress low-level depression on demand. The ability to dematerialise suddenly and reappear in the smoking area.

Tasha (Viper Tongue)
Height: 5 ft 2
Look: Sheer top from slow-fashion designer EMRLD, statement red lip, cat eyeliner, platinum blonde hair in loose waves, black cycling shorts.

Superpowers: Can read[26] a bitch better than a librarian with binoculars. The ability to maintain wit when inebriated.

Evie (Ankara the Forest Witch)
Height: 5 ft 6
Look: Green gipsy skirt. The 'Palma' top by local slow-fashion brand Before July, which flattered her enormous breasts. Dangling diamanté earrings. Auburn hair flowing freely, majestic, regal. Smokey eye. Salomon trainers.
Superpowers: Interacts with schoolchildren daily and doesn't commit suicide. The ability to go from quite shy to unstoppable seductress in T-minus 4 drinks.

Dan (The Shadow)
Height: 5 ft 11
Look: Short-back-and-sides haircut. Black crew neck. Black trousers. Black low-top Dr. Martens. Slightly ill appearance, but in a young kind of Pete Doherty way.
Superpower: related to Gabriel.

The effect of four young, attractive, well-dressed people (and Mitchell) rounding a street corner would usually be a dramatic one. But seeing as this constituted every other person that inhabited Canal Street of a weekend, we went largely unnoticed outside of our own perception. There was a widespread epidemic of Main Character Syndrome[27] in

---

[26] To 'read', or the act of 'reading', is a concept stemming from the underground ballroom scene in 1980s New York. It is, in essence, to articulately and artfully tear someone a new one. To psychoanalyse, critique, and destroy using wit and humour, but often without the full negative intention of an insult

[27] Main Character Syndrome is an affliction that forces one to believe that they are the protagonist of life – that the world and every happenstance

The Village that had been left untreated since it first spread in the 1990s. Before this, Canal Street was a haven for gay people, where they would congregate behind foggy-windowed bars, but in secret – as homosexuality was, of course, still criminalised. It was during this time that the chief cuntstable[28] James Anderton made his infamous statement that Canal Street consisted of 'gay men swirling in a cesspit of their own making'. As we stepped onto the sticky floors of Via, elbowing past sweaty throngs of scantily clad men dancing provocatively, I was reminded how wrong James Anderton was in his statement. It wasn't just gay men who had created Canal Street; it was also the lesbians – proud and fierce – who met each other on the dance floor, forging intense relationships with each other and leaving them again more quickly than a mum popping to the Co-op for some loo roll. It was the transfolk, in all their defiant glory, who still face the same persecution today as we did all those years ago but who never back down, and insist on living within their truth. The drag queens, statuesque pillars of brashness and kindness and venom and beauty, chaperoned the atmosphere in any venue; deciding whether you would laugh, dance, or cry at the click of a button or the tap of a dusty mic. And, yes, it was the gay men in all of their different forms – vested and muscular, feminine and glamorous, chic and hairy, all battered and bruised after their arduous journey on the winding road of life with shoes that didn't quite fit – but all healing, and doing it together, around love and hope and music. This wasn't a cesspit. Yes, it stank of old wallpaper and sweat and out-of-date Paco Robane. Yes, the floors were filthy, the drinks were watered down, and eighty per cent of the clientele was on a potentially fatal cocktail of ketamine and cocaine. But at its heart, it was a sanctuary – a refuge that traded the isolating

---

in it orbits around their existence. It's similar to narcissism, but a bit more theatrical and less dangerous

[28] Oh my god autocorrect, how could you?!

chaos of the outside world for joyous pandemonium. I'd not been in ages and hadn't realised how much I missed it.

'Gabe?' Dan shouted in my ear over the euphoric sound of Taylor Swift's 'Cruel Summer'.

'Yeah?'

'Can you hurry up and push through to the bar? I've had my arse slapped three times.'

'Two of them were me!' crowed Mitchell, who grabbed us both by the shoulder and pulled us to the counter.

★ ★ ★

We progressed through the night in a dream-like autopilot, two drinks at Via culminating in a dance to a Sugababes megamix. On to G-A-Y. Three more drinks each. At this point, we'd all reached various stages of inebriation that could be categorised by our exploits:

Tasha – Had a go at the bouncer for IDing her. Intimidated him so much that he let her in without any. Requested 'Blurred Lines' by Robin Thicke from the DJ as a joke and got told to piss off.

Evie – Took an edible. Passionately snogged Dan during Kylie Minogue – 'Padam'. Took a photo with a stranger in the toilet and set it as her WhatsApp display picture. Asked if said stranger from toilet could join the group chat.

Me – Became fixated on finding someone to shag. Smoked one cig every thirty minutes.

Dan – Passionately snogged Evie again during Dua Lipa – 'Physical'. Two slurring conversations with strangers about how he's a committed 'ally'.

Mitchell – Threw his cowboy hat at a drug dealer on the way to the club. Snogged a man in his fifties wearing an ill-fitting blazer who looked like he'd wandered in by accident. Last seen being escorted out by a bouncer after going behind the bar to pour himself a drink. Could be overheard shouting, 'This is live homophobia! ARE YOU ALL SEEING THIS? I basically pay rent here, ya fat shit!'

We all left G-A-Y and put Mitchell in a taxi home, watching as he waved from the window and then instantly clasped his hand to his mouth to stop the rise of vomit as the car jerked into motion.

'Gabe, it's getting late. Shall we go to Kiss?' asked Evie, who was now holding hands with a grinning Dan. It was the question I'd been worried about facing all night. Kiss was the bar where Seamus had worked part-time while we both studied at university. It was a lively little hole in the wall that we'd often visit mid-week for the drag bingo or just to catch up with the locals and other staff we'd become close to, and it was usually the last place open in The Village. They regularly had lock-ins, and attending one was seen as a privilege gifted only to their most trusted clientele. I'd been dreading going back there, especially after Mitchell had informed me that 'everyone' knew what had happened between my ex and my stepbrother. Unfortunately, the voice of wisdom in my head, which was quiet at the best of times, was drowned by the alcohol in my bloodstream and remained silent. So, we headed there without further ado, completing the four-minute walk in fifteen due to our drunken pace. We arrived to Clark the bouncer grinning, hugging me and saying it was good to see me. Down the narrow staircase that led to the dance floor. Four shots. Dance. Toilet. Offered poppers. Declined because they gave me a headache. Bought a lollipop from a lucky-lucky man in what could be considered a disturbingly infantile display of sexiness. Baby Guinness shot. Tasha abruptly left after a phone call from Scott, or maybe she hated the vision of me with the lollipop. I was too pissed to care at this point. Grace Period, one of the resident drag queens, noticed me from across the bar. Either her colossal scarlet wig had a motor concealed inside, causing it to move from side to side, or I was steaming.

'As I live and fuckin' breathe. I thought you were dead!' she said, slapping me around the face. 'GET OUTTA MY PUB!' We both descended into laughter. Evie and Dan were nowhere to be seen. Grace regaled me with a story about another queen she knew who sucked their own faeces from a penis the other week to stop her sexual partner from realising her accident. I was undeniably steaming, so began discussing what happened with Seamus and Luca. She looked awkward and said she knew all about it and was sorry. But the lights were bright. It was all blurry. I needed breathing room. Grace Period left to greet some other excitable punters. I knew I needed to find Dan and Evie. It was home time. Then:

'Gabe?' There was a tap on my shoulder.

I hadn't taken any drugs that night, so I couldn't have been hallucinating. It was Luca. Not out in Nottingham, where he studied Sports Science at university. Here. In front of me. I heard the red sirens from *Kill Bill* sound in my head. I hadn't seen my stepbrother since the whole muddy affair. I hated him, obviously. I felt like I was going to be sick. He looked good, shock. He always looked good. Tall. Ginger. Muscular because his personality was the gym. Dressed alright, but fashion didn't matter as much when hidden underneath was sculpted aesthetic perfection. I hated him. I shoved him aside and headed towards the narrow staircase. Dan and Evie would be fine, and I needed to go home.

'Gabe, wait . . . Please...' Luca called, chasing me up the staircase. I ran out, gasping lungfuls of the frosty night air. It was cold – freezing, actually. I walked quickly; it was 4 a.m., and I needed to get back to my safe place and away from the leech who had sucked the life force from my relationship.

'GABRIEL. Listen to me!' A hand grasped my upper arm and pulled hard. The force shocked me. I turned to face my stepbrother, and my vision zoomed out. I saw him standing in place, the edges of his frame clear against the blurred city backdrop, like he was on the cover of a shit, early-2000s thriller DVD with a cringeworthy one-word title. The sight of his face and the force of his grasp made fury bubble to the surface, causing me to do something I'd never done before in my life: I turned around and punched Luca in the face.

***

INTERROGATION
By Gabriel Lanes

<u>Scene 1/2</u>

EXT – FRESH BITES CHICKEN SHOP. MANCHESTER. NIGHT.

Establishing shot of chicken shop FRESH BITES. The sign glows yellow. The 'E' on BITES has been scribbled out with graffiti. A few customers can be seen through dirty windows. Distant sounds of cars screeching, a muffled police siren, dim thud of music from an apartment nearby.

Two men appear in the shot, arm in arm, panting heavily. They both appear to be drunk and injured.

Camera switches to a tracking shot, following the men as they enter FRESH BITES.

INT – FRESH BITES CHICKEN SHOP.

Shot of Gabriel and Luca exhausted in the shop entrance from the POV of the two FRESH BITES servers. A couple leans against the wall, lazily feeding each other chips. The place is dingy but comfortably so. Metallic silver interior with bright white, clinical lighting. There's no way it has a food hygiene rating above 2.

Close-up shot of Gabriel, who looks extremely worried and has blood covering his shirt.

Close-up shot of Luca, who is wincing in pain, has a nosebleed and lots of redness around the right eye socket.

Extreme close-up of Luca's bleeding nose.

Extreme close-up of Gabriel's right hand – swollen and red and hanging in an awkward position.

Shoulder shot over Gabriel. The two servers can be seen behind the counter, assessing the pair's injuries. One rolls their eyes and walks back into the kitchen; the other beckons them in to offer help.

FADE OUT.

INT – CONTINUOUS. FRESH BITES CHICKEN SHOP.
Down shot. A bright white spotlight appears over Gabriel and Luca sat opposite each other at a small, square metal table. The background of the chicken shop is now black, and nothing is visible but the two men, lit in clinical white. The chiaroscuro lighting makes the scene resemble a detective interrogation sequence in a neo-noir film.

Mid shot of Gabriel, sat opposite Luca, with a bag of frozen chips over his swollen hand.

CLASSIC WESTERN MUSIC BEGINS TO PLAY, TO COMEDIC, TARANTINO-ESQUE EFFECT.

Extreme close-up of Gabriel's eyes, bloodshot with alcohol consumption, narrowing as he stares at his rival with fierce determination.

Mid shot of Luca, sitting opposite Gabriel, fidgeting. He has two rolled-up pieces of tissue paper plugging his nose to stop the bleeding.

Extreme close-up of Luca's eyes, also bloodshot with alcohol consumption, widening with worry as he faces his stepbrother.

Camera switches to wide shot of the two sat opposite at the table, western music stops abruptly, the background of the scene is still blacked out. The interrogation begins.

LUCA
I can't believe you punched me.
GABRIEL
(*in mocking disbelief*) You CAN'T?!
LUCA
It was a pretty good hit.
(*Luca smirks nervously*)
GABRIEL
(*disgusted*) Don't try and placate me. It was a great hit. You moved your fat ginger head.
LUCA
How's your hand?

Close-up of Gabriel's hand, which is now almost entirely concealed by a wilting bag of McCain oven chips.

GABRIEL
In one piece, at least.
LUCA
And how're you?
(*Beat*)
GABRIEL
Slightly more fractured.

(*Beat. There is a moment where Gabriel's expression softens from derision to pain*)
LUCA
Look, Gabe—
GABRIEL
How the fuck can you even look me in the eye?
LUCA
Because I have to. I need you to know how sorry I am.
GABRIEL
(*scoffs, but visibly upset*) You're sorry?
LUCA
Of course I'm sorry. I've not stopped thinking about it all since it went down. I—
The lighting switches from chiaroscuro to a deep red, close-up on Gabriel.
GABRIEL
(*menacing*) You've not stopped thinking about it? That must've been solid, Luca. Don't apologise. You're the victim here. How're you holding up, after fucking my boyfriend behind my back IN OUR FAMILY HOME?
(*Gabriel's voice becomes warped and altered until it sounds demonic. His silhouette becomes darker and more imposing*)
GABRIEL
ARE YOU DOING WELL, LUCA? IS YOUR SLEEP INTERRUPTED BY TORTUROUS FLASHBACKS OF A TEXT THAT TORE YOUR LIFE APART? HAVE YOU CALLED ME ONCE? HAVE YOU REACHED OUT TO APOLOGISE? OR HAVE YOU BEEN TOO BUSY *THINKING*?
(*The roar from Gabriel's monologue has caused his breath to become an otherworldly cyclone.*

The camera switches to Luca, whose hair is being blown back and he is clinging to the metal table to avoid being blown into the void. Chips, bottles of condiments and chicken nuggets are swirling around the room)

GABRIEL

HAVE YOU MANAGED TO TAKE A BREAK FROM YOUR NONSTOP *THINKING* TO EMPTY THE CORROSIVE CUM FROM INSIDE YOUR DEMONIC, GAPING, HAGGARD SPHINCTER? HAVE YOUR INFINITESIMAL, PROTEIN-ADDLED MICRO-THOUGHTS MANAGED TO COME TO ANY PLAUSIBLE CONCLUSION OTHER THAN THAT YOU ARE AN EMOTIONALLY STUNTED, DICK-HUNGRY SOCIOPATH WHO WILL RIP OUT THE HEART OF HIS RELATIVES IF IT MEANS BEING GIFTED THE OPPORTUNITY TO GIVE A TOOTHY CHRISTMAS BLOW JOB TO A PART-TIME POET WITH A FOUR-AND-A-HALF-INCH COCK?

(The red light dissipates slowly, and the white clinical lighting returns. Gabriel's size and voice return to normal)

GABRIEL

(exhausted from his outburst) Have you *really* thought about what you did, Luca? What you've done to me? I can't even face seeing my dad because it means stepping into that house.

(Camera moves to Luca, who looks devastated. He is shaking, and his lip looks unstable)

LUCA

I don't think I'm the victim, Gabe. I'm disgusted with myself. And with...

(He considers saying Seamus's name but changes his mind after noticing the expression on Gabriel's face)

LUCA

Him. It wasn't just shagging, Gabriel. I know you think it was, and I don't know if this makes it worse, but it wasn't.

GABRIEL

What do you mean?

LUCA

I thought I loved him, Gabe.

GABRIEL

(*baffled*) you... what?

LUCA

It started about nine months before you found out. We'd stay up, you know, when everyone had gone to bed and just talk shit. Mostly about you, at first. He would go on about how you met, how much he loved you, all of that. I'd talk about how much I did, too, how I'd always wanted a brother.

GABRIEL

Oh please.

(*Luca's eyes are filling with tears now; he is earnest. It is a pitiful sight to see his nose plugged, covered in blood, on the edge of tears*)

LUCA

I mean it. Then, something changed. He started going to the gym more – we had that in common – and he'd message me a lot about it on Instagram, for tips and that. I think, because you two were struggling, I think that's what motivated him to start working out, maybe. That's what he said anyway, that you two weren't doing well. He said that he thought you hated him, Gabe. It did seem like you did, sometimes.

(*Camera on Gabriel, who also looks shaken. The amalgamation of different emotions, thoughts and memories flying around his brain results in a deep frown*)

LUCA

He cried to me about it, Gabe. He opened up, and was sensitive and honest and stuff, and I'd never... no one had ever done that to me. Then, he started writing things for me. It was... nice. He'd call me quite a lot, would check in and that. Then it grew from there; he told me he liked me, that you two had been over for months, that he loved me an—

GABRIEL

Stop. That's enough.

(*Beat. Silence. Both boys have tear-stained faces*)

LUCA

It was all a lie, anyway. He didn't love me. Or even like me, really. It was just shagging, for him. I think he got off on... on behind-the-back stuff. He'd always call me his naughty boy and—

GABRIEL

Are you serious? Did you have a sex tape of you both that you wanted to show me as well, or . . .?

LUCA

Nah, I'm not saying it to rub it in. Just to make you understand. He played me. He played us both. He was shagging someone else the same time as me too, some 'straight' guy. It was probably the same thing with them two, just a fetish, a sneaky thing. I don't know. I'm not that experienced in this sort of shit. It was all a

headfuck. He's older than me, and he played off that too, I think.
(*Gabriel softens for the first time*)
GABRIEL
I always forget you're a foetus. God, that makes it worse. It's almost sinister from him. How old are you again?
LUCA
Twenty, it was my birthday last week.
GABRIEL
The Moonpig card slipped my mind.
(*Luca laughs. Gabriel does, too, reluctantly*)
LUCA
I'm so, so sorry, Gabe. I'll do anything to make it up to you. I hate him. I hate myself.
(*Luca starts sobbing, sculpted shoulders bobbing up and down. Gabriel hands Luca a grease-stained napkin from the table to wipe his tears*)
GABRIEL
Why didn't you get in touch with me, Luca? It's been months. Nothing.
LUCA
(*sniffling*) I was too ashamed. I told Mum, and—
GABRIEL
(*shocked*) Ivy knows?
LUCA
Yeah. I had to talk to her about it, Gabe. After Christmas. I made her swear not to tell your dad, or let on to you or anyone. She hasn't, I promise. I just needed someone to talk to; I was going mad. She said to give you some space. So I did, but then I didn't know how to word it. I'm not good with words like you or him. I know it's pathetic. I was hoping I'd bump into you at one

of your dad's get-togethers or something, and we would talk then, in person. I've been struggling, Gabe. Not in a victim way, but I want you to know that it's hurt me. And it makes me sick that I hurt you. I meant what I said, Gabe; I do see you as a brother. Do you think we can get past this? I'll never do anything like it again. I swear—

(*Gabriel bursts out laughing*)

GABRIEL

If I ever get another boyfriend, I'm not letting you anywhere near him, you little demon twink. You won't have the chance.

(*Luca laughs tearfully. The lighting changes, the scene returns to normal. The chicken shop has emptied except for an old man with a guide dog leaning on the counter*)

SERVER 1

We're closing up, boys; better get going.

GABRIEL

Sure, sorry. And thanks for the ...

(*He nods to the chips, walks over to place a tip on the counter, and then heads to the door*)

GABRIEL

(*to Luca*) Come on. You can walk me home. And you can take those tissues out of your nose too, you faggot, I barely touched you.

(*FADE OUT*)

Scene 2/2
EXT – COURTYARD OUTSIDE BROADGATE TOWERS. MANCHESTER. SUNRISE.

Establishing shot of Manchester skyline as the sun rises.

Over-the-shoulder shot of Paul's bald head, as he sits at his reception desk and sees two young men come into view outside. One is Gabriel, the other is unknown to him. Both look haggard. We hear him sigh and he puts down the pamphlet he was reading before their arrival.

LUCA
(*Turning to face Gabriel*) So . . .
GABRIEL
So.
LUCA
(*looking up towards building*) This is where you live?
GABRIEL
No, this is where my Grindr meet lives.
LUCA
Seriously? But . . . your hand.
GABRIEL
I like a challenge.
LUCA
(*realises he's joking*) Oh. Dan's here too now, I hear?
GABRIEL
Yep. Has been for a couple of months.
LUCA
How's that going?
GABRIEL
Well, it WAS going alright, but I think he might be shagging my best mate as we speak.
LUCA
Ah. Messy.
GABRIEL
Isn't it always?

LUCA
I suppose so.
(*Beat*)
LUCA
Maybe I can come over next time I'm visiting? It's going to be funny explaining this one (*he points to his nose*) to my mates back at the flat . . . But I'd love to see you both, for dinner or something?
GABRIEL
Maybe. Let's give it some time. We eat actual food too by the way. So you might need to bring your own Huel, or whatever.
LUCA
(*laughing*) That's fine. (*sombre, once more*) I really am sorry, Gabe.
GABRIEL
It's okay, Luca. I forgive you. I don't think we're at sharing-protein-pancake stage but, it's a start.
LUCA
That's good enough for me.
(*Luca moves in for a hug, but Gabriel brandishes his swollen hand*)
LUCA
Well, night Gabe. Take care.
GABRIEL
You too.
(*Over-the-shoulder shot of Paul, who has been watching the whole time. He shakes his head and chuckles to himself. Gabriel heads inside alone. Paul opens a drawer in his desk and places the pamphlet he was reading at the start of the scene inside. Before he can close the drawer, the phone rings*)

PAUL
Good morning, Broadgate Towers. How can I help you? Ah, Benny, you old bastard. Thought it was someone important . . .

(*Front shot of Paul walking off from his desk and around the corner with his phone, sound trails off and becomes muffled.*

Close-up shot of pamphlet resting in the drawer.

Extreme close-up reveals its cover:

NHS-supported self-management for patients with a recent cancer diagnosis)

(FADE TO BLACK)

PART TWO

8

A Birth and a Bribe

As the lead-up to summer arrived, so did my new nephew – Milo. Anna, my older sister, looked so exhausted as she lay in the hospital bed that I didn't have the heart to tell her the truth – that I hated her choice of name as it reminded me of either something you'd call a springer spaniel, a disobedient American kindergartener or one of The Tweenies.

'Do you want to hold him, Gabe?' Anna asked. It had been a difficult birth. She'd been in labour for over three days and lost a lot of blood. Milo had to be delivered using a device called a ventouse, which was essentially a metal suction cup placed on his head to help pull him out of the birth canal. As a result of this, Milo looked even less like a human than most newborn babies. His head was conical and had a blue ring on the crown, which made him look as though he might one day grow into an Avatar. I had been informed that he was an average weight and perfectly healthy – but to the uninitiated eye, he looked dangerously tiny and worryingly red.

'Of course!' I said, picking up the wriggling bundle from Anna's breast and cradling him in my arms. His tiny eyes were closed as he lay fast asleep, and he still had little flakey spots in the spaces where his brows should have been.

'Aw. He's bald!' I laughed, stating the obvious, not sure what else was appropriate. I'd always despised any occasion with a prescribed set of positive emotions – birthdays, celebrations, reunions – as they pressured and forced everything and made me feel uncomfortable.

'Like his dad,' said Ed, Anna's boyfriend, who wasn't totally bald but was receding enough for the joke to land.

'When will he, you know, grow hair?' I asked with earnest curiosity.

'For fuck's sake, Gabriel,' Mum shouted, sitting in a deck chair in the corner of the hospital room in skinny jeans, a turtle-neck jumper from the charity shop and a pair of old Converse.

'What?!' I said.

'What do you mean "what"? You've just met the lad, and the first thing you're worried about is his bloody haircare routine. Pass him here now. It's the last thing your sister needs.' She stood up and plucked my nephew from my hands before I could protest.

'He's gorgeous, Anna,' I said, turning to my sister, who looked knackered but amused by the exchange nonetheless.

'Gabriel,' Mum said sternly.

'What now?' I asked.

'Don't be fake. I can't be arsed with it, and neither can your sister. He's minging,' said Mum.

'Mum, don't call the baby minging,' Dan gasped.

'He is minging.' Anna laughed, sitting up against the pillow.

'He is! And so were both of you. Dan, you came out face first instead of head, so you looked like Quasimodo until you were four months old. I'll never forget having Aunty Diane and Uncle Rob round and watching them trying to come up with a compliment for you.'

'What did they say again, Mum?' Dan asked politely. We'd grown up hearing these stories on repeat, but we still liked them, as we were the main characters.

'Diane said you looked "hardy". I pretended to be offended for weeks.' Mum cackled. 'She bought me a pram to say sorry. Anna won't be one of *those* mums, will you, love?'

'What mums? The ones that love their children?' Dan asked.

'The mums who put their newborn on Facebook covered in amniotic fluid and pretend it's "gorgeous", Dan,' said Mum. 'Because he's not. But he will be. And he'll be kind and clever and funny. Like everyone in this family, and he's part of it now, whether he likes it or not . . . aren't you, my little Coney Woney Milo Wilo . . .' Her voice trailed off into cooing-baby sounds and she planted a fuchsia-lipstick kiss on Milo's forehead.

'God help him,' Anna said, laughing. I sent a picture of Milo into the group chat.

```
[15:01] Evie: Oh my god, Gabe, you're an un-
cle! He's so cute. Give Anna all my love. I bet
she's over the moon
[15:01] Tasha: Has he got the Zika virus
[15:01] Gabriel: No, Tasha, he hasn't got the
Zika virus. his head's like that because he had
to get sucked out by a hoover called a ventouse
[15:02] Tasha: Everything in your family is
always so dramatic
[15:02] Gabriel: Because yours is so
functional
[15:02] Tasha: Fairs
[15:02] Evie: Did Dan get a picture with him,
Gabe?
[15:02] Tasha: Jesus, Evie, can you calm down?
your ovaries are showing
[15:03] Gabriel: Yeah, Evie don't be gross
```

Dan and Evie had been sleeping together intermittently since our last big night out. My coping mechanism so far had been to bury my head firmly in the proverbial sand, but it was becoming difficult.

'Dan, Evie wants a picture of you holding the baby,' I said for a reaction. Everybody in the room subsided into 'OOHs'. Gotcha.

'Are you seeing our Evie, Dan?' Mum asked, visibly excited at the prospect of Dan's days as a chlamydia-riddled lothario coming to an end.

'No, no, it's not that deep,' Dan said, blushing. 'We've just been . . . spending time together. Casually.'

'Right, well, make sure it isn't "that deep", or we'll have another one on our hands before Christmas,' Mum warned, nodding to Milo, who was now fast asleep in her arms.

'I hope you're being careful, Dan,' said Anna with a frown. 'Evie's not like you. She's a lot more sensitive.'

'Most of the time,' said Mum. 'I've not forgotten what she was like at your twenty-first, Gabe.'

'She is a freak after a drink,' I conceded.

'I am being careful. She knows what's up. It's chill.' Dan shrugged. I let out an exasperated 'eugh'.

'Hmm. Are you seeing anyone, Gabe?' Anna's voice was lightly interested.

'No, but I did have the best sex of my life last week,' I said with unconcealed pride. It was true. Ethan. Twenty-six years old. Flying over from New York for a photography project in the city. He was only coming for a week, but he made me cum three times. Great arms. Liked slapping.

'Good for you!' Anna smiled as Mum covered Milo's ears with her hands. 'And how's the job?'

'The job is . . . well, put it this way, I've started writing again!' I said. It was true. I'd worked EnsureInsure for over six weeks, and it had only taken that amount of time within the corporate world to show me that it was a universe in which I was utterly unfit to reside. Although the initially esoteric language of acronyms and corporate shorthand was becoming increasingly familiar to me, and I found the day-to-day easier as time passed, I had something akin to imposter syndrome. Not in the traditional sense that I felt as though I wasn't skilled enough to belong, but in the sense that I was surrounded by a cast of colleagues who seemed to actually *care* about insurance policies. They seemed to draw stimulation from a corporate environment and fulfilment from making money for somebody else, and, in my view, had abandoned all worldly hope of the pursuit of what I considered meaningful ambition: leaving a positive mark on the world, besides a higher number on a spreadsheet or a piece of positive feedback from a manager. This realisation and subsequent desperation not to fall into the corporate trap of my mid-twenties pushed me to blow the dust off my writing notebook, where I'd finally felt sparks of creativity and a glimmer of motivation return.

'That's brilliant, love!' Mum exclaimed, who still kept the short story I wrote in Year 4 in her handbag.

'What have you been writing, Gabe?' Anna asked.

'Well, I don't know what I want to write. Or what my style is. Or what I have to say, or anything really, yet. So I've just been writing whatever I feel like. Until something comes to me. I wrote a poem the other day, which I think is pretty good.'

'Come on, let's hear it, then!' said Mum excitedly.

'Okay, fine . . . let me just . . .' I pulled the document up on my phone. 'It's called "Pantoum for Grindr".'

'What's a pantoum?' Dan asked.

'It's a Malaysian style of poem that consists of a series of four-line stanzas, the second and fourth lines of each stanza serving as the first and third lines of the next. It's meant to create a haunting, waltz-like structure. A bit like a lullaby. I wanted to contrast that pleasant – almost musical – rhythm by highlighting the attitudes of some of the worst types of people who use Grindr – shallow, racist, promiscuous, dishonest . . . you know.' The room was silent. Mum's mouth was open as she tried to process what I'd just said. Dan scratched his head.

'What's Grindr[29]?' Ed asked.

'Oh, come on, Ed,' Anna said.

'What?!' he said, indignantly.

Anna tutted, ignoring Ed. 'Go ahead, Gabe.'

---

[29] Grindr is the leading dating app for gay men. I use the term 'dating' here loosely. It's location-based, so it's mostly used to see if there is anyone in close proximity that might be willing to engage in intercourse with you. Or you and your boyfriend. People also use it to buy and sell drugs. It's a riot

'You might want to cover Milo's ears again for this one, Mum,' I said, clearing my throat:

> 'Pop up! Don't be shy, but please
> no more fats, femmes or asians
> If you want me choking on my knees
> You must respect my persuasions
>
> No more fats, femmes or asians
> I'm a fussy power top
> You must respect my persuasions
> Until I beg you to stop
>
> I'm a fussy power top
> With seething internal hatred
> Until I beg you to stop
> Rip my clothes off till I'm naked'

Dan had begun to persistently cough at a rude volume, but I ignored it and continued:

> 'With seething internal hatred
> Watch me rim your boyfriend's hole
> Rip my clothes off till I'm naked
> Wait, twenty-four is too old
>
> Watch me rim your boyfriend's hole
> I'll leave the way I came
> Wait, twenty-four is too old
> Remind me again, what's your name?'

Someone really needed to get Dan a Strepsil.

> 'I'll leave the way I came

And check my messages, just to see
Remind me again, what's your name?
Boring, fucked that guy last week

Maybe I'm addicted to the grind
Pop up! Don't be shy, but please
Bring your body, leave your soul and mind
If you want me choking on my knees.'

I finished. Everyone looked awestruck. They'd been stunned into silence, and Dan's cough had miraculously healed. It was only a warm-up back into the field, so I was shocked to see it elicit such a positive reception.

'Well?' I asked.

'Well, indeed,' came the baritone drawl of my father from behind me.

★ ★ ★

There weren't many times since my parents' divorce over a decade ago when they'd been forced into a room together. Dad had attended my grandpa's (on my mother's side) funeral out of respect; she'd done the same for my father's mother. They'd both come to my graduation, but I'd managed to swindle Mum and Ian Beale, her boyfriend at the time[30], seats two rows away from Dad and my stepmother, Ivy. Many divorced parents take the morally correct position of pursuing an at least amicable relationship for the benefit of their shared children. Unfortunately for Dan, Anna, and me, our parents' relationship had only soured further as years went on; arguments over finances

---

[30] Mum's ex-boyfriend was a miserable yet harmless man, who unfortunately happened to be called Ian and have red hair. Thus, the nickname arose and stuck

and parenting decisions (or lack thereof) ensued, Chinese whispers passed back and forth, and an entire step-family was introduced. Like many adult children of divorced parents, I now found it almost impossible to imagine a world in which Mum and Dad had ever been in love. Or even a world where they would date successfully, they were so antithetical in personality.

My father was tall, bespectacled and wiry. He was handsome when he smiled, which was rare, and he wore a lot of brown. He'd worked his whole life in risk assessment, and it was a case of chicken versus egg in terms of whether he was relentlessly serious, painfully guarded, and exhaustingly sensible because of his job or pursued that career due to those attributes. Ivy, his second wife, was a lot more colourful in appearance and sunnier in nature. She was a retired hand model and freelance interior designer with an obvious, yet still excellent, boob job. They weren't as big as Mum's, though, which were all natural and still in great condition after breastfeeding three kids. Mum has a gun to my head as I'm writing this. Please call the police. The hospital address is aihsgwbrb g,w,b3 . . .

***

I'd not seen my father since the Seamus/Luca debacle at Christmas (of which he was blissfully unaware); however, it still wasn't ideal that the first words he'd heard me say in half a year were, 'Bring your body, leave your soul and mind, if you want me choking on your knees'.

'Dad! Hi,' I said as Ed and Mum stifled laughs behind me.

'Hello, son. Was that some of your work you were reciting there?' he said, trying and failing to conceal a cringe of discomfort.

'No. Well, yes. It's just a little pantoum. I've started writing again.'

'Ah! I didn't realise you'd stopped. Well, that's good news, I should think.'

In an act of mercy, Ivy hugged me and ended the interaction. She gave fantastic hugs – genuine, earnest and filled with a warmth that isn't often associated with 150cc of military-grade silicone. She did nothing to let on that she knew anything about her son's involvement with my ex-boyfriend. There wasn't a hint of pity in her turquoise eyes, and I was grateful.

'It's good to see you, darling,' she said before she and Dad began a greeting tour of the hospital room. The walls seemed to hold their breath as they approached my mother, who hadn't yet acknowledged their presence.

```
[15:17] Gabriel: Mum and Dad on a collision
course in the hospital room
[15:17] Tasha: This is the safest place for it
to happen, Gabe
[15:18] Evie: Is Ivy there?
[15:18] Gabriel: Yeah
[15:18] Evie: Oh nooo
[15:18] Tasha: Gabe, will you send a father/
son picture of Dan with your dad for Evie,
please <3
[15:18] Evie: I actually hate you
[15:18] Gabriel: Hahahahaha
```

'Fiona. Good to see you,' said Dad, holding up a stiff hand in an attempted wave that became a half-hearted Native American salute.

'You too, Jeremy. Hello, Ivy,' said Mum with an unhinged grin.

'Hi, Fiona. Congratulations, you're a grandmother!' Ivy announced with an exuberance that matched the array of brightly coloured plastic jewellery she was wearing. Mum stiffened in her chair. I watched intently to see if her upper lip was thinning into dangerous 'thin angry Mum lips' territory but only noticed a 1mm decrease.

'Thank you, Ivy. So are you!' Mum said.

'Yes. Again! My eldest, Jessica, gave birth last year. It's so fulfilling. All the joys of parenthood without any of the responsibility!' Ivy giggled.

'Hear, hear!' agreed Dad. Mum's neck swivelled towards my father with such alarming speed, I could've sworn I heard a crack.

'"All the joys of parenthood without any of the responsibility!" What a lovely thought. I couldn't even begin to imagine what that must be like. Could you, Jeremy?' I witnessed another 2mm lip decrease.

'Well, I—' blustered Dad.

'Of course you bloody could. Every divorced father should be forced to get that tattooed, if you ask me. Or as a bumper sticker on their new Mercedes.' Anna, Dan and I were frozen in anticipation. Ivy's forced smile had lost its curvature and become horizontal. 'Speaking of grandmothers, Anna mentioned you had a big birthday recently,' Mum said, turning to Ivy after an uncomfortably long pause. 'Recently' was last September, when Ivy had turned sixty.

'Well, yes – in a sense.' Ivy seemed relieved to change of subject.

'Happy seventieth for then!' Mum said. 'I'd better get going, anyway.' Ivy looked dumbstruck.

'Take care of yourself, love.' Mum kissed Anna on her forehead. 'I'm so proud of you. I love you very much. Look after her, Ed. And you be a good boy for your mummy,' she whispered to Milo, leaving the hospital room without further ado.

★ ★ ★

'I'm going to grab a snack from the vending machine. I'm starving.' After another forty minutes of pleasantries, including Dad deciding that Milo would be a golfer because of the posture of his shoulders, I decided I needed a break. I headed into the corridor outside and began surveying the selection of snacks, all at absolutely insane prices. A 30g pack of Skittles – £1.60. I paid on contactless, picked them up and almost jumped out of my skin when I turned to see Ivy standing alone in the corridor, waiting for me.

'Gabriel, sorry, didn't mean to make you jump. I wondered if I could have a moment?'

'Of course, Ivy. Are you okay? I'm sorry about Mum before; she was only winding you up.'

'Oh, no. Don't be silly. No bother at all. Funny. Funny Fiona!' She giggled manically.

'Yeah . . .' I said. There was a pause. I couldn't guess what this could be about, but I'd be fine as long as she didn't mention either Luca or Seamus.

'About Luca and Seamus,' she began. Great. 'It's . . . I'm . . .'

'It's fine, Ivy. We don't have to do this. I've seen Luca, we've spoken. It's water under the bridge.'

Ivy looked at me with an emotion I couldn't quite place. It seemed to exist between admiration and befuddlement. 'That's big of you, darling. There are no excuses for what he did . . .' she said. Brace for 'but'.

'But he's so young. And his father is nothing like yours, you know. Des can be ruthless. He was never kind about the way Luca is.' Ivy had a rose-tinted view about my father's attitude towards my sexuality. At best, he'd been indifferent, and at worst he'd made me feel ashamed during my tender developmental years, potentially contributing to my low self-esteem and general feelings of anxiety. If you don't feel safe and secure at home, it's hard to feel safe and secure anywhere. I didn't like to dwell on it, though. Nobody wants to be a cliché.

'I know. We all do stupid shit, Ivy. Honestly, it's okay.'

'It's not. I feel terrible, too. I should've called. Shoulda woulda coulda. Take this.' She thrust a brown paper envelope into my hand that didn't contain a bag of Skittles. It felt heavy.

'What's . . .' I asked, peering inside before seeing a wad of cash. Of course. When in doubt, throw money at the problem. The failsafe British middle-class alternative to processing emotions. 'Oh, Ivy, I can't.'

'You can and you will, and we'll. Say. No. More. Of. It.' She patted the bag lightly with each utterance. There was something almost threatening about her smile.

'You deserve a break. Go on holiday somewhere nice. Treat yourself. And don't let it get back to your father. The money, or . . .'

I nodded, realising what this gesture really was. A bribe.

'It's for the best,' she finished, before turning on her wedged heel and leaving a trail of Chanel N°5 in her wake. I hadn't thought I'd ever be the direct recipient of a wad of cash in a brown envelope, but I also hadn't thought I'd ever punch anyone in the face; life is nothing if not a jumbled series of defied expectations[31].

```
[16:13] Tasha: How did it go with Mum squared,
Gabe?
   [16:15] Gabriel: Yeah, fine-ish. no casualties
this time, but guys, there has been an unexpect-
ed and extremely welcome surprise
   [16:15] Evie: Yay! I need something to cheer
me up. I've still not been able to eat lunch to-
day, and I'm hungry and cranky
   [16:15] Tasha: Why?
   [16:15] Evie: One of my Year 1s stayed inside
with me for the whole of the lunch break and
spent the entire time crying because I said I
couldn't adopt her
   [16:16] Tasha: Brutal, why does she want
you to adopt her? Are her parents awful or
something?
   [16:16] Evie: No, we're reading Matilda by
Roald Dahl, and I think she's taking it a tad
too seriously
   [16:16] Gabriel: Make sure to check your
Chilly's bottle for newts. Anyway, the surprise
```

---

[31] You'd be saying shit like this too if you'd just received a grand tax-free

is that Ivy just gave me a grand in a brown envelope

[16:17] **Evie**: A grand, as in one thousand pounds?

[16:17] **Gabriel**: Yes

[16:17] **Tasha**: Wtf - why?

[16:18] **Gabriel**: I would assume it's to assuage the massive amounts of guilt she's feeling for her son riding my boyfriend's cock for Christmas. She also told me not to tell my Dad about what happened with Luca and Seamus.

[16:18] **Evie**: She bribed you?!

[16:18] **Tasha**: Who knew she had it in her!!

[16:19] **Gabriel**: It was honestly kind of fierce

[16:19] **Evie**: Were you going to tell your dad?

[16:19] **Gabriel**: Absolutely not. As far as I'm concerned, nothing's changed except I'm a grand richer

I'd never had this amount of cold, hard cash in my life – it felt sinister. I'd have to go and deposit it in the bank tomorrow. Besides, I'd known what I wanted to do with the money as soon as Ivy passed it to me. The rational thing would've been to pay off a chunk of the credit card debt I'd racked up during my brief stint of unemployment. I had something more fun in mind.

[16:19] **Tasha**: I'd let Scott fuck my real brother for a grand in a paper bag

[16:19] **Evie**: Hahaha. Yeah right! Anyway, Gabe. What have we been saying? We told you everything would work out in the end, and look at you - a new job, dating again, looking amazing, a grand!!! I'm so so proud of you. It just goes to show that the old saying is true, patience IS a Gertrude!

[16:20] **Tasha:** What?

[16:20] **Gabriel:** Patience is a Gertrude? What are you on about, Evie?

[16:20] **Evie:** What do you mean? Stop being thick, patience is a Gertrude! The saying!

I snorted with laughter and almost choked on a Skittle.

[16:20] **Gabriel:** Do you mean 'patience is a virtue'?

[16:20] **Tasha:** Evie, SURELY you didn't mean that because that would make no sense whatsoever

[16:21] **Evie:** Oh, I always thought it was that. I thought it meant like an old woman called Gertrude who had been patient or something

[16:21] **Tasha:** I'm so glad you're in charge of shaping the minds of the future

[16:21] **Evie:** Hahahaha. God I've been saying that for years.

[16:21] **Gabriel:** I love you so much, Evie. You idiot.

I really did. She really was.

[16:22] **Gabriel:** And you, Tash.

[16:22] **Tasha:** Stop making it weird

[16:23] **Gabriel:** Well, I know what I'm spending the money on anyway.

[16:23] **Evie:** An air fryer at last?!

[16:24] **Tasha:** A new gay card?

[16:24] **Gabriel:** No, I'm taking you both on holiday

[16:25] **Tasha:** WHAT?! Well, now I almost feel bad

[16:25] **Evie:** Stop it!!!!

[16:26] **Gabriel:** Yep! I can't put into words how much I appreciate your friendship over the last few months, guys, so I won't bother. Hopefully, this will do instead. How does a long weekend in Seville sound? June? I'll get the flights and Airbnb and all you need to bring is suncream and spends.

[16:26] **Evie:** And a sombrero! (Maracas emoji)

[16:27] **Tasha:** Oh my god, Evie, that's Mexico.

[16:27] **Gabriel:** Evie, have you had a lobotomy that we don't know about

I paced up and down with excitement. We'd not been away together since the halcyon days of university holidays on a budget.

[16:27] **Gabriel:** So, you're in?

[16:27] **Evie:** IN!!!

[16:28] **Tasha:** I can't believe it. Yes! IN!

[16:28] **Evie:** I love you both so much

[16:28] **Gabriel:** Me too!!!!

[16:29] **Tasha:** I love you both very much

9

The Score

The EnsureInsure workspace was on the fourteenth floor of City Tower and had nine enormous windows lining the back wall, meaning that, when the sun was out, it was in the office too and everyone was in a good mood. I was especially chipper because it was a Friday and I was going to do something tonight that I'd never done before: watch a football match, live, in a stadium. With trepidation and excitement, I agreed to watch Manchester City play Burnley with Paul, whose friend had dropped out at the last minute. The plan (and boredom with my current project – an email campaign about the benefits of individualised versus generalised home insurance) led me to reminisce on my own experience with the sport. I'd had a brief foray into footy during my primary school years. Still, I had a similar experience to most of the gay men I knew – a feeling of alienation from other young lads that led me to stop indulging in 'the beautiful game' once high school and the onset of puberty arrived. The law of the jungle that ran rife on the playground turned a football match into a battlefield, where the most skilled survived and became the most respected by the other boys. This didn't fit with the teenage me, a sensitive soul who, at that point, preferred gossip and listening to Fergie's debut solo album out of the tinny speaker of a Sony Ericsson mobile phone. Of course, the fact that I was shit at football also put me off. Being bad at football aligned with being feminine, so avoiding this marker and spending your break time doing something else was best. Many lads were good at football because their dads or older brothers had played with them. A lot of gay men had a resentment towards the sport and the community that surrounds it. This is both fair and unfair, rational and irrational. It was arguably necessary for gay men to extend caution when interacting with members of the football community who were, to make a generalisation, pretty homophobic. There was a reason why there had been barely any openly gay footballers in the premiership of British football since its inception. Statistics showed that one in five British people now identify as something other than straight, yet in the nine-hundred-plus players in the premiership and championship, that study didn't apply, apparently. This was not because of some sort of statistical anomaly – playing football, as far as I knew, was not the 'cure' for homosexuality – but existing within that environment seemingly poisoned the ability to embrace it. I'd always felt that the football industry at large was a microcosm of the worst attributes of heterosexual men. When our national team lost, domestic violence instances increased. Footballers would wear rainbow laces as an apparent show of support for the LGBT community before choosing to play in Qatar – a country that stones gay people to death – without speaking out in protest. That's the rational part. I understood why a lot of gay men were wary when interacting with fans of the sport. It was undeniable, though, that football was an integral mechanism for men to explore areas of their lives that are unfortunately unexplored. They could express emotion in a safe environment, there was a strong sense of community and an unrivalled opportunity to bond with their family, friends, and strangers. It was an almost universal language shared across countries and creeds, but one that I'd never learnt how to speak.

The clock at work ticked slower than usual as I wished the afternoon away. I'd finished arranging our holiday to Seville and was knee-deep in every possible dating app at every opportunity. I opened Grindr to kill time, and a message popped up.

DiscreetHung: Hey

'Discreet' on Grindr means 'something to hide'. They're in the closet. They're in a relationship. Both. They're not usually the type of people I'd interact with, but this profile had the same age as me, was only a couple of kilometres away (meaning he lived in one of the surrounding Manchester districts) and, after saying 'Hey', he instantly sent a phenomenal dick pic. Well-lit, with an angle that included a full view of a perfect pair of balls. Well-kempt pubes. It was thick, about six and a half inches (manageable) and looked very clean.

```
Angel44: Hi! Discreet?
DiscreetHung: Yeah, I'm not out
Angel44: That's ok. Nice dick. You're not lying about the 'hung' part
DiscreetHung: Haha, nope. I'm an honest guy.
Angel44: Except for the whole secret identity thing.
DiscreetHung: Well, yeah, except that ;)
```

Apparently, having a new job, being freed from the ties of my old relationship and shedding my heartbreak weight had imbued me with newfound confidence. I threw caution to the wind and sent a faceless nude of myself back.

```
DiscreetHung: Wow. Can I see your face?
```

Still not quite enough confidence that a validatory compliment from an anonymous stranger didn't make my heart flutter excitedly. I hadn't put my face as my profile picture on Grindr. It felt uncomfortable to be on a grid smiling next to other profile pictures, which were usually either anonymous grey silhouettes or a close-up shot of a white jockstrap. I also didn't include my real name as my username, as I generally shared it in the first couple of interactions.

```
Angel44: You can see mine when I can see yours.
DiscreetHung: Ok. Let's get to know each other first a bit.
```

'Gabe?' The voice of my line manager, Eric, came from behind me. I pocketed my phone.

'Hi Eric, are you alright? How did the meeting about the business cards go?'

'Excellent, thanks. All sorted. Listen, I know it's not our one-to-one until next week, but I just wanted to say well done on the campaign content you produced for the twenty-four-hour turnaround insurance package. You managed to get all the info across but still keep that signature sense of humour.' He smiled. After my first four weeks, we were permitted to switch to a 'hybrid' working model, which meant I could work from home two days a week, and these were my favourite days. Not just because, in a stroke of luck, they were the opposite days to when Scott worked from home, meaning I rarely[32] saw him, which suited me just fine, but because it meant I had autonomy over my work schedule. In truth, this autonomy led to writing the campaign copy in two hours, then spending the rest of the day playing *Overwatch* on the PS5 and working on one of my current projects – a script about a modern-day version of Snow White where the Wicked Witch wants to murder Ms White due to her higher follower count on Tik Tok.

'Thanks, Eric! It's all starting to make sense now. I know my CRM from my OoO!' I joked. People in the corporate world have an AFE[33].

'Seems that way! Well, Gabe, have an early finish today. You've earned it. Are you doing anything fun this evening?'

---

[32] By rarely, I mean I had seen Scott twice. The first time, he'd been all perfect smiles, acting like the entire Buffalo Sauce debacle had never taken place, making small talk with me about my workload. The other time, he had sauntered over, asked Eric 'how his protegé was doing', then retreated to the kitchen to commit the cardinal office sin of microwaving seafood

[33] Acronym for everything

Fantastic news. I was keen to get home and prepare for the footy (have a candlelit wank over the pictures DiscreetHung had sent me). 'Nice one, Eric! Nothing major; I'm just going to watch the football with my friend,' I said. My phone was vibrating in my pocket, and I knew who it was.

'What about you?' I added reluctantly.

'Ah, sorry, Gabe. Got to run. Just realised the time. Conference call. Wait – *you're* going to watch the football? No, no, I have to go. Explain yourself on Monday,' he said before sprinting out of the office and to one of the meeting rooms.

`DiscreetHung:` What are you doing right now?

Another picture. This time he sent a shot of his sculpted torso, in the reflection of a gym mirror. He had an amazing physique, looked tall (with the gym equipment as a frame of reference), and had a river of light brown body hair that ran from the top of his chest, just below where the picture was cropped, all the way down past his naval.

`Angel44:` Just finished work. On my way home now
`DiscreetHung:` Message me when you're naked

★ ★ ★

Exchanging nudes was not a dance that I knew all the steps to. Though it's a commonplace rung in the modern dating ladder for many across all sexualities. Seamus and I tried it a few times at the start, but never felt it necessary, especially once we'd moved in together. Unfortunately, the dance didn't last long. Two nudes sent back and forth before I got overexcited and had to masturbate. Upon completion, I felt a sudden wave of post-cum clarity: what had I become? Exchanging nude images with a stranger to pleasure myself to, in lieu of real physical and emotional connection? It felt like a slippery slope to something akin to a porn addiction, so I quickly asked two of the guys I'd matched with on Tinder on dates next week to make sure that I halted the descent to wanky inceldom before it could go any further. Once I left the flat, I found Paul pacing in the lobby like a nervous prom date, though in dark denim bootcut jeans and a tight-fitting Manchester City jersey rather than a tuxedo. When I greeted him, and he wrapped me in an excited bear hug, I was surprised not to feel the familiar press of his beer belly against my body.

'Have you been dieting?' I asked.

'Off the booze fully now, Gabe! Gone straight edge, 'aven't I! How do I look?'

The truth was, Paul was undeniably trimmer, but overall, he looked a lot less healthy. His eyes — usually abuzz with excitement — looked weary and dim, with dark circles underlining them. His smile didn't contain any of its regular cheekiness but was closer to a wince. His skin was sallow. Even his scalp, which was usually so shiny that it could blind a bushbaby, had lost some of its lustre.

'I would,' I said, getting a guffaw from Paul in return. If the two dates I was organising next week didn't go well and I was still Captain Shagless, then that joke might end up worryingly close to the truth. We walked down the winding canal in New Islington and through the industrial estates bordering the road leading to the stadium. It felt exhilarating to be part of the procession of spectators marching dutifully towards the arena. Usually, I was against the tide, cowering in the corner of a tram as the drunk fans burst into chants that sounded like they'd been written by an angry five-year-old, but it felt strangely comforting to be part of the swarm. Throngs of teenagers clad in Stone Island, families in matching powder-blue, and boomers in unseasonal puffer jackets all walked as one, and the silhouette of the Etihad appeared under the setting June sun. I waited until Paul's monologue on UAE money being pumped into Manchester City was over.

'So, why have you stopped drinking, then?' I asked. 'You love a pint more than anyone I've ever met.' It was true. I hadn't even been able to stand the taste of beer until I'd met Paul, and he'd slowly introduced my palette to Moretti and Estrella over the course of a few post-work bevvies.

He inhaled sharply as if the question had made him lose his breath. 'My wife. Kaye. Her orders. Well, and the doctors.'

I knew something was off. 'Is everything okay?'

'Would be if I could have a pint. Yeah, it's nothing major. I'm fifty-nine now, mate, and I'd carried that baby around for two decades.' He slapped a hand on the place where his beer belly had once been. 'I want to be around to see my kids grow up, Gabe.' This was the most sombre I'd ever heard him. 'And you!' he said, the cheeky glint back, albeit diluted, for a fleeting moment.

'WITWOOO, LADIES!' The distorted voice of one of the Stone Island teenagers mocked from across the road. He'd put on an affected camp accent and had thrown both hands forward into limp wrists. His friends burst into a chorus of hyena cackles.

'Is that your sugar daddy?' called another one of the teenagers.

While my flight mode kicked in, Paul's fighting spirit did the same.

'Paul, don't . . .' I pleaded, knowing what was about to happen.

'YOU FUCKING WHAT?' Paul boomed before throwing his arms out to the sides in challenge. There was too much traffic for him to attempt to cross Ashton New Road, and he couldn't have done it anyway because, after he'd finished his exclamation, he descended into a violent coughing fit. The teenagers stomped off laughing while Paul doubled over, his back heaving. I put my arm around him and handed him some water, which he drank through splutters.

'They're not worth it, Paul. It's fine, I'm used to it.' I was, in fact, shocked, because I thought I'd done an admirable job at curating a relatively plain 'heterosexual-passing' outfit today. I decided to take it as a compliment that, even when dressing down, I was so effortlessly chic that it warranted a mild homophobic assault.

'Scum. You shouldn't have to put up with that shite,' Paul said after catching his breath.

'You're right, but I do. I've had it my whole life. I promise it doesn't get to me.' It was true. As a child, I had been more effeminate than most other boys, and I was taught to be ashamed of this, either by the passive distaste of my father, by the mistreatment of similar personalities in the media, or by the active bullying of my peers. As a teenager and young adult, after coming out, I'd been harassed and degraded by strangers, sometimes violently. At the time, this had been crushing. As a young person, I didn't understand the reason for this abuse, so the natural conclusion was to assume that there was something wrong. That *I* was something wrong. As an adult, I understood this behaviour to be an externalisation of a deep inner sadness, of a dissatisfaction with the self, or a profound and ignorant state of confusion, to be treated with pity, or when I could be arsed, patient education. I would never allow homophobia or the people who espoused it to take up any more time in my life than they already had.

'How? Do you not want to kick the shit out of them?' Paul asked.

'I don't have many violent impulses, Paul, surprisingly. Besides, it's pointless. In all honesty, I see them as beneath me. Anyone who does stuff like that, who tries to hurt other people. They're not worth it. You know that feeling you get when you look back at your life and think about when you did something you weren't proud of? Usually in doctors' waiting rooms or at night when you're trying to fall asleep because you've got work in the morning?' I asked. Paul nodded. 'Well, we do that over small stuff. Saying something awkward. Offending someone by accident. Getting pissed and snogging married men.'

'What?' Paul said, confused.

'Doesn't matter. The point is, one day, they'll remember that, and they'll feel ashamed. That's enough punishment, I think. There's nothing to gain by losing control and making it worse for ourselves by causing a scene or getting battered.'

'Pffft – getting battered? Speak for yourself, lad. They'd be wearing their arses as hats by the time I'd finished with them,' Paul fumed.

I wasn't sure what that could possibly mean, but appreciated the sentiment. 'Why, what were you going to do? Cough in their eyes? Whip them with a blood-stained handkerchief?' I teased. 'Seriously, though, Paul, what was that, before? Are you sure everything's alright?'

He gave me a stern look that said, 'If you press me any further on this, I will flip.' So I didn't.

'Anyway, I think you're being naive, mate,' Paul said as we continued walking towards section L3, where our seats were. The stadium loomed overhead as we walked to the turnstile entrance. It was enormous – a gigantic spaceship adorned with a twenty-metre Puma logo.

'Why is that naive?'

'Because not everyone thinks like you, Gabe. These lads that are dickheads to gays or blacks or women. They're nothing like you. They aren't the kind to be kept awake thinking about their mistakes. They don't care, lad, take it from me.'

'Maybe they don't, but that's even worse, right?' I said. A surly steward in a hi-vis jacket held out a card-reader and I opened my phone, pulled up my Apple Wallet and held the electronic ticket to the reader.

`DiscreetHung:` You're close by. Are you at the City game?

He was two hundred metres away. I felt a curious rush of adrenaline and started taking more of an interest in the people around me, looking for signs of someone who looked like a closeted gay man in their late twenties, whatever that might be.

`Angel44:` Big City fan, obviously. Are you?

'What do you mean, that's even worse?' Paul shouted over the roaring din as we headed up corrugated iron stairs, bordered with bright yellow paint that made them look like we were heading towards the *Robot Wars* arena instead of our seats.

'Because that's the best way to grow and become better people, isn't it? By being self-aware? By looking back at your own mistakes and learning from them, so you're not a piece of shit,' I shouted.

Paul looked contemplative and then smiled. 'No, it's not.'

'What is, then?' I asked.

'The Bible,' he replied with a sarcastic grin.

DiscreetHung: Not really. just here to look after my old man, he certainly is.

'You're a good lad, Gabe. It's a lovely way to think. Very, what's the word . . . empathetic. Tolerant,' Paul said, slapping me on my back as we finished our ascent and reached the double doors leading into the stadium's interior and to our seats. 'Sometimes I wish my lad were more like that.' It was the first time Paul had brought up his son to me unprompted. He was somewhat of an enigma. I was dying to ask more, but before I could, he threw open the double doors, and we were met with a wall of sound from the crowd. It was like nothing I'd heard before. Fifty thousand people stamping, cheering, and clapping their hands, shouting 'CITY!' in unison. As we walked to our seats in the nosebleed section, I felt a rush of excitement for the gladiatorial battle about to commence. In my anticipation for this, the most heterosexual of events, I considered that maybe my uncle, most Conservatives, and my Year 11 Science teacher were right – maybe being gay was a phase after all. Then I remembered that I'd gotten butterflies a moment ago at a secretly closeted man opening up slightly to me on Grindr, and I sat my little gay ass down in seat L319.

★ ★ ★

The first half of the game was relatively eventless; there had been some near misses from both sides, a couple of tense corners and a free kick awarded to Burnley for a foul by Kevin De Bruyne that had elicited roars from the crowd and twenty seconds of expletive-filled protests from Paul, who was sat between me and a six-year-old, also screaming and swearing. Even so, I was having a great time. It warmed me to see families united in their support for our city and their team – arms around each other, grinning and grimacing in union. The entire experience was a sensory thrill ride: the noises of the crowd, reacting in real-time to every movement, the vibrant green of the pitch illuminated under gigantic white floodlights, the smell of beer and cheap deodorant and hazy summer air. Paul and I didn't talk much, transfixed as he was by every development, but that gave me time to occasionally swap messages with DiscreetHung. I'd found out that he didn't live too far from the stadium, owned his own home, grew up in Wilmslow, had a millenial enthusiasm for both smiley face emojis and Harry Potter references, and, judging by the barrage of faceless pics, didn't quite love his sexuality, but did love the sight of his own abs. As half-time began, we headed from our seats towards the drinking lounge. Paul went for a piss, and I looked at the food on offer.

```
[20:31] Gabriel: Just at the City game, guys
[20:31] Tasha: Words I thought I'd never
hear
[20:32] Evie: Is Dan there, Gabe?
```

Annoying.

```
[20:33] Gabriel: No, I've gone with Paul
[20:33] Tasha: I've been forced a few times,
it's mind-numbing
[20:33] Gabriel: I'm actually enjoying it
[20:33] Evie: Good for you!
```

[20:33] **Tasha:** More like masc4masc[34]

[20:34] **Gabriel:** Speaking of, how funny is male-led marketing? I simply want to buy a pie, and they've called it 'XL PREMIUM STEAK PIE', it's so aggressive

[20:34] **Tasha:** Alpecin: German Engineering For Your Hair - what?!?!?!

[20:34] **Gabriel:** That!!! It's so fragile! why does it always have to be hyper-masculine, it's so stupid

[20:35] **Tasha:** The only way they'll wash their balls is if their shower gel is like BLACK PEPPER & OAK

[20:36] **Gabriel:** There's a makeup line for men and it's called 'War Paint'. Like, come ON, Jack. You're concealing your under-eye. You're not going into battle

[20:36] **Tasha:** Your World War 2 veteran grandfather is turning in his grave, Jack

[20:36] **Evie:** WHAT HAS HAPPENED TO OUR COUNTRY?!

[20:36] **Gabriel:** LET MEN BE MEN AGAIN!

I grabbed a pint and a cheese and onion pie. Paul returned from the loo to buy a water and an XL NON-VEGAN STEAK AND COARSE BLACK PEPPER MEGA PIE, and we found a corner to stand and chat.

---

[34] 'Masc4masc' is a term used by some gay men on dating sites. It is usually accompanied by statements like 'I'm gay – I like my men to be men' and 'no sissies'. What it translates to is, 'I may have come out of the closet, but I still hate myself and hold a societally instilled disgust towards feminine traits. I am going to spend the rest of my life carrying out a beleaguered, embarrassing performance of masculinity that is so absurd that it eats its own tail and becomes camp. Squeeze my pec, bro'

'Bloody nightmare. Hundred and twenty million they've spent this year, and we can't put one in the net against bloody Burnley,' Paul huffed, rubbing his fingers, which had remained sausage-like even after his recent weight loss, against his ruddy forehead.

'Only halfway through!' I offered. I said a silent prayer that this wouldn't start to transform into some sort of in-depth game analysis.

'It's lazy midfielding, mate, at the end of the day. No finesse from Burnley whatsoever, so it has to be our fault. Defence is strong, been some solid little passes down the line, but Foden spends too long dancing around the ball to get it to any of the strikers. Probably too busy worrying about his hair.' He tutted. 'What do you think?'

'About Foden's hair?' I asked.

'No, you fanny. About the match!'

'I mean, I've got no idea what you're talking about, and I don't *really* care. But I'm having a great time.' I smiled.

'You've been on your phone a lot. New fella?' I told him that I had a couple of dates lined up next week, and about my excellent shag last month, and then I explained the newly burgeoning situation with DiscreetHung. By the time I'd finished, we were back in our seats, and the match had resumed. Paul was still transfixed but took occasional breaks to continue interrogating me.

'So this lad you're talking to on Grinder, where's he from? How old is he? What does 'e do for a living?'

'He's local. Same age as me. Hasn't said yet, but he's got his own house. He looks like he might be a personal trainer or something, seems to spend a lot of time in the gym.'

'All sounds good, except for the obvious. You know, the hiding away part. Twenty eight and still living like that. Wasting the best years of his life.' He sighed.

'Yep. Not everyone has the support system to come out, though. He's not much of a City fan, but is at the match with his dad, which, if I were to jump to conclusions based on barely any information – one of my biggest hobbies – I'd assume he was surrounded by a lot of intense masculinity, views being gay as a threat to that, and so stays in the closet.'

Paul looked uncomfortable. There were oohs and ahhs from the crowd as Burnley appeared to come close to a goal, but his eyes remained set on me. 'Can I ask you something, Gabe?' His energy had shifted; he was holding his weight strangely, so his posture was slanted as though he were being pushed down by a force on one of his shoulders.

'Go for it,' I said.

'When did you know? You know. That you were . . . gay?'

It's a question I'd been posed a hundred times by people in the smoking area of nightclubs, by overfamiliar colleagues and by the voices in my head – I couldn't believe it had taken Paul this long to ask me. Still, after all these years, there wasn't a solid answer.

'It's not the same for everone, I don't think. Maybe when I first saw H from Steps on the TV. Those curtains. Wow.' I laughed.

'Really?'

'Yeah. I mean, I was only four years old. I remember wishing he was my 'best friend'. Then it was Hercules from the Disney film. In hindsight, I had a crush on him. And then, when everyone else was growing up and wanting to kiss girls and the rest, I didn't get any of those urges at all. I got them for men instead.'

'You told me you used to get off with girls!' Paul said.

'I only did that because then I thought no one would think I was gay. I should have never done it. For their sake and mine, really.'

'Were you that bad a kisser?'

'No! I mean, I hope not.' I laughed. 'It's not right to use people, for any reason.'

'Ah, mate. It's shit, isn't it.'

'It doesn't have to be. And it's definitely getting better. But yeah, I suppose I knew I was gay for sure once I'd had sexual experiences with girls and felt nothing, and once I'd had them with lads and felt like that's what I was put on the planet to do.'

'Steady on.'

'Why do you ask?' I said. The stadium erupted. City had scored. Paul dragged his fist backwards, shouted 'YES!' in a restrained but enthusiastic way, and then returned to the conversation as the crowd bellowed.

'Well, my son. Midge. We call him that. His name's Michael. I've always wondered about him.' Paul shook his head slightly, like his thoughts would fall out of one of his ears and dissolve into the floor.

'That he might be gay?' I asked. I was on the edge of my seat. Paul hadn't mentioned his son to anyone; until now, it had felt like a forbidden topic.

'I guess so. Yeah.'

'And would that be a problem?' I asked as gently as I could.

'Well . . .' said Paul, screwing up his mouth as if trying to find the right words.

'Paul?!' I couldn't believe that the man who I'd spent the last year discussing my innermost thoughts with, who had shared his favourite memories and beers with me, might be a homophobe.

'No – fuck off, Gabe. Not like that. You know it's not like that. It wouldn't be a problem now. But I've not always been the bloke that's sat next to you, Gabe. I spent a lot of my life being a bit of a nobhead, really. Sometimes, a lot of a nobhead. What you said before – looking back on our mistakes to stop being shitty people. I've done a lot of that. It's not an excuse, Gabe, but it was a different time I grew up in. Being different wasn't good. Not in that way, not in my neck of the woods. Not with my old man.' He laughed a hollow laugh and shook his head. 'Midge doesn't know, though, that I'm not that same man I was ten, twenty years ago back when he was a kid. He won't talk to me. Changed his number. I can't get in touch with him,' Paul said, staring at the pitch absent-mindedly.

Something clicked. 'You're worried that Midge might be afraid to come out because of you?'

'Something like that. I don't know. He doesn't want to see me, Gabe, and barely sees his mam either. Which kills her. And sometimes, I replay these moments in my mind of what I was like when he was younger. I don't know. I had this idea of what I wanted my son to be like. What my dad wanted me to be like. We all have them. And he just wasn't. But I think I let him know that, in one way or another. And now . . .' He buried his head in his hands, rubbing his temples with his fingers, bouncing his knees up and down anxiously. My instinct was to reassure him, even though I knew what he had done must have been dark if his only son had cut off all contact.

'You wanted an easy life for him, Paul. That's what all parents want for their kids. You were probably just worried it would've been harder for him,' I suggested.

'Nah. That's a cop-out. It wasn't that. It wasn't that one bit. I hated it, Gabe. I'll be honest, I did. Cause I was taught to mind, but I still did. He'd always play with girls instead of lads, so I'd rinse him for it. He didn't like footy, so I didn't bother to find out what he did like. He was soft. Not like me. Cared too much. Kind. And now it might be too late.' He sniffed.

'Jesus, Paul. He's not dead. Look at me,' I said. Paul looked up, the whites of his eyes red. 'You did the best you could by who you were then. You're not that person anymore, whatever you said or did. I know that. To be brutally honest, I wouldn't waste a second on you if I thought otherwise. He'll come round. You just need to show him,' I said, wrapping my arm around his giant shoulders. 'I'll help you when the time's right. We could get a text to him or a letter or something?' I suggested.

'You'd do that, would you, mate?' Paul asked, hope returning light to his rough features.

'Of course, you idiot.' I laughed. And I pulled him in to lean on my shoulder. Whoever Paul had been, he was different now, at least from my experience. Midge deserved to know the kind, caring, selfless man his father had become.

City had scored another goal, and full-time was called. The two kids in the row in front jumped into their parents' arms, and they swung them around and kissed their cheeks. Groups of drunk men got into huge scrums, waving their tops around their heads and cheering at full might. And Paul, whose movements had become more laboured as the evening went on, stood up silently and started leading the way to the exit.

★ ★ ★

2 January 2018

    Paul:
Hi son. Don't like how we left things last night. Don't like how you spoke to me or your mother. Think you should think twice before coming back to this house if you're gonna disrespect us like that. Its not how we raised you.

    Michael:
Hi Dad, neither do I - but you keep pushing me to that point. Jackson is my mate. You were rude to him, laughing at the way he looks and all that.

    Paul:
It's my house my rules, Midge. Your nan was round she doesn't need to see all that.

    Michael:
I don't think she's the problem here, Dad.

    Paul:
So who is then?

    Paul:
?

19 May 2018

  Michael:
Just so you know, I saw your posts on Facebook. Your views are disgusting.
What if I was gay? How would you feel then?

  Paul:
Which posts? Well - are you?

30 July 2018

  Paul:
Hi son, we've not seen you in a while. How's tricks?

17 April 2019

  Paul:
Hi Midge, your mum was upset tonight. She says you had a go at her for defending me. She's not defending me, son, she just sees it from my point of view too. You could have a go at that as well some time. Come round if you're free.

10

Red Flags and Icks

The time between Paul opening up about his son at the Etihad and our group trip to Seville could be mapped by the sheer number of dates I went on: Tinder, Grindr, The Co-op – no online platform or local mini-market was safe from my desire to meet someone to share stimulating conversation and glorious sex with. While I swiped and flirted, called bars and reserved tables, keeping Evie and Tasha involved at every junction, there was an omnipresent fixture on my phone screen: that of DiscreetHung, in all his mystery. I hadn't mentioned my undercover flirtationship to either of my best friends; I was worried that they would externalise the internalised judgement that I was already applying to myself, and I didn't want to be put off from a back-and-forth that I was enjoying while I tried to invigorate my offline sex life. I confided in my brother, Dan, about the situation, but he was of little to no help. He laughed about 'DiscreetHung' as a username and asked if I wanted to play online poker with him. The more I discovered about DiscreetHung's personality, the more pictures of his sculpted form he sent me in different lighting (all faceless), the more I realised we had a lot in common and the more curious I became to see what he looked like. He would, of course, beg to see pictures of me – but I was standing firm. We either sent them together or not at all. I suggested meeting multiple times, but building trust was paramount for him. I discovered that he worked a corporate job, like most people in their mid to late-twenties, and that he also resented it. He was cagey about what and where, but we laughed about our workplaces' various office caricatures. He began an ongoing joke where he would start his messages with 'I hope this finds you well', and if I crossed a boundary, he'd respond with 'Let's circle back to that later'. One Friday night, he'd poured his heart out to me about how he'd always thought he might be gay, or bisexual, but never knew how to explore this possibility. He insisted that his family wouldn't be supportive; he'd often heard them say homophobic things behind closed doors. We'd clashed during both political conversations we'd had (one about traditionally Christian gay weddings, the other about the necessity for LGBT education within schools), but it hadn't bothered me, as all debates were nuanced and respectful. Problematically, I found the disagreement arousing – like two stags locked in battle. I had, however, started to become introspective about why I was engaging with a person when I had no idea what they looked like. I worried that I had become an 'I can fix him!' kind of person, that maybe I always had been. There was a niggling inkling in the back of my mind, which kept suggesting that I was entertaining this cyber-fantasy as a form of self-preservation. In the real world, I could be hurt. I could be cheated on. I could be made to feel worthless, and ugly, and shit in bed. With DiscreetHung, behind our phone screens, I felt shielded, at least for the present, from any pain or humiliation that he might inflict on me. This, although comforting, made me anxious about the current state of my self-esteem. I was concerned that, if I was willing to invest time in what was essentially a stranger, with no concrete plans of making our online tête-à-tête a real-life dick-to-ass, I might be becoming, god forbid, lonely. With all of these swirling neuroses in mind, and the desire to be on top form during my upcoming girls' trip to Seville, I propelled myself on a three-week back-to-back dating extravaganza that began on a sticky leather sofa in a dark corner of the Northern Quarter cocktail bar, The Lost Cat.

Date One: Henry. Friday 10 May. 3 weeks until holiday
Location: The Lost Cat, Northern Quarter
Met: On Tinder

Henry and I had been chatting on Tinder for about a week before I asked him out for a drink. He said yes, but he was skint – so naturally happy hour at The Lost Cat was the place to go. I fancied Henry from the moment I saw him. He was tall, had scruffy auburn facial hair, a trendy haircut that flirted with the idea of being a mullet, and an outfit that wouldn't have looked out of place on Machine Gun Kelly. The feature that seemed to be the most significant contributing factor towards his physical attractiveness was a prominent brow bone that wasn't strong enough to make him appear Neanderthal-esque but did make his eyes look dark and brooding – almost shark-like – as though he was on the hunt and my ass was in the crosshairs. He was twenty-four and a Master's student at The University of Manchester, studying Maths. I had, for now, written him off as a potential romantic partner and was purely looking to ride him into the Mancunian sunset.

'So, what made you decide to study the worst subject in the world?' I asked after our third cocktail.

'What did you study?' he replied. Evidently, his learnings so far had yet to extend to the knowledge that it's annoying to answer a question with another question.

'English Literature,' I said.

'Because I want my degree to lead to a job?' He grinned. Ouch.

'Fair point. I am a copywriter, though, by trade,' I said, trying not to sound defensive and failing spectacularly.

'And is that what you want to pursue? Copywriting?' he asked, licking his lips. He'd done that a few times while maintaining eye contact with me. It was hot. He was hot. He had a Scottish accent. Hot.

'No. I want to publish a book, eventually. Or a poetry anthology. Or maybe be a scriptwriter. I don't know. I haven't decided yet. I do know one thing, though, and I don't want to be dramatic, but I hate the corporate world and everyone in it. They all shag spreadsheets and Steven Bartlett, and I can't be arsed with it.'

'Not a fan of Stevie?' asked Henry.

'I have nothing against him per se. He just makes me cringe. He's "Live Laugh Love" but for middle management,' I replied. He laughed.

'I hear you. You're writing off a lot of people there, though, with that sweeping statement about hating everyone in the corporate world. There's gotta be some things you like about it?' said Henry Browbone. I became temporarily paranoid that I was coming across as one of those embittered Gen X gay men who were mean about everything and everyone and put #rantover on sprawling Facebook posts about bad customer service when everyone knew their attitude was the problem.

'I love the social element. I am being facetious; I obviously don't hate everyone in that world. I'm a lover, not a fighter.' I instantly regretted the final quip.

'Oh really?' he asked, raising a bushy eyebrow. Well, I'm in it now.

'I am . . . are you?' I asked, extending one of my legs and rubbing it against his under the table. He smirked.

'I'll show you later,' he said. Fit!

'Why wait?' I asked, trapping one of his legs between mine and squeezing. He exhaled and stared at me with a look of hunger. 'You're in danger, boy.' I had a semi and needed a piss – awful combination. I released his leg and stood up to head to the toilets. As I walked past Henry, he pulled me in hard and kissed me, his coarse facial hair rubbing against my cheek.

'Let's get home so I can fuck your brains out.' His breath was warm against my neck, making the tiny hairs stand on end. I grinned at him, then continued to the toilets. The facilities at The Lost Cat were unisex, and the plywood walls were always painted with graffiti. Inside the cubicle, someone had written 'Tonight I will suck a big fat beautiful cock, and he will remember it forever!! <3' on the door. Heartwarming.

```
[22:06] Gabriel: He's fit, guys. Says he's go-
ing to fuck my brains out
   [22:06] Tasha: That shouldn't take long
   [22:06] Evie: Ooo, think there's gonna be a
second date?
```

[22:06] **Gabriel**: No, but if the sex is good, I'll shag him again
[22:06] **Evie**: Why not?
[22:06] **Gabriel**: He's a bit immature, and he's not very funny
[22:07] **Tasha**: I'm pretty sure Seamus never told one successful joke
[22:07] **Gabriel**: Seamus is not the standard I want to base my next partner on
[22:07] **Tasha**: Fairs
[22:08] **Evie**: Fairs! Me and Dan are watching Shrek 2
[22:08] **Tasha**: Cuties!!!!!!
[22:08] **Gabriel**: No one asked

My brother and Evie's annoyingly persistent romance made me feel nervous and uncomfortable, two emotions that did not align with the levels of sexual adrenaline that Henry Browbone was causing to course through my body. I still had doubts on Dan's ability to commit and how this might affect Evie or our friendship if (and when) everything went south. There was a distinct possibility that their mutual weed inclinations might lead them to enter a joint cannabis-induced psychosis, like Marcus, my chef-date from spring, had told me had happened to his friend. What if they had a kid? Uncle to TWO children before I'd even hit thirty? NOT chic.

[10:08] **Evie**: Don't be mean! Do you think Lord Farquaard is based on Napoleon?
[10:08] **Tasha**: I can't say I've ever thought about it, Evie. Why do you ask? I didn't know you knew who Napoleon was
[10:09] **Evie**: Shut up, I have to teach about him. he's on the curriculem
[10:09] **Gabriel**: Is spelling?

[10:09] **Evie:** When I deep[35] it, I always saw him as the personification of short man syndrome, but then I guess that's what Napoleon is too
   [10:09] **Tasha:** Evie, are you stoned?
   [10:09] **Evie:** Absolutely baked
   [10:10] **Gabriel:** Hahahaha

I headed to the mirror to fix my hair and was greeted by my drunk reflection: IE, somebody who seemed to be approximately 3.7 times more attractive than my usual, sober self. It couldn't be denied, though, that trauma had done my body good. I was the healthiest I'd ever been. I'd been working out, so my bone structure had returned with a vengeance. My dark brown curls, which had been lacklustre and verging on grey, looked more glossy due to my commitment to eating well and cutting down on cigs. I also had my pre-Seamus glow back. Someone walked through the doors as I ran my damp hands through my hair to style it into the lazy, pushed-back waves I favoured. It was Henry Browbone. My first thought was that it was bad manners to go into the toilet when you know your date is in there, but that was quickly quashed by the sudden realisation that he wasn't here for a piss. He had that sharky look in his eyes again. Without saying anything, he strolled towards me, grabbed me by both wrists and kissed me, pushing me against the bathroom wall. All of my Evie-and-Dan worries were jolted from my mind, and I was back in the moment, and in my body. I felt the stiffness of his cock through his trousers as he ran his hands up my shirt and rubbed the sides of my torso. He was forceful and slightly taller than me, and

---

[35] To 'deep' something (verb), is to think about something critically. It usually applies to subjects that don't necessarily require deeper levels of analysis, like the creative inspiration for villains from twenty-year-old animated films

the exchange was so erotic that I felt myself melt as he reached his arms around my body and pressed me tightly to him.

'Come on . . .' he whispered into my ear with that irresistible Scottish twang. I ignored the intrusive group-chat-induced thought that he sounded a bit like Shrek and followed him into the empty toilet cubicle, locking the door behind me.

★★★

DiscreetHung: I hope this finds you well. What have you done tonight? you're up late
Angel44: Went to The Lost Cat
DiscreetHung: It's grim there! you're better than that, who did you go with?
Angel44: Don't be such a snob, it's fine. Good vibes and cheap drinks.
DiscreetHung: Stop avoiding the question
Angel44: I'm not! Hahaha, I went on a date, actually
DiscreetHung: Oh right
Angel44: You're not . . . jealous?
DiscreetHung: Nah. I'm going to sleep
Angel44: Ok. Let's circle back tomorrow ;)
DiscreetHung: Night

★★★

Date Two: Fergus. Thursday 16 May. 2 weeks until holiday
Location: The Edinburgh Castle, Ancoats
Met: Set up via Jay, the receptionist at work

Fergus was a thirty-year-old graphic designer from Surrey. Jay, the gay receptionist at EnsureInsure, had set us up. He'd promised me that

Fergus was 'self-made, rich, clever and always smelled amazing.' He didn't know him too well but had met him at one of his best friend's weddings earlier in the year, soon after his latest relationship had dissolved, and promised to hook Fergus up if he ever met anyone that was 'his type'. This did make me slightly anxious as I'd wondered what type of box that put me into and what adjectives Jay had used to describe me. The nerves had melted away after forty minutes, one and a half glasses of red, and a delicious starter of cavolo nero with too many elements for me to remember. The atmosphere upstairs in Edinburgh Castle was rustic and warm, which, along with the outstanding food, made it almost impossible to feel anything other than a bit jolly. Fergus, at first, seemed to be exactly as Jay had described. He'd started the meal by saying, 'This is on me. I got my commission for a project at NVidia last week', in a *very* posh accent, so he was wealthy. This was not a pre-requisite for me, and could even lean into ick[36] territory. However, considering my last relationship consisted of two struggling writers arguing over what brand of butter to go halves on, it was a welcome relief. He smelled glorious – not in an expensive aftershave way, but in an excellent skincare, takes his clothes to an upmarket dry-cleaners kind of way. He wore a crisp white shirt that was well-fitted enough to show the hint of a nonchalant belly; he struck me as the kind of man who deemed working out a waste of his time. His hair was dark brown and lazily combed over.

---

[36] An 'ick' is a character trait that someone may have that has the power to completely turn you off them. It can also be an event that happens to them that is beyond their control, or a reaction to said event. Where 'red flags' are objective and universally accepted, 'icks' are subjective and often shared and debated. Example:
Red Flag – a man who tells you he doesn't want you to wear that top because it shows too much cleavage.
Ick – a man who is eating a sandwich outdoors at a café, and their napkins blow away in the wind

He had a 'back from holiday' tan that made his teeth luminescent. The conversation so far had flowed with ease. We'd flirted and laughed, kept eye contact and sparred about which city was better between Manchester and London. He spoke with his hands and had a flair for dramatic overexpression, which I initially found cute. Things took a turn once we'd reached the second glass of wine.

'So, Jay mentioned that you're recently single?' he enquired in his musical drawl.

'Yeah,' I replied. 'How about you? When was your last relationship?' I deflected.

'Ah, it ended about a year ago now. Rather spectacularly, actually. At least it went out with a bang rather than a fizzle.' Fergus laughed, nodding his glass towards me. 'Since then, I've been... you know, playing the field.'

There was something about the way he was speaking that made me squirm. I was on the precipice of getting the 'ick'. He'd crossed over from confident to slightly arrogant during the first twenty minutes, and now he was edging perilously close to cocky.

'Went out with a bang?' I asked. In any other instance, I wouldn't press, but he'd given me enough information up front to suggest that he was open to discussing it.

'Yes. Well. We had a misunderstanding about . . . the boundaries in our relationship.' He rolled his eyes.

'What does that mean?' I said.

'Well, I've never been a big believer in monogamy. And I thought he wasn't either. Turns out . . .' His voice trailed off as he sipped his drink.

'So . . . you cheated?' I asked, feeling the blood rise to my face.

'No. Cheated. Puh.' He chuckled with contempt. 'Does that exist for us? It's so archaic. Haven't we moved beyond the need to imprison ourselves with Judeo-Christian rules?'

'Okay . . . so you had an open relationship?' I asked, chewing furiously on the end of the cocktail stick I'd used for my second starter of Kalamata olives.

'I thought so, yes. Well, I misread. We'd always aligned on how regressive monogamy was. How fifty per cent of heterosexual marriages end in divorce, and a big driver is infidelity. All their desires are stifled by these restrictive relationships that lead them to resent the person they're with. It doesn't work. He'd agreed,' Fergus said, then beckoned to the waiter with three fingers. Red flag.

'So I'd taken that as the green flag. I thought, if the moment arose, we were permitted to snatch it. And it did, so I did. Then he found out at our mutual friend's thirtieth and dumped me. On a karaoke machine,' he said, eyes widening at the drama of it all.

'Right. So . . . he thought you were monogamous? You'd never had that conversation directly?' I asked.

'HE had been putting topless photos of himself all over his Instagram feed for months. Apparently, that didn't cross his line, but my behaviour did. I do think you're right. Our mistake was that we didn't establish clear enough boundaries, I suppose, but god, that's so unsexy, isn't it?' He wrinkled his nose. 'You can't do this, and I can't do that, and blah blah blah blah. So much "no". I prefer "yes" and to lead by instinct,' he said, reaching over and stroking my hand. I flinched instinctively. He noticed and withdrew. 'We're friends now. We know where we both went wrong. Anyway, he's seeing somebody new, and they're totally open. Verging on a throuple[37].'

I was gobsmacked. In the gay community, open relationships weren't uncommon and came in varying shades and hues. Some couples allowed sex outside the relationship on holiday. Some had regular threesomes. Others saw love as separate from sex entirely. I wasn't alien to this notion, even though I didn't subscribe to it personally, but there was something about the nonchalant way with which he discussed his ex-partner's emotions that triggered me. I could feel all the negative emotions I'd experienced in the aftermath

---

[37] A relationship between three people instead of two. I've heard they get larger beds custom made especially. Bet they save a fortune on bills

of my breakup with Seamus and it made him, in an instant, repulsive to me.

'I'm not sure I agree with you,' I said, trying to remain calm.

'How so?' He smirked.

'I think, if you haven't established clear boundaries in that relationship, and you slept with somebody else, you've cheated. The default is still monogamy. Regardless of how many thirst traps you post.'

'Wow.' He raised an eyebrow. 'Jay told me that you were a progressive thinker.'

'I *am* a progressive thinker, Fergus. I just don't like people who use their 'progressive' beliefs as a justification for their shitty ethics,' I snapped.

'Well, Gabriel, I don't like people who stick their noses into other relationships without knowing the full story!' he said.

'YOU BROUGHT IT UP!' I shouted. The restaurant was temporarily silent. I felt my cheeks turn purple. I couldn't believe we'd become nemeses before the main course had arrived. A heavy and uncomfortable silence followed, during which he repeatedly folded and unfolded his napkin in some sort of panicked origami display and I re-read the drinks menu for no apparent reason.

'So you play that game, then?' asked Fergus after two horrible minutes.

'What game?' I said.

'Monogamy. The big competition for who can best pretend to be satisfied, to meet society's expectations, while all of their personal identity and sexual satisfaction ebbs away.'

'That's not how I see it, Fergus,' I said, grinding my teeth. He was so unbelievably irritating.

'How *do* you see it then, Gabriel?'

I hesitated. 'Well, I clearly haven't given it as much thought as you.'

'Clearly!' He laughed.

I clenched my fists under the table. 'But I don't think you can write off the entire belief system of monogamy when it has created loving, happy, fulfilling relationships for millions of people all over the world for thousands of years. Yes, it doesn't work for everyone. Yes, a lot of it is societal conditioning, and heteronormative, and restrictive. And YES, I do think people, especially queer people, should be free to decide their own rules and how to forge their own relationships in the way that works best for them. But what I DON'T think . . .' The waitress arrived with the food, placing a steaming hot beef and bone marrow sharing pie on the table between us. 'Is that you can retroactively apply your own set of rules after fucking someone behind your partner's back. That is insanity.' The waitress hurried back to the kitchen to grab the chips.

'You're clearly not evolved enough for this kind of discussion. Maybe we should change the subject.'

'Maybe you should change your mindset, you insufferable dickhead. I'm leaving.' I stood up and walked the ten paces to the bar to pay my share of the bill. The waitress looked at me with concern as I swiped my card across the reader.

'Everything alright?' she asked.

I was proud of myself for defending my principles and speaking my mind. Historically, I would've acted out of anxiety and stayed quiet, but I'd managed to retain most of my dignity and still make my position clear. Was this . . . *growth*?

'Great, thanks. Can I get a box for half of that beef and bone marrow pie, please?'

★ ★ ★

Angel44: Do you believe in monogamy?
DiscreetHung: Of course! What other option is there? Who wants to live like a Persian emperor . . . actually, now that I think about it, I

do like the thought of you and another guy doing exactly what I say ;)
  Angel44: Shut up. That's hot, but shut up.
  DiscreetHung: Why do you ask?
  Angel44: No reason. Just been thinking about it.
  DiscreetHung: If you're as hot as I think you are, I could see myself being with you
  Angel44: That's stupid, we've never even met
  DiscreetHung: Yet
  Angel44: Yet.

★★★

Date Three: Marcus. Friday 24 May. 1 week until holiday
Location: My flat
Met: Months ago at the post office

My final date before the holiday found me emotionally exhausted from the previous two. I'd gone from honouring the ghosts of my gay ancestors by giving a Scotsman a blow job in a toilet cubicle to hurriedly boxing up half a beef pie to escape a date with the white Nick Cannon. The date with Fergus had played on my mind all week, leading to several existential quandaries over whether or not my disinterest in polygamy made me a prude, self-loathing, or heteronormative. Did I value sexual and romantic exclusivity purely because the landscape of my brain had been pruned by the subliminal messaging of my youth? Was Walt Disney responsible for sowing the seed? Were the childhood stories of pre-destined monogamy at the root of my longing for an unshared love? Had the perma-propagated concept of 'the one' muddied my chances of cultivating modern romance? Was I producing a surplus of gardening metaphors because I longed for the great outdoors (to explore fields and forests with a man who marathons and makes jam) rather than live an urban lifestyle in a two-bed with my brother? This led me to question my recent decisions, namely, writing off hot chef Marcus, simply because we were both bottoms. I sent him a text after work on Friday:

Gabriel: `Hi Marcus, long time no speak. I know this is out of the blue, and you might be seeing someone now or whatever, but . . . I have no plans tonight, and I enjoyed your company last time. How does a Deliveroo (on me) and some shit TV sound?`

I got a reply within ten minutes:

Marcus: `Hi Gabriel, It's good to hear from you! I'm working until 9, but could come over after that?`

Marcus arrived at twenty past nine, and nothing about our reunification was frosty. He was wearing his chef clothes, I was in a Fiorucci (sale) hoody and shorts, and my asshole, this time, remained unwilling and unprepared. Just as the other times I'd met him, I was bowled over by how handsome he was. He had a new buzzcut that suited him (a luxury only afforded to men with proportionate foreheads and symmetrical features). It didn't take long for us to laugh about our date's climax over a couple of (Dan's) Strongbow Dark Fruits.

'You know, Marcus, even though our status as dual-bottoms makes us incompatible for anal . . . we could still do other stuff?' I suggested on a whim.

'I'm vers, actually, Gabe,' he said, with a barely concealed smile.

'Don't talk shit. I saw the coffee table book,' I said.

He burst out laughing. 'Fair enough. I should put that away, didn't realise it would be such a cock block. Is "we could still do other stuff" your way of coming on to me?'

'I'm not sure . . . I think I'm just analysing the possibilities. Sorry, I've had a rough week.'

'WOW. So sexy, Gabe. Let's just be friends.' He laughed. And so we were. We exchanged dating disaster stories (I won), ordered a Northern Soul Grilled Cheese and watched an old series of *The Real Housewives of Beverly Hills*. By the night's end, we were cuddling on the sofa as Brandi Glanville insulted Lisa Rinna's hair, and it was the best date I'd had all week.

* * *

Ick Lists

Evie:
- Skinny jeans
- People who 'don't like kids'
- Eating an apple while walking
- Pressing the button before crossing the road
- Dressing gowns
- 'You decide!'
- Keeping a festival wristband on

Gabriel:
- Singing along to 'Come on Eileen'
- Unqualified DJs behind DJ decks
- DJs
- Scarves
- Having a DVD rack (mega ick it if it includes *The Hangover*, *Superbad*, etc.)
- When they get pumped up in the barber's chair
- Reading a book in public that they've visibly just started
- When a dog sniffs his crotch

- Dropping coins
- Monster Munch

Tasha:
- Crying at films
- Shaking out a picnic blanket
- Wearing gloves
- When they ask 'What's still hot?' at Greggs
- Trying to get out of the sea when it's moderately wavy
- Inhaling a helium balloon and doing a funny voice
- Quoting *Gavin and Stacey*
- When they're middle class and white but love rap
- Ankles
- When you're in a perfectly respectable and safe bar and they say 'who's going to watch the bags?' when it's time to get a round
- Buying a beige linen shirt to wear on a European city break where the architecture is also beige
- When the bus brakes and their body jolts slightly
- When they have a sip of beer and turn the can around to start reading the label
- When they try on a pair of shoes in a shoe shop and they're just sat waiting in their socks
- When they stamp to try and scare away a pigeon but it doesn't move
- When they try to merge in traffic and no one will let them in
- The little 'awh' before saying 'nice one'

Paul:
- Small tits

11

Viva España

Our holiday began with the obligatory journey from Platform 14 at Manchester Piccadilly, directly to the airport on one of the best train routes in the world. Gone was the amalgamation of dreary commuters or drunk weekenders, to be replaced by the bustle of eager travellers clutching handles to their hold-alls, everyone united by the thrill of escape, the promise of sunshine, the draw of experiences new, and even the potential for romance. The sky was the typical shade of slate as we stood outside Terminal 3 to allow me to have my final cigarette. It was 8 a.m., and our flight was at 10:50. Tasha read out a checklist to everyone for the umpteenth time ('Passport?' Check. 'Liquids separated?' Check. 'Boarding passes? Oh, I've got them on the app . . .') while I revelled in the schadenfreudic knowledge that we were leaving behind everyone in Manchester to wilt under a British summer while we bloomed on the scorching streets of Seville. Was I a psycho for wanting the UK general public to have terrible weather in my absence? Nah. They elected Boris Johnson and allowed the Mars Delight to go out of circulation; they were the psychos. Tasha was *actually* a psycho by the time we reached airport security. All of her usual levelheadedness dissolved at the airport, but it was the final straw when the purple-haired lady at security announced:

'Yous all need to make sure your liquids are under 100 ml and in one of the clear bags provided. If your luggage fails the scan, the queue to have it searched is over an hour. Separate your large electricals for scanning; this includes laptops, iPads, smartwatches, hair straighteners, kettles, toasters, microwaves and flat-screen TVs.'

Most of the queue rewarded her half-hearted routine with a reluctant murmur of laughter, but Tasha devolved into what could only be described as some sort of administrative chimera. She dropped to all fours and began tearing through her bags, searching for anything that might break the security rules. Finding nothing, and without invitation, she did the same to my bag and then Evie's. A nearby middle-aged couple, witnessing the performance, covered their mouths with their hands in concern.

'Are you alright, Tash?' Evie asked, pulling her bag back gently so as not to provoke another attack.

'Yes, fine,' she said with pursed red lips. 'I just don't want to miss the flight. You know what they're like.' She nodded to the security staff.

'We won't miss the flight; they always say it takes an hour to wait to be searched, but it never does. It's a scare tactic, so they don't have to do their jobs,' I tried to reassure her.

'Gabe, where's your lighter?' she asked. I looked in the plastic wallet that held all my worldly liquids. No lighter. I checked my pocket. Lighter.

'Got it!' I grinned, placing it securely in the plastic wallet and turning to Evie to wink.

'It's not fucking funny, Gabe. You won't be laughing on the train home. I had to fight to get these holiday days, please don't ruin it with any of your bullshit,' she snapped.

'WOAH NELLY! Less of that. We'll be fine. Come on. Where are those holiday vibes?' I said.

She grumbled to herself until we reached the security desk. Before long, we were completing the mandatory post-check-in routine:

1. Go to WHSmith to purchase a few too many snacks 'just in case'.
2. Browse sunglasses shop at duty-free, try on two pairs, pretend to yourself and store assistant that you're in a position to drop £130 on accessories.
3. Walk past fragrance shop and almost pass out from the fumes.
4. Check if your gate information has been released at the appropriate time (it hasn't).
5. Settle down for a well-earned pint.

There's just something about that morning pint post-check-in and pre-flight. The shit bit is done and dusted, and only excitement remains. I'd paid a ridiculous amount for a badly poured Heineken, but knowing I was about to start paying EuroPrices for delicious wine made it all better. There was an obnoxious group of lads on a stag do at the table next to us, but for once, their prehistoric grunts didn't bother me. I felt a sense of camaraderie with everyone at Terminal 3 and, most importantly, with my two best friends.

'Cheers, guys!' I said, raising my glass to clink with Evie and (a now much calmer) Tasha. 'To Ryanair! Let's make this a trip to remember!'

'That's aimed at you, Evie. No blacking out,' said Tasha, whose ice-blonde locks were tied in her signature 'I've got shit to do' bun.

'What about on the last night?' asked Evie, who was re-applying the metallic array of bangles, bracelets and necklaces that she'd had to remove before being X-rayed at security.

'I guess that's okay. Are you sure you want to be hanging for the flight home though? Especially wi . . .' Tasha's reply to Evie faded into an inaudible mumble as a tall, thin, beautiful Spanish man dressed in all black walked past our table.

'Sorry,' he says as he brushes past your shoulder, pulling a suitcase behind him. You meet his eyes and nod to indicate it's okay. His eyes linger, and your gaze locks to his for a moment too long. They are dark amber, wide-set and long-lashed. They glisten, and the upper corners of his full mouth reach upwards into the hint of a smile, but there is something sad about his aura. Not sad in the sense that he'd just been told he had to pay the fee for extra baggage, but deeply sad, in a tortured way — as though he was mourning the state of the world and dressing for it, too. As he turns his head and walks to the only free table at the other end of the bar, you catch his scent, and it's curious, totally alien, but somehow familiar. You steal another glance and notice that he's done the same. Your heart races, but you aren't aware of it, as if you were exercising or having a panic attack. You feel it as a buzz, as though every atom in your body is bouncing up and down in unison. Your

stomach flips, and you wonder if you should take a Rennie before the flight. You look downwards at your pint, feeling the heat rise in your face.

'Gabe? What do you think?' Evie asked.

'About what?' I said, jolting back to the present moment.

'About the chances of me making it through sec — Wait, were you even listening?' Evie said.

'Sorry, no. I zoned out. Did you see that guy? Don't look now. The one that just walked past. Spanish. All black outfit,' I said, unable to look up from my pint unless I was caught unawares by those eyes again.

'The one that bumped into you? Yeah, why?' asked Evie.

'I don't know. I don't want to be dramatic, but don't you think he's the most beautiful man you've ever seen?' I whispered, looking up from my pint but keeping my head fixed in one place.

'Erm . . .' mumbled Evie.

'I didn't see too much of him, but he had weird eyes, kind of like a giraffe?'

I ignored Tasha. My phone buzzed.

```
DiscreetHung: Hey, what're you doing? I've got a
song I want you to listen to, think you'll love it
  Angel44: Hey, sorry, I'm actually gonna be
busy thi—
```

'GABE!' yelled Tasha. The volume should've drawn more attention but the stag do had burst into a chorus of 'Take Me Home, Country Roads'.

'Are you serious? This is the first drink of the holiday. We're trying to set the mood here?' Tasha's voice had the same edge she'd utilised earlier in the security queue.

'What, by micro-managing Evie's alcohol intake?' I said. Evie snorted.

'Can you not? You've spent the last month going on and on *about* men. And dating. And sex. And men. Can this trip not just be about us? Rather than the nameless Spanish guy in the muddy shoes? Or whoever that . . . wait, is that Grindr?' Tasha seethed.

I minimised the app. She was right. She'd verbalised a thought I'd started having over the last few days after raising my head out of the Grindrverse, looking around and realising I'd not asked anybody how they were for an embarrassing amount of time. It was decided. I'd stay away from my online paramour for the weekend. DiscreetHung was becoming a bit intense, and Tasha clearly was, too.

'Okay. Okay. I'm sorry. Heard. You're right. This holiday is about us. It's to say thank you to you both for being such amazing friends and supporting me during my post-breakup, self-centred phase.'

'Self-centred *phase*?' Tasha sneered.

'No men. No pursuing men. If they happen upon us, then that can't be helped. We're irresistible. Especially you, Tasha. Look at you with that widdle frown and widdle angwy tracksuit . . .' I leaned forward and squeezed her cheeks while saying it. When I annoyed Tasha, sometimes the best way to get her to lay off was to become so obnoxiously irritating that she just found it funny.

'You're a dickhead.' She laughed. I couldn't get the Spanish guy's face out of my head.

'I'll drink to that. Come on, ONE MORE BEFORE WE BOARD, BITCHES!' I shouted.

'AYYYYYYY!' cheered the stag do next to us in agreement.

★ ★ ★

Five hours, four miniature bottles of Ryanair's finest vino, three *Take a Break* crosswords, two terse exchanges with the passengers next to us over luggage space, one taxi journey and a partridge in a pear tree later, we'd arrived at our Airbnb. As soon as we finished the ascent up the stone staircase to the top of the narrow building situated slap-bang in the city's centre, I knew I'd smashed it. Finding holiday accommodation that was gorgeous and fit for purpose but still within budget was #189 on my list of impressive talents. The apartment was a crisp white with exposed wooden beams; sunlight spilt through windows lined with light pine shutters. The living space had a row of hanging plants tumbling down from a mezzanine, a large corner sofa, and, for a deranged yet aesthetically successful reason, an old bicycle mounted to the wall. We had our own terrace, with several ashtrays for the million cigs we would all be smoking (on holiday, everyone becomes a twenty-a-day fiend), and a BBQ that we wouldn't use. We lasted about five minutes on the terrace before we headed back inside, defeated, to turn the air-con on. Seville was known as 'the frying pan of Spain' to locals, and upon arrival, it was easy to understand why. We were still technically in spring, and the mercury was pushing forty degrees.

'It's unreal, Gabe!' Evie marvelled.

'You've smashed it,' Tasha said.

'It's boiling,' I whinged. We agreed to take a moment to unpack and get our bearings, then meet for dinner. Long cold shower. Cig on the balcony in my underwear to dry off instead of a towel. Unpacked clothes and hung them in the wardrobe. Applied factor 50[38] suncream liberally. Took a moment to inhale the incredible scent of said suncream. Sat on the edge of the bed watching TikToks. Called Mum and showed her the Airbnb.

'Just remember, Ivy might be able to throw money at you when she wants, but she didn't birth you. I sat and played with you for hours. I wiped your arse for two years, Gabriel. Remember that.'

'I'd rather not, thanks, Mum.'

---

[38] It was only in the last two years that I'd admitted defeat and stopped trying to develop any kind of tan. My skin type was pale and freckly, and after a particularly vicious sunburn on my calf after a day at the beach in Portugal, I'd finally realised that my lifelong dream of having the same skin as Jennifer Lopez might be unachievable. It's a hard pill to swallow, watching your friends become golden and sun-kissed while the only thing you face is the potential for a worrying new mole

Got changed. Wore the new red shirt I'd been saving. Back to the living space.

It was 6 p.m., and Evie played Sabrina Carpenter on the speaker; she looked breathtaking. Evie had the opposite skin type to me — she tanned at the merest suggestion of sunlight. She'd been sat on the balcony and already had a glow, like her body had absorbed the energy from the sun and was now emanating it back out. She was wearing a skirt shaped like a butterfly wing, which she'd bought from TallulahBelle, a designer in Manchester, and a baby-pink lace crop top. Her ochre hair was clipped up at the sides, giving her typically round eyes a feline quality.

'Jesus, Evie, you look fire,' I told her as we sat on the terrace with a glass of white.

'Thanks, babe! I feel it!' She smiled. I felt a wave of guilt over my attitude towards her and Dan. Evie looked — and seemed — the happiest she had in ages. The thought that my brother might have something to do with this was almost unbelievable to me, but the possibility that they might not be a mutually destructive disaster-coupling crossed my mind for the first time. Tasha was still getting ready, so I took the chance to get something more urgent off my chest.

'Evie, do you think Tasha's alright with me?' I whispered.

She frowned slightly. 'What makes you say that?' she whispered back. I could barely hear her over the sound of Sabrina pleading 'Please Please Please' from the speaker.

'I don't know. Just instinct, I suppose. She was snappy at the airport. Not her usual snappy. It felt venomous, I don't know,' I said.

Evie paused for a second and looked deep in thought. 'Well, I know things haven't been great with Scott. She's been down about that, and you know what she gets like at airports.' Evie widened her eyes at me. I nodded, as if I had the faintest idea that Tasha and Scott were struggling. I suddenly envisioned myself on trial for being a bad friend.

'NOT GUILTY!' screamed the imaginary judge. 'Natasha has made it explicitly clear that she will come directly to Gabriel when she feels comfortable to talk about emotional matters, and not a moment before.'

'GUILTY!' screamed an opposing judge. 'Gabriel has been emotionally unavailable, selfish, and concerned only with matters of the penis for an unforgivable amount of time.'

'Airports do make people weird!' I said, wincing at the hypocrisy of having called someone else weird directly after having some kind of judiciary hallucination.

'Yeah, and I don't know, Gabe. Maybe she's just taking it out on you a bit. Or it might be . . .' Her voice trailed off as she wrestled with what she was about to say.

'Might be what?' I whispered.

'I think she might be frustrated because she feels she can't talk to you about Scott. I think she might resent that she helps you with a lot of your stuff, but when she needs help, to vent about her relationship or whatever, she can't come to you,' Evie said methodically as if a conveyor belt of different words had moved across her brain and she'd hand-selected each with thought and care.

'Why do you think she thinks that?' I asked.

'Gabe, come on,' said Evie, taking a sip of her wine.

'What?'

'It's so obvious that you don't like him,' Evie said.

I stifled a gasp. I thought I'd done a masterful job of disguising my disdain for Scott. 'It's not that I don't *like* him. It's just . . .' I started.

'No, you don't like him, Gabe. It's obvious when you like people, and it's obvious when you're pretending. It's the other way around, too. For example, you pretend not to like Mitchell when really you do, but you pretend to like Scott when really you don't.'

'Evie, I will accept your analysis of my feelings towards Scott, but I draw the line at you insinuating that I have a single positive feeling towards Mitchell,' I said, his neon face flashing through my brain like an orange aneurysm.

She laughed. 'I get it. I don't love Scott. He always says "Wow... look at you!" when he sees my clothes, and he hasn't got a sense of humour. But Gabe, you can't decide who your friends choose to be in relationships with.' Evie's voice rose from a whisper to a regular volume with the last sentence, and I cautioned her to keep it down with a waft of my hand.

'But I don't want to decide who my friends are in relationships with. I just want them to be with someone who is right for them and makes them happy. I don't *think* he's right for Tasha, and I don't *think* he makes her happy. I *think* I'm entitled to think that!' I said, accidentally ignoring my own calls for quiet.

'Gabe, you don't know *who's* right for *who*!' Evie's tone changed, and it was clear she wasn't only referring to Tasha and Scott. 'You only see them when they're together in front of you. You don't know Scott like Tasha does, and neither do I. You're being naive. What's that saying? *Only a fool presumes to know someone's relationship*. You're not a fool. But it would be foolish to carry on being this judgey,' Evie said, looking me dead in the eye. Evie had an odd habit of occasionally producing the shiniest pearls of wisdom.

'Be out in a sec! I've just come on my fucking period, for fuck's sake. It's early. Evie, have you got a pad?' shouted Tasha from the other room over the sound of Chappell Roan.

'Top drawer of my bedside table!' shouted Evie in return.

We were silent for a moment as I thought about what she said. The sound of people milling about the streets below for the pre-dinner rush was now loud enough to permeate Chappell Roan wailing 'Hot to Go!'.

'Okay. Maybe you're right. I just wish she'd spoken to me about it if it was pissing her off,' I said.

'She probably feels uncomfortable speaking to you about it. You're stubborn when you make up your mind about people, especially when it comes to straight men. I bet that contributes to why she's resonant to be vulnerable with you over this kind of thing,' Evie said.

'You mean hesitant,' I replied.

'What did I say?' Evie asked, shocked.

'Resonant,' I said. We both burst out laughing.

Evie leaned forward and pulled me into a hug. She smelled like roses and mosquito repellant.

'On the subject of choosing who people can and can't be in a relationship with, how do you feel about me and Dan?' she asked earnestly, holding one of my hands in hers.

'Erm . . . I didn't think it was "holding my hand on the terrace" levels of seriousness, to be honest,' I said.

'What if . . . what if it was?' asked Evie (resonantly). I looked at my best friend and saw how much this meant to her. The truth was I didn't feel happy that someone so close to me was dating my brother. The truth was I'd always suspected she had a crush on him, and I was scared that he'd always known that and was taking advantage of it because he'd moved to a new city and wanted some comfort. The truth was I was scared they'd be a bad influence on each other, that they'd disappear down a weed-infused wormhole and spend the next ten years watching 'News Anchor Fails' compilations on YouTube, ordering Oreo waffles on Just Eat and arguing over who had to be forced into having a social interaction with the delivery guy while high as a kite on cheap street cannabis. Above everything, I was scared about him hurting her and what that might do to her and our friendship. But these were all fears, and if poet laureate Evie was to produce another recycled pearl of wisdom here, it would be something along the lines of 'act through love, not fear', so, at that moment, I made the conscious decision to change my perspective. My current tactic of sitting on the sidelines of my friends' relationships and silently judging them clearly wasn't working for anybody. If Evie and Dan worked out, which they feasibly could, my best friend and brother, two of the people I loved most, would be happy. Evie would be part of my family, which was worth the risk.

'Then I'd say good fucking luck to you both, and I'd be your biggest cheerleader. And I'd say, PLEASE do something to make his dress sense a bit better. I'm knackered from the effort.' I sighed.

Evie looked on the verge of tears. She said nothing, but enveloped me in another hug. This one lasted uncomfortably long and our arms stuck together in the Spanish heat.

'Oh, and Gabe, don't say anything about what we spoke about to Tasha on holiday, about how you feel about Scott. Let's just have a good time,' Evie said.

'I won't,' I lied.

'Right, guys, let's go! My pussy just turned toilet water into wine, and I am ready to BLESS THIS TOWN!' shouted Tasha from the living room. I thanked god that the neighbours probably couldn't understand English, and we headed out.

12

Idiots Abroad

After a delicious welcome meal of seafood paella at a restaurant two streets away from our Airbnb, we were all so tired from the travelling and exhausted by the heat that we agreed to have an early night and seize the day . . . tomorrow. On Saturday, the holiday began: we headed out of the Airbnb by 10:30 a.m. and weaved around Seville's narrow, cobbled streets. The architecture was awe-inspiring: five-storey terraces of pale yellow and sun-washed peach stood daintily against the turquoise morning sky. Early risers hung washing to dry in the scorching air from black iron balconies. Locals and tourists alike drifted leisurely, taking in the sound of birdsong and the chirp of insects; the provincial scents of bread baking and fresh fruit juice pouring filled the air.

'God, everyone here dresses like shite, don't they,' Tasha announced as we walked down a wide promenade bordered with orange blossom trees.

'What do you mean?!' asked Evie.

'I know this is shallow, don't judge me, we're on holiday – but, like, I haven't seen one person our age in a cool fit,' said Tasha.

'I doubt they fuss about what they look like as much as we do back home.' Evie tutted.

'Why do you think that is?' Tasha asked, biting on some fresh breakfast churros we'd picked up from a friendly street vendor.

'Because they're happy,' I said. 'Who gives a shit when you live somewhere this gorgeous, and you're as gorgeous as most of them. If I looked that good in a Fruit of the Loom Disney slogan T-shirt, that's all you'd catch me in too.'

'Yeah, sure, Gabe,' laughed Evie.

'Okay, Saint Gabriel, you *are* somewhere as gorgeous as them, and although it pains me to say it, you *are* as gorgeous as *most* of them – yet you've brought twelve different pairs of socks for a weekend break so that you can match them to your shoes,' said Tasha.

'Fair point,' I conceded. By 11:30, we'd arrived at our first Seville-sight seeing stop, the Alcázar and its adjoining cathedral. We hadn't booked a guided walking tour because Tasha argued that those were for over-fifties who hadn't learnt to use the internet, and Evie said that they always overloaded you with too much information, so we ditched the guide for google. I volunteered to do some background research as we wandered so we could get some context. The Alcázar was jaw-dropping, an almost thousand-year-old palace that combined ancient Islamic and Gothic architecture. We walked through the Patio del Yeso, and I marvelled at the ancient stone porticoes; elaborate archways bled into intricate patterns atop smooth pillars.

'So this portico . . .' I said, pointing to the southernmost structure on the Patio. 'It was built in the twelfth century and is one of the many parts of the Alcázar that still maintains its Islamic influence!'

'Islamic influence? If I wanted that, I'd just go to bloody Bradford!' Tasha grumbled, doing her best gammon impression.

'The word *alcázar* itself has Arabic etymology and can mean "palace" or "c—"'

'Gabe, could you take a picture of us here, please? It's so pretty,' Evie interrupted. I put my Philomena Cunk performance on hold and did a small photoshoot of Tasha and Evie, who moved between an unfeasible amount of poses in the space of two minutes, slowing down only to bark commands at me.

'Higher, Gabe. Move the camera higher!' instructed Tasha.

'Brightness up on the camera, Gabe, look, slide like this . . .' Evie said, waving her hand up.

'Gabe, for fuck's sake, take three per pose. Three. Pictures. Per. Pose. Stop using the phone like it's a disposable camera,' Tasha shouted across the Patio.

'Okay, Gabe, can we try a candid one?' asked Evie. I didn't quite understand what about Evie, with her head resting on her hands directly in in the centre of one of the archways, was 'candid' until she turned her face twenty degrees sideways and looked aimlessly into the distance.

'Okay, Gabe, you need to be in one now. Excuse me . . . erm . . . Perdona, señor?' Tasha turned to a nearby stranger. 'Fotografía, por favor?'

'Wow, Penelope Cruz, look at you!' I whispered as I put my arm around her for the group photograph.

'Duolingo,' she said, smiling for the camera. 'Gracias!' she said as the man walked away, mumbling 'de nada'. This routine continued over the next hour as we strolled through the Alcázar, the sun's heat tickling our necks. Despite initial protests, I read facts out loud about the Sala de Justicia and the Salón de los Embajadores, and Tasha and Evie looked around in awe for a moment, then continued to curate photoshoots for us all, carefully selecting the best backdrops and lighting to make sure that they matched the mood of the palace. I was conflicted. On the one hand, I lamented my friends' focus on creating content and disdain towards my thoughtfully Wikipediaed factoids, but on the other, their photography skills were impressive. By the time we'd reached the cathedral, we had an album of memories to preserve and look back at for years to come, even if the 'present moment' might have eluded us.

'Right, guys, I think I want to go in and light a candle for my nan. Shall we do this bit alone and then meet back up afterwards?' Cathedrals were a solitary place, and it always felt inappropriate to walk around in a group, however small.

'All our nans are dead, Gabe. Why don't we do it together?' Evie said.

'Are all of our nans dead? All six? Evie, yours aren't, are they?' I asked, surprised.

'Of course they are!' Evie laughed, presumedly at the absurdity of her best friend not knowing this rather than at her grandmother being dead.

'When did Granny Mavis die?' Granny Mavis was Evie's grandmother on her mother's side. She lived in Alicante, so she'd never seen much of her, but whenever Mavis did one of her annual visits, I made it my mission to go over to Evie's house. Upon the untimely death of her husband, who she'd been cheating on – undiscovered – for over a decade, Mavis had emigrated to Alicante and bought a house by the beach, leaving her family behind to become a raisin under the Spanish sun.

'She died during Covid!' Evie said, absent-mindedly flicking through her camera roll. 'That's probably why. It was hectic, and you know she and I weren't that close, so I didn't bother to mention it.'

'Aw, I'm sorry, Evie,' Tasha said, looking just as surprised as I felt. 'She died of Covid, did she?'

'What? No, *during* Covid,' said Evie.

'Oh . . . how did Granny Mavis die, if you don't mind me asking?' I asked gently.

'She got licked out to death,' Evie proclaimed in her airy voice. Tasha and I exchanged a momentary look of horror. I stared down at my trainers, trying not to laugh.

'What do you mean?' Tasha asked.

Evie looked up from her phone. 'What's hard to understand? She was having an affair with the married towel boy in the resort where she lived, and he was licking her out on one of the sun loungers. The resort was closed down because of Covid, so they must've thought they could get away with it. Anyway, they got caught by the manager, and she died.'

There was a moment of silence as the cathedral loomed overhead.

'Wow,' I said, finally.

'What a way to go,' conceded Tasha.

'I think it was a heart attack, officially. That's what the coroner said in his report,' said Evie.

Bet that was an interesting one to write up.

'So I guess . . . she didn't get, you know, licked out to death, Evie. The shock of being caught might've had something to do with it,' I suggested.

Evie looked thoughtful. 'Maybe. I suppose we'll never know. But it's fine. She left him her savings, her flat, and her cat. The towel boy. Mum got nothing. She was fuming.'

'I bet!' I said.

'Anyway, you're right. I probably should light a candle for her.' Evie relented.

'She died how she lived,' Tasha said.

We all agreed to meet outside in half an hour, and I headed through the enormous double doors that led inside the cathedral.

★ ★ ★

Cathedrals were hit-and-miss for me as an agnostic man who had never been surrounded by any kind of major religious influence aside from primary school hymns and 'Judas' by Lady Gaga. Sometimes, I would walk in, look around, try and fail to take a decent picture of a stained-glass window, and then walk out. Occasionally, though, I would walk into one that would make the hairs on my arms stand on end and fill me with so much awe that it would bring tears to my eyes – and every golden memory I'd shared with those I'd loved and lost would come drifting back. Seville Cathedral was the latter. It was an enormous structure; the light from the stained-glass windows cast an orange glow and bathed the statues of unknown religious figures in an amber hue. A priest stood at the top at a lectern, shuffling papers and preparing for his next service. As I walked, mouth ajar, taking in the sparsely dotted worshippers who sat praying on pews and the soft sound of quiet choral music coming from an antechamber, I felt the presence of my own nan's hand on my shoulder, comforting me. I closed my eyes for a moment, and the barrier of time felt paper-thin, as though I could turn around and she'd be there – opening the kitchen door to come in and plant a kiss on my forehead and ask me about my day. For a moment, she felt so close, as though all of the memories in my life weren't structured in a straight line, rigid and immovable, but rather were all happening at once and hadn't ended but lived on, in tandem, glistening and infinite. I didn't believe in a Christian god. No god worth worshipping would've made me gay and then punished me for it (what a waste of time and effort, especially when you only have seven days to create all of existence). But there was something about being in a cathedral, a place that had housed the emotions of thousands of people over hundreds of years, that held memories of joyous weddings and the heartache of funerals, that made me feel connected to myself and my past. I reached the end of the cathedral and turned left to a large wooden structure where candles could be placed and lit to remember those who had passed. There were only four or five candles lit, and it made me realise that, for a Saturday morning, the cathedral was relatively empty. I popped a euro into the donation box, understanding that a god worth worshipping would be pro-capitalism, and lit a candle. I stood in silence, taking another left down Memory Lane, lost in the adventures of my childhood and swimming in a pervasive sense of gratitude. How lucky was I to have had such amazing grandparents and, at my age, how lucky was I that they were the only people who I'd lost? Someone walked past me to place a candle in one of the wooden holes. Even through the haze of my nostalgia, his scent pierced. He smelled amazing. Different, but also familiar. I looked him up and down. Dressed again in all black, tall and skinny. It was the Spanish man from Terminal 3. I couldn't believe it. What were the chances? Miraculous, some might say. I didn't even notice him on our flight – surely Evie or Tasha would've mentioned if they did? Not that it mattered anyway; he was a stranger. For all I knew, he could've been straight. Or gay, but think that I was a gangly pale minger. The area with the candles was slightly sequestered from the main hall of the cathedral, and there was no one else around, meaning that I could potentially talk to him. That was out of the question, surely? This was a sacred place. He could be mourning. Maybe he'd be getting the same flight back as me? Although he was Spanish, so perhaps he'd flown home, never to return to our TotallyNormalIsland™. This was ridiculous. First, my pathetic situationship with the faceless 'DiscreetHung', and now my maladaptive daydreaming about a man I barely knew while trying to pay tribute to my beloved grandmother. I'd been single for less than a year and was regressing to my seventeen-year-old self. I felt pathetic. And suffocated. And scared to meet those incredible eyes again and have him see me in my state of weaselly hopefulness. I needed to leave. Church clearly didn't agree with me. Except, I'd placed my backpack underneath the candle structure when I'd lit mine earlier. I'd have to move past him to get the bag. I stepped forward and bent down to grab the backpack, trying to be subtle so as not to draw his attention. It worked, but as I straightened back up, backpack in hand, he, having not noticed me in my artful stealthiness, leaned forward to place his candle in one of the holders. We met somewhere in the middle and crashed to the floor, his candle and my backpack toppling with us, the Chilly's water bottle in the bottom corner sending a 'CLANG' reverberating around the hallowed halls for everyone to hear.

'Mierda. Lo siento! Lo siento mucho. Ha sido mi culpa. Estas bien?'

'SHIT. I'm so sorry. That was me. I'm a ridiculous oaf. I'm sorry, are you okay?'

We spoke at once, our words, like our bodies, crashing together. I grabbed my backpack and returned the candle; the flame snuffed in the fall.

'Here. I really am sorry. I don't know if you speak English. I don't speak Spanish, but . . . Sorry. Sorero? Sonoro? Sorry,' I spluttered, avoiding his gaze because I was too scared to look in those eyes again and concerned that I might've just been racist.

'Wait,' he said as I turned to leave. His voice was soft but commanding. 'You were at the airport. I saw you.' I looked up to meet his gaze for the first time, and my legs suddenly felt as if they weren't strong enough to support my torso. He smiled, all crooked teeth behind full lips and unkempt stubble.

'Airport?' I asked, trying to play it cool but instead sounding like a toddler who had just learnt a new word. 'The . . . oh yeah, the airport. Yesterday! I saw you, too. At the bar,' I managed. God, those eyes. Like melted copper, swimming in suspension somewhere between a liquid and a solid and heaven. Those lashes, too. He was so handsome but so pretty, like God had chosen the best facial features from both sexes, smashed them together and placed them on top of a skinny stick figure.

'Do you mind?' He gestured towards the candle. 'One moment, please.'

He turned around to light the candle again, placing it gingerly in one of the holders. As he faced away, I took advantage of being out of his line of sight and reached into my pocket for Vaseline. I hastily applied it to my lips, which felt dry with anxiety after the whole exchange, and pocketed the little tin again before he turned around.

'So, what are you doing in Seville?' he asked, frowning slightly as he glanced down at my lips. Shit. Overapplication of Vaseline. Probably looked like I'd just been drooling. I don't know whether it was the effort he was taking to speak at a respectful volume in the cathedral, but his voice was such a seductive, gentle rumble. I made the same effort but knew I'd still sound like a shrill foghorn.

'Just here for the weekend! With friends,' I said, trying to subtly wipe the Vaseline from my chin.

'The friends from the airport? I remember. You were making them laugh.'

'Yes. Those,' I said, revelling in the realisation that he'd also taken something away from our airport connection.

'How do you like the city so far?'

'I love it. It's beautiful. And SO hot.' I laughed.

'Sí, mucho calor.'

All my newfound confidence crashed to the floor with the candle earlier. He was a skinny stallion, and I was the guy at the front of the class from *Mean Girls* who 'farts a lot'. I had the personality of a jacket potato. I didn't know what to say or do; I wanted to get out, but I also wanted nothing more than to hear him relay every detail of his life so far in those dulcet tones.

'Are you from Seville?' I assumptively asked. Potentially racist again.

'Andalusia, yes. Seville, no. I'm from a town that is much smaller.'

'Me too,' was all that I could muster. I needed air. 'My friends are waiting outside. I should probably get going.'

'What's your name?'

'Gabriel. Gabe. What's yours?'

'Nicolas. It's nice to meet you. This may not be appropriate in a place like this.' He looked around with a smile. My heart leapt. 'But maybe I could get your number? I know Seville well, if you wanted to go somewhere . . . how to say it in English, "mas escondido" erm . . . off the road? Off the road well walked?' He frowned in concentration. He was adorable.

'Off the beaten track?' I offered.

'Sí! Yes. Off the beaten track. Beaten. I don't know this word. Excuse me, you must think I am stupid.'

'Absolutely not. You should hear my Spanish. In fact, I think you did before.' I laughed, feeling my face flush.

'Ah yes – sonoro. That means sound. You meant siento. And it's okay, don't worry about it.'

'Yes, you can have my number.' I inputted it into his phone and turned to leave, awkwardly waving, hoisting my backpack over my shoulders, eager to return to the girls and tell them about my miraculous encounter.

★ ★ ★

'It must've been the spirit of Granny Mavis, Gabe,' said Evie after dinner. We'd filled our afternoon with more sightseeing, strolling around the Parque de María Luisa in the afternoon before having a few sangrias outside the Plaza de España. The heat hadn't relented, but, as we'd reached 9 p.m., the air was breathable at least. The sun was low in the sky, and we had just finished an incredible tapas banquet.

'How do you mean?' I said, finishing the last mouthful of salmorejo.

'It's too much of a coincidence. Granny Mavis loved men. Her spirit must have sent that boy to you in the cathedral.'

'How pissed are you, Evie?' I laughed.

'Steaming.' She burped.

'Same.' I was. We all were. We'd been drinking for about five hours intermittently.

'You're going to marry him,' Evie said.

'Evie. I've literally met the guy once. We know nothing about him. He could be a narcissist. Or a murderer. Or an astrology person,' I said, horrified at the thought.

'Or worse – A TAURUS!' Tasha gasped.

'Shut up, guys. You two just don't get it.' Evie rolled her eyes, scowling. She had an almost Angelenos infatuation with horoscopes. 'But you could end up marrying him, Gabe. From what I've heard anyway. It sounds like love at first sight.'

'I think we all know who will get married first out of us three,' I said, raising my eyebrows in Tasha's direction.

'Get fucked. Really? You think I'm most likely to jump headfirst into the world's biggest PDA, sponsored by Christianity?' Tasha laughed. Her ice-blonde hair shimmered against the unusually twee floral dress she wore for the evening's meal. I remembered my conversation with Evie on the terrace and decided to take this as my opportunity to silence the imaginary courtroom.

'That aside, how is stuff with Scott, Tash? I don't see him much in the office. Our work-from-home calendars are opposite,' I said.

Tasha looked me in the eyes as if searching for an ulterior motive. 'Not great, to be honest, gayboy[39],' she conceded, finding none.

'Why, what's up?' I dared.

---

[39] Tasha would often playfully insult me after showing any sign of vulnerability in order to offset the potential for her to sound earnestly emotional about anything

To my surprise, she proceeded to launch into a ten-minute monologue, peppered with an uncharacteristic amount of 'do you know what I mean?'s. According to Tasha, Scott had been distant from her, disconnected during their time together, and keen to get out of the house whenever he could. She reassured us that she thought a relationship should be the coming together of two independent adults who build a life together but still have one apart, but said that she felt as if Scott now only wants to spend his free time with his mates or his colleagues. Their sex life had become non-existent, which he blamed on stress from work, but she was worried something else was afoot.

'In hindsight, did you notice anything with Seamus, Gabe? Any signs that he might have been, you know . . . cheating?' Tasha asked. She looked crestfallen, as though saying it out loud confirmed suspicions that had been swirling in her head for weeks.

'Yeah, of course. But Tasha, we were nothing like you two. The more I look back at our relationship, the more I doubt whether we ever even loved each other. I'm not sure whether it was circumstantial. Two lonely, damaged people with enough in common to make a united front. I don't know. But no way, Scott. He's not the type. Plus, everyone at work respects him. And you.' It was true. There were people around the office with a reputation for a wandering eye at work socials or a wandering dick at Christmas parties, but Scott wasn't one of them.

'I've got a surprise for everybody,' Evie announced with a devilish glint in her eye.

'What is it?' asked Tasha nervously.

Evie reached into her handbag and pulled out a small cube of tin foil. 'A little cake!' She unwrapped the foil and revealed a home-baked brownie.

'Is that a . . . space cake, Evie? Did you smuggle a cannabis-laced brownie through Manchester Airport?' I asked.

'Oh, it's only tiny! I wrapped it tight. That's why I was so nervous when you were rooting through my bag at customs, Tasha!' She laughed.

'Evie . . . you're insane. You're actually insane. What would you have done if you'd gotten caught? You're a school-teacher!' said Tasha, but I could tell she was impressed.

'Anyway . . . shall we? Come on, it'll be like old times. Let's split it. It's only small!' Evie smiled. We all used to enjoy weed together regularly at uni, but Evie was the only one who had held on to the habit.

'I will if Tasha does.'

Tasha looked at me, then back to Evie. 'Fine. Fuck it, we're on holiday.'

Evie wasted no time, grabbed a butter knife and split the brownie into three pieces.

'Bottoms up!' she said, and we all ate our third. She moved to put her handbag back under the table.

'Guys. SHIT, I've just realised. I left my purse on the bar on the terrace where we were just sitting. Be right back!' Evie stumbled out of her chair. She was wearing a low-cut embroidered top, and as she jumped up, a crescent of areola became visible to us and the giggling couple at the neighbouring table.

'Evie, NIPPLE!' Tasha shouted. I had assumed there was some kind of subtle code word for this kind of happenstance, but apparently not. Evie sheathed her tit. 'Should we come with you? Are you sure you're alright to go grab it alone?'

'It's a two-minute walk, I'm fine. It won't kick in until I'm back. You guys sort the bill, and I'll transfer you after! WHEN WE GET SPACEY!' she shouted, waltzing off from the table in a swirl.

'She'll be fine. Won't she? It's fine. It's still light out.' Tasha seemed to be wrestling with the moral implications of having allowed Evie's solo mission to go ahead. 'Anyway, thanks, Gabe. So you've not noticed anything weird? In fact . . .' Tasha started. Clearly, wanting to continue the conversation won the bout over defending Evie from daylight robbery.

'Do you like Scott, Gabe?' she continued, with an earnestness that could only have been made possible by the CannaBrownie. 'I feel like you don't. It doesn't matter if you don't. I didn't like Seamus. I don't like most people. But I do want to know why. If, you know, you don't.'

I considered lying before quickly realising that I'd been doing that for the last year. The thought of telling the truth scared me. There was still a splinter of mistrust for Tasha after the Buffalo Sauce incident. What if that's what Scott had wanted all along? Did he know I didn't like him? Did he know how much the opinions of Tasha's friends meant to her? Was that why he did it? It would make sense, considering how forced his kindness seemed around us. I felt torn. Hiding my feelings due to fear of overstepping, or meddling, or any kind of negative consequence, had got me to a point where there was a weird underlying friction with my best friend. I'd changed my perspective on Evie and Dan, and it had felt good; perhaps it was time to switch directions here, too[40]. My heart was racing, and my head felt bizarrely heavy[41], but I decided to be honest.

'Not really, Tash. I don't know. He got me this job, which obviously I'm grateful for. And I like that he *seems* to make you happy. But sometimes I wonder whether he does . . . make you happy . . . or if the idea of him makes you happy, and in practice, he actually makes you angry. Or sad. I don't know. It's not my business,' I finished.

'When has that ever stopped you before?' she said with a smirk.

'True,' I said.

'So go on. Let it out. You've *obviously* been waiting for this.'

'Well, he doesn't make you properly laugh. He doesn't laugh at your jokes – and you're fucking hilarious. He's arrogant. He doesn't make any effort with any of us, not really. He's good at the niceties . . . but I'm not sure if he likes me, to be honest, never mind me liking him,' I said with reckless abandon, wondering if the brownie had kicked in already. It had tasted potent.

---

[40] Social Darwinism in action!

[41] Cannabis brownie starting to *take* action!

'Neither am I,' said Tasha. 'But you are well annoying.'

Then, she walked from her seat to where I was sitting and bundled me in a bear hug. This was a rarity from Tasha; it was quick and stiff, but it conveyed how much our conversation meant to her.

'Good job there's no cream carpets nearby.' I laughed into the warmth of her shoulder. She sat in the chair beside me where Evie had been before leaving to retrieve her purse. I looked into her eyes, which looked suddenly sleepy and bloodshot, and I posited that a lot of the reasons for me disliking Scott might also have been due to me feeling possessive over Tasha. So, I apologised for being a shitty best friend.

'Thank you for being honest. I get what you're saying. But he is good to me, Gabe,' Tasha said, turning red at her own honesty. 'He's self-sufficient, and intelligent, and he can be thoughtful. He's a good cook. He makes good money, he's ambitious. He has his faults, a lot of them, and they're weighing us down at the moment, but I do want to make it work. That would be a lot easier if I had your support, which for some insane reason means a lot to me.'

'That makes sense. It does. If that's what you want, I won't stand in your way, obviously. You know I only want what's best for you, don't you?'

'You want what's best for me, but also someone fun for you,' she said.

'Fine. True. But you know what I mean.' We hugged again, and a thought sprung to my mind: the night when we'd knocked the buffalo sauce over onto the carpet, and what Scott had said to me after the fact.

'Actually, Tash, before we bury this. Do you remember that night at yours earlier in the year, just before I got the job at EnsureInsure?'

'Of course! After your date with the chef?'

'Yeah, that night,' I said.

'Yeah! The night when we dyed Scott's carpet orange?' She laughed. I knew by her nonchalant reaction that the suspicions I'd had at the time were about to be confirmed.

'Yeah. Well. Scott said something strange to me later that week after I'd got the job. He said that you'd been upset about it, that I'd lunged at you. Basically, that I'd been violent and I'd scared you.' I chose to leave out the part where he'd been casually homophobic. I'd agreed to have a fresh start, and all I truly cared about at this point were Tasha's feelings.

'What the fuck? Are you serious?' Tasha asked.

'Deadly. So you didn't say that? Or insinuate it?'

'Not even slightly. I'm baffled.'

'So was I.' I laughed. There was no doubt about it at this point: the edges of my vision were blurry, and I was constantly suppressing the urge to laugh or speak in a strange accent, even though the subject matter was serious. The space cake was doing its job.

'Why didn't you say anything at the time?' Tasha asked.

'I don't know, it was awkward. And I'd just got the job. I didn't want to wade into your relationship or anything. I never wanted you to know I didn't like Scott, so I guess I just—'

'Gabe.' Tasha interrupted me, her face suddenly horror-stricken.

'What?'

'Where's Evie?!' she said, frenzied as she leapt to her feet. I looked at the time. We'd been so engrossed in our conversation and steadily slipping into a dark green haze that neither of us had noticed. It was 10:14 p.m., and she'd left her iPhone on the table when she'd gone to collect her missing purse over half an hour ago.

'Shit. SHIT. Gabe. Pay the bill. We need to go. NOW.'

The urgency in Tasha's tone didn't match the smile that had appeared on her face and that I felt spreading on my own. This was no time for frivolity, but just as we both realised that Evie had gone missing, the colours around us began to pop, our vision distorted, and it was clear that the full effects of the space cake had kicked in.

★ ★ ★

THE DISAPPEARANCE OF EVIE MORRALL

The two friends sprinted from their table, leaving a wad of euros pinned under an ashtray to pay for their meal. As they reached the street outside the restaurant, they subsided into laughter.

Tasha: Your eyes are red. You look like a mole.

Gabriel: You look so dry. You're like the crisps from the table earlier. Remember the ones in a bowl? Like they were tapas . . . that's . . . so . . . silly . . .

They propped each other up for support as their bodies shook with uncontrollable giggles.

Tasha: Wait. Gabriel. Seriously. This is serious. We have to find Evie, she could be in trouble.

Gabriel: Oh, is it! It is very serious, isn't it, Sergeant?

The streets shifted, colours bounced, and edges blurred – but through this, their joint mission became clear. By day, they were Gabriel Lanes and Natasha Campbell, but in the wake of the sudden and horrifying Disappearance of Evie Morrall and the ingestion of a cannabis brownie, they became Inspector Lanes and DCI Campbell – two fully trained crime-fighting professionals, seasoned in locating missing people.

Inspector Lanes: What on earth do we do, DCI Campbell?

DCI Campbell: Elementary, my dear Gabriel. We retrace Evie's steps. First to La Terrazza Del Eme, that's where the missing person left her purse!

Inspector Lanes: Okay, can you map it? I've not got much charge.

DCI Campbell: No, cartography remains your responsibility, Inspector. Lead the way.

Inspector Lanes: Seriously, Tash, I'm on nine per cent battery.

DCI Campbell: For god's sake. Okay, fine, follow me

LOCATION ONE: *LA TERRAZZA DEL EME*

The detectives arrived back at the rooftop bar around three hours after they had last paid an exorbitant amount for a watered-down cocktail there. The views of the cathedral were even more stunning by twilight, and they stopped, arm in arm, to drink them in before realising that they had more pressing matters to attend to. They headed to the bar and spotted their server from earlier in the evening.

Inspector Lanes: Excuse me – sir? Señor?
Disgruntled Bartender 1: Hola. ¿Cómo puedo ayudarle?
Inspector Lanes: Hi. Erm. No comprende.
DCI Campbell: Hola, *Disgruntled Bartender 1*. DCI Campbell.

She put out a hand for him to shake, but he ignored it.

DCI Campbell: As you were, señor. We're looking for this woman; it's a matter of state urgency, and you'd do well to comply.

She held up her phone to show a picture of Evie.

Disgruntled Bartender 1: Ah, sí. La pelirroja tetona. Vino a buscar su bolso y se fue con dos chicas. Parecía borracha, pero es inglesa, ¿qué le vamos a hacer?

The two friends looked back and forth at each other, nonplussed.

Obnoxiously Loud American Diner 1: Hello! Well, I'll be – do neither of you speak Spanish?
Inspector Lanes and DCI Campbell: NO.
Obnoxiously Loud American Diner 1: Estos ingleses, ¿verdad?

Disgruntled Bartender 1 started laughing and nodded, walking away to collect some empty wine glasses.

Obnoxiously Loud American Diner 1: My friend here said that the girl you're looking for came by earlier to collect her purse. She left with a couple other girls she met at the bar. What brings you two to sunny Seville? You're both European, right?

Inspector Lanes: Thanks very much. Do you have any idea where they went?

Obnoxiously Loud American Diner 1: Search me. That's all he said, kid.

DCI Campbell: God dammit, man – go and ask him for us, if you don't want to find yourself blacklisted from British Airways or worse . . .

Inspector Lanes: Please! She meant please.

The Obnoxiously Loud American Diner got up from his chair, shooting them both a disdainful look before walking over to consult with Disgruntled Bartender 1.

Disgruntled Bartender 2: Would you two like a drink?

The detectives looked at each other.

Inspector Lanes: We're on the job, but . . .
DCI Campbell: Two tequilas, please.

By the time they'd finished their shots, The Obnoxiously Loud American Diner had returned.

Obnoxiously Loud American Diner 1: They went to the bodega at the top of the street. One of them needed to grab a vape. I don't think they're the only two who have been smoking something tonight, judging by the look of y'all!

Inspector Lanes: Thank you, Obnoxiously Loud American Diner.

Obnoxiously Loud American Diner 2: Don't speak to my husband like that!

Inspector Lanes: Let's go, Tash. We have our first clue.

The two detectives ran from the bar holding hands, one step closer to solving the case of The Disappearance of Evie Morrall.

LOCATION TWO: TIENDA DE TABACO

The 'Tienda De Tabaco', aka the shop at the top of the street that had housed the missing Evie at some point this evening, stayed open late – meaning it was rammed with locals and tourists alike. The two detectives burst through the door.

DCI Campbell: FREEZE! POLICE!

The shoppers looked up for a moment, then returned to their browsing.

DCI Campbell: No respect for the law in this place, Lanes. All the more reason for us to get Evie home and safe.
Inspector Lanes: Yeah, what do you think happened in the last bar? Who are the other girls?
DCI Campbell: Suspects.
Inspector Lanes: Seriously, Tash.
DCI Campbell: Are you questioning me? ANYONE could be a suspect, Lanes, in fact . . . where were you the moment Evie Morrall disappeared?
Inspector Lanes: I was literally sat opposite you, you absolute freak
DCI Campbell: A likely story!
Inspector Lanes: Let's chat to the shopkeeper.
Cheerful Shopkeeper: Hola! Lots of English people tonight. What can I do for you?
Inspector Lanes: Lovely to meet you! Wow – seven euros for twenty Marlboro Gold? Can I get two packs and a ligh—
DCI Campbell: LANES!
Inspector Lanes: Sorry.
DCI Campbell: We're investigating a missing person's case. Have you seen this girl?

DCI Campbell held up her phone to show the shopkeeper a picture of Evie.

Cheerful Shopkeeper: Ah, yes. Beautiful girl. Huge . . . never mind. She was in earlier with two others. I think she'd had too much to drink. Same story with every English.
Inspector Lanes: Did she seem safe?

The shopkeeper laughed.

Cheerful Shopkeeper: Yes, of course! She was with friends. I know the girls that she's with. They both speak English. They're local girls. Lovely.

The two detectives breathed a sigh of relief.

DCI Campbell: We know they came in here to buy a vape . . . do you have any idea where they went?
Cheerful Shopkeeper: That's not all they bought! Yes, I know where they went. But there is a queue, and you two have not bought anything yet.
DCI Campbell: Reveal your information or face the full force of the British Constabulary.
Cheerful Shopkeeper: You two are not police. You are tourists. What are you talking about? What is going on?
Inspector Lanes: I honestly have no idea at this point.
DCI Campbell: If he buys those cigs, will you tell us?
Cheerful Shopkeeper: How many packs did you say, chaval?
Inspector Lanes: Two. Please. Por Favor.
Cheerful Shopkeeper: Just two, for all this help?

He grinned.

Inspector Lanes: Fine, three. Four, actually. I'll take some back with me. Make it five. I'll take some for my brother, too. Actually, I'm craving sweets. Tash, are you craving sweets, too? Also, my mouth is . . . so dry . . .

DCI Campbell nodded and ambled to the sweet aisle to fetch them both some Haribo Peaches and two litres of water.

The shopkeeper rummaged behind him before producing five packs of Marlboro Gold and placing them in Gabriel's hands. He pointed at a stand to the left of the queue, piled high with plastic red roses. A sign above it read: FLAMENCO ROSES – BUY FOR SHOW.

Cheerful Shopkeeper: That's what they all bought.

LOCATION THREE: CANTINA DE FLAMENCO

The flamenco bar consisted of several tiny but huddled tables facing a small, shiny stage at the back end where the dancing occurred. As the two detectives shuffled towards the bar, the lights dimmed further, and the barwoman signalled that the performance was about to begin. The air was thick with heat and a sense of anticipation; the flamenco was a revered tradition in Spain, and the dancers in Seville were known as some of the best in the country.

DCI Campbell: Excuse me, have you seen this girl?

The barwoman pointed to the table closest to the little stage. There, front and centre, was the back of Evie's head. She had a plastic rose nestled in her auburn hair, as she sat intently next to her two new Spanish friends.

SUSPECT LOCATED. MISSING PERSON'S CASE CLOSED.

'Should we shout to her?' I asked, barely holding back laughter. All the colour had returned to Tasha's face as she smiled with relief. The high-vis jacket that she would've sworn I was wearing only moments ago had faded away.

'No. We've found her. Let's get her after the show; for now, let's just find a seat – my legs are like jelly.' Tasha smiled. We carried our jelly legs to a pair of empty chairs near the back of the audience and waited for the show to start. The delicate prang of a guitar indicated that the dance had begun. I felt the vibrations of each note like wobbling tentacles tickling my skin. The space-cake-trip may have ended, but my senses were still wonderfully warped. A beautiful woman, hair tied into a slick brown side bun, walked onto the stage to whoops and 'ah's from the crowd.

'She's copied your hairstyle,' I whispered to Tasha, who accidentally spat out some of her water.

The woman twirled to the music, clicking her castanets and singing in a heavenly voice. I felt every note transport me across a timeline of Spanish history – I was floating above the Barcelona coast, over the terracotta roofs of Marbella, skipping down whitewashed Andalucian streets. I witnessed a thousand Spanish love stories across five minutes. The woman exited the stage with her first performance finished, and a man took to the centre. His sleeves were puffy, coloured crimson and gold to match his country's flag. I might've said he was the most beautiful man I'd ever seen, but no one could take that accolade from Nicolas. He bowed to the crowd, extending an arm outwards, and then – the unthinkable happened. Another arm extended upwards from one of the front tables and grabbed the dancer's, hoisting her body onto the stage. Evie stood proudly in front of the crowd as though she was a scheduled performer. There was a moment's hesitation before the bailador[42] smiled and lifted Evie's hand into the air as if she were a seasoned bailadora[43]. The audience clapped, but even in my cannabis-infused state, I knew that she'd shattered the illusion. The male dancer was pristine, and Evie looked like she'd spent an hour with Diana Vickers's hairdresser. Her auburn locks were static and looked backcombed, and her skin was pink and heat-blotched. Her crop top, which had accidentally exposed part of her areola at dinner earlier,

---

[42] The Spanish word for a male flamenco dancer

[43] The Spanish word for a female flamenco dancer

was perilously low again, her sizeable breasts glowing under the glare of the spotlight.

'Now, we dance!' exclaimed the bailador in a delicious accent before taking both of Evie's hands and assuming the position. The audience applauded, laughing and clapping at the scene unfolding before them. Tasha turned to me, tears streaming from her eyes in hysterics.

'What is happening?' I gasped, holding my sides to stop them from splitting. We had a clear view of Evie's face; she looked delighted – proud of herself, even, as though she'd been waiting her entire life for this debut. The music started. Slow at first, the bailador all but carried Evie across the stage. His skill made her look competent, majestic, even. By the grace of an unknown deity – or secret after-school lessons that neither of us knew about – Evie managed to keep step. The speed of the music increased, and the two glided back and forth to rapturous reactions from the audience. I turned to Tasha, who couldn't breathe for laughing.

'Is that your friend? She's very talented!' an elderly woman said from the table next to me. The dance went on, and Evie spotted me in the crowd. I waved, and she blew a kiss back – to more shrieks of approval from the audience. As the music built to a thundering crescendo, the audience clapped along on beat, and Tasha crossed her legs so as not to wet herself. For the finale, the bailador took Evie's waist and, for the last beat of the song, thrust her backwards so her back was arched and her body was parallel to the floor. Evie extended her arm, and with an almightly wobble, both of her breasts fell out of the confines of her crop top. The crowd held its breath, and Evie was frozen in position like a graceful Pornhub swan. Suspended in mid-air, she was held in situ by the dancer as her naked tits took centre stage, one nipple pointing northward and the other in direct eye contact with the first row of the audience. I turned to see the elderly woman doing the sign of the cross. Evie broke free of the position and, still not realising what had occurred, bowed to the crowd, both breasts hanging, to wink at the front row.

'Gabe. Gabe. I've weed. I've wet myself. We need to go,' said Tasha, with tears streaming down her face and a small puddle of urine underneath her seat.

The crowd were gasping and shouting aggressively for Evie to cover 'Las tetas!' 'Guarra!'

But Evie didn't realise. She continued to stand and wave, a vacant expression on her stoned face as her British boobs sat proud and glowing in front of the mortified onlookers. I rushed forward to the stage, plucked her from the arms of the bailador, and ran for the exit.

'Adios! Adios, my beautiful fans!' shouted Evie as Tasha tucked her bust back into her crop top and away from the eyes of the Spanish public.

13

Complex on the Beach

'Morning, tiny dancer!' I whispered, braving the stench in Evie's room to bring her a fresh glass of iced water. 'How're you feeling today?' I asked as I perched on the side of the bed. The room, which was pristine only two days ago, was now a mosaic of bras, shoes, and toiletries. It smelled somewhere between an aged Jo Malone perfume and raw onions.

'Eugh, hiii,' Evie mumbled into her pillow. Her auburn hair was parted into three matted tufts, the plastic corner-shop rose tangled somewhere within one, and last night's makeup was bruised across her face. 'Not good. I'm sorry, Gabe. Was it awful? I don't remember anything.'

'Nah, it was just funny. You were just funny,' I half-lied, remembering Evie's double Ds centre stage.

'Are you sure?' she asked, leaning up to glug the entire glass of water in one.

'Yeah. You scared the shit out of us, though. You disappeared. It was lucky that we found you.'

'I'm so sorry. How did you find me?'

'WELL . . .' I began before unpacking Inspector Lanes's and DCI Campbell's case as Evie listened intently.

'That's amazing. It's a bit like Hansel and Gretel!' exclaimed Evie.

'Well . . . maybe, but instead of following breadcrumbs, we were interviewing strangers while we were tripping balls, and instead of ending up in a gingerbread house, we were led to a flamenco bar. Apart from that, it's dead similar.'

'Flamenco bar?' Evie asked, confused. She really had been black-out. She was still fragile, so the full tale would have to wait for when her serotonin levels had returned to normal.

'It doesn't matter. Shall we watch a Superbowl performance? Tasha has gone out to get breakfast,'

'YES! Madonna, please. Then old *X-Factor* auditions,' Evie suggested excitedly. 'And Gabe?'

'Yes?'

'Do you still love me?' she asked pathetically, jutting out her bottom lip. I crawled into bed next to her and grabbed the iPad.

'How else could I put up with your breath right now?' I replied.

We watched two Superbowl half-time performances on YouTube before our attention waned and we switched to chatting. Evie maligned her inability to 'just have a few drinks and be sensible', and I reassured her that it was part of being in her twenties, English, and on holiday. She made the solemn oath (for the seventeenth time) that she would never drink again. I suggested that mixing the alcohol with a space cake was the main culprit for her misdemeanours. Then, I relayed my conversation with Tasha, how we'd cleared the air, and we both discussed Tasha's worries: that Scott was distant, whether we thought the relationship would last and whether she even wanted it to. We spoke briefly about Tasha's suspicion that he was cheating, and both agreed that he wasn't.

'On the subject of ending relationships . . .' I started, deciding to tell Evie about my situation with DiscreetHung.

'God, Gabe. I didn't realise this still happened at our age,' Evie said, having now recuperated somewhat and put on clothes.

'People stay in the closet into their fifties. Sometimes, their whole life. They have kids and everything. It's a scary thing to do, coming out.'

'So what're you going to do?'

'End it, obviously. It's not even a thing, anyway. We've just been exchanging nudes, but I think he's starting to like me, and I've been through all that already. The self-hatred, the questioning what moves to make so that no one realises I'm gay, the hiding on Grindr. It's not a place I want to go back to.' I sighed.

'Aren't you still hiding on Grindr?' Evie said.

'No. Well, yes. But only from DiscreetHung. So it's fair.'

'Do you like him, even though you've never met him?' she asked, with as much judgement as I'd expect from Evie – absolutely none.

'I don't think so, no. He's sweet. I think I feel sorrier for him than anything. We don't know anything real about each other, not properly. And I've still not seen his face. I can't see him ever getting to a point where we'd have anything fulfilling, so...' I finished, leaving the thought hanging. I wasn't sure whether it was the in-depth conversations with my friends about their relationships, the feeling I got when I saw Nicolas, or the hypnotic powers of Evie's pendulous tits – but I'd broken out of whatever DiscreetHung trance I was in. I didn't want to be somebody's secret. I'd done too much to process and move past any shame attached to my sexuality to regress into an undercover tryst. Whatever internal romanticisation I'd had had evaporated into the muggy Seville air.

'Makes sense, Gabe. I think you're right, and it's time to end it. Besides, you've got a new boy now, what's his name again? Enrique?' asked Evie, inadvertently joining the potentially racist club.

'You're right. No, it's Nicolas,' I said before my phone started ringing next to me.

'Wow, what the . . . Evie – it's him. It's Nicolas,' I said, my mouth dropping open.

'OH MY GOD!' Evie screamed. 'Gabe. Oh my god. He's the one. That timing, GABE, ANSWER—'

'I WILL IF YOU SHUT THE FUCK UP – Hello?' I said.

'Hi, is this Gabriel?'

'Yes, hi Nicolas, how are you?' I said, my voice breaking on the 'hi' like I'd just begun puberty. Evie clasped her hands to her mouth to stifle a laugh. She mouthed the word 'speaker' twice until I switched the call to speakerphone so she could listen.

'I am great! What did you get up to last night?' he asked. I told him about the tapas we'd had, and he told me it was a great choice and one of his favourite places to eat in the city.

'Listen, I haven't got long because I will pick up my friend. We are going to the beach today. I have room in my car for three of you. Would you and your friends like to come?' he asked. Before I could sit with the thought of going on a first date surrounded by my mates, and even more nerve-wracking, going on a first date in swimwear, Evie burst into a 'Yes!!!'

And the plan was made.

★ ★ ★

Tasha arrived with a bundle of freshly baked bread, eggs, jamon, and tomato conserve but was perturbed when we informed her that we had an hour to prepare it, eat it, and get ready before heading to an unknown beach with two Spanish strangers.

'There *must* be more than this provincial life.' She sighed as she placed her basket down on the Airbnb countertop.

'You pissed yourself last night, Belle. Hardly provincial.' I laughed.

'Less of that, Inspector,' Tasha said with a wink. 'I'm excited to meet Nicolas!'

Luckily, our conversation at dinner had obviously changed Tasha's attitude towards me.

'Weird that we'll be getting to know him at the same time as you, Gabe,' she said as she hastily packed a beach bag.

'I know. And his mate. Anyway, shut up. I can't dwell on it, or I'll get panicky. Right, which pair, guys?' I showed them the first of two sets of swimming shorts, a bright red pair I'd rush-purchased from Asos.

'Not those. Too Mowgli,' Tasha said. She was right. I pulled down the swimming shorts.

'Gabe, what the hell!' Tasha shouted.

'GABE!' Evie joined in.

'What?' I asked, naked and confused.

'Oh, nothing; please, by all means, insert your penis into our eyes,' Tasha scoffed. I burst out laughing, suddenly remembering that we hadn't been in a situation for years where they might've seen me fully naked.

'Oh, I'm sorry, ladies – are we now being modest after Evie's display last night? Tits Akimbo can turn her areolas into Beyblades, but I can't *accidentally* get my dick out in the privacy of our own home?'

'Tits Akimbo? I don't get it,' said Evie.

'It looks a bit bigger than I remember,' said Tasha.

'Thanks for the boost. I needed that today.' I pulled on the second pair of swimming shorts (powder-blue Calvin Klein) to murmurs of approval. I threw on a light viscose shirt from Red Cow Vintage, Evie necked a pint of water with two paracetamols, and Tasha did a roll call of all the things we'd need for the beach:

> 'Towel?' – *'Got three!'*
> 'Sun cream?' – *'In my bag!'*
> 'Water?' – *'Evie, refill the big bottles!'*
> 'Football or tennis rackets, maybe?' – *'Huh?'*

Nicolas and his friend Pepe were sat outside our Airbnb, waiting in an old green Ford Fiesta.

'Hola!' they shouted, waving excitedly in unison. Pepe, it turned out, was also gay, and also attractive, but in a completely different way. Nicolas had an unconventional, almost androgynous beauty, while Pepe looked like a model from a 2009 Next catalogue – tall, defined biceps, a swooping fringe and a grill to kill for. I also realised, as we were crammed into their backseat in thirty-seven-degree heat with only the feeble gasps of a dying air conditioning unit for support, that they had opposing personalities, too. Pepe was loud and cheeky. His English wasn't as good as Nicolas's, but he spoke a lot more, even though he was the designated driver, offering jokes and sarcasm and laughing loudly at Evie's music choices. Nicolas was more reserved but attentive whenever I spoke, laughing at all my jokes and often catching my eye in the rear-view mirror. The ninety-minute car journey to Matalascanas flew by.

I learnt that Nicolas was from a small town an hour from Seville, still in the province of Andalucia. He was twenty-nine and had moved to Manchester a couple of years ago because the economic situation in Spain was 'mierda'. My heart leapt when he revealed that he was living in Manchester and was only home visiting his friends and family over the summer holidays. I swooned when he disclosed that he'd read Spanish Literature at university (the same degree as me, just a different language), and Evie was ecstatic to hear the news that he was a teacher by trade. They exchanged stories about their best and worst classroom experiences while Pepe, Tasha and I taught one another swear words in our respective languages[44]. Nicolas had brought lunch for us all, comprising of homemade tortilla wedged between two slices of crusty bread, with extra virgin olive oil, mayo, and salt and pepper. The car was filled with sounds of awe as we ate.

'Did you make that? The sandwich?' I asked Nicolas as we stepped out of the car and started unloading, ready to add 'excellent cook' to the growing list of his green flags.

'No, my father. He's a great cook but is . . . what's the word . . . reacio . . . reluctive?'

'Reluctant!' I offered. This happened often, and every time I taught him a new word, he'd blush and smile, and I'd do the same. He was endearing but also very sexy. He was clearly intelligent but didn't wear it heavily.

'Reluctant. Sí. My mother cooks most of the time, which is bad for all of us. It's one of the main reasons I had to emigrate.' He laughed.

'HAHAHA!' I roared, instantly regretting my overenthusiastic approval of Nicolas's first proper joke of the day. Tasha threw me a withering glare. We unpacked the car and headed to the beach.

---

[44] The de facto bonding experience for any interlinguistic friendship wherein one or both parties have a maturity deficiency

'What's that for?' I asked Nicolas, who, amongst other miscellanea, had a frying pan attached to his back.

'You will see!' He winked and patted my back. I momentarily worried whether I'd agreed to a beach day with Armie Hammer but discarded all anxiety when the feeling of warm sand touched my toes.

'I'm pleased you said yes to this,' Nicolas said as we walked closer to the ocean, ahead of the other three who had stayed behind to pay for a lounger, searching for a place for us all to pitch for the day.

'I am, too.' I smiled. 'Thanks for asking us.'

We found a pair of free loungers and unloaded our stuff. Nicolas immediately removed his T-shirt, revealing glistening amber skin and a toned, skinny torso. Luckily for me, the anxiety of my encroaching body reveal was enough to stop a semi. I took a deep breath and removed my shirt, not looking Nicolas in the eye. Immediately feeling the sting of the sun against my semi-skimmed skin, I reached into my backpack for my trusty factor 50. Nicolas reached over and grabbed it from me.

'Want some help with that?' he asked. His alchemy of confidence and shyness was intoxicating.

'Go on, then, and don't be stingy with it,' I said.

'What is stingy?'

'Tight. Don't be tight with it.'

'What are you talking about?'

'Just put fucking loads on.' I laughed. He laughed, too, and began massaging the cream into my body. As he rubbed his hands up and down my back in rhythmic motions, pressing the cream into my shoulders, his touch sent currents of electricity through my body. I looked at him to see if he'd felt the same sensation, and he met my eyes.

'Your skin is beautiful,' he said earnestly. The unstoppable force of my semi overcame the immovable object of my nerves around Nicolas, and I had to sit on the sun lounger.

'Thank you. Yours is. It's golden. I hate mine, especially at the beach. I feel so out of place. You look like you belong here, and I look like Tilda Swinton after Lockdown 2.' I sighed. He laughed, even though I was sure the reference went over his head.

'You shouldn't hate it, it's regal. Like something Botticelli would paint. It's so clear. You look like a prince,' said Nicolas. In a vacuum, I would've cringed at this, but he was so genuine in his delivery. No one had ever complimented my skin tone before, and early 2000s tanning culture had made my naturally pale skin a point of self-consciousness. Seeing it from his perspective was refreshing – not pasty and poorly, but regal and clear. I remembered the frying pan.

'Wait, you're not going to cook me and eat me, are you?' I nodded to the frying pan he'd laid on a towel by the lounger. He burst out laughing again. I thought that it might be the most brilliant sound I'd ever heard.

'Not cook you. Maybe eat you, but not on the first date,' he said, grinning and blushing.

'So, what's it for?' I asked, trying to keep my voice steady through the elated rush of hearing him refer to this as a first date.

'Well, we should spend the day having a bathe, and then we can have some Cruzcampo and collect some coquinas. Then we'll cook them on the beach. They are delicious, you'll see.'

'WOW!' came the sound of an approaching Pepe, who had reached the lounger with Evie and Tasha in tow.

'You can tell who is the British one!' He laughed, seeing me standing by the bed. 'Please stay in the shade, or you might die!'

Princely and regal indeed.

★ ★ ★

We spent the afternoon drinking progressively warmer cans of Cruzcampo (the delicious local beer) and frolicking on the beach like the Gaymous Five. There was a micro-drama when Tasha thought she was being attacked by a jellyfish that turned out to be a plastic bag[45]. Nicolas and Pepe had brought their own volleyball, which meant that I was subjected to team sports, which turned out to be fun, even if every team that included me lost.

'You don't play much sport at home?' Nicolas asked between rounds. I was pouring with sweat, and my cigarette-shrunken lungs were working overtime to make sure that I didn't collapse.

'What gave it away?' I panted.

Volleyball kept us entertained until Nicolas announced that it was coquinas time and explained what on earth coquinas were.

'Coquinas are tiny shellfish that live under the sand on these beaches. You stamp your foot like this . . .' he said, giving a demonstration. 'To bring them to the surface, and then you go through the sand like this . . .' he said, moving his hand through the loamy sand. 'Until you get this!' he exclaimed, proudly holding up a tiny beige shellfish.

'And this is for our dinner?' asked Tasha, confused.

'Yes! We will cook them and they are delicious. Trust us. Que rico, que rico.' Pepe was insistent.

'Sorry – not to be ungrateful, but we're growing girls, and it's 6 p.m. Surely it will take us years to forage enough to make a meal for five?' Tasha asked.

'No – just a few. We already brought some from yesterday!' said Pepe, and in Spanish he said, 'Here's one I made earlier!' thrusting his hand into the cool box and producing a brown net filled with previously harvested coquinas.

'Plus, we have bread. To dip,' he reassured us as our stomachs grumbled. Sure enough, we got to work, all of us tipsy, in a meandering zig-zag, stamping and grabbing at the sand to catch enough of the tiny coquinas. Evie got the giggles and fell over multiple times until Nicolas and Pepe leg-and-a-winged her into the ocean, where she floundered about for a moment before returning to the task with

---

[45] Drifting through the sea, wanting to start again

seaweed attached to her leg. We were all sitting by half past seven with a sizzling bowl of coquinas. Nicolas had cooked them in white wine, garlic, and parsley sauce. We sat under the sinking sun and sucked the tiny fish from their shells. We dipped the crusty loaf into the sauce, all of us grinning in unison and silent for the first time that day, the sign of a great meal. We'd spent the day being so present that everyone silently took this moment to go on their phones while they finished the last of the meal. I took the opportunity to have a sneaky debrief with the girls.

    [19:49] **Gabriel:** This has been the best day
    [19:49] **Evie:** It actually has. I wish Pepe wasn't gay
    [19:49] **Gabriel:** Jesus, Evie, fickle'inell. You were asking for my Dan blessing two days ago, and now you want to sack him off for fish fingers over there
    [19:50] **Tasha:** Hahahaha. What do you think of Nicolas, Gabe?
    [19:50] **Gabriel:** I think he's amazing
    [19:50] **Evie:** He seems so lovely
    [19:51] **Tasha:** He's not stopped looking at you all day, you know

'Anyway, girls, let us go and get some more Cruzcampo. Leave the boys alone for a while,' announced Pepe suddenly. He took the girls on a short pilgrimage to a nearby beach shop, and Nicolas suggested we walk along the shore. The sun was setting by then, and the beach, which had been relatively uninhabited all day, was now deserted. We walked as the waves lapped against the shore; the air had that warm, salty stillness that only came on a Mediterranean evening by the coast. Nicolas walked parallel to me at all times, synchronous without any effort, both of us chugging on what was left of the homemade sangria.

'I've enjoyed today so much,' he said, slurring his words slightly.

'So have I.' I grinned drunkenly.

'I think you are hilarious, very bright and beautiful,' he admitted. This time, it was he who would not meet my gaze.

I found, to my surprise, that I could reply sincerely. 'I think you are kind, very interesting and beautiful.'

I turned to look at him, and the strangest sensation made the hairs on my arms fizzle. Each step across the sand felt lighter than the last. I'd known him for less than a day, but I felt safe in his presence.

'I can tell you have a lot on your mind, though,' he said.

'How so?' I asked, mortified that he might have perceived any of my psychological flaws.

'You are never still. You are always moving.'

'I mean, to be fair, you did just make us hunt our own dinner. You wouldn't catch many coquinas sitting down,' I retorted. We both laughed.

'You know what I mean,' he said, looking up at me, eyes filled with golden light.

'Well, I can be anxious. I'm quite an anxious person, which probably makes me fidget a lot. But a lot is going on in my life, I guess, at home. But we've only just met. I don't want to throw all my shit at you,' I lied, as the combination of Cruzcampo, sangria and this newfound feeling of safety meant that the only thing I wanted to do was be vulnerable and overshare.

'Don't do that. I asked you. You can throw it at me. Or you can tell me to fuck off.' The 'fuck off' sounded like 'folk oaf' in his accent.

'Fine. Get ready to catch,' I said. He laughed, and the waves seemed to pause and the orange sun got brighter.

'I hate my job. It's draining, and I have to wake up every day and pretend that I'm not wasting my life reaching for some greasy rung on a wonky ladder, being forced to be a part of a shitty "high school never ends" corporate hierarchy that would just end up with me being able to get a mortgage on a soulless new-build property and fret about deadlines. Living my life only to make some horrible multimillionaire even richer.'

'Everyone hates their job,' he said.

'That's not true.'

'It is.' He was smiling, like he was enjoying baiting me.

'Do you?' I asked.

'No, but I do something I love.'

'Exactly, then.'

'That isn't a job. It is a passion. An art. The lucky ones use that to make money. It's different,' he said.

I rolled my eyes. The last thing I needed was pedanticism. Why ask me about my feelings if you were just going to semantically dissect them like Ben Shapiro in a debate with a university student.

'What do you love? What's your passion?' he asked. His European openness disarmed what was left of my British reservation. That or those long and fanned eyelashes — he was so pretty, handsome, and safe. I was drunk.

'I love to write.' It was the first time I'd said this out loud, and it felt like an otherworldly truth, like what I'd have answered if Oprah had asked me, 'What do you know for sure?'

'Then write!' he exclaimed.

'I do. Sometimes. I've been writing poetry. And short stories, little scripts, and diaries in my free time. But it's frantic and disjointed. I don't know what to write about. My head is too busy. I have too many ideas but not enough, I guess. If that makes sense,' I said, stuck in the struggle between wanting to remain mysterious and the impulse to want to share my innermost thoughts with this skinny Spaniard semi-stranger.

'It doesn't.' He laughed.

'Must be the language barrier,' I said.

'The ideas thing that you say makes sense, but why you are sad doesn't.' He shrugged. I wasn't used to having my emotions prized open like this by anyone other than my best friends or Mum.

'I never said I was sad, Nicolas,' I said defensively.

'That's true. You don't seem sad. You have a lot of light. People love being around you. Then, what is it?' he asked.

'I suppose I was sad. But I'm angry, now, I think.' A bubble rose in my chest as I said it out loud. The sorrow that I'd carried over the years at my mistreatment for an unchangeable part of myself, that had weighed me down and made me question my identity, my value and my worth, had for the most part disappeared – but what it had left behind was a kind of righteous fury, a surety that I didn't deserve any of it, and an anger that I ever wasted any time believing that I did.

'That makes more sense,' he said. He wasn't smiling anymore.

'Why?' I asked.

'Because you are gay. You should be angry. My father is a Muslim, and my mother is a Catholic; you can imagine that it hasn't been easy for me, either. Being gay. But we will speak about that another time, I'm sure,' he said, sitting on the sand and staring at the rumbling ocean. I sat beside him, hands behind me, steadying myself under the evening glow.

'There are a lot of things for us to be angry about,' he said. He was right. The anger wasn't just a residual from the past.

'There are. I suppose I just don't like to acknowledge them. It's easier. Part of me feels guilty, like I should be fucking grateful for being tolerated, or something. I thought I was done with healing from it all, but . . .' My words were spurred on by flashes of memory: the awful date with Fergus, Paul's fractured relationship with his son, DiscreetHung and his digital existence shrouded in shame.

'But . . .' Nicolas prompted.

'But is it even over? Being gay as an adult can be just as hard as being gay when you're younger. And I didn't realise that it would still be this difficult. And I don't want to talk about it or even think about it. It makes me feel guilty and pathetic for not just shutting up and being relieved that we've got it so much better than people in the eighties, in the UK, anyway. Because we fought for our rights, and we got them. We don't get arrested for existing anymore. The media doesn't obsess over someone's sexuality like it's some kind of perverse freak show. We can get married. RuPaul releases a new season of *Drag Race* every two weeks. But we still can't have kids, not biologically; surrogacy laws in the UK are archaic. Nearly every religion condemns us – and a *lot* of people still follow religions. Their right to chastise us supersedes our right to exist peacefully and proudly. Their belief is more important than this unchangeable – not that we should want to – facet of ourselves. And if we're not the enemy, we're only a novelty. Something interesting to them. Similar in just enough ways to keep around – and tolerate – but too different to treat the same. Something to be suspicious of. Or mistrust. We're reduced to the act of sex. When all we want is what everyone wants, to love and be loved. And to have sex – don't get me wrong – but you know what I mean. Not to mention, the beauty standards are INSANE. I know they're bad for women and straight men too, but my god: if you don't have three per cent body fat in the gay community, and if you're not white or if you're not twenty-four years old, what's the point? And I feel like this, and I've assimilated! I've done *the thing*. God knows how Mitchell feels,' I said, feeling a sudden wave of guilt about my attitude towards my neon neighbour.

'What thing?' asked Nicolas, who had moved his hand so that the edge of it touched the edge of mine, jolting me back to my monologue.

'The straight thing. The *expectation*. I've got the job. I dress well, but I don't wear makeup. I've built a passable relationship with my dad. I want monogamy. I don't know if that's conditioned, Disney's fault, or what, but I do. I don't want to do the polygamy thing, but I still feel, sometimes, not all the time, like an outsider. Like the faggot who forgot their PE kit on purpose again, like the jester at the party who gets tossed aside when people are bored or if they have "serious" matters or "proper relationships" to attend to.' My face felt flushed with emotion.

'I understand how you feel. I do. Every part of it,' Nicolas said, his fingers stroking mine. We sat like this for a moment, silent except for the push and pull of the waves. 'You're in pain,' he said.

I saw myself lying in bed at my mum's house as a teenager, depressed, catatonic, scared to face my own reality. I visualised Seamus on our first date after a lecture together at uni, grinning at me with a twinkle in his eye across a table in the corner of Revs. I pictured Paul on our move-in date, helping me with our boxes while Seamus complained about the state of the lobby. And finally, the images of the text messages between my ex-boyfriend and stepbrother last Christmas rose to the forefront of my mind.

'Yes,' I said. I was happy to share, but only a little.

'I do not want to undermine what you're saying by blaming it on that. I agree with everything you said. But I think you are forgetting a lot of the joy,' he said, his finger still moving along my hand as we stared at the water. 'The freedom. We do not have to put on an act; we spend our time doing that and learn how much it hurts, and once that's over, we have no other choice but to be ourselves. There is liberation in that. You talk of "they", society as a whole, but what about the people you love? Those bonds have depth that is very hard for most people to achieve. Most people never have the friendships we have because we have to value them. At times, they are all we have. It's difficult for me to express. And I know it's shite sometimes . . .' he said with a wink, causing me to erupt into laughter. He must've overheard the conversation about British swear words earlier. 'But it's also amazing. And thank you for speaking like that. I don't want to be too dramatic . . .' I couldn't believe he was saying this after my monologue. 'But I think you're amazing too.'

Facing each other, he grabbed my hand properly and pulled me closer. The universe split in two. All the confusion and anger that I'd felt at its zenith moments ago, that had bubbled beneath the surface and spilt out at points over the last year, all evaporated into the salty air. Every part of my body burst into currents. Vibrations of colour, elation, and weightlessness. Nico pulled me in and kissed me; the physical sensation was lost to something higher, a feeling of belonging and magnetism, and then it was over. I saw my reflection in his eyes as he smiled. I briefly wondered if this alien feeling was a hallucination or a panic attack, but I knew it wasn't. I brushed my cheek against his stubble and rested my head on his shoulder. Shutting my eyes and breathing in his scent of warm milk and fresh earth, I was still. He held me, ran his fingers through my hair, and kissed me deeply again. We were suspended in stillness and movement over the waves of the ocean, into the orange sky, past Jupiter, and even beyond the four humming Easter Island heads I'd seen on a mushroom trip in Amsterdam once, into infinity.

'And there is that. We do have that.' Nicolas laughed, looking at me with a feverish curiosity.

'We do,' I said, resting my head on his shoulder once more.

The sound of Pepe and the girls returning to the beach chanting 'CRUZ-CAM-PO, CRUZ-CAM-PO' interrupted our sanctuary.

'When will I see you again?' Nicolas asked. I felt a rush at the possibility that maybe he felt what I'd felt when we kissed and that he didn't find my speech annoying or masturbatory.

'Manchester!' I grinned.

'Yes. Manchester.'

★★★

The journey to the airport the following day wasn't painful for hangover reasons but because it felt sombre to say goodbye to beautiful Seville and all the unforgettable experiences we'd had. As I sat in Ryanair seat 18D, poring over my camera roll while Evie and Tasha slept soundly in the seats next to me, I felt overwhelmed with gratitude. This holiday was the best (hush) money I'd ever spent, and the best trip I'd ever been on. I felt grateful for Ivy's gesture, even though her intentions were questionable. We'd eaten wonderful food. We'd shared golden moments. Evie was almost arrested for indecent exposure. Tasha and I had healed whatever tension had built up in our friendship. I had met Nicolas and, at the risk of sounding like a *Love Island contestant*, had forged a connection like nothing I'd ever felt before. As we veered closer to the runway at Terminal 3, greeted by slate clouds and a fine summer drizzle, I felt renewed and excited for whatever lay in this next chapter. I decided to head to the toilet, knowing that soon the seatbelt sign would light up overhead, and I couldn't go again until after passport control. As I sat on the rickety lavatory, the signal returned to my phone, and I received a cascade of notifications. Mum had wished me a safe flight over Facebook Messenger for some reason. Dan had asked me for the Amazon Prime password. Three Grindr notifications. I recalled my conversation with Evie back at the Airbnb and my experience with Nicolas. I replayed our conversation on the beach and decided that there was no time like the present (having a shit on a Ryanair toilet) to end my situation with DiscreetHung.

Friday
   DiscreetHung: Hello? Why've you just gone quiet?
   DiscreetHung: Bit out of order

Saturday
   DiscreetHung: Hey, I hope this finds you well. you OK?
   DiscreetHung: This is out of order. I know it's taken me a while, but I think I'm ready now. If you promise not to show anyone, I'll send you a picture of my face. I think I like you

Sunday
   DiscreetHung: Please, this isn't fair

Apparently, absence does make the heart grow fonder! He was online, so I decided to rip the band-aid off.

   Angel44: Hi. Listen, I need to be honest. I don't think we should speak anymore. I'm going

```
to delete Grindr. It's not good for me here, and
we're not good for each other. I think you're
lovely and sexy, but I've done my time sneaking
around. I need something real. Take care
```

The writing symbol appeared almost instantly. He was typing a reply.

```
DiscreetHung: Wait
DiscreetHung: At least let me show you what
I actually look like. Maybe then you'll realise
what you'd be missing ;)
```

I never believed he'd send a picture. A part of me wishes that, in that moment, I'd not let curiosity get the better of me. That in that moment, I'd closed the conversation, deleted my account and never heard from DiscreetHung again. But I didn't. As I stood up to wash my hands, I received the notification:

Grindr: One Image Received

It would be the second time this year that a message on a screen would force my breathing to go shallow and my heart rate to increase. It would be the second time in a year that a message on my phone screen would change the course of my life and the lives of the people around me. When I opened the image from DiscreetHung, I dropped my phone in horror and revulsion, hearing it land in the empty sink with a sickening thud. There was no mistaking that face. The blond hair atop the smirking head, attached to the athletic body, which I now realised I knew. It was the face of my colleague and my best friend Tasha's boyfriend – Scott.

PART THREE

14

Spiralling

The days following my revelation in the aeroplane bathroom were a cyclone of unadulterated panic. Somehow, I'd managed to keep up appearances with the girls as we'd gone through passport control. Usually, they'd have noticed my change in energy, but they were both flat out after the holiday and desperate to get back to their own beds. *Thank god*. My levels of anxiety, which up to that point had been verging on stable, had gone off the charts and into the stratosphere. There was no escape from my mind. My phone, the weight of it in my hand, was a trigger. The thought of going into the office was impossible – the potential for bumping into Scott was a risk I was in no fit state to consider. I rang in sick with fauxvid[46] and informed HR that it was severe so I could take the full week off. The chains that tied me to sanity – my best friends, the routine of work, the belief that I was a good person – had been severed. Eventually, when my fight-or-flight response had exhausted itself, the panic transformed into shame. Its dark tendrils curled their way outwards from my centre, writhing and whispering and conniving: you have had an affair with your best friend's boyfriend. You knew there was potential for something like this, but you continued anyway. You are everything society told you that you were when you were younger. You are dirty. You are selfish. You are wrong. You are a burden. Shame is not guilt; guilt says 'you have done wrong'. Shame is 'you are wrong'. Guilt could be helpful, a tool to grow and to learn. Shame was a malicious pollutant. Guilt was a visitor – often unwelcome but usually necessary. Shame was a squatter. Shame wasn't new to me. Many of us, as queer people, harboured it in some form from an early age. It mutated and presented differently, but the results were

---

[46] Fake Covid

the same: you became heavier, weighed down by its presence. Shame altered your view of yourself, dragged you down and tried to keep you there, in a haunted cavern at the pit of your soul. If you were to sit with it for too long, if you let it grow and fester, it would become a magnet. You'd be drawn to others who were acting through its influence. Shame was a cannibal. It wanted to feed on itself, to grow stronger, and it was good at it.

My first experience with shame – upsettingly – was as an eight-year-old child. I was taught what the word 'gay' meant, told that it was wrong, and I knew it applied to me. 'Gay is when a boy likes another boy! Boyfriend and boyfriend, not boyfriend and girlfriend,' I was told in the school playground, followed by a chorus of 'ewws' from other children. As a kid, this terrified me – that a part of myself I had no control over was something to be concealed or I would be judged or hated. The lens through which I viewed the world as a child (my family, the media, my teachers: the caretakers of my prefrontal cortex) had taught me to be ashamed. The message on the screen from Scott, the realisation of what I'd done, had sent me spiralling downwards, hurtling back into that dark, destructive feeling. I couldn't stay there. I wouldn't. There was only one antidote that I knew to shame: empathy. Three days after discovering that DiscreetHung was Scott, I knew I had to kill it at the source.

I pulled myself from bed, had a shower, got changed, and went for a walk. It was a muggy Wednesday, the best we could hope for during a Manchester summer. I stomped through the Northern Quarter and beyond, no AirPods in, no music playing, just the sound of the city. My body felt unsafe. This was the first time I'd been out of the cocoon of my bedroom since the revelation, and it sensed threats everywhere. I knew I had to ground myself and do my best to come out of fight-or-flight if I had any hope of winning my duel with shame.

I could **hear** incessant chatter at a bus stop, nonchalant, friendly, comforting.
I could **smell** the warm tang of petrol.

I could **feel** the gravelly surface of the pavement beneath my feet supporting me.
I could **taste** Airwaves cherry menthol.
I could **see** punters in chino shorts, smoking merrily on the windowsills at The Peveril of the Peak.

I found a seat on one of the benches opposite the Pev[47] and sat down, vision blurred, unfocused – but with the chartreuse brickwork of its exterior in my peripheral. I shut my eyes and breathed in and out. I cleared my mind of its racing thoughts. Inhale. Exhale. Inhale. Exhale. I opened my eyes and looked down Chepstow Street at the red-brick terraces that characterised my city. The punters at the pub, some already three pints deep, were guffawing at something indecipherable. I replayed the last six weeks in my head. I tried to comb through, looking for an instance that would corroborate the accusation that shame was repeating in my head: that I knew what I was doing and was responsible for what had happened with Scott – but there wasn't one.

I had no idea it was him. I *couldn't* have had any idea that it was him. If I had met up with him and it had been revealed to be Scott, I would've been sick on his brogues. A light breeze cooled the air and combatted the mugginess. I wiped the thin layer of sweat from my forehead. I was not the type of person to betray somebody I loved. I knew what that felt like. I was not malicious, hateful, or sneaky. I was a good person who loved my friends. I looked around at the streets, the city that had done so much for me, the battleground where I had rid myself of anyone else's hurtful perceptions and found who I was. I couldn't let it down. My phone buzzed in my pocket, and I found the strength to pick it up for the first time in days. Nicolas had texted me but, as much as I longed to read it,

---

[47] One of Manchester's most iconic pubs. It used to be a brothel, way back when. The landlady that runs it now has been doing so for over fifty years. *There's* a memoir I'd like to read

there were more urgent things to deal with. The group chat had been quiet, as it usually was after we'd spent an extended period together. Nevertheless, my silence had been noticed.

```
[18:03] Gabriel: Sorry I've been dead, guys,
I've had the worst covid
[18:05] Tasha: Oh, what the fuck, retro!
[18:06] Evie: Get better soon! Tell Dan to
take a test, I'm meant to be seeing him later
[18:06] Gabriel: Will do
[18:06] Tasha: Get well soon, inspector
```

Note to self: would need to explain fauxvid situation to Dan. I felt hot tears fill my eyes at Tasha's well wishes. I stood up and started heading back to my flat, looking down at the streets as I walked, allowing my feet to go into autopilot. I had been selfish. I was not the victim in this situation. Tasha was. Her whole life would be torn apart when she found out about Scott. The things she valued most from their relationship – safety and surety – were about to be ripped from her. But I was not responsible, I insisted to my own brain. Scott would have been doing this for a while. It would've been with someone else if it wasn't with me. It probably already was. I was sure of one thing: Tasha needed to know that Scott could not be trusted. I couldn't sit idly by and let my best friend be a beard[48]. I rounded the street corner and reached the entrance lobby.

'Ay-up, dickhead!' croaked a voice from behind me. I turned to see Paul walking towards me, struggling with the weight of a small pile of Amazon parcels. The last time I had seen Paul properly, a few weeks ago at the football match, he looked thin and unwell. He now looked

---

[48] A 'beard' is a term for a woman that a gay man dates in order to retain the illusion of heterosexuality. The idea being that to be gay is to be feminine, so attaining a 'beard' will remedy that. Gross!

even worse as he laid the boxes gingerly on the stone floor. His skin was sallow, and his cheekbones were all pinched. Paul had always been bald, but now he had no eyebrows. His collarbones were visible through his uniform, and his face contorted into a grimace when he smiled at me. Whatever pain I had been feeling was minimised by my friend's suffering.

'Hi, Paul.' I gave him a hug; his body felt brittle.

'How are you, mate?' His was voice dim and raspy.

'I'm alright . . . Paul?' I looked him dead in the eye. He was panting from carrying the little Amazon boxes, and there were only three.

'You don't look well. Come up to mine, Dan's at work,' I insisted.

'And why aren't you, you little skiver! I'm fine, Gabe. How was Seville, then? I wan—'

'NO! Stop it. Stop lying, Paul. Something's not right. I'm your friend. Stop doing this,' I said, the hot sting returning to my eyes, forcing me to look to the ground again.

Paul sighed deeply. 'Alright, mate. Well, I've just brewed up in the office. Let's go there. Things might be a bit shit, but there's no need to waste a good cuppa.'

★ ★ ★

'The big C! Bastard. Fucking cancer.' Paul sniffed, taking a gulp of his coffee. He'd just finished telling me his story. He'd been diagnosed a year ago, and his doctors had tried a combination of drugs to destroy it, which hadn't worked, then a round of chemotherapy. I felt my heart slice into pieces as his words floated in the air. Was Paul another casualty of my self-absorption over the last few weeks? I'd known something was wrong, but should I have known it was this dire?

'Why didn't you say anything?' I asked.

'I haven't told anyone, really, mate. Just Kaye. I don't want to bother my daughter when she's got that new life in Oz, and as for

Midge . . .' His voice trailed off. 'I don't suppose he's bothered if I live or die.'

I wrestled with this concept. My instinct was that Paul should've told his family of his illness, but he'd never judged me or my decisions, so I owed him the courtesy of returning the favour.

'I didn't want to tell them in case I was alright and worried them for no good reason,' he said, as if reading my mind.

'And are you going to be?' I asked. I didn't want to know the answer to that question, but if I were to judge it based solely on how Paul looked, I already did.

He shrugged. 'There's an operation in a few weeks. It's a complicated one, so I've heard. They're taking out a tumour apparently, but . . .' Paul shook his head. 'We'll know after that.'

'Can I come to the hospital when you have it? I'd like to be there,' I said.

'No, mate. That's sound of you, like. But our Kaye's made of strong stuff. And I have told my daughter now, gave her a bell last night. She's flying home next week, bringing her fella with her n'all. Which is a relief. It's good to know she's happy.'

There was a silence. He'd be okay. He was a brick shithouse. He was built to withstand worse.

'On the subject, though, there *is* something you could do to help me, mate,' Paul said, twiddling his thumbs.

'You don't want me to euthanise you, do you?'

'Not before the cup final!' he bellowed.

'Wait, you *don't* want me to go to another football game?'

'No, but I want you to help me with what you said you would. At the match,' Paul said. I thought back to our conversation where Paul had said he wanted to reconnect with his son.

'Of course. What's the plan?'

'I—' There was a knock at the office door. Paul rolled his eyes. 'It's way past closing, for Christ's sake. I'll be glad to see the back of this job, one way or another,' he said, hoisting himself to his feet. He headed out of the office, shutting the door behind him. I heard a muffled conversation between him and what sounded like my *favourite neighbour*, Mitchell. Paul re-entered and sat back down at the table.

'Mitchell. The Amazon parcels were for him. Seemed shifty. Nice lad. Bit strange, like.' Paul laughed.

'His heart's in the right place.' I shrugged. 'I think.'

'I'd have thought you two would've gotten on!'

'We do get on. In a manner of speaking. Anyway, why would you have thought that? Because we're both gay?' I asked.

'Well . . . yeah,' Paul admitted.

'It doesn't work like that.'

'I don't see why it shouldn't,' he said. 'Anyway, as I was saying. Ah, fuck it.' Paul reached under the desk and pulled out the bottle of whiskey I'd bought him as a thank-you gift months ago.

'You said whiskey gave you gout!' I gasped.

'Gabe, I've got cancer, mate. Gout's a fart at a fishmonger. Bottoms up.' He handed me a glass. I toasted to him and shot the whiskey.

'My son, Midge. I've done wrong by him, Gabe. I've not treated him right, for being . . . for being gay. He's never told me directly, but I know he is. And I know why he wouldn't have told me. I've known for a while that I did him wrong, and he gave me the chance to apologise and speak about it proper, but . . .' He picked up the whiskey and poured us another glass. 'I bottled it. And now he wants fuck-all to do with me. He's still in touch with his mam and his sister, but he doesn't give me the time of day, and he's forbidden them from talking to him about it.'

'Haven't Kaye or Kristen said anything about your illness? To Midge?' I asked.

'Kaye hasn't. She begged me. But I didn't want it. I don't want him to come back to me out of pity. I don't deserve that, and neither does he. Kristen might've now, with the operation and everything, but I've not heard anything from him.' Paul looked broken.

'What happened? Why won't he speak to you?'

'I'll tell you. But I need your help. I need to write Midge a letter explaining how I feel. He won't pick up my calls, and I wouldn't be able to get my words together if he did. I'm not good with this sort of thing, but I've read your writing, and it's bloody brilliant. You're still at it, aren't you?'

'Occasionally,' I replied. 'So, you want help writing this letter?'

'If you don't mind, mate,' Paul said, his eyes desolate and regretful.

'Of course not. Fill us up again, then get me a pen and paper.'

'By hand?!' Paul asked, baffled.

'Of course! You want this to mean something, don't you? It's hard to be personal if you type it out and print it. It's too Gmail. Too HR.'

'Blinkin' eck, do you make a habit out of forcing cancer patients to do manual labour?'

★ ★ ★

After two hours of familial reminiscing, writing and whiskeying, Paul held up the finished letter for his son in front of him.

'Thanks, Gabe. I won't forget this.'

'I'm proud of you, Paul. This will mean a lot to him.' Throwing myself into Paul's problem had given me a welcome break from my own, and I'd come to realise that I wasn't the only one in the pokey office who was in a fist-fight with shame.

'What made you change your mind, by the way? About Midge? About your . . .' There was no easy way for me to say it. 'What made you stop being homophobic?'

Paul twitched uncomfortably in his seat. 'It's hard, hearing it as plain as that. But you're right, mate. That's what it was. I was taught that being gay was a bad thing. My whole life, growing up. By me dad. Then by my mates, who were taught the same. There weren't as many ways to be men, back then, Gabe. It was all I knew. I know it's not an excuse, but it's a reason, I suppose. But after the diagnosis . . . I had a lot of time to think. That thing you said at the footie match about looking back at your life and changing the bad bits of yourself? Well, I'd never done that. Not even once. Never 'ad to. Then the cancer happened. And . . . well, it made me think. About my past. And my future, if I had one. And the people I loved. And also, well . . .' He took a sip of whiskey. 'I suppose getting to know you, too, mate. But you see them everywhere, don't you, gays? On TV. In the street. But I'd never got to know one properly until you.'

I wasn't sure how to feel about this. On the one hand, it was great to have confirmation of something that I'd suspected for years (that my personality was the cure for homophobia) but on the other, I lamented that it took a close personal bond to push someone to move away from the default of discrimination. If Paul wasn't terminally ill, the instinct to cancel him might've been more prominent, but instead, I simply said, 'I love you, Paul.' And through all his flaws, I meant it.

'I love you too, mate.' And through all of mine, so did he. 'Will you promise me something, Gabe?'

'Jesus. Did I sign up to the Make A Wish Foundation without knowing it?' I said.

He laughed, then was sombre again. 'Promise me you'll stick with your writing. Not the writing at that job you hate. The proper stuff. The real stuff. You've got a talent, Gabe. Don't let fear get in the way of it. Regret is the only thing you should be really frightened of, mate, take it from me. Will you promise me?'

'I promise. But stop talking like you're going to die. You're gonna be fine, Paul, I know it.'

'We'll see. If you break that promise, I'll haunt the fuck out of you. Now, tell me about Seville, I could do with a distraction.'

And so I did. I told him about meeting Nicolas and how I'd felt during our time together at the beach.

'You're in love, mate! That's what it feels like. I remember it with our Kaye. It feels like that at first, then before long, you're passing the other one bog roll through the door and forcing yourself to have sex once a month.' He laughed.

'I think it's a bit soon to throw "love" around,' I said. Then, there was a shuffling at the office door.

'What was that?' I asked.

'Ah, nothing, mate. It'll be Benny doing the rounds,' Paul said. 'Go on, then. It's you, so I doubt that's the end of it. What else happened?'

I told Paul all about DiscreetHung, Scott, and how I was at an absolute loss as to what to do next. By the time I'd finished, Paul was laughing. It seemed an inappropriate reaction to one of the worst things that had ever happened to me.

'I'm sorry, mate. I shouldn't laugh. It's just . . . what a year you've had. Never a dull moment, eh? She needs to know, that's for sure. That her cunt of a boyfriend is snooping behind her back on that bloody app.'

'I know,' I said.

'But, if you ask me, it's not the time to tell her about what happened between you two. No good can come of it, mate. Some things are best left in the dark.'

'The thought of keeping a secret from her makes me sick, and the thought that I was complicit . . .' I let the sentence trail off before burying my face in my hands. The idea of Tasha thinking that I might've knowingly betrayed her was too much to bear.

'I can't tell you what to do, Gabe, and I understand if after tonight you think my moral compass is a bit bloody rusty – but that's my advice. I know it feels wrong, but knowing about your mistake will only add insult to injury. That's what it was, Gabe,' Paul said, his face scrunched in concentration as he seemingly read my mind once more. 'A mistake. You weren't to know, and she'll need friends around her when she realises what's been happening, as you know.'

'But how can I let her know that Scott is likely cheating, potentially gay, maybe bi, but definitely on Grindr, without her knowing what went on between us?' I asked.

'That's for you to figure out.'

The shuffling at the door was more pronounced this time. There was a thud as someone dropped something outside, then a high-pitched 'Shit!'.

Paul leapt up and went to the door. 'We're closed, mate. What are you doing here?'

'I forgot one of my packages, Paul, sorry!' Mitchell said.

'I don't see why that would bring you to my office door. Parcel room's on t'other side. You've not been eavesdropping, have you?' I heard Paul ask, and my heart sank.

'No, babe! Of course not. I . . .' Mitchell was lying.

15

Plans and Pac-Man

'It's simple,' Dan said a few days later, splaying out across the sofa with a pack of chilli heatwave Doritos. 'You have to engineer a situation where Tasha catches Scott in the act. He's obviously good at this, the sneaking around cheating thing, if he's been getting away with it for so long.'

'Pray tell, dear brother, how is that simple?' I asked. 'And do you have to eat Doritos on the sofa?'

'It's a small price to pay for my advice.'

'Oh really?'

'The way I see it, it's obvious. We've got Evie's birthday in a couple of weeks, right?' Dan said.

'Yes . . .' I said, wondering where he was possibly going with this.

'And she's doing that little bottomless brunch with everyone at House of Fu, then they want to have an afters. I told her we could have it here, actually,' Dan said.

I didn't know what was worse, my brother knowing more about my best friend's birthday plans than me, his new haircut, which looked even more like someone had put a pudding bowl on his head and cut around it with garden shears, or the specks of red Dorito dust on my cream Dunelm throw.

'Right. Thanks for the heads-up. Can't wait for you to do the clean-up the day after,' I remarked, already having war flashbacks to the state of the living room whenever Dan had people around after nights out.

'Whatever. But look, there's an opportunity there. We need to figure out what it is. Everyone's invited, it's a big group, Scott will be there. Even Mitchell's going.'

'That's a good point. I barely ever see Scott out. Shit, Dan, there's something I forgot to tell you . . .' I spilt the beans to my brother about how Paul had found Mitchell suspiciously close to the office door when I'd been spilling the tea.

'Bollocks, so you're telling me Mitchell might know?' Dan asked, visibly nervous.

'Yeah. That's exactly what I'm saying.'

'Gabe, I can't lie, that's bad. You need to do some damage control on that one. Booze, Mitchell and a secret doesn't sound like it's gonna end well.' Dan grimaced. 'Have you still got the package? The one that Paul forgot to put in the postage room?'

'Yeah. It's under the sink. Shall I ask Mitchell round to collect it?' I sighed.

'I think you're gonna have to; give me a sec, and I'll get changed,' Dan said, indignantly. He was wearing stained tracksuit bottoms and a T-shirt.

'Huh? It's only Mitchell. Why do you give a shit?'

'He obviously thinks I'm fit, and I want to maintain appearances.' Dan laughed.

'You've got to be joking. Is your ego that fragile?'

'Yep!' Dan shouted while scuttling to his bedroom to change into a slightly less dirty but just as dull fit.

★ ★ ★

'Not heard from you in a while, babe! Nothing new there!' Mitchell said as he sauntered into the apartment and sat next to Dan on the sofa. He was wearing a denim-print vest, his signature jorts, and a backwards snapback cap that said 'Daddy' on it. Charming.

'I've been on holiday, Mitch! How've you been?' I said, carrying over a cup of tea to him and sitting on the armchair opposite.

'Can't complain. Well, I could, but we'd be here all day! Have you got my parcel?'

'Sure, yeah . . .' I said, handing him the Amazon box. 'What is it?'

'Don't be so nosy!' He cackled. *The nerve*.

'Well, on the subject . . . I wanted to ask you something now that you're here.'

'I know what you're going to say, babe. And the answer's yes.' He smiled mischievously. I felt my legs turn to jelly, a similar sensation to when I was in the flamenco bar in Seville, but this time for an entirely different reason. 'But don't worry, I can be discreet.' He winked.

I turned to Dan, horrified and lost for words.

'So . . . Mitchell . . . you *did* hear Paul and Gabriel's conversation?' Dan asked as if needing any more confirmation.

'Oh yeah! Everything. Couldn't help but hear.' He tore open the Amazon cardboard, pulling out an Eyelure eyebrow tinting set.

Rage enveloped me. 'What the fuck do you mean, couldn't help but hear? You had your ear to the door. You must have done. There was a full fucking office between us, you—'

'What Gabe means to say is that it was a private conversation. Why did you listen in to it?' Dan finished for me as I sipped my scalding tea to quell my anger, accidentally burning the roof of my mouth.

'Thanks, Dan. Glad one of you two was raised right. Honestly, I was only there to get my package. I didn't think it would be open, because Paul normally locks up around five on weekdays, but it was. When I went to get it, I heard your voice, Gabe, and you mentioned Grindr. Don't tell me for a second if you heard a secret convo about Grindr you wouldn't listen in, babe.' Mitchell was grinning at me.

I felt myself seethe at his nonchalance towards the gravity of the situation – towards Tasha's feelings. And underneath my anger, guilt that I had tried to take solace in my most trusted friends to handle this situation as sensitively as possible, and in doing so, had inadvertently given the least trusted person in my wider circle ammunition to be a messy bitch. Inhale. Exhale. Inhale. Exhale.

'Are you alright, Gabe? You sound like a broken hoover,' said Mitchell obnoxiously.

'Mitchell, what you heard — I know it's probably just tea to you, but I need you to understand something,' I started.

'Oh, go on, Chuck. What is it you *need* me to understand?' he asked, giggling.

'Oh my god, Mitchell. How about you *try* and think about other people's feelings for once in your life?' I snapped. 'I know it's hard to divorce yourself from the idea that some people have lives beyond preening their hair and choosing how much of your ass to have on display on any given day, but—'

'Don't PATRONISE ME, GABRIEL!' shouted Mitchell, standing up from the sofa. 'Do you know what? You have no idea, do you?' He'd become irate; his eyes held a furious gleam, and he was gesticulating wildly. I looked up at him, alarmed. 'You have no idea how you come across. Or how you make me feel. How you make so many people feel! So many queer people at Kiss have said the *exact* same thing. You are judgmental, Gabe. You sit there in your trendy clothes with your stable job and your lovely straight mates, and you turn that big fucking nose up at me,' he spat, blushing through his tan.

'Mitch, come on mate, let's just—' Dan attempted.

'No, I've wanted to give you a piece of my mind for a while, Gabriel Lanes,' said Mitchell, sounding momentarily like a supply teacher on the edge of a nervous breakdown. 'You think you're better than me, don't you? Why? Is it because of the way I look? Is it because I'm not as "serious" as you? Do you see me as just some tacky faggot? Because I'm not as quick with my words? Because I've been single for longer than you?'

I'd never seen Mitchell this angry; it was mildly terrifying. I'd always thought our relationship was built on a foundation of banter, that he enjoyed the ribbing, and it hurt me that I'd hurt him.

'Do you know what I think?' he seethed. I really didn't want to know. 'I think you see all the things in me you hate about yourself. Or hated, and do your bloody best to hide. Well, I don't care! Just stop speaking to me like I'm something you scraped off the bottom of your shoe.' Mitchell sat down, out of breath.

I closed my mouth, which had fallen open during Mitchell's rant. The worst thing about someone reading you is when they're (at least partly) right.

'Mitchell, I'm sorry.' I meant it. Every negative experience that I'd been through due to my sexuality, Mitchell probably had too, and tenfold. His queerness was so visible, so external. I cringed at his words as I recalled my own to Nico on the beach. Had I been a hypocrite? Had I internalised the 'every gay for themselves' mindset from Romiley and rejected Mitchell's olive branches due to my own lack of self-worth? 'I really am sorry, I hate that I've made you feel like that.' One thing I was sure of was that I could be callous towards him; it was easy to forget he had genuine emotions when his personality, most of the time, was that of a Real Housewife of Ancoats.

'Be fair, though, Mitch – it's not just me. Your behaviour is sometimes . . . challenging to deal with. You must know this.' Mitchell tried to interrupt, but I talked over him. 'BUT . . . I think what you're saying about me looking down on you for whatever reason might be right, to an extent. I've not done it on purpose, and I'm so sorry about that. I'll do my best to stop it. I don't have the capacity right now to analyse the complexities of my inter-queer insecurities, but at some point, I will. For now, will an apology do?'

'Yes. Thank you, Gabe,' he mumbled.

'For what?' I asked.

'For understanding,' he said. 'And I'm sorry too. I'm sorry for being a cunt that time when I came for drinks with you and Shay. I'm sorry for being sloppy. I'm sorry for being a bitch. And for bringing up your nose.'

'That's okay. We all have our moments,' I said.

'And I'm sorry for stealing the samples of Clinique moisturiser that came to your letterbox that time.' He blurted the last part out, the tips of his ears still managing to turn red through the layers of St. Tropez.

'That was you?!' I gasped. He nodded.

'It's fine,' I said through gritted teeth. 'Judging by your skin, it wasn't worth the money anyway.' This was a risk, but Mitchell laughed, and Dan, who had done a sharp inhale after the joke, laughed with relief, too.

I got out of the chair and kneeled on the carpet before him. It was instinctive, but I did worry that it might've come across like Drew Barrymore on her chat show.

'Tasha's been in a relationship with Scott for a long time. She loves him. They have a *home* together. They spend Christmas together. She's never had a relationship like this before and she had a tough childhood. This is going to uproot her whole life. Please. Please do not tell anyone about this, Mitchell. I am begging you. I have to find the best way to break it to her myself.'

Mitchell looked contemplative. 'Girl, of course. I'm not a total demon, you know. I haven't told anyone, and I won't. I promise, and – as my nan used to say – "me word is me bond!". But Gabe, do you not think the best way to tell her is just . . . to tell her? Don't you owe her the truth?' Mitchell looked earnest.

'No. I've given it a lot of thought. I know Tasha. It's too painful, all at once. She needs to find out about Scott, and that's going to be shit enough as it is. But I can't tell her everything, not yet. It's not the right thing to do.'

'You're sure about that, babe?' asked Mitchell.

Dan turned to look at me. I felt myself shrink slightly under their gaze.

'No. But it's the decision that I've made, and I'm sticking to it,' I insisted. The room was quiet. The churn of the washing machine was the only noise in the apartment.

'You're both going to Evie's birthday bottomless brunch, right?' Mitchell asked.

'Yes,' we replied in unison.

'Well, I think I've got an idea.' Mitchell's voice buzzed with excitement. Then, we sat together on the sofa, like the three witches in *Macbeth*, and began concocting a plan to gently break my best friend's heart.

※ ※ ※

Finding out that your friend has cancer and that you've accidentally had an affair with your other friend's long-term partner makes for quite the week. Once I'd waded through the turgid marshes of emotion, started to process the former, and devised a plan to address the latter, I needed a distraction. That distraction came in the form of my holiday romance: Spanish teacher Nicolas, who it turned out, lived in the Green Quarter. When he'd first moved to England, he didn't have any friends here, so he agreed to a flatshare with a Slovakian woman who was so lacking in exuberance that she made Keir Starmer seem like he'd be fun at a house party. She greeted me at the door and led me into their flat. Nicolas was busy getting ready, so we sat in the lounge and enjoyed painful small talk. She was a tiny woman, with her mousy hair pulled back into a ponytail and severe facial features. I hadn't seen her smile yet and had difficulty imagining what that might look like. Julia was thirty-eight and didn't want anything to do with my bullshit.

'You are a loud person. You do not need to slam the doors or stomp, please,' she informed me after I came back from the bathroom.

'Sorry! It's these shoes.' I said, nodding towards my new suede double platform Dr Marten boots with a smile.

'They are not shoes. They are boots for hunting vampires. Van Helsing – have you heard of him?' she asked.

'Yes. I've read *Dracula*. It's brilliant. And a film about Van Helsing came out when I was growing up. It was . . . okay. I wouldn't recommend it, actually.'

Julia was silent, surveying me with an expression that hovered between confusion and disgust.

'Nico!' she called as she got up from the sofa and left the room. 'The very chatty boy is waiting for you. Don't be rude and keep him waiting any longer!'

I found it ironic that she'd just called Nicolas rude after insulting my footwear and then abandoning me mid-conversation. Ten minutes later, Nicolas and I walked through town towards NQ64 – his choice – for our first date on Mancunian soil.

'I don't think your flatmate is too taken with me,' I observed as we strolled (or stomped, apparently) past the AO arena.

'Don't take Julia personally. I was scared of her when I first moved in. You have to get used to her.'

'She told me my boots made me look like Van Helsing,' I snitched.

'Did she lie?' Nicolas laughed.

'No. Do you like them?' I asked.

'Yes, you have cool clothes. I thought this in Seville. You dress like somebody creative, so it made sense when you told me about your writing.' He smiled. The butterflies that had been flitting softly at the bottom of my stomach rose at his compliment. I loved that he'd remembered that.

In the most predictable twist of the year so far, it started to rain. In the second most predictable twist, I'd forgotten my umbrella.

'Ah, shit,' I said.

'Don't worry,' said Nicolas, who reached into his jacket pocket and pulled out an umbrella. When he popped it open, I gasped in surprise.

'Cool, right?' he asked.

No. *Not* cool. The umbrella had an enormous Poké Ball emblazoned on top and two pointy 3D Pikachu ears.

'If you drink three cans of Monster a day and pay rent at Comic Con maybe,' I said before I could help myself.

'Come on! It was a gift!' He laughed. 'You said you're a gamer. You must like *Pokémon*, no?'

'LIKE *Pokémon*?! I absolutely love those games. Do you remember the first ever Game Boy? Where you had to use actual batteries before rechargeable ones were introduced? Well, once I did Rock Tunnel – completely in the dark. I never found the HM for flash – and the batteries . . .' We walked side by side, exchanging childhood stories about our favourite games, underneath a Pikachu umbrella, and by the time we'd reached NQ64 I'd forgotten to feel self-conscious.

★ ★ ★

NQ64 was a neon dive bar inside a basement in the Northern Quarter. It was stacked to the rafters at every angle with arcade-style game machines, both old and new. They had everything from *Pac-Man* to *Tetris* by way of *Space Invaders*. Walking into NQ64 would be fatal for your epileptic cousin or young niece who gets overstimulated and cries easily. It was undeniably an assault on the senses. The ceilings were plastered with retro gaming posters – old adverts from SEGA, Nintendo, Sony and Atari in a colourful tapestry of thumb-pushing history. The lighting was dark and dingy except for neon lights in hues of ultraviolet and lime-green that flashed about the place, illuminating the punters. NQ64 was populated mainly by some of my favourite types of people (actual nerds), but also spiked with Blazer/Brunch/Bulldog[49] girlies who want an Instagram post posing with the plastic *Resident Evil* guns, and Ralph/Races/Racist[50] lads who need somewhere dimly lit and unsupervised to have a carefree key of coke. The combination of the music blaring from floor-length speakers and people screaming at the games they were playing didn't make it an accessible venue for communication, but this didn't bother me: Nicolas and I did *more* than enough talking on our first date, so I was okay with a more practical jaunt. We grabbed two hideously bright cocktails from the bar and collected our coins in a red plastic cup to begin our session.

Game 1 – *Guitar Hero*
Song Selected: 'Paint It Black' by The Rolling Stones

---

[49] Turn to page 95
[50] Turn to page 95, again. Try not to get a papercut.

Difficulty: Medium (my fingers didn't stretch far enough to include five buttons for hard mode. Nicolas found this hilarious.)
  WINNER: ME! NOT SO FUNNY NOW!
Notable moments: Nicolas slapping my ass during a punishing guitar solo. I would've demanded a rematch because this was technically a distraction fault, but I won, so I didn't have to.
Intrusive thought: Did I tense my bum too suddenly when he slapped it? Did Nicolas now think[51] I had a pointy, parallelogram ass?

Game 2 – *Tetris*
Difficulty: Advanced
  WINNER: NICOLAS
Notable moments: Being bowled over by Nicolas's spatial awareness and problem-solving skills. Big brain.
Intrusive thought: Was it alright for me to be having fun? Should I have been inside and alone, readying myself for the Tasha task ahead?

Game 3 – *Dance Dance Revolution*
Difficulty: Medium
  WINNER: NICOLAS
Notable moments: Nicolas was so unbelievably talented at the game that his performance garnered a small crowd, who videoed his feet stamping on the coloured arrows at astonishing speed. It became impossible to keep up with him, so I stopped playing and joined the crowd. I understood and respected why he chose NQ64 as the spot for our second date – to show off.
  Intrusive thought: Was Nicolas a bottom?

Game 4 – *Resident Evil 2*
Difficulty: Medium
  WINNER: THE ZOMBIES. *Resident Evil* is a co-op game.

---

[51] know

Notable moments: Me shouting 'For fuck's SAKE, Nicolas' and him telling me to call him Nico.

Intrusive thoughts: Why does every second I spend with this man feel like a part of me is healing itself?

After a couple more cocktails, we moved on to some solo games. Nico hugged me from behind as I played *Ms. Pac-Man*, kissing my neck and making me extremely horny but incredibly crap at the game in equal measure.

'Shall we go back to mine?' Nico suggested after three hours of non-stop gaming.

'Yes, please. My corneas can't take any more of this lighting,' I admitted. He reached out his hand to me with a smile, and I didn't let go until we reached his flat.

When we returned, Julia had gone out, so we had the whole apartment to ourselves. It was the first time Nico and I had been alone together (that wasn't in a place of worship) and we wasted no time. Nico's touch gave me the same sensation I'd felt on the beach, intensifying as we took off our clothes and our bare chests pressed together. The warmth of his flesh, the feeling of his heartbeat in rhythm, the pulse from his underwear as I felt the hardness of his dick against mine.

'Are you sure you want to do this?' he whispered in my ear, nibbling the top once he'd finished his question. The consent was hot. I felt his nails digging into my shoulder blades. Hot.

'Sure,' was all I could muster as he pushed me down onto the sofa and took off the rest of my clothes. The connection between us was so intense there was only impulse, no worry about what he was thinking or if he was enjoying it as much as me, just instinct, leading us together and into each other. He was attentive, hungry to satisfy me before himself, and by the time we'd finished and lay back, our mutual response was to laugh.

'That . . .' I began.

'Wow,' he said and turned his head, which was only an inch from mine, and gazed into my eyes. We stared at one another. Only his prominent chin, covered in a layer of black stubble, interrupted his androgynous handsomeness. We lay there naked, our hands running over each other's skin, grinning intermittently as we swam together through the ocean of these new sensations. Then we made love again, and it was just as earth-shattering as the first time. After another half an hour, Nico tried to instigate a third round, and I told him that I would but I was concerned for the structural integrity of my rectum, so we lay in bed together instead. We talked for hours about his life in Spain – his family, friends, and dog. He told me stories about his lesbian aunty who defied their Catholic grandmother and ran away to a town in the north. He talked about his favourite food and all the dishes he wanted me to try. We discussed the political situation there (here he became fierce), rueing the global swing to the right and its implications for the future. We agreed to start a new file on *Bloodborne*, one of his favourite games and one I'd never played, together. Before I knew it, my face was buried into the back of his neck, the scent of his hair and the feeling of security allowing me to forget, for a moment, the anxiety of the situation with Tasha and the horror of what could happen to Paul. I fell into a dreamless sleep.

* * *

The Plan
Devised by Gabriel Lanes, Daniel Lanes
and Mitchell Roberts

The date: Evie's Birthday
The venue: House of Fu / Our flat

Phase One:
It was crucial that, although we had a mission, Evie still had a birthday that made her feel loved and special.[52] The day would start with a bottomless brunch at the Korean restaurant House of Fu. We had to all be on top form – attentive, fun, thoughtful and present.

Phase Two:
We would take everyone back to our flat when the time was right. We'd need to make Scott feel comfortable. He'd likely be slightly on edge as he was weird socially, especially around me, likely due to my gayness. This meant that the presence of another gay (Mitchell) might make him more withdrawn. We all had to make him feel welcome, so he stayed long enough for Phase Three.

Phase Three:
Scott was an Aux Lord[53]. He would no doubt be in charge of the speaker at some point in the evening. We would welcome this, even ask for it. At some point, after Scott was set up, it was Dan's responsibility to bond over music and ask to put a song on. He needed to pretend it was one he thought Scott would like. This was the key moment. This had to be manufactured so that Scott would give Dan his phone passcode and not think much of it. Dan would need to channel his GCSE drama skills here.

---

[52] I'd never kept Evie in the dark about anything before, but this unfortunate coincidence meant that her birthday was the only opportunity we'd have to allow Tasha to unearth Scott's behaviour in the least harmful way possible. I hated lying to her. I hated lying to Tasha. But this felt like the best way out for everybody.

[53] Somebody who never allows anyone else to control the music. Be it in a car, in a club, or at a party – they're doing everything they can to make sure their superior music taste is the one that propels the evening

Spiralling

Phase Four:

Before we start playing the new song, Dan must head into Scott's phone settings and go to the notifications centre. There, he'd need to change the permissions on Grindr so notifications were on loud. Scott would have silenced these notifications so that no one was alerted to his despicable deeds.

Phase Five:

With Grindr notifications set to loud, Mitchell would be in prime position to innocently pop up to DiscreetHung. When the time was right, he'd be able to send several messages through to set off a string of notifications that would alert Tasha, who, having spent enough time around homosexuals, knew the Grindr notification sound well enough to realise what was going on.

Phase Six:

This is where I would need to get my hands dirty. Dirtier. I'd have to pull Tasha and Scott aside and ask them to come downstairs for some reason, perhaps because I'd 'ordered some weed for Evie as an extra birthday surprise' and didn't want to collect it alone. We three would then go downstairs together.

Phase Seven:

When I'd got them downstairs, this would signal Mitchell to go onto Grindr and send the messages to DiscreetHung, aka Scott. By this point, his notifications would be on loud, so Tasha, and Tasha alone, would be immediately alerted to Scott's behaviour.

Phase Eight:

The plan would be complete; Tasha would be free to leave the confines of her horrible relationship, and we would all be able to love her back to life.

POTENTIAL PROS
- Tasha would be made aware that her boyfriend was a cheat (in private) and would get to keep her dignity.
- We wouldn't out[54] Scott to anybody except his girlfriend.
- Tasha would not be made aware of the fact that I'd been accidentally having a cyber-affair with her boyfriend, which would be too much to handle all at once.
- Scott would be out of our lives forever.

POTENTIAL CONS
- This could negatively affect Evie's birthday. We'd make it up to her next year.
- The scheme felt underhand, calculated, and shameful.
- I still wouldn't have told my best friend the full truth.

---

[54] Out (verb). A concept whereby somebody is forced 'out of the closet' by somebody else. When somebody is outed, it is when someone else has revealed their sexuality without their consent. Choosing when to come out should be a personal decision that you have autonomy over. I could make a moral exception in the case of outing Scott to Tasha, as she was my best friend and he was betraying her with his actions, but it was crucial to me that absolutely no one else found out unless he chose to tell them himself, however disgusting I found him

16

The Calm

'Another round of prosecco, please, girly! Whenever you're ready!' Mitchell cooed to the waitress at House of Fu.

'I'm sorry – I can only refill if you've finished your drinks, guys,' the waitress said to the table at large. The whole group (me, Evie, Tasha, Scott, Dan, Mitchell, Evie's best friend from work, Elisa) all picked up our flutes and downed whatever prosecco was left.

'Alright, then!' the waitress laughed, heading off to grab another bottle.

```
[15:15] Nico: Have an amazing time
today. See you on Tuesday :)
[15:16] Gabriel: I will! I'm looking forward
to drunk texting you something
embarrassing later
[15:16] Nico: Not as much as I am!
```

I smiled at my phone. My stomach had been in a knot all day at the thought of enacting the plan later. The knot had tightened when I greeted Scott, seeing him for the first time since his face-pic bombshell in the aeroplane bathroom. I'd deleted my account, and the app, without replying to him. The texts from Nico loosened the knot somewhat.

'What're you grinning at, you big buffoon?' Tasha asked from across the table.

Evie – who was, of course, already the most pissed – giggled. 'I bet it's Nico! I told you to bring him today, Gabe! He is your booooyyyyfriend!'

'He's not my boyfriend,' I said abruptly. I hated boasting about my blossoming romance in front of Tasha when I knew hers was about to be blown to smithereens. But I quickly remembered Phase One of the plan (that we had to keep up appearances) and added, 'YET!' with a beam. Evie had instructed me to invite Nico, but I didn't want any more distractions from what I knew we had to do. The waitress arrived back with the prosecco. We'd just enjoyed a delicious brunch of Korean fried chicken, with enough kimchi to reset Ronald McDonald's gut bacteria, and now Evie tapped her glass for silence and stood to give a speech.

'Well, everyone, thanks for coming!' she began. She looked like a beautiful fairy, dressed in pastel colours, with a sky-blue asymmetrical satin skirt and a halter-neck top in the same colourway as a Flump marshmallow. 'It's not many people this year. I wanted to keep it nearest-and-dearest because that's what life is about! I don't want to go on and on, because the karaoke room is booked and I'm not good at stuff like this, but I just wanted to say I love you all. So much. LET'S GET DRUNK! WOOO!' She squealed to a 'wahey' from the table and a slap on her ass from Dan as she sat back down. I paid my slice of the bill, then headed to the toilets before the karaoke began. I'd only just unzipped the fly of my new Bermuda shorts when I heard the door go, and someone immediately broke one of the unspoken rules of urinal usage by starting to piss in the one directly next to me. I was steadfast in my adherence to the rules and continued to look straight ahead.

'It's good to see you, Gabe; it's been a while.' Came Scott's voice from next to me. A chill ran down my spine. Instinctively, I turned to face him, and he stared at me with a wicked smile. I'd always thought of Scott as objectively handsome, even if I'd never found him appealing, but now I saw his pristine blond hair, his slight tan and his three-quarter-zip top, light brown chest hair peeking out, and all I could think was how anyone could ever deem this slippery eel of a man to be attractive. I saw his eyes briefly dart down to my penis and back up again.

'There's nothing there for you, Scott,' I said. I was meant to be doing my best to be cordial until the plan was complete, but this *was* my best. I wanted to gouge his eyes out with the chopsticks I'd just used to eat kimchi.

'You are funny,' Scott said, letting out a hollow laugh. 'It's a shame our work calendars are opposite. I've seen you less since you started at EnsureInsure than I did before.' I knew this wasn't strictly true.

'Yeah. It is a shame,' I said, finishing what felt like the longest piss in history and heading over to the sink to wash my hands. I wanted to scream. I wanted to scream at him to fuck off, that I thought he was disgusting, that I knew he was cheating on my best friend, that I'd found out his secret and that in a matter of hours, so would Tasha. But I didn't. 'Love the hybrid working model, though. How are things going? At work?' My voice echoed off the tiled bathroom walls.

'Well, mate. I had my best quarter yet and so did my team. We did 130 per cent of target.' He joined me at the sink. He began washing his hands, careful not to get water on the expensive silver watch on his wrist.

'That's amazing. Nice one,' I said, chewing on the inside of my cheek to stop myself from gritting my teeth.

'Couldn't have done it without all that copy you've been producing. Great collateral for outreach. You're smashing it, Gabe. I'm proud, mate!' he said, slapping my back. His touch made me want to unpeel my skin.

'Cheers, Scott. I can't take all the credit, though. Eric's a great manager,' I said.

'Meh, he's alright. Anyway, want one of these?' He had produced a tiny plastic bag of cocaine and a set of keys from his pocket.

'Nah, too early for me.' I forced a laugh.

'Since when!' Scott said before dipping the key into the bag and withdrawing a tiny bump of coke.

'Maybe at the afters later,' I lied. I needed my wits about me.

'Good lad! It's at yours, isn't it?' He leaned forward, doing a deep, scratchy inhale through one nostril. I couldn't believe he didn't even have the grace and decorum to head into one of the cubicles parallel to us.

'Yeah, you coming?'

'If I'm invited,' he said with a cheeky smirk. *I hate him. I hate him. I hate him.*

'Of course! As long as you don't get any buffalo sauce on my carpet.' I fake-laughed.

Scott let out another hollow, false laugh, too. 'Oh mate, be real, there are no carpets in those high-rises, Anyway, let's get back to the party – don't want the girls thinking we're doing anything weird!'

★ ★ ★

The performances had already begun when we returned from the toilet and entered the karaoke booth. The room was painted an offensively bright shade of pumpkin and sequestered from the rest of the bar, meaning we had total privacy and two microphones to swap between us. Evie and her friend Elisa were doing a rousing duet of 'Still Into You' by Paramore, but Evie somehow still got the lyrics wrong even as they flashed up on the television screen before her. Next, Scott – with cocaine-infused confidence – treated us all to an enthusiastic yet unbearably pitchy solo rendition of 'Fly Me to the Moon' by Frank Sinatra. He finished to a round of applause.

'Look at you, Mr Swing!' said Mitchell.

'The only thing swinging is that jaw.' Dan laughed. Scott sat beside him and offered him a key, which he excitedly accepted.

'Come on, Gabe! It's you and me, baby,' Mitchell shrieked, leaping out of his seat and grabbing a mic for us both. 'Gaga?'

'Okay. *Born This Way* album track?' I said.

'No, let's please the breeders[55], girl. We LIVE for the applause. 'Shallow'?' he suggested.

'Fine. But I want to be Bradley,' I said.

'Obviously! Gags is more my key anyway.'

After our performance, my mood shifted somewhat. The booth was just too much fun, and we were drinking too much prosecco for me to be able to dwell on anything other than having a good time. At one point, Dan, Elisa, Scott and Tasha shared the mics and scream-sang 'When The Sun Goes Down' by Arctic Monkeys. Once Evie had concluded the session with a horrifying rendition of 'I Have Nothing' by Whitney Houston, we headed out of House of Fu and into the city. We bar-hopped through the late summer sun and into the night – Oast House, Albert Schloss, Behind Closed Doors and then Sammy's. My anxious anticipation had been kept at bay for most of the day so far. Dan had done an excellent job of befriending Scott, to the point where I wasn't even sure if the bond was real or (the most likely option) the cocaine. When he wasn't talking to Dan, or anyone, Scott appeared glued to his phone and I was reminded of the plan. After the obligatory table-dancing at Sammy's, it was almost 11 p.m. Elisa had headed home because she needed to mark some papers for the next week, and I headed out to the smoking area for a cigarette. I had barely lit up before Tasha appeared, taking the seat opposite me.

---

[55] 'Breeders' is a derogatory term used by some gay people to describe heterosexuals. It of course refers to their natural predisposition to reproduce. I don't like it; it makes me think of some shitty undergrad dystopian concept about a world in which the roles are reversed and gay people are the majority and straight people are running for their lives, being forced to complete their natural function just to keep the population alive. Wait, maybe that's actually not a bad idea for a script

'If Evie "drops it low" one more time on one of those fragile little tables, she's going to herniate one of her discs and several of Mitchell's.' She laughed, leaning forward and taking a cig from my packet.

'She's having a nice time, at least,' I shouted over the sound of the Abba remix blasting from inside.

'Of course! The vibes are good. How are you? You've been quiet on the chat!' she said. 'It's been glorious. I've finally been able to come out of my shell.'

'Ha. I'm alright, I suppose,' I said, failing another acting challenge.

'Alright, you *suppose*? What the hell – I thought things were heating up with Nico. Have you done any writing?' Tasha asked.

'They are. I think I like him, actually. In fact, I know I like him. I know I really like him. But I'm trying not to get carried away,' I said. *Trying not to rub it in*, more like. 'And no. I haven't done any writing whatsoever.' It was true. I'd been so preoccupied with everything else, I hadn't produced so much as a haiku in weeks.

'Well, for what it's worth, we're all rooting for you two. He seems sweet – and sometimes opposites attract.' Tasha laughed, taking a sip of her double gin and tonic.

'How are you and Scott? Did you chat to him about any of the shit we spoke about on holiday?' I asked. I said a silent prayer that they'd had a conversation and Tasha had decided that she no longer loved him, that the realisation had washed over her that she was better off without him and was looking for a way out.

'Yeah, we had a huge talk after I got back. You know how much I *love* those.'

Come on, I thought, say it ended with you screaming at each other that you're both gaslighters.

'It went really well, though. It feels like a fresh start. It's a weight off my shoulders, to be honest. Also, I've noticed how much you and Dan have been making an effort with him today . . . and, thanks, I guess, Gabe.'

'Of course. Any boyfriend of yours is a friend of mine!' I blurted.

'You're a freak. Let's go inside.'

After another hour of dancing and drinking, we began the journey back to our apartment. I could picture an enormous intimidating clock, like the one on *Countdown* or Big Ben's (before he got a facelift and buccal fat removal), counting down to Armageddon.

'Are you ready, babe?' Mitchell whispered to me when I had a moment apart from the pack on the walk back.

'I think so. You remember what we have to do, right?' I asked.

'Yeah. I spoke to Dan earlier. We're hot to go.'

'Okay.' We rounded the corner, and Broadgate Towers loomed into view. What usually comforted me made the hairs on my arm stand on end.

'Dan, take the guys inside. I'm just going to run and chat with Paul for a sec!' I shouted back to the group.

'Roger!' Dan called back.

'Roger, Todger!' cackled an inebriated Evie from underneath Dan's arm.

As the group headed up the stairs, I buzzed the bell on the office and waited for Paul to answer.

'Hello, mate!' he said as I walked inside. 'Y'alright? Is tonight the night?'

'No. And yes. But more importantly, how are you?' I asked.

'As far as people with terminal illnesses go, I'm pretty fucking splendid, to be honest. Tonight's my last shift here. I've been given medical leave.' Paul smiled, his thin skin stretching. He looked ten years older than when I'd first met him.

'It's about time. Thank god. Get some rest,' I said.

'Oh aye, I will. Got that operation on Tuesday.' Paul cringed.

'It'll be sound. You'll be fine. Once it's done, I'll visit you and Kaye. We could have dinner?' I suggested.

'Jesus, mate, if the cancer doesn't kill me, Kaye's cooking will. Don't do it to yourself.' He laughed. 'Give me a bell, and we'll sort something.'

'Have you posted that letter yet? To Midge?' I asked, raising my eyebrows at him.

'No, but don't say anything. I've been busy doing my handovers. I'm posting it first thing tomorrow,' he insisted.

'Alright. I'll be checking. Do me a favour, Paul. Do you mind keeping an eye out tonight? You and Benny. In case anything goes wrong? He's on coke, too, Scott. I'm probably being dramatic, but cognitive dissonance is a powerful thing,' I said.

'I don't know what cognitive discipline means, but I do know that cocaine is a powerful thing, so yes, mate, I will. Give me a bell or a knock if you need me. I've got a button here to call the police. You know, like in *Thunderbirds*,' he said, looking self-important.

'I don't, because I'm not ancient. But thanks, Paul.' I went behind the desk to hug him, then left the office and began the ascent into the belly of the beast.

17

The Storm

Usually, I would've pitied the walls of my apartment for having to hear a drum and bass remix of Mr. Brightside, but as I entered the flat and saw Scott crouched on the rug next to the Sonos speaker, I was comforted. Phase Two was complete, and we'd successfully entered Phase Three of the plan. Scott was in control of the music. Mitchell had brought round his disco ball lighting set, and the flat shone with a thousand dancing diamonds. There was a hardback copy of an as-of-yet unused cookbook by Jamie Oliver – *VEG* – that now had a thin layer of cocaine residue across the cover. Scott had seemingly continued to share his bottomless gram. I rummaged around in the plastic Spar bag on the kitchen side, withdrew the pink gin and lime cordial, and poured myself a glass with the remaining ice cube from the freezer. I felt someone grab me from behind.

'Thank god you're here. Have you heard what's playing? On MY birthday of all days?' Evie whispered. 'Shall I chuck him off the speaker, or do you wanna?'

'Ah, let him have his moment for a bit, Evie! I know it's all about you tonight, but remember what I promised Tasha about making an effort. Plus, my brother seems to be enjoying it.' Dan was sitting by Scott, pumping his fist in rhythm with the beat. I hoped this was him playing his part well rather than a genuine reaction to the cacophony.

'Wow. Ick,' cringed Evie. 'Okay, fine. One hour, that's all I'm giving him, then it's quarter past Billie.'

The Armageddon clock in my head moved perilously close to midnight. We had an hour to complete the plan.

'ALRIGHT, BITCHES!' shouted Mitchell from the sofa. 'PRESENTS! Time to see who loves Evie the most! Turn this shite – I mean, banger – down for a sec, please, Scott!'

The group gathered in a circle around the coffee table, where we had all deposited Evie's birthday presents. We completed a rousing chorus of 'Happy Birthday', with Mitchell pulling off a surprisingly impressive Christina Aguilera-style run on the final note of 'you'. Evie unwrapped the largest present first. It was an original Mathmos lava lamp, the kind you'd find in the nineties.

'OBSESSED! This is perfect for my room! For the bedside table. Thanks, babe, that's so thoughtful,' Evie said, leaning over and giving Dan a (far too passionate) kiss. The lava lamp momentarily rekindled my fears of them descending into a life of permanent stonerdom. They were one good high away from buying rainbow beanies and getting matching Adventureland tattoos.

Evie unwrapped Tasha's gift next, an emerald tartan skirt from House of Sunny.

'Tasha!!! It's beautiful!' she said, standing up and holding the skirt to her midriff.

'It's from Scott, too.' Tasha smiled.

'Thanks, Scott!' Evie said, leaning down and kissing him on his revolting cheek.

'I'll have to get into the habit of buying you gifts, if that's the outcome, Evie!' Scott joked.

'Can you calm your boner, please?' Tasha snapped, playfully slapping him around the head. Yeah, right.

Evie opened my gift next; it was an envelope rather than a parcel.

'What's this, Gabe . . .?' she said, opening the envelope and reading the letter inside.

'OH MY GOD! THE WICKED TOUR!' she shrieked upon unveiling the tickets, leaping across the room, knocking over a half-empty glass of vodka lemonade and pinning me to the sofa. 'I LOVE YOU. I LOVE YOU. I LOVE YOU.'

'Evie, you're crushing my lungs. "Thanks" is fine. Dan, can you grab some kitchen roll, please? There's a new one on the side.'

After Mitchell had given her his gift (a satin blindfold from Lovehoney plus a Trixie Cosmetics blush set) and she'd opened the one left behind by her colleague Elisa (a mug with a photo of them both on it), twenty minutes had passed. I knew we only had a short time to execute the plan's next phases. I stole a knowing glance at Dan.

'Scott, show me that Andy C beat you were on about before . . .' Dan said. A moment later, the flat was filled once more with the rump and pump of what had to be the worst sub-genre of electronic music besides dubstep. The entire group struggled to dance, and after a few attempts, factions broke off to have intense, narcotic-fuelled conversations. My friendship group wasn't in the habit of taking class As anymore, but if the occasion called (and someone brought some along), they were unlikely to turn them down. Dan and Scott sat by the speaker at the far side of the room, locked in a fierce exchange of words about Pendulum's discography. Tasha was parked at the kitchen table with Evie, who was regaling her with an uninterruptable monologue about how their friendship was stronger than ever and how she thought that, when they were older, rich and had kids, they should buy houses in Prestbury next to one another. Mitchell was alone on the sofa, tensing his jaw, so I went and sat next to him.

'Hey. Did you do a line?' I asked, accidentally sounding like an undercover cop.

'Yeah, babe. Couldn't resist. It's power!' He laughed, his pupils wide.

'I mean, you could. And should. But we're here now. I'm so nervous.' I was quiet for a moment in contemplation. 'Do you think it'll work?'

Everyone was enraptured by their conversations, and the music was blasting at a volume that could kill certain smaller breeds of guinea pig, so I felt like we were safe enough to discuss the plan.

'Of course it will. It's genius. I should know – I helped come up with it. Try and relax for now, babe. Can I ask you something?' Mitchell said, his jaw swinging.

'Go on . . .'

'Do you think I'm ugly? Be honest.' He smiled, and my heart ached. It hurt that he had ever considered this.

'Absolutely not. In no world, Mitch. You've got a banging body and great features. Is your overall aesthetic to my taste? Absolutely not! But there's no denying that you're a handsome guy,' I said. I looked over to see Scott stand up and head to the toilet. 'I'll put something on the speaker, mate; what's your password . . .?' Dan asked as Scott walked towards the loo.

'Thanks, Gabe. I just feel ugly sometimes. Don't get me wrong, we both know I'm not short of dick . . . but they don't . . .' Mitchell's voice trailed off as we saw Dan in action. He quickly put a song on the speaker – Hannah Diamond 'Concrete Angel' – then continued to move and swipe his fingers across the screen of Scott's phone at a brilliant speed. The faint flush from the toilet could be heard through the first instrumental opening of the song. Then Dan put the phone down and walked over to us both, sitting on the sofa beside Mitchell.

'It's done, guys,' he whispered.

'Everything?' I asked, feeling suddenly clammy.

'Yep. Grindr notifications are on loud. His phone's off silent mode. I also changed the keylogging so the button on the side doesn't take it off silent mode. He's done for. Gabe, you need to get them both downstairs, if you want it to be only those two that find out. Remember, text Mitchell when you need him to send the Grindr messages. Go, now.'

The pounding chorus to Concrete Angel began as Scott arrived back from the bathroom triumphantly. Bass shook the apartment.

'Mate, this is a thumper. Where did you find this little bitch? She's brilliant!' he said as he walked over. I jumped to my feet as inconspicuously as possible and headed over to Tasha and Evie.

'And if I had to choose anyone to read a speech at my funeral, it would always be you—'

'Tasha, can I have a word for a moment? Sorry Evie, I'll bring her back; it's a good thing, I promise!' I pleaded.

'Oh, hi Gabe, yeah, sure, take her! But don't be long!' said Evie.

Tasha stood from the table and walked around the corner with me into the hallway.

'What the *HELL* do you want with me on a night such as this?' Tasha said in a butchered RP accent. My heart felt like it might leap from my chest and land in her hands.

The song was reaching its conclusion.

'S-so,' I stammered. I took a deep breath to steady myself. The walls in the hallway felt like they were getting narrower, like they were closing in and would squeeze me and Tasha together until our bodies had fused into a bloodied 2D cut-out. 'So, I ordered some weed as a surprise for E-Evie's birthday. Obviously, she won't be smoking it tonight, but I still want to give it to her. Will you come and p-pick it up with me?' I said.

'Er, yeah, that's fine. What's with the stammer? Why have you turned into Joe Biden? Are you nervous – wait, is this that dealer you got with after Parklife that—'

'No. No, it's not him. Sorry, it must be the erm – coke. Shall we bring Scott, too?' I asked.

'Aw, that's cute from you, but he seems pretty obsessed with Dan and his music taste. Let's go. Is he here now? The dealer?'

The last beats of the song petered off, and a new sound burst through over the closing instrumental notes. The familiar Grindr trill. As it did, I froze, staring open-mouthed at Tasha who said, 'Oops – which ruthless power bottom is connected to the speaker? That's so funny.'

The sound went off again, more distinct now, as no music was playing. I felt my body start to shake. The echoing sound that was unmistakably the Grindr notification pulsated at full volume through the speaker and bounced off the walls for everyone in the flat, and potentially the street below, to hear. Tasha headed back down the hallway and around the corner, and it took each ounce of conviction in my body to follow her and not turn tail and run out of the flat and into oncoming traffic. When we rounded the corner, every person in the room was completely still. Dan sat by the speaker. Evie, Mitchell and Scott huddled together on the sofa, staring at a phone on the coffee table.

'God, who am I, Medusa or something? You're all so still, you weirdos.' Tasha laughed. 'What's wrong with you?'

The sound went off again, making everyone in the room jump.

'DAN, UNPLUG THE SPEAKER!' I shrieked. He hurried forward and pulled the plug from the wall. I looked at Mitchell, and he met my glare, widening his eyes and shaking his head. He wasn't even touching his phone. It wasn't him who had sent the Grindr messages at the wrong time. Scott, aka DiscreetHung, must have got them from someone else. At no point in our plotting, at no juncture of us formulating the perfect plan to protect Tasha from the worst of this revelation, did we consider that Scott was enough of a Grindrholic to receive messages from someone else in that tiny timeframe. Evie was staring at Scott in disbelief. He had turned a curious shade of green and his whole face looked like it might blow away in the slightest gust of wind, leaving only a slack-jawed skeleton behind.

'Who's connected to the Bluetooth?' Tasha asked. The realisation had dawned on her now, and the change in the room's atmosphere had caused her brow to lower and her lip to quiver. 'Scott. Scott? Is it your phone? Are you connected to the speaker?' Tasha jumped to the sofa. Scott quickly picked up his phone and started maniacally swiping, but before he could do anything effective, Tasha had reached him and plucked his phone from his hands. She held it before her face and began to scroll and read.

'Tash – don't, wait –' Scott tried to stand up, but Evie pounced on him, a blaze of auburn hair and flowing satin, to pin him to the sofa.

'What have you done, Scott?!' Evie howled, her fingertips gripping into the sleeves of his three-quarter zip until they were white. We were all frozen, watching Tasha's face lose colour under the reflection of the phone screen.

'Tash, please . . . ' But it was too late. Tasha found whatever she was looking for and, as she read through Scott's Grindr profile, the messages she saw in his inbox, and the pictures she uncovered in his sent box, she had to steady herself so as not to fall, placing one hand on the kitchen table for support. She wobbled for a second, then threw the phone to the floor at full force and ran to the toilet to vomit.

'What the fuck have you done, Scott?' Evie screamed. 'What the FUCK HAVE YOU DONE TO MY BEST FRIEND? ON MY BIRTHDAY!' She released him from her grip, and tried to leap up to attack him, but Dan held her back as she wriggled and screeched his name over and over again, tears of fury streaming down her face. Tasha ran from the bathroom and out of the apartment, the door slamming shut behind her. Scott shook his head in disbelief, then jolted to his feet to pursue Tasha. There was stunned silence. It dragged on and on as we all tried and failed to process the scene that had just unfolded. Dan was hugging Evie, who was lying in his arms, sobbing and clenching and unclenching her fists.

'Is she gonna be okay down there?' Dan asked after what felt like an age. The words seemed heavy after so much silence.

'Let's give them a bit longer.' The sound of my own voice shocked me. 'Then I'll go down.'

★★★

I pressed the 'G' button and waited as the lift slowly whirred into action. How could this have gone so wrong? My head was swimming. In our attempt to save Tasha from further trauma or humiliation, we had triple-handedly made the situation even worse. It had been such an appalling conclusion that I even found thoughts for Scott's wellbeing flashing through my mind. None of us had wanted to out him like this. Mitchell was meant to send the Grindr messages when Scott and Tasha were alone downstairs. None of it was meant to happen like this. Even though I despised Scott for what he'd done to my friend, for what he'd done to me, I never would've wanted his sexuality to be revealed to a room of people, over a Bluetooth speaker. And Tasha. She was meant to find out downstairs, with Scott. Not with an audience.

But my guilt could wait. The steel doors opened, and I ran into the lobby. I could see Tasha sitting on the courtyard bench outside through the giant windows, and Scott pacing back and forward nearby. As I left the building and walked towards them, I was shocked not to hear screams, swearing, or wailing. The wind whistled past my ears, but their voices didn't. Tasha had her head in her hands, rocking slightly, and Scott was still pacing, his eyes deadened as if all the light inside him had evaporated into the breeze. I leaned down next to Tasha.

'Are you okay, Tash?' I asked. She shook her head from side to side.

'Is it okay if I give you a hug?' I asked. She nodded. I wrapped her in my arms.

Scott, through all his apparent despair, still managed to stop pacing for a moment and flash me a dirty look, as though somebody with greasy fingers had just picked up his favourite watch.

'I can't believe it, Gabe,' she whispered softly, her fragile form shivering through cold or shock or both.

'I don't understand how my phone . . . the notifications . . .' said Scott, who was now standing opposite us, shaking his head maddeningly.

'Is that the *primary* issue right now, Scott?' I seethed. The thought I'd had for his wellbeing earlier seemed misplaced. Scott's dickheadedness clearly knew no bounds.

'You're right. Tasha, Tash, please look at me so I can explain,' he pleaded.

Tasha raised her head from my lap and turned to face Scott.

'Look, this has been . . . I know this is horrible. I feel sick – really, I do – but Tasha, it doesn't mean anything. Those messages – that's all they were. I didn't actually meet anyone. I never cheated!'

Tasha was unusually calm. She sat up from my lap and stared at Scott, her voice deadpan, her movements stiff and lifeless. 'I will never believe a single word you say again, Scott. You have cheated. Even if you haven't fucked anyone else. Or been fucked yourself . . .'

Scott scoffed and rolled his eyes.

'You've still cheated. It's over, obviously. It was over before this. I was just in denial. I don't want to be with you anymore,' she said with blank finality.

Scott moved his hands around wildly, searching for the words.

'Don't say that, Tash. It doesn't have to be. I'm not gay!' He laughed. 'Honestly, I'm not gay! I thought I might be bi, but I'm not. I'm sure of it now. Especially after tonight. Give me another chance, please, Tash,' he pleaded.

'I don't care if you're gay, bi or whatever, Scott. You've betrayed me.'

'I'm not gay,' he repeated as if that was the crux of the issue.

I couldn't stay silent any longer. 'What the fuck is wrong with you? Not even an apology? Nothing?' I asked. The sadness and shock, which had drifted through Tasha and left her almost comatose, had funnelled through my body and transformed into rage.

'Sorry, Saint Gabriel, but what *exactly* has this got to do with you?' Scott shouted. A bright light turned on in the office behind the bench.

'Hmm. Good question, Scott. What DOES this have to do with me?' I shouted back, standing up from the bench to face him. 'You've been fucking, or trying to fuck, half of Manchester for god knows how long behind my best mate's back and you've broken her heart, in my apartment, may I add, but you're right. That has nothing to do with me. I'll go up and pour you a drink if you want. Actually, do you need a note to do another fucking line?'

'He was arranging to meet up with someone tonight. He was going to go to their house after the party. He sent them pictures of his dick,' said Tasha, unblinking, unmoving.

'Tash, please, that wasn't *serious*. I'm sorry. I am. Of course I am! I've told you. I'm not gay, I—' he spluttered.

'I need you to go. Please.' Her head fell back into her hands.

'Scott, you need to leave. Tasha is staying at mine.' My voice was firm. I knew Tasha couldn't stand to hear any more.

At the sound of more raised voices, Paul appeared from his office.

'Iya. No trouble out here, I hope?' he asked, looking Scott up and down with suspicion.

'Jesus, and who the hell is this?!' Scott shouted, enraged that another person had arrived who might attempt to stop Tasha from taking him back.

'Should I call you an Uber, mate?' Paul asked, his voice tinged with menace.

'Don't worry, Paul. He's leaving. Nobody wants him here,' I said.

'Scott. Go home,' Tasha commanded calmly.

Something inside Scott seemed to snap as he realised that he was no longer able to control the situation, or the people around him. He started to flap and stomp like a petulant toddler.

'This is why you know I'm not gay, Tash. Just look at these lot. It's *The Rocky Horror fucking Picture Show*, and you're LISTENING to them! You're letting them turn you against me! Look at the state of that Mitchell. I don't know how he even makes it down the street without getting battered, and he'd be all the better for it. And YOU! You're even worse!' he said, pointing at me. 'And now we've got GCSE Bricklaying to come and shout the odds!'

Paul looked unbothered, his arms folded, staring at Scott intently, but I was bothered. I lunged at Scott, knocking him to the floor. We tumbled on the concrete, rolling, scraping, and punching while Tasha and Paul shouted indiscernible protests. Hits and kicks were landed and missed, and after a minute, we were pulled apart, panting, Paul holding my arms behind my back and Tasha doing the same to Scott.

'Tasha. Please, come back with me. I want to explain. I deserve that chance. You've got the wrong end of the stick completely. This is a set-up. It's a plant! My phone was on silent! *They* sent the messages! They set me up!' he screamed. His face was red from the tumble, and it was the first time I'd seen his hair look anything other than perfect.

'As if we'd let her go anywhere with you. She's staying here. You need to go home, sober up, delete Grindr and call a therapist,' I said, spitting blood onto the floor from the split lip Scott had given me.

'*I* need therapy, do I? *Me*?' Scott laughed. If he wasn't already, he was manic now.

Evie, Mitchell and Dan burst through the double doors at the sound of the furore, surveying the scene before them.

'You're a walking advert for psychological disturbance, mate. And to think I got you that job. You should be kissing my shoes.'

'You'd like that, wouldn't you!' I shouted.

'I. AM. NOT. GAY!' he roared. 'I am NOTHING like you lot. You make me sick! You parade around like you're some sad little victims of life with your rainbow flags and your pride bullshit, forcing kids to watch all of your depravity. I am NOT one of you. Fuck me, Gabriel, you think I would shag someone in a toilet cubicle? Do you think I would pose around in prissy little clothes and go on about pop music to anybody with two ears and a spare minute? You're a joke, mate. And I will make sure you get fired, too. I'm not having you anywhere near my office. It's no wonder you got sacked from your last job. Who would want you anywhere near them?! At least then, you'll have more time to piss out more unpublishable poetry. It's no wonder Seamus cheated on you. With someone from your shitty little Fraggle family too. He was the only one with any sen—'

But Scott couldn't finish his rant. Paul let go of my hands and stepped forward to where Scott stood. Even with the weight loss from his illness, Paul was a formidable man. He was a head taller than Scott and still twice as wide. He didn't even clench his fist; before Scott could finish his tirade, he backhanded him with a slap so hard that the sound reverberated through the courtyard and onto the main road. Scott fell to the kerb – face first – in a heap, blood pouring from his nose.

What happened next happened quickly. I pulled a bellowing Paul away from the scene and back to his office as his shouts subsided into guttural coughs. Scott staggered to his feet, screaming at Paul that he would report him to the police. With last-ditch strength, Tasha bundled Scott into an Uber and sent him home. Evie, Dan, and Mitchell carried Tasha back up to the flat to start to repair the damage that had been inflicted. Once we were back in the office and alone, the emotions of the evening and the last few weeks overcame me. I latched on to Paul and burst into tears.

'I'm so sorry, Paul. It wasn't meant to happen like that. I'm sorry you had to be involved. Is your hand alright? For fuck's sake, this is such a disaster.' I sobbed.

'It's alright, Gabe! It's done. She'll be fine. She's a strong lass. She's made of solid stuff.' He hugged me tighter. 'It's over, Gabe.'

'But what if it's not? What if she doesn't leave him? She might believe him! Why was she ever with such a BASTARD? And Paul – what if he does report you to the police? You'll lose your job. There are cameras everywhere.'

'She will leave him, Gabe. It might not be this time, but she will leave him. Mate, it's my last shift. And do you think I need to learn how to handle the pigs? Stop being a fanny. It's going to be fine. He's all mouth; he won't do a thing.' But Paul was wrong. Scott, who blamed everybody but himself for his castle of cards tumbling down, did call the police on Paul. The first thing he did when he woke up with a pounding head and a dry mouth the following morning was not to get in touch with Tasha or reflect on the hurt he'd inflicted but to try and enact revenge on the man who had embarrassed him. The police came to the house in Didsbury, where he was packing his clothes and furniture up at Tasha's request, making sure he could stuff whatever utensils and ornaments he felt he had claims to into boxes. He sat with the two officers and filed a report. The police, having heard his twisted version of events and seen his broken nose and bruised eye sockets, assured him that they'd do everything they could to deliver justice. They returned to the station and inputted Paul's details into their computer. They found no major previous offences, only a couple of minors. There was an instance of drunk driving a decade ago. There was an incident a few years prior where his neighbours had worriedly called the police about raised voices coming from his home. There was a caution for the possession of speed outside the Hacienda back in 1984. But by the time the police had compiled their preliminary findings and pulled up outside Paul's house in Salford to take a statement, it didn't matter. None of it did. Because earlier that week, after the doctors at Manchester Royal

Infirmary had done all they could for his ailing body during a complicated surgery, Paul had passed away.

***

To: GabrielLanes@gmail.com
From: paul@BroadgateTowers.co.uk

Hello my mate,

Your number's on the system, but I thought it might be a bit weird to text you out of the blue, like. As I said when we moved you in the other day, welcome to Broadgate, don't flick any of them cig ends out your window, the pigeons eat them.

Been laughing all week about what you said about that delivery guy, you're a funny fucker! You mentioned going for a drink to say thanks. I don't know how you feel about beer, but let's grab a pint. My number's below. Give me a text whenever you're free. Your fella's welcome to come n'all, but he didn't seem too keen on me. Or heavy lifting. Those hands have never seen a hard day's work in their life. I probably shouldn't put that on email, but here we are lol.

Don't be a stranger!

PS – If you lose your key fob, don't go to Benny. Come to me. I won't charge you.

Stay safe,

PAUL

18

Send-Off

'There,' Nico said, straightening the knot on my tie. I turned to look in the mirror, checking that the final result was one I was satisfied with.

'Have you got the letter?' I asked. 'The last thing I want to do is forget that.'

'Right here.' Nico patted the breast pocket on his navy blazer before placing his hands on my shoulders. 'How're you doing?'

'Yeah. Good. Fine,' I said. The funeral itself, a humanist arrangement, was a private affair, with only Paul's immediate family in attendance at the crematorium. His daughter, Kristen, had messaged me on Facebook to let me know the details of the wake, which was being held at The Kings Arms, his local pub in Salford.

'It'll be nice to meet them all – his friends and family, I mean,' I said.

'And his son?' Nico asked. 'Have you thought about when you will give him the letter?'

A few days after his death, Benny, Paul's co-worker at Broadgate Towers, knocked on the apartment door and handed me the letter we'd written to Midge, Paul's son. It was unsealed and unposted but paperclipped to a note saying:

Gabe. Couldn't do it. If everything goes to pot with the op, you'll have to. Be good!!!!
Paul.

'Before we head home, I think,' I said. 'Emotions will be high today, so I'll suggest that he reads it alone another day or something.'

We knocked on Mitchell's door and hopped onto a tram. Mitchell had been running late, so he found a corner alone at the back of the carriage to put his face on while Nico and I grabbed seats together. I leaned against the window, watching the slipstream of pedestrians, scattered trees, and concrete towers pass by on our way to Salford. Once I'd finished pretending to be in a devastating music video, I turned to look at Nico. He looked so handsome in his suit.

Evie and Dan couldn't get the time off work, and Tasha wasn't in the right headspace to attend a wake, but Nicolas had offered to come with me as soon as I'd mentioned it was happening. He'd been a rock over the last three weeks – listening, advising, empathising. I worried that he might take a 'you're surrounded by drama and I don't want any part of this' approach, and I wouldn't have blamed him, but he didn't. Evie, Mitchell, and I had taken turns staying over at Tasha's so she didn't have to sleep in her home alone with the ghost of her relationship rattling around the corridors. For the first few days, she'd verged on catatonic, not saying much and eating even less. After a week, she'd been able to get invested in films and TV, so we'd watched all of her favourite comfort series: *Buffy the Vampire Slayer*. She'd started chatting more, but not about Scott. She insisted she didn't want to talk about it; instead, she only wanted to discuss memories from college or what our old classmates were up to. After two weeks, she'd laughed at a joke I made. And two nights ago, during one of my stays, she'd made one of her own – a witty put-down about a new jacket I'd bought. The first real sign that she was returning to herself.

When the three of us reached The Kings Arms, my heart leapt. The pub was packed to the brim and then some, so much so that gaggles of people flocked outside, crowded round wooden tables, dressed to the nines and clutching pints. Heading inside the pub was like stepping through a portal back to 1970. The acrid smell of tobacco, lager, and urine hit your nostrils like a bottle of expired Amsterdam Gold[56]. Around the corner from the bar in the central area was an enormous table and, at its centre, a giant portrait of the man himself, with both of his children as babies on his knee, while Paul stuck his middle finger up at the camera. The sight of Paul noncha-

---

[56] Amsterdam Gold are the best poppers on the market (#ad)

lantly swearing around his two young children wasn't nearly as disturbing as seeing him with a full head of hair. Not just any head of hair, but a dusty brown mod cut, complete with a full fringe. I nudged Mitchell, who had somehow already procured a drink.

'I'll go and get us one, Gabe. What would you like?' Nico asked.

'A pint of Estrella, please,' I said. It was the first pint I'd had with Paul, back at The Crown & Kettle when he'd introduced my otherwise vehemently homosexual palette to the taste of lager. A fitting tribute.

'Maybe going bald isn't so bad when that's the alternative,' I said to Mitchell under my breath, nodding at the portrait.

'You would say that with your hairline, babe.' He laughed.

Like Nico, Mitchell had risen to the occasion since the events of Evie's birthday. The devastation had brought us closer. We'd bonded over our guilt at how awry the plan had gone, and helped to support each other through it. Once Paul had died, we'd started regularly texting, and I discovered that I actually quite liked him after all. Things I'd previously seen as insurmountable, offputting flaws, had morphed into charming – even loveable – quirks. I started to understand that nothing Mitch did came with bad intent, and we were actually, though it pained me to admit it, similar in a lot of ways. The impossible had happened: I'd started to consider him a – dare I think it – dare I say it – a friend.

Laid out across the enormous table and surrounding the giant portrait of Paul were different tributes that his friends and family had placed there for him. There were Manchester City football shirts, rusty-framed photos of Paul and his friends, a scarf, a small sculpture of the Colosseum, different vinyls – ELO, Blur and Manic Street Preachers – and an old dartboard, that at one point must have been nailed into a pub wall somewhere, with three darts still protruding from the triple 20 score – a perfect 180. I leaned over the table to examine it further.

'Legendary,' croaked a forty-a-day voice from somewhere behind me. I turned to see an enormous man with an unkempt ginger beard and only three visible teeth.

'Graham,' he said, holding out a hand the size of a rowing oar. I felt my fingers fold over under the weight of his grip. He turned and introduced himself to Mitchell, who looked at him with the fear of god in his eyes.

'Was this from the night he did it?' I asked, pointing to the dartboard.

'It certainly is.' Graham smiled.

'That's amazing. I didn't realise he was so good.'

'Good?' He laughed. 'Don't be bloody thick, lad. Paul was the worst dartsman from here to Hazel Grove.'

'Then . . .' I said, confused.

'He'd gotten a reputation, our Paul, for losing at darts. People used to put money against him. Proud man, to a fault. Anyway, one night after a few scoops – City had lost to Newcastle, so it must have been what, 88? 89? – he'd challenged us, me and Terry – the one there at the bar – to a friendly. No stakes, think he just wanted to practise.'

Mitchell and I were both listening intently. It was uplifting to hear stories from Paul's history, from a life before we were in it.

'Anyway, he was losing badly, as usual. I went for a slash, and Terry over there went to get another round in. When we got back, Paul stood with a face like someone who'd just matched their two fat ladies and called BINGO! I looked over at the dartboard and, lo and behold, three darts, right in the centre of the 20. 180. First time I'd ever seen him hit a red, never mind three 20s.' Graham shook his head and smiled wistfully as he spoke, his three teeth like kernels of corn in a wind tunnel. 'Good job I'd just been for a piss, or I would've gone again in my Levi's, it were that funny. Him thinking it was believable. Couldn't control ourselves, our kid and me.' He gestured towards Terry from the story, who was stooped over the bar. '"WHAT'S FUNNY? WHAT'S FUNNY?"' He imitated Paul, arms by his side, and Mitchell and I subsided into laughter with him. The impression of Paul's 'angry face' was spot on. 'He was so fuming, he ended up storming off and going to our rival pub up th'road. The Goose. Good job we took the piss, cause he met his wife, Kaye, that night. At The Goose. She was collecting glasses. Good man. Good woman. Anyway, he'd never admit he went and put them there himself, the darts. But we knew. We knew,' he finished with a nostalgic sigh.

'How did you manage to keep the dartboard?' I asked. 'It looks like it was nailed on.'

'Ah, it was mine to begin with. I was landlord at The Fox & Nettle back then. It needed replacing anyway. Told Paul it must be faulty if he managed to get a 180. Always kept it, in me loft. As a reminder, you know, of times gone by. Funny thing, time. And what's that thing you kids say – "everything happens for a reason"?' He looked again at the portrait of Paul and paused for a moment. 'What a load of shite. Anyway, lads, I best mingle.' He headed over to Terry at the bar.

The rest of the evening was more of the same. An event typically associated with tears saw the opposite: endless laughter at anecdotes about Paul. There were banterous disagreements about the validity of specific details in people's stories, arguments over who was there and who wasn't, times and places, and Paul's various hairstyles at the time.

```
     [19:49] Gabriel: Guys. Look at this.
```

I sent a picture of non-bald Paul.

```
     [19:49] Evie: That's not . . .
     [19:50] Tasha: Oh my god! Remember when you
used to see Homer with hair in flashbacks in The
Simpsons?
     [19:50] Gabriel: It's LITERALLY THAT
     [19:50] Evie: Hahaha, how's the wake
Gabe? Thinking of you both x
```

[19:51] **Gabriel**: It's lovely. Perfect. For Paul. I'll stay for a couple of hours, give Midge the letter, and then probably head off

[19:52] **Tasha**: Do you want to come to mine after, Gabe?

[19:52] **Gabriel**: Deffo! Can Nico come?

[19:52] **Tasha**: Ofc!

[19:54] **Tasha**: And Mitchell. But remind him to put his phone on silent. If I ever hear another Grindr notification, it might push me to start organising straight pride rallies

[19:54] **Gabriel**: There's definitely an audience. I think a lot of it might be in this pub

'Hey,' said Nico from the seat next to me.

'Hey!' I said, looking up to meet his smiling face. 'What're you grinning at?'

He leaned in and kissed me tenderly. I loved how he did that. When I was with Seamus, we were always conscious of being affectionate in public. Nico was fearless in that regard, and different to me. He was so stoic in his non-concern for the judgement of others that I found it emboldened me.

'Just you,' he said. I leaned forward and kissed him again.

A pretty, tall, tanned girl with beachy blonde waves beelined towards us, with a tall, tanned, handsome man in tow.

'Hi – are you Gabriel?' she asked, in one of the strangest accents I'd ever encountered.

'Yeah, nice to meet you. What's your name?' I replied.

'Kristen. I'm Paul's daughter.' She smiled.

'Oh – oh my god! Kristen! I'm sorry, hi! And I'm so sorry for your loss,' I added, reaching out and touching her hand.

'Thanks. I've heard so much about you, Gabriel, the writer. You meant a lot to him. I hope you know that,' she said without letting go, her eyes red.

'I do. Paul meant a great deal to me, too,' I said, feeling a lump in my throat for the first time that evening, partly from the sentiment and partly from the embarrassment of being called a writer when I hadn't published so much as a *Take a Break* article.

'This is André, my boyfriend.' She gestured to the tall, handsome man.

'G'day!' he stereotyped.

'André, it's lovely to meet you. This is . . .' I turned to Nico, and the word caught in my throat for a second. SHIT. WHAT IS HE? WHAT ARE WE? WHY DIDN'T I ANTICIPATE AND PLAN FOR THIS MOMENT?

'This is my . . . This is Nico! He's Spanish!' I added in a panic. André laughed.

'Nice to meet you both. I'm sorry for your loss,' Nico said before throwing me a look that translated to 'We will be discussing this as soon as humanly possible'. We all sat together with our pints and listened to Kristen and André chat about their life in Australia. I could tell she was relieved to think about something else. Kristen had a similar energy to her father. They spoke about their lifestyle in Australia and how different it was from Kristen's old one – she spent her days surfing, snorkelling, enjoying the sunshine. I knew Paul would be brimming with pride to see his daughter so full of joy.

'Have you met my brother Midge yet, guys?' she asked. 'That's him over there.' She turned her head to a slight boy, not much older than nineteen, sitting with an elderly woman. His skinny-fit black shirt hugged his hunched shoulders, and he had unfortunately started to inherit Paul's hair genetics, though this was the only thing he shared with his father. He was a wisp of a man, and Paul was a tornado.

'Go and say hi afterwards! I'm sure he'd love to meet you, but now . . .

'EVERYONE!!!!' she hollered at a volume that made me, Nico and a recently returned Mitchell jump out of our skins. She could boom like her father. 'GO FOR A PISS IF YOU NEED TO,

THEN GRAB A PINT AND GATHER ROUND HERE FOR SPEECHES.'

* * *

Arranging over a hundred attendees at a wake into a giant circle was no mean feat, but somehow Kristen managed it. She barked commands (with a warmth that clearly ran in the family) until we were all standing in a large hoop with three rows of people that extended back into the bar space. Mitchell, Nico, and I were in the second row, with a row of people in front of us who mostly seemed to be over sixty. This meant I had a clear view of the centrepiece – the tribute to Paul, with the portrait and the trinkets. There was no microphone, but the room had fallen into a respectful silence.

'A few of you heard my speech at the service earlier. I don't want to go there again, if that's okay. I've said my piece,' laughed Kristen nervously, holding back tears. 'But I guess this, losing a parent, makes me a part of that club no one wants to be in. Many of you are in it, too, so you'll know how this feels. As far as I know, there are no rules in the club, and Christ knows my dad wouldn't have followed them if there were, so say as much or as little as you like. If you want to speak, speak. If you want to grieve, grieve. If you'd like to go outside for some air, feel free. Thank you – so much – to all of you for coming today; it's testament to how much my dad meant to everyone.'

I nodded solemnly, noticing others do the same. Paul's wife Kaye was too overcome to speak and fell into her daughter's arms. Graham retold the story about the dartboard to rings of laughter, cheers, and applause, bringing Kaye back to her feet.

'My 'usband,' she began. Black marks from smudged mascara mixed with tears circled her eyes. Her voice was hoarse and raspy, and her words slurred slightly. 'Twenty-four years we were married. Fifteen of them were good. Five were a struggle. Four were bloody disastrous. I'd say that's good going.' There was a murmur of tittering and cheers of approval from the crowd.

'The stuff that kept me going through those four years was the same stuff that made the fifteen so brilliant. Laughter. God, he was funny. Kindness. And loyalty: I never had to worry about him looking elsewhere, even when other women were on the prowl. Elaine.' Kaye looked across to a skinny woman in a skirt-suit who turned scarlet and became suddenly interested in her shoes. Kristen covered her face with her hands in embarrassment.

'And he's been the best father I could ask for to our kids. They'll miss him dearly. And so will I. God knows, so will I. To be honest with you all, I don't know how I'll cope...' She subsided into tears again. The people closer to her wrapped her in a group embrace.

'You've got us, Kaye!' shouted Terry.

'We're not going anywhere,' came another voice from the crowd.

'We've only ever had . . . your best interests at heart, love!' squeaked Elaine, who had moved back a row so as to be obscured from view.

The speeches from the rest of the crowd ranged from short ('I'll miss you, big lad') to extremely long (a full reading of a John Cooper Clarke poem), from humorous to heartbreaking. Michael, Paul's son, stood three spaces across from me, also in the second row. I found it confusing initially that he wasn't standing with his sister and her boyfriend. But when I let my gaze linger, I noticed he looked uncomfortable, arms folded, staring at the floor, as though he'd rather be standing at the back or not there at all.

'Are you going to say something, babe?' Mitchell said, attempting a whisper.

'I think so, yeah. Are you?' I asked him. I didn't need to wait for an answer because the lady beside Mitchell had finished speaking, and now all eyes were on him.

'Er . . .' He hesitated. I'd never seen Mitchell appear anxious at the prospect of attention. 'Paul really looked after us. He worked at our building. Didn't he, Gabe?' He turned to me for reassurance. I nodded, turning red as eyes in the circle shifted to me. 'He worked there but became a friend... in the end. He used to helped me set up my council tax when I got stuck. He got me out of paying it a couple of times, actually! He was a bit like that. Like a dad to us, I suppose. Better than mine, that's for sure. At least Paul never tried to chuck me out!' He laughed. There was a murmur of nervous laughter from the crowd. Someone from the back shouted, 'Hear, hear!' I saw Midge dissolve backwards from his place in my row before hearing the front door of the pub open and close, and then it was my turn to speak. Adrenaline coursed through my body. I was too nervous to give a long eulogy – nor would I have wanted to; as much as I adored Paul, there were people here who had known him and loved him for decades.

'Paul had the rare ability to lift people up. Even when he might've been having a time of it himself. Paul and laughter were never far away from each other. He knew how to heal with it and be healed by it. I don't know where I'd have been without his support this past year. And I'll never, ever forget him,' I said, adrenaline being replaced with grief. 'Thank you for everything,' I said, looking into the eyes of the portrait in the centre. Nico leaned closer and held my hand, squeezing it.

'Can I have the letter, please?' I asked him.

'Now?'

'Now. I saw Michael go outside. He looked bad. No idea how much longer he'll stay.'

'I'll come with you,' Nico said, squeezing my hand again before passing me the letter.

'It's okay, I'll go.'

'Are you sure?'

'Yeah. Can you make sure Mitchell's alright here, please?' I said and made for the exit.

The tables in the seating area outside were deserted now, except for the hunched silhouette of Midge, seated alone, his hands between his knees, as if in prayer.

'Michael?' I asked as I walked over. 'Is it alright if I sit for a moment?' He looked up nervously, barely able to meet my eyes. Cars rushed past on the busy road opposite.

'I'm Gabriel. I was friends with your dad. I'm very sorry for your loss.'

'Nice to meet you. Thanks, I appreciate it,' he mumbled, bouncing his feet.

'Do you prefer Michael or Midge?' I asked. 'I've heard different names.'

'M-Michael's fine,' he stammered. His breathing seemed laboured.

'Are you okay?' I asked, sitting next to him.

'I will be, I think. My breathing feels weird. I sometimes have these p-panic attacks I think . . .' Midge said, scrunching the dark-grey material of his trousers with his palms.

'That's okay. Me too. They're the worst, aren't they,' I said, in my best attempt at a soothing tone. He nodded and took a heavy, urgent inhale.

'I found this trick that works for me. Try this . . .' I spoke quietly as I guided him through the sensework that I often utilised to stop my own panic attacks. After we'd finished, we sat together listening to the cars still rushing by and the dull hum of music and chatter from inside the pub, breathing deeply in unison.

'Thank you,' Michael said after a while. A bit of colour had returned to his mousy face, and when he smiled he looked like his father for the first time. 'Sorry, how did you know my dad again?'

'I lived in the building where Paul worked. We became close. He was a brilliant person.' I smiled. The pub doors swung open, and Nicolas appeared. He walked over to where we were sat and kissed me on the forehead.

'Hi, I'm Nicolas.' He held out a hand for Michael to shake.

'Hi. Wait . . . are you gay?' Michael asked me. I smiled. I'd not heard that question for so long.

'Erm . . . yes. Extremely.'

He laughed slightly at the floor, as Nicolas sat down next to me.

'Are you?' I chanced.

He flinched. 'Yeah.'

'Thank god. That would've been awkward. Wouldn't want to add insult to injury,' I said, nodding towards the ongoing wake. He laughed, properly now, and looked up to face us, his hunched shoulders regaining a bit of posture. His watery eyes were bloodshot slits.

'I'm surprised, I have to say. I didn't think my dad had ever spoken to another gay person. If it's okay, do you mind if I have some time alone?'

'Of course. I don't want to intrude. But . . . before Paul, before your dad died, he . . .' I searched for the words. 'He expressed a lot of regret to me about how things went down with you two. I don't know exactly what went on, and I don't need to, but I do know that he was sorry and loved you very much.' I felt Nico's hand squeeze my knee underneath the table as I tried to hold it together. Michael stared steadfastly at a piece of chewing gum stuck to the tarmac. 'He wanted to express this to you but didn't know how. He asked me to help him write this letter a few weeks ago. He told me he would post it to you, but—'

'But he was too scared,' interrupted Michael.

I grimaced slightly, and pulled out the envelope to hand to him. He hesitated for a moment, then reached out and pocketed it. I thought about cautioning him not to open it today or advising him around the best time to do so, but the last attempt I'd made to micro-manage someone's emotions hadn't exactly gone to plan – and there was moving traffic nearby – so I didn't.

'Thank you. My taxi's here, so I'm going to go now,' he said.

'Okay, take care, Michael.' I smiled.

'And Michael,' said Nico. 'If you ever want someone to talk to or to grab a drink with, we'd love to.'

My heart lifted at Nico's gesture. 'Absolutely. Here.' I took a pen from my pocket and wrote my number on the envelope.

'I'd like that. Well, see ya.' He all but ran to the black Mercedes parked against the kerb. I thought about Michael sitting alone, reading the contents of the letter, unable to have any effect – even if he wanted to — on the passing of time, and for the first time that day, I wept. I cried for Paul, for Midge, for Mitchell, for myself, and for all of our dads, too. Nico scooped me up into his arms and told me he'd book us a taxi. We went inside to collect Mitchell, but when we signalled him to leave, he waved us off and continued to dance to Abba, arm in arm with André the Australian and Elaine.

```
[22:49] Gabriel: In the taxi to yours now,
Tasha
[22:52] Evie: I've got FOMO[57], can me and Dan
come over?
[22:52] Gabriel: Please, I'd love to see you
all. It's been a day.
[22:52] Tasha: Go on then. But pick up some
Echo Falls on the way.
[22:53] Gabriel: Echo Falls? Someone's fell
from grace
[22:53] Tasha: I'm paying rent for two people,
dickhead
[22:53] Evie: See you soon!
[22:54] Tasha: Is Nico coming, Gabe?
[22:54] Gabriel: He is!
[22:54] Evie: YAY!
[22:54] Tasha: What about Mitch?
[22:54] Gabriel: She's in Dancing Queen mode
[22:54] Tasha: Of course she is
```

The taxi trundled through the grey streets, and Nico and I discussed the day's events. He told me how much he wished he could've met Paul. I agreed. We discussed the differences between funerals and wakes in England and Spain and whether we wanted to be cremated or buried. Usually, these would be morbid conversations, but

---

[57] Fear Of Missing Out

although I was emotionally exhausted after the exchange with Michael, I also felt fulfilled. Happy, even, to know that, in life, Paul had been surrounded by so many people who loved him, and in death, so many who could look back with joy at all he had given to them. As we got closer to Didsbury, Nico brought up something that had slipped my mind, but had clearly remained in his.

'So, when you introduced me to the girl. Paul's daughter. Kristen, was it? "That's Nico . . . He's Spanish!"' he mimicked.

I couldn't help but laugh. 'I'm sorry; what was I meant to say?!'

'The truth!' he insisted.

I rested my head on his shoulder. 'And what's that?'

'That's Nico . . . he's my boyfriend,' he said. I tilted my head upwards and looked into his eyes. He was silent, staring back at me with a warm determination.

'Okay. I'll say that next time,' I replied , then nestled into the nook between his warm neck and the cool leather car seat and fell fast asleep.

★★★

To Midge,

Hi son. This isn't an easy one to write and I doubt it's an easy one to read, so take a seat. Firstly, I want to apologise for how long it has taken me to write this letter. I have tried to call you and tried to text you but I haven't tried hard enough. I haven't tried hard enough to make amends and I didn't try hard enough to be the father you deserve. I also want to apologise for what happened at your 16th birthday and how I reacted to you and that other lad. And for my attitude afterwards. It was disgusting, and I am ashamed of myself. I should have known better, and been better, but I didn't and I wasn't. I regret it every day, mate.

Secondly, I want to give you reasons for why I acted the way that I did. I have never told you this, because I didn't want to make excuses, but my friend Gabriel here insists there is a difference between the two. The reason it took me so long to write this letter was because, when I realised the amount of damage I'd caused you by having a horrible outlook that felt natural to me, I didn't know how to face up to it. I still don't really, but I've had some bad news about my health, so I thought I best had now, in case anything goes wrong. It's nothing to worry about, but better to be safe than sorry. Part of the reason I think I couldn't be the father you deserve, Midge, is because I didn't know how. My father was a cruel man, from a cruel time. For all my faults in the last few years or so, we've shared some brilliant times and some big laughs together that I'll always remember. I never had that with my old man, not one bit. It's why we never liked you kids to see much of him. He didn't know how to love, and most of what I know about how to love, I learnt from your mam – believe it or not. I did try, you know, Midge, to be good to you. But nothing prepared me for it, son. To realise you might be gay. After what I overheard at your 16th, I panicked. Panicked because I didn't understand it, panicked because it was out of my control. And because I'd been taught to hate it. I pushed that on to you and I'm so, so sorry, Midge.

    Lastly, I want to talk about the future. Hopefully, if we can talk, just us two, man to man, then I think we'll have a bright one. Do you want to go for a coffee? Or a pint? Or some wine? On me, of course. Let your mam know and she'll tell me. I'll come to you, or you can come to me. I'll answer any questions, and I promise I'll listen to everything you've got to say. I've seen pictures of you and you look taller! Sorry about the hairline, that's my genetics. I need you to know how proud I am of you, son. Your mam tells me about your grades at uni. The first in the family to go. You'll never know how much that means to both of us. You look like you've made a good group of mates too. On the subject, you've got to meet our Gabriel at some point – I know you'd get on. There's another lad at work too, Mitchell, who's a riot. Think about what I've said, Midge. And even through all the shite, all those mistakes I made, I hope you never doubted, son. I know it's not much, but I hope you never doubted how much I love you with everything that I've got.

    Take care and chat soon,
    Your Dad x

SIX WEEKS LATER

19

Eureka

'SHIT!' I leapt up from Nico's bed at the realisation of the time.

'What, did I hurt you?' he asked.

I pulled on one of my socks and one of his in the rush. 'No, don't worry,' I said, leaning down to kiss him on top of his head. 'It was a very tender and meaningful hand-job.'

'Thanks. I'm glad you felt the emotion,' said Nico, still hard, and slowly but surely adapting to my sarcasm.

'I'm late. I was supposed to meet the girls at Flawd twenty minutes ago,' I said, pulling on an undershirt and a fleece.

'It's only drinks. They'll be fine. Come back to bed, let's finish first,' he coaxed.

'Er, disrespecting people's time is a turn-off for me, as you may have noticed,' I said, my flaccid cock wobbling around as I searched for my SCRT jeans.

'Babe, Evie was three hours late to your birthday meal! And that was for a special occasion! Come on, just twenty minutes,' he said, referencing Evie turning up to Sparrow – after we'd all finished our starters – in a cloud of cannabis smoke last week.

'Nico, this *is* an occasion! Evie and Tasha signed on their new flat together, and she and Dan made it official last night. So actually, it's a double,' I said, pulling on my underwear.

'Can I come?' he asked, jutting out his lower lip playfully.

'Sure, just give it a few tugs yourself,' I said.

'You know what I mean!' He laughed.

'No, it's just the girls tonight,' I said, slinging my backpack over my shoulder.

'So, Mitchell isn't going?' he pouted.

'Yes, he is. What does that change?' I laughed. I headed to the door and began to ease it open gently so as not to disturb Nico's flatmate, Julia.

'Fair enough. Wait, before you go . . .'

I hesitated in the doorway.

'Look in your backpack.' He smiled.

'What? Have I forgotten my water bottle or something? Or my charger?' I asked. I took the backpack off and found a sizeable rectangular-shaped object wrapped in metallic blue paper.

'Babe! What's this!' I said with excitement. 'My birthday was last week, and you already—'

'Do I need a reason to treat you?'

'Won't argue with that,' I replied, eagerly tearing off the wrapping paper. Within it was a Moleskine notebook bound in maroon leather.

'She's gorgeous. Thank you,' I said, kissing him on the lips.

'I've split it into sections so you can organise your writing properly,' he said proudly.

'You're too good for me.' I sighed. I'd been writing a lot more often during the last several weeks. Although a concrete idea for a more extended project still evaded me, I felt more inspired and motivated than ever.

'And . . . Look under the pillow.'

'For god's sake. What now?' I smiled, trying to appear modest but, in reality, becoming increasingly anxious about my lateness. I lifted the pillow, and underneath it was a brand-new copy of *Baldur's Gate 3*, a PlayStation game I'd wanted to play since its release.

'How do you ever expect me to get any writing done with *that* around?' I asked.

'It's two players. And I'll only play with you when I know you've been writing,' he said with a wink.

'Wow. Creative authoritarianism. What do they teach you in Andalucia?' I laughed. 'Thank you, babe. So much.' I gave him another kiss and stomped out the door to head to Flawd.

★ ★ ★

'Oh. Fancied joining us, did you?' Tasha said as I took a seat at the table outside the bar. The season had changed, and you could feel it. It was midday on a Saturday, and the sun was casting shimmering jewels over the water of New Islington marina. Still, the air was frosted and crisp, and the leaves had started their autumn dance, blazing vermillion against a clear sky.

'Sorry. Nico started tossing me off, and I forgot the time. I did sacrifice my orgasm for you guys, though.'

'So noble. Could you not have thought of a more palatable excuse on the way over?' Tasha asked.

'Is this your Scott-induced homophobia coming out to play again?' I smirked. All three of us burst out laughing. I couldn't remember when Tasha had reached the joking stage about what had happened with her ex, and there was no doubt she was still hurting from it, but we had 'humour as a coping mechanism' in common.

'On that subject, I'll have you both know that last night, in a moment of either personal progression or outright horniness, I may or may not have downloaded . . . THE APPS![58]' she said.

'Tasha! That's huge!' squealed Evie. 'We can swipe through them together next week!'

'Okay, okay, okay. Let's get this out of the way,' I announced as the pretty waitress brought me over the glass of orange Norwegian wine that was their recommendation of the day.

'A toast! First, to my two best friends moving in together. Am I burning with jealousy? Yes. Am I slightly offended that they didn't ask me to abandon my flat contract with my brother and join them? Yes. Will I be around there all the time so it will seem as if I'm living there anyway—'

---

[58] The collective term for the trifecta of dating apps used by heterosexuals: Tinder, Hinge and Bumble

'Erm, obviously not, Honeymoon Period. Aren't you basically paying rent at Nico's nowadays?' interrupted Tasha.

'Will I be round there often enough so that neither of you accuse me of being one of those friends that disappear at the merest whiff of a romantic partner? Yes! But most of all, am I so excited for this new era, and do I think this will bring you both to dizzying new heights of fun, frolics and self-actualisation? YES, YES, YES!' I shouted, taking a sip of my wine.

'Are you having a manic episode?' asked Tasha with genuine concern.

'Gabe, aren't you forgetting something? With your toast?' Evie asked.

'Oh, yeah – where the hell is Orange Thunder?' I laughed.

'He can't come. He's got this new personal trainer, and he's got him on a strict workout and diet plan, apparently,' said Evie.

'Wait. Do not tell me Mitchell is transitioning into a gym gay[59]. Please. Not on a day of celebration. Not before me,' I pleaded.

'How *ever* will you maintain your sense of superiority now?!' teased Tasha, leaning over to squeeze my cheek.

'No, aren't you forgetting about . . .' Evie started.

'Oh yeah. Sorry. And let's also raise a glass to Evie, who has now made it official with my horrible, infantile, wouldn't load the dishwasher if it popped out a tenner as a reward, brother – Dan! To you guys!' I announced. Tasha laughed, but Evie looked pissed off. 'I'm only messing. I'm so excited for you, E. You're practically my sister-in-law now.'

'One day, maybe!' Evie exclaimed gleefully.

---

[59] At a certain point, vast swathes of the community begin their transition into gym gays. This is where they will devote their time, revolve their personality, and meet their equally gorgeous partners. I had begun to fear my day would never come

'God, give me strength. You've been going out for twenty-four hours,' 'Tasha said, rolling her eyes.

'They have been seeing each other for absolutely ages, in her defence,' I said.

'Not really, you just operate on gay time when it comes to relationships,' Tasha said.

'There she goes again with the homophobia!' I laughed. I sipped the wine – tart, refreshing, and slightly different in a good way. 'It feels like ages since we've been here.'

'It is! The last time we were here was when Seamus uploaded that poem about you, Gabe, on his blog, remember?' Evie asked, the picture of innocence.

'Yes – thanks, Evie. Each stanza is burned into my mind. Did you know, though, that he's deleted it? His blog? I checked the other week. I finally told Nico about everything that had happened, so he was on my mind – and yeah, gone. The entire blog. Kaput,' I said triumphantly.

```
Dad: Hello, Gabriel. Are you still coming over
next weekend?
Gabriel: Hi, Dad, yeah. I think Dan is bring-
ing his new girlfriend, Evie.
Dad: I've heard! Will you be bringing Nicolas?
Gabriel: Yeah! He's excited to meet you
Dad: Likewise. I'm doing casserole especially.
Gabriel: Especially? Do casseroles have some
kind of Spanish roots that I don't know about
Dad: No. But they're delicious.
Gabriel: OK, see you next weekend.
```

As the sun lowered in the sky, and we had to put an extra layer on, we gabbed the evening away. Both girls showed me more pictures of the new apartment and described their completely opposing interior design plans in detail. Evie told us the story of how Dan had asked her out, and drunkenly expressed her desire to start cutting down on her cannabis intake. We all discussed provisional costume ideas for Mitchell's upcoming Halloween party. I told the girls about how I'd been writing more than ever but still felt directionless, like I hadn't quite found my 'thing'.

'You could write a series of novels from the perspective of a broken record? I think you'd be able to deliver that narrative voice convincingly,' Tasha said, cutting as ever.

Evie went into detail about a new series of crocheting TikToks that she'd found, announcing with glee that she was aiming to be able to knit us our Christmas presents this year. Tasha spoke about how she was disillusioned with her job and felt as though, after leaving Scott, she'd realised that she had stayed in her stable career path to support his goals.

'I miss him, you know,' she said, in one of her only moments of vulnerability since everything had happened.

'Of course you do, Tash. He was a huge part of your life,' Evie said, stroking her arm.

'I keep replaying times together and thinking about how cagey he was with his phone. It makes me feel stupid, and naive. Like I saw him for what I wanted him to be, not who he really was. There's something about it all that makes me feel so . . . I don't know, so . . . pathetic, I guess.'

'You're the least pathetic person I know, Tash,' reassured Evie.

'Yeah, come on, Tash, being cheated on doesn't make you pathetic. Flip it around. It happened to me, and you don't think I'm pathetic, do you?' I asked hopefully.

There was a moment of prolonged silence. And another. Then we all burst out laughing.

'No, of course I don't. I just can't *believe* I didn't know something so fundamental about him. I knew the name of the guy who bullied him for having a 'squeaky voice' in Year 3. I knew that he hated the feeling of mud on his shoes. I knew that his favourite animal was an alligator. But I didn't know his sexuality? It doesn't make sense. I keep looking back for something I might've missed, searching for clues that he was gay.'

'Did you find any?' asked Evie.

'I mean, he liked a finger up his arse. Regularly,' said Tasha.

'Oh, come on, that's not gay. That's every man. Dan likes—'

'Evie, OH MY GOD!' I screamed.

She panicked. 'SORRY, Gabe, sorry I forgot. Forget I said anything.'

'Easier said than done. Jesus. Carry on, Tasha, please.'

'Well then, no. He hid it so well. I'm still not sure if he even knows it himself. Remember what he was saying, Gabe, on the bench that time? It's still a blur in my head, but he was obsessed. "I'm not gay", over and over,' Tasha said, looking off into the distance as if replaying the night in her head.

'Do you know what he's doing for work now, Tash? Gabe?' Evie asked. Scott had handed in his notice shortly after his unmasking at Evie's birthday. The EnsureInsure office had been shocked to its core; he was one of their top salesmen.

'I haven't heard anything, but I'll keep you updated,' I said.

'Me neither,' Tasha replied. The ripple of the water and the hum of chatter sounded around us. 'I think the strangest thing is, I'm not angry at him. I was, at first, but it went so quickly. I don't hate him. I feel sorry for him. What a life to lead.'

'I'm angry at him. I hate him for what he did. But I'm proud of you for feeling that way. You won,' said Evie.

'You really did,' I echoed.

'So, you had no idea, Gabe?' Tasha asked. 'Your gaydar's usually pretty good.'

I felt something wriggling underneath my skin, something that had been there since the night at my apartment. Since the aeroplane bathroom. Temporarily quietened, but still there, waiting, until I finally found the right moment to tell Tasha the whole truth. Shame.

'No. I honestly didn't, until the Grindr stuff, obviously.' I did my best to frame it so I wasn't technically telling a lie. 'But you know I was never a fan of him, Tash. I'm glad to see him gone. It's a cliché, but it's a cliché for a reason – you deserve so much better.'

'I know.' She sighed, but a deep pain lurked: a concealed agony. 'I know,' she repeated, pushing it back and smiling.

'You're right, though. I feel sorry for him, in a way, too. I feel sorry for them all. The happier I get, the more I can look back clearly and understand.'

'Them all? What do you mean, Gabe?' asked Evie.

'Scott, not being able to accept himself. Paul's son not being able to come out properly to his dad until it was too late. Paul's inability to accept his son for who he was. Mitchell's dad and even mine, to an extent. Luca and the choices he made. Seamus. It's all the same thing, really, isn't it?'

'What?' said Tasha.

Shame. I felt the dark force at the pit of my stomach, small, sleeping, but present. Although, I had the antidote. Empathy. Pride. Love. Whatever the fuck you want to call it. As I sat with my two best friends, with a phone in my pocket that buzzed with a text from a man I was falling in love with, I felt it in spades, hovering around me and pushing the dark force downwards until it was nothing but a bleak speck of grey in a sea of technicolour.

'The gay agenda,' I replied. And we all laughed.

'HELLO BITCHES!' came a familiar warble from down the street. We turned in unison to see Mitchell sauntering towards us in lycra shorts and a string vest the size of an average handkerchief.

'Mitch!' I called excitedly.

'I thought you were at the gym?' said Evie.

'Where does it look like I've been, babe?' replied Mitchell sarcastically, pushing Evie up a space and completing the foursome on the bench.

'In all fairness, Mitchell, you dress similarly to that, whatever the occasion. I'm surprised you weren't in a vest for Paul's funeral.'

'Terry would've loved that, wouldn't he, Gabe.' He winked, referencing the middle-aged man he'd danced the night away with at Paul's wake.

'He would.' I laughed. 'I think Paul would've done, too.'

'No doubt. Anyway, girlies, I can't stay for long. I just douched, and by my calculations, I've only got three hours with no risk. I've got to go and meet this old Welsh couple from my Yoga class that I've been shagging.' *That's one way to reach enlightenment.* 'But I've got tea. Gabe, you're gonna wanna hear this, babe,' Mitchell said, a frenzied look in his eyes.

'What is it?' I asked.

'I came over as soon as I saw him,' Mitchell said.

'Saw who, Mitch?' asked Tasha.

'Seamus! He's back. Like full on back, in Manchester,' Mitchell said, smiling at the stunned silence his words elicited.

'How do you know?' asked Evie. Tasha downed the rest of her wine.

'As I was leaving the gym just now, someone slapped my arse. I got excited because the receptionist has been giving me the eye since he saw me in action at SoulCycle, but no. I turned around, and there he was. He's moved back to Manny. To Endside Grange, down the road from Broadgate. Not far from us, Gabe. Anyway, that's it. I've got to dash – I'm on the clock and need to be on the cock! HA! Text me, Gabe!' Mitchell jogged off down the canal.

It started to rain.

'Let's go inside,' said Tasha.

★ ★ ★

We huddled in a corner table. I'd panic-bought a full bottle of a New Zealand white to myself and was pouring my second glass.

'I just don't get why he's come back. He hated Manchester. He was only here because I wanted to stay.'

'Maybe it's just temporary, Gabe. For a few weeks or something?' Evie suggested.

'Are you alright?' Tasha asked.

I wasn't sure how to respond. What I knew was I *needed* answers. It felt like I'd just found a maggot in my Reese's Peanut Butter Cup.

Or like I'd walked into my living room and discovered an ugly assailant sitting on the sofa. Like my home had been invaded; because that's what Manchester was, *my* home. There was no place for him here, not anymore.

'I think so. I don't know. There's nothing I can do about it, is there? I thought I'd made peace with it all, but that was under the condition that I never had to see him again.'

'You might not, Gabe,' said Evie.

'He's practically my neighbour, Evie.'

'Mitchell to the left of you, Seamus to the right . . . here I am . . .' Tasha began.

'STUCK IN THE MIDDLE WITH YOU!' Evie finished, and we all laughed.

'I need to know what he's doing here. Why he's back. For closure, I guess. I hope I'm with Nico when I do see him. I hope my hair looks incredible. And that Nico's doing that face he does, you know, the pout when he's deep in thought? He's even more gorgeous when he does that.' Thinking of my current boyfriend drowned out any worries about my ex. Whatever happened when Seamus and my paths crossed again wouldn't – couldn't – be worse than everything else I'd been through in the past year.

'What a fucking year, though. And it's not even over. Madness,' Tasha said, reading my mind. Couples in trendy outfits sheltered under half-broken brollies, an old man clutched a dog lead to his hip as his sodden dachshund meandered over damp cobbles, a father struggled with the weight of a pram and two bulging Aldi bags. We both nodded in agreement with her statement.

'You couldn't write it,' she sighed.

The events of the last twelve months flashed before my eyes. Kaleidoscopic memories, sorrow, love, fury, and joy, twisting and turning, before arranging themselves in sequence. I felt the weight of my backpack and the gift from Nico that lay inside it, the maroon Moleskine notebook, heavy and leatherbound. There was a rush from the bottom of my feet to the top of my skull as I envisioned the memories, experiences, conversations and complications as pieces of a puzzle, but with their edges malleable and pulsating, longing to be joined together.

'Actually, Tasha . . . I think I can.'

ACKNOWLEDGEMENTS

First and foremost, I'd like to thank Becky Percival, who has been an incredible agent and an even better friend throughout the tumultuous process of crafting a debut novel. It's not even close to hyperbole to say that *Spiralling* (or indeed, my status as "person with self-belief") wouldn't exist without Becky's boundless kindness, incomparable brain, and unshakeable faith. You're the best, Beck. Thank you to my editor, Megan Jones, who, with her wealth of talent, has shepherded me through the publishing process with determination, dynamic vision, and, this one is key - patience. Thanks also to the extended team at HarperNorth who brought *Spiralling* to life and into your hands through their creativity.

I doubt that, while teaching the works of William Shakespeare, Harper Lee and Kate Chopin, any of my English teachers hoped that one of their students would go on to publish a detailed, step-by-step guide to… douching. And yet, they nurtured individuality, encouraged vulnerability, and celebrated authenticity while performing one of society's most underacknowledged yet vital roles, always with a wry smile and witty aside. For all the imaginations you've expanded, and for providing sanctuary when I needed it most: Kirsty Cunningham, Mary Dooley, Nikki Jackson, Lisa Linde and Helen Mort, thank you.

The beating heart of *Spiralling* is, of course, the friendships at its centre. That dusty old adage "write what you know" holds true here. And if there's one thing I've been lucky enough to know intimately, it's the wonder of true friendship. Without it, I'm not convinced I'd be alive today, and if I don't thank the people responsible individually, I fear I won't be tomorrow.

Alicia, nothing feels too heavy when we've got each other to help carry it. Your selflessness, humour and unique outlook on life fuels me every single day. From snogs in Greggs to wedding bells, for the full bellies and belly laughs. Amber, when I said, "I'm going to write a book, and I'm going to get it published," you looked at me across the table and said, "Obviously." Thank you for reminding me of who I am whenever I forget. Bex, happy 20th friendiversary, my SM4L. Nath, for the nights in, the nights out, and the unforgettable adventures, the quality of my life (and my ability to pursue my passion) increased tenfold when you came into it. Do the math! Raff, my whole university experience in one human being. Your endless effervescence is an unimitable gift. Raya, for the Pecan years, the 'pffft' potato, Priss... for every cackle and every tear, for the music, the mania, the magic. Ruby, the main character in the best chapters of my life so far. My co-pilot on the road to who-the-fuck-knows and who-the-fuck-cares, as long as I look to my right and you're still there. Anna, Ed, Elena, Grace, KR—thank you all.

From my chosen family to my actual family, *Spiralling* wouldn't have sashayed into the world without the influence of my kin. I've been lucky enough to gain a second Mum and a group of extraordinary siblings through my stepfamily. Gill, Rich, Phil, and Mark—there aren't many people I'd happily stay up past 1 a.m. with at my age. In fact, it's just you lot. Dad, thank you for everything you've taught me, from Crash Bandicoot to cooking dinner to being a man I can be proud of. Thank you for all your guidance and support, through it all, no matter what. Molly, your empathy, brightness, and hilarity have often been the light that helped me find my way through the dark and eventually see a creative project through to the end (sorry it wasn't the bamboo cane duelling school). Joe! My brother, my captain, my king. This book, and so much else I treasure, has only been fully realised due to being in proximity to your genius. Mum, everything I do is to make you proud, and even if I never did any of it, you still would be. At work, you've given countless children a voice, the confidence to use it, and the imagination to create brilliance. At home, you gave us all of that and so, so much more. I love you, Mum, thank you! And finally, on the subject of love—my Ol. Gracias por todo. Te amo, mi vida.

Harper North

BOOK CREDITS

HarperNorth would like to thank the following staff and contributors for their involvement in making this book a reality:

Sarah Allen-Sutter
Fionnuala Barrett
Peter Borcsok
Laura Braggs
Sarah Burke
Alan Cracknell
Jonathan de Peyer
Anna Derkacz
Tom Dunstan
Kate Elton
Sarah Emsley
Simon Gerratt
Lydia Grainge
Monica Green
Natassa Hadjinicolaou
Emma Hatlen
Jess Haycox
Megan Jones
Jean-Marie Kelly
Taslima Khatun
Holly Kyte
Emily Langford
Rachel McCarron
Alice Murphy-Pyle
Adam Murray
Genevieve Pegg
Amanda Percival
Dean Russell
Florence Shepherd
Colleen Simpson
Eleanor Slater
Hilary Stein
Emma Sullivan
Katrina Troy
Claire Ward
Ben Wright

For more unmissable reads,
sign up to the HarperNorth newsletter at
www.harpernorth.co.uk

or find us on socials at
@HarperNorthUK